POISONED BLOOD

PHILIP E. GINSBURG

WARNER BOOKS

A Warner Communications Company

WARNER BOOKS EDITION

Material on pages 11–12 reprinted with permission from Gonzales,
Vance, Helpern, and Umberger, *Legal Medicine, Pathology, and
Toxicology*, 2nd edition (New York: Appleton-Century-Crofts,
1954).

This Warner Books Edition is published by arrangement with
Charles Scribner's Sons, a division of Macmillan Publishing Company,
866 Third Avenue, New York, NY 10022.

Cover design by Anthony Russo

Warner Books, Inc.
666 Fifth Avenue
New York, N.Y. 10103

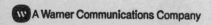 A Warner Communications Company

Printed in the United States of America

First Warner Books Printing: May, 1989

10 9 8 7 6 5 4 3 2 1

For my late father, Aaron Ginsburg,
who made me want to understand,
and for my mother, Libby Fisher Ginsburg,
who has been my foundation,
with love and gratitude

Author's Note

This is the true story of a real person, Audrey Marie Hilley. The personalities, events, actions, and conversations portrayed here have been reconstructed from extensive research, using court documents, letters, personal papers, press accounts, and the memories of participants, gathered in dozens of interviews. The reader should be aware that when gaps in the sources or the logic of the narrative required it, the author has contributed his own interpretation and extrapolation of the facts. In an effort to safeguard the privacy of certain individuals, the author has changed their names and in some cases altered otherwise identifying characteristics. Events involving such characters happened as described; only minor details have been changed.

Author's Note

Contents

Contents

Acknowledgments

The world thinks of a writer as a solitary figure, laboring unaided to produce words on a page. Sometimes a writer thinks of a writer that way, too. But the truth is otherwise. From beginning to end, a writer needs the cooperation, or at least the tolerant regard, of many others in order to produce a book such as this.

In my case, toleration began with a number of people in Marlow and Keene, New Hampshire, who were willing to give me their time and their thoughts about the woman they had known as Robbi Homan and later as Teri Martin. Among them I am especially grateful to Peter Homan and his wife, Shelley, who were generous with their hospitality and their memories, and to Barry Hunter, who showed me how intelligent persistence could become a craft.

I found southerners just as hospitable as New Hampshire folks, and among them I particularly appreciated the help of Gary Carroll, who showed me the thoughtful person behind the taciturn professional lawman, and the Reverend Michael Hilley, whose trust is the more valued for being hard won. Carol Hilley, whose courage became more impressive the more I learned about what she had experienced, gave me as much assistance as she could.

In Florida I was taken briefly into the family life of Greer Parker and her husband, Rick, who gave me something it was not easy for them to share.

Among the scores of people who talked with me or provided materials, a number were especially kind and informative. Among these I want to thank in particular Freeda Adcock, Robbie Grace Daigle, Tim Doherty, Larry Dollar of the Broward County State Attorney's Office, Jan Earnest of the Anniston Public Library, Carol

Hammann, Sergeant Bob Hardy of the Keene Police Department, Tom Harmon, Joe Hubbard of the Seventh Circuit District Attorney's Office, Jack McKenzie, Wilford Lane, Sergeant Mike LeClair of the Vermont State Police, Charles Lecroy, Robert March, Jerry Montgomery (for his help with photographs), Eddie Motes of the *Anniston Star,* Ron Oja, Sandra Peace, Lieutenant Lyn Presbie of the New Hampshire State Police, Jerry Scadova, Karen Shughart, Agent David Steele of the FBI, Cynthia Stewart, Parian Tidwell of the Calhoun County Circuit Court, and Roger Williams. There were a number of others who did as much and asked in return only anonymity, which I hereby maintain with appreciation. They and I know who they are. There were a few others, remarkably few, who felt for a variety of reasons that they could not talk to me; I don't blame them, and in their place I might have done the same. Their refusal emphasizes by contrast the generosity of those who helped. A writer is utterly dependent upon that species of kindness.

I began work on *Poisoned Blood* during a sabbatical leave from the New Hampshire Council for the Humanities, which might have preferred to be associated with more scholarly work but which nevertheless helped me get started.

The advice of Dr. Edward Rowan and Dr. Denny Carlson was helpful in my understanding of certain medical and psychological questions. I had another form of professional help from Nancy Ray, who provided excellent transcriptions even before she had a word processor, and Anne Dubois, whose skill as a photographer was matched only by her patience in pursuing an acceptable image.

I was fortunate in the literary professionals who took an interest in me and my book. My agent, Elizabeth Knappman, of New England Publishing Associates, has been a gentle teacher and enthusiastic supporter since long before this book was a book. Susanne Kirk has been a discerning editor and deserves full credit for any superiority of the book over the first draft. The multitude of little pencil marks placed on the manuscript by Carrie Chase were manifestly the traces of a superior literary taste. Milly Marmur was generous with her interest in both the manuscript and its author.

It had never occurred to me until I started seeking advice how many of my friends had the kind of feeling for writing I could trust as a measure of my work. Jennifer Lee, Phyllis Bennett, Barry Lane, and Mary Strayer McGowan read early versions of parts of this book. I hope they will see evidence of their suggestions here, and that they will think it improved. Alan Lelchuk and Tom Williams offered counsel from the writer's perspective at critical moments.

In retrospect, *Poisoned Blood* was destined to become a book from the moment I talked to my cousin and friend Rachel Ginsburg about it. She has given me virtually everything that I have thanked others for in these paragraphs, and more. She may measure my appreciation by summing the sentiments I have expressed to them.

And finally I express my love and appreciation to two people who have not read a word of any outline, draft, or manuscript of this book, who will probably be too busy with homework, violins, soccer, and life to read the book itself, but who have shared every moment of its existence and played an active role in shaping the author's world. They are my sons, Adam and Matthew.

Prologue

When it was all over, when it was possible at last to begin gathering the fragments of the story—a story of deceit and betrayal, of lust and murder and the destruction of life's most sacred bonds—it seemed unlikely that the small, plain town of Marlow could ever have held this woman. There was so little to the town, a mere wide spot in the road with a tiny post office, a general store with two gas pumps out front, a few hundred houses strewn across the low hills in the southwestern corner of New Hampshire near the Vermont border.

Afterward, when they recalled the ways her life had touched theirs, the people who had known her still seemed bemused. They talked of her as if she were someone they remembered from a tale read in childhood or a movie seen on television. In their minds the story was surrounded by a mist of unreality, so incongruous did it appear amid the persistent ordinariness of their town. Many, like a person awaking in the middle of a dream, lived with the sense that the story was unfinished, and some found themselves wondering at times if it had ever happened at all.

But of course it *had* happened, and it was the peculiar power of the woman that so many people in so many places felt they had been part of the story. Like an actor who is moved by one part above all the others he has played, each of them would live with the experience for the rest of his life.

Part One

Arrested

1

A Mysterious Woman

Sally called Teri Martin at Book Press in the middle of the afternoon. The weather report was predicting snow, Sally said. Her faculty meeting had been canceled and she felt like going home an hour early. Could Teri get off between four and four-thirty? Teri checked with her boss and he didn't mind. She'd meet Sally in the parking lot.

Usually the lot was almost empty when Sally got there, but today they were leaving before the rest of the employees. It gave the place a different feeling as she drove between the long rows of cars, crowded and a little uncomfortable. As she turned left near the front of the lot, starting to pull in next to the curb, she noticed a car parked facing outward at the end of the row, a big, nondescript American sedan. There were people inside. It was a group of men, she saw, big ones, filling the car, looming large in the windows.

Strange, she thought, bringing the little white Honda to a stop where the walkway from the front door reached the curb. They seemed to be staring at her. They were directly behind her as she secured her hand brake. She left the motor running, watching them in the rearview mirror. What would four men be doing sitting in a parked car like that?

The front door of Book Press opened and Teri, on time as usual, headed down the walkway toward the passenger side of the car. She had barely taken her first steps when the doors of the big sedan started opening. Sally went rigid, watching in the mirror. She had an impression of trench coats and shiny shoes, an ominous look that she associated with the Mafia and TV thugs. It fitted with her uneasiness about Teri Martin.

3

They came from both sides of the sedan and they seemed to be walking forward in parallel formation, as if to surround her own tiny car and prevent her from leaving. What could they want with her? She locked the door next to her, imagining herself jamming the gas pedal to the floor as Teri leaped into the passenger seat, the Honda screeching away through the crowded parking lot. Her hands trembled on the steering wheel.

One of the men closer to the walkway spoke to Teri. She turned immediately from the walk and moved a few steps toward him and his partner. The one who had been heading for the driver's side of the Honda moved toward the curb and joined the little group. The man in the lead reached into his pocket. Sally was afraid to turn around or do anything that might draw attention to herself. She turned her eyes upward to the rearview mirror, trying to watch without moving her head. The man was pulling a wallet from his pocket. He held it in his hand and let it flop open. A moment passed before she realized it held a badge, and next to the shiny metal she thought she saw large letters, reversed in the mirror, IBF. What was going on?

The men talked with Teri for a moment, then she turned from them and came to the passenger side of the car. She opened the door and put her head in. There was no expression on her face.

"I've got a ride," she said. "I'll see you later."

Teri closed the door, walked back to the sedan, and got in with the men. Sally sat at the steering wheel for several minutes, her heart pounding. "I've got a ride"? "I'll see you later"? Just like that? That's it? *What* was going on?

Just a little bit longer, Barry Hunter thought as they headed for the Brattleboro police station. The woman was ready to talk, you could see it as soon as LeClair spoke to her in the parking lot.

When they saw her come out of Book Press, Hunter had slipped out of the driver's seat and walked around the front of the car, a few steps behind LeClair and Steele, who were getting out of the passenger side. He had moved up behind them as Steele showed her his FBI identification, introduced himself, and identified the two state troopers. The blond woman looked at Steele impassively. There was a sharp, self-possessed quality to her gaze. She was smaller than they had thought, Hunter noticed, a good two or three inches shorter.

Hunter had been following her trail in New Hampshire for more than a week now, but Book Press was just across the border in Brattleboro, LeClair's jurisdiction. The Vermont trooper spoke for them all.

"We have reason to believe you're not who you claim to be," LeClair said.

Hunter stared into her face, looking for a sign, and poised to move. Even with an apparently harmless person like this small woman, the moment of confrontation was a tense one. No matter how many times you had done it, you never knew what was going to happen. Sometimes they just gave up, tired of running and hiding, but sometimes they bolted, and sometimes they fought. Cops got killed that way, and suspects, too.

As the meaning of LeClair's words sank in, the woman's face seemed to lose its shape, like a slow-motion mud slide. Hunter knew in that moment, there was no resistance in her. Her features relaxed, her shoulders slumped, she deflated before their eyes. There was a pause before she spoke.

"Yes," she said, softly, still looking at LeClair. It was an admission, not a question.

"We'd like to ask you some questions," the trooper said gently. "It's kind of cold out here. Could you accompany us to the Brattleboro Police Station?" He explained that it would be voluntary on her part; she was not being arrested.

She seemed to revive slightly. "I've got somebody waiting for me here." She nodded toward the white Honda. Steele assured her they would have her driven wherever she wanted to go when they had finished talking with her. She walked to the curb and opened the door of the Honda. Somebody wrote down the license plate number of the little white car, just in case they needed it later. LeClair stayed close behind her but made no move to interfere as she spoke briefly to the driver; then he escorted her to the unmarked car.

There were a few moments of tense silence as Steele drove off through the parking lot, heading for Route 5. LeClair sat in back with the woman. Hunter finally turned to face her.

"We understand that Teri Martin isn't your real name," Hunter said.

"That's right," she answered. She had recovered her composure.

She seemed resigned but calm. Hunter was struck by her attractiveness. Even in these circumstances she seemed graceful and composed, as if she carried an inner poise that was not touched by the rough suspicions of a carful of cops.

"Did you have some problem with the police?" LeClair asked.

"Yes," she replied quietly, and looked out the window for a moment. She sensed that LeClair was going to follow up his question.

"Look," she said, "would you mind waiting until we get to the station?" There was no impatience in her tone; it was just a courteous request for a favor. She looked from LeClair to Hunter. "I'll answer all your questions when we get there." Nobody responded.

"I'd just rather not talk about it in the car," she added.

The two troopers exchanged looks. She seemed ready to talk. Why not let her do it her own way? They had nothing to lose.

"Sure, we'll wait," LeClair said. "We'll be there in a few minutes."

There was no sign out front to indicate the presence of the Brattleboro Police Department. Steele turned into a driveway next to a broad lawn that sloped upward at one end of the main shopping district. At the top of the lawn stood a brick building that looked like a nineteenth-century big-city high school, but the sign out front called it the "Municipal Center," and the police shared the building with the selectmen, town manager, and other Brattleboro officials.

The building was deeper than the proportions of the front suggested, and the police were at the back. LeClair led the way inside, the three men forming a convoy with the small blond woman loosely but firmly secured in their midst. They were directed past a low front desk into a small maze of rooms that looked like the result of a fifty-year-old renovation project. Inside one of the offices, LeClair guided her to the desk chair, a wall with a small window at her back. There were a few minutes of awkward shuffling while someone brought an extra chair from another office. Hunter sat facing her with LeClair at his left, his back to a large wooden locker. Steele leaned against the door behind them; there was no room for another chair.

Hunter was the most familiar with the case, but as a New Hampshire trooper he had no jurisdiction in Vermont. She would have to be questioned under Vermont or federal law, and LeClair knew more about the investigation than Steele. LeClair took the lead. He began by reciting the litany of her rights: She didn't have to talk to them, she could have a lawyer, a public defender if necessary. He came to the last steps.

"Now, do you understand what your rights are?" LeClair asked. She said she did.

"And having your rights in mind," he went on, "are you willing to talk with us now?" There was a gathering of stillness in the room as they watched for her response.

"Yes," she said simply. The resignation Hunter had seen before was in her voice. There was a moment of relaxed shifting before LeClair began again.

"You told us in the car that Teri Martin isn't your real name," he said. She nodded assent.

"Could you tell us your real name?" he asked politely, not wanting to jeopardize her cooperative mood.

"Audrey Marie Hilley," she said.

"What?" someone asked. Hunter realized he had still been expecting to hear something about Terry Lynn Clifton, the fugitive they had tentatively matched her up with earlier in the week. The three detectives exchanged a roundrobin of looks. Nobody seemed to recognize the name. They asked her to spell it out. There were a few moments of questions and checking before they all got it written down correctly.

"And your date of birth?" LeClair asked.

"June fourth, 1933." Almost fifty years old, Hunter thought. That was at least ten years older than they had estimated after secretly observing her last week. And it was twelve years older than the age she was claiming as Teri Martin. She had gotten away with it; she wore her age well.

Now they had reached a critical moment. LeClair spoke carefully:

"Do you have any involvement with being wanted by the police?"

"Yes," she answered. She was waiting to be asked another question.

"Where was that?" Hunter picked up the questioning. His curiosity was getting the better of him.

"I'm wanted in Alabama for some check charges," she said. She was very matter-of-fact.

That's it, Hunter thought: a real person, with a real name, and outstanding charges for a real crime. Here were the last pieces for the puzzle, the ones that finish the picture and make sense of all the rest.

And he felt relieved, too: Her admission put them on firmer ground. Their suspicions had been justified; now they had a legal pretext to hold and question her.

But nothing he had learned or heard so far prepared Hunter for the real mystery of Audrey Marie Hilley.

LeClair excused himself and turned toward the door. "I'll put this on the wire," he said to Hunter. Steele followed him out the door. They walked back out past the desk and across the hall to the dispatcher's office, where a teletype machine connected the Police Department to the National Crime Information Center's computer. They could get a fast check on the charges and the accuracy of the information she had given them.

Hunter felt the need to maintain some connection with the woman, but he didn't want to talk about Alabama; he didn't know anything about it. The subject was all new to him. He asked her instead about the false name, Teri Martin. She had used it about three months, she said. She was starting to tell him about her life in New Hampshire when she was interrupted by a sound at the door behind Hunter.

Hunter turned as LeClair and Steele returned to the room. LeClair's eyes sparkled with excitement. He handed a ragged piece of teletype paper to Hunter. LeClair's gaze fastened on the woman as Hunter looked down at the printed message.

"Audrey Marie Hilley," it said, and gave the date of birth. He looked for the bad-check charges. She was wanted on two counts of passing bad checks. But there was more. The words leaped off the paper. She was wanted in Anniston, Alabama, on charges of murder and attempted murder!

"You said there were some check charges," LeClair was saying to her.

Hunter looked up as LeClair spoke again.

"Is there anything else you might be wanted for?" he asked.

She looked annoyed, like someone remembering a dental appointment fifteen minutes after it was supposed to begin. She moved slightly in the chair.

"Well, the police down there accused me of poisoning my daughter." She looked from face to face, measuring the reaction. "That's so ridiculous," she said. "Why would I do that to my own daughter?

Part Two

Audrey Marie Hilley

*Inorganic Arsenic compounds . . . are carried by the blood to different parts
of the body, where they attack the tissues vigorously, producing their most
pronounced effects on the capillaries. The intensity of the toxemia depends
on the amount of the drug administered and the rapidity with which it is
absorbed.*

Four types of poisoning occur:

*1. The acute paralytic form, in which the deceased has received a large
quantity of inorganic arsenic compounds with rapid absorption into the
system. . . . The most striking manifestations are a profound circulatory
collapse with low blood pressure, rapid weak pulse, shallow or difficult
respiration, a semicomatose or profound stupor, and sometimes convulsions.
. . . Death supervenes in less than 24 hours.*

*2. The gastrointestinal type is the most common. . . . Soon after the
ingestion of the arsenic compound, vomiting occurs, followed by diarrhea
after an hour or two. [Other symptoms include] burning pain in the
abdomen and abdominal cramps, sore throat, urgent thirst and dryness about
the mouth . . . a livid and anxious face, a cold clammy skin, cramps in the
calves of the legs, delirium . . . and dehydration. Death occurs in a few
hours to several days.*

*3. A subacute type of poisoning may develop if the arsenic compounds are
administered in small doses repeated at intervals, or it may even follow the
administration of a single large dose which does not cause death rapidly but
remains in the body. . . . The victims linger on from weeks to months:
some may develop a toxic degeneration of the liver, which progresses to
. . . yellow atrophy accompanied by an intense toxic jaundice . . .*

11

persistent diarrhea, cramps, and dehydration; the kidneys may show a
nephrosis, with albuminuria and bloody urine; skin eruptions [and]
eczematous [rash] areas . . . appear on the skin in some instances. . . .
The patient loses weight, becomes emaciated and quite ill before death
supervenes.

4. A chronic type of poisoning may develop in some cases after the acute
symptoms subside. [It may display] a chronic neuritis . . . with
degeneration of the nerve fibers which starts at the periphery [of the body]
and extends toward the center . . . characterized by paralyses of the muscles
of the hands and feet. . . . In some cases [there is] chronic gastroenteritis
. . . with anorexia, nausea, and diarrhea . . . progressive weakness . . .
loss of weight, anemia, pallor, and general ill health. . . . These
syndromes may be evoked by . . . the continual ingestion of small amounts
in the food. . . . The chronic forms of poisoning may not be preceded by
acute symptoms and may make their appearance insidiously.

Gonzales, Vance, Helpern, and Umberger, Legal Medicine, Pathology, and
Toxicology, 2nd ed.

There is something in human nature that refuses to accept a mystery, that
requires an explanation. If the mystery concerns human motivation, why
somebody did something, we are satisfied to find a craving for money, or sex,
or control over others. In the case of Audrey Marie Hilley, we are not
disappointed. We find all of these.

And yet there is something curiously incomplete about this kind of
explanation. Some of her crimes are so small, so apparently purposeless as to
seem hardly worth the trouble. In retrospect, some even seem comical. And
some of her crimes are so horrible as to far outweigh the promise of any
reward that might have come to her.

It is our custom in a case like this to seek out the expert, one who may help
trace the mental processes that lead to such destruction. But Audrey Marie
Hilley's only publicly known examination by a psychiatrist brings us no
closer to an understanding of why she did what she did; it was designed only
to test her competency, and it found her competent. Audrey Marie Hilley
was always competent. But the examination sidestepped the other, more
interesting questions.

Finally, we are left with only one recourse: We may ask Audrey Marie
Hilley herself, "What was in your mind? Why did you do what you did?"
But Audrey Marie Hilley does not answer. Even at the end, she admitted
nothing, accepted nothing, repented nothing.

If we are not to be offered a great insight, a sudden, simple revelation of the principle, the passion, or the need that drove this woman, we must find the answer ourselves. We must look at her beginnings, at the small choices that became big ones, at the pressures that became urges, at the desires that became desperate needs. This is not easy, because of all the kinds of passion that made Audrey Marie Hilley what she became, the greatest was her passion for stealth, for secrecy, for concealment. So overwhelming was this need that Audrey Marie Hilley became one of its chief victims. She took the human capacity for occasional self-delusion and built an entire life around it, hiding the truth of herself even from herself. To the end, she was devoted to keeping hidden what we have come to find. She was the ultimate defender of her own mystery.

But a life is not a painting or a paragraph, where every detail may be kept under control and every secret may remain hidden, even by a genius of deception like Audrey Marie Hilley. It is an accumulation of actions and responses, of words and deeds, of decisions made and possibilities neglected. It is here, in her daily reality of many years, in her own actions and in the reflections of others, that we begin to find the solution to the mystery of Audrey Marie Hilley.

2

A Country Girl

She was four years younger, not quite fourteen, but Frank Hilley knew immediately: He was going to marry this girl one day. She was just a skinny little thing, with a big cloud of brown hair down to her shoulders, but you could already see the woman in her, in the big, glistening eyes, so deep and so changeable, full of mirth one minute, far off and serious the next. "She always dresses so nice," someone said, and it was true, even when she was in seventh grade down at Quintard Junior High. Her parents worked in the mill up at Blue Mountain and they didn't have a lot of money, but she always looked so neat in her sweaters and slim, pleated skirts.

Frank wasn't the only one taken with Marie Hilley. She was picked as "Prettiest Girl" at Quintard that year. You could see it in that picture of her, sitting up on the high front fender of somebody's '41 Ford coupe in the parking lot, even with her legs hanging down, her feet well off the ground, and her skirt not quite reaching her knees. The legs were already shapely like a woman's, and you could see she already knew who she was, with the nice smile but not too much, not trying too hard for it, and her hands cupped together comfortably in her lap, and her ankles in the rolled-down bobby socks crossed neatly, everything in line, everything composed, such a contrast to Jimmy Marbut, voted "Most Handsome Boy," standing next to her, with his big ears and his eyes squinted in a sweet, kid's smile, gangly and pigeon-toed, all bones and angles leaning against the fender, looking like the seventh-grader he was.

Marie Frazier had already come a long way by then, and that was her parents' doing, especially her mother's. Lucille Meads had been born in 1912, when the Civil War was still a living memory in

Alabama and the changes it had set in motion were just beginning to work themselves out. She was one of five children, all of them determined to better themselves. One brother became the longtime, highly respected sheriff of a town near Anniston, and one sister was rumored to be involved with shady people and suspicious dealings. Lucille devoted her great energy to making a comfortable life for the next generation. She would live to see a time when leaders were proclaiming the achievements of a New South, and she would die on the very day her only child fled Alabama, accused of attempting the most horrible crime against her posterity.

On the other side of the family there were farmers back a few generations, but Marie's paternal grandfather, Ernest Frazier, had started the transition from the farm to the factory, following the slow trend of the South as a whole. At twenty-two he had come over from Georgia and married an eighteen-year-old Alabama girl. Ernest and Leila Frazier settled down to try farming in Chambers County, but within a few years they had given it up and moved to Anniston. That was just after the turn of the century. In the summer of 1909, Ernest was working as a carpenter in Blue Mountain, five miles out from Anniston, when his appendix burst. He was thirty-seven when he died, leaving Leila with six children.

Ernest Frazier was put in the ground at the Edgemont Cemetery. American Net and Twine had built a mill at Blue Mountain a dozen years before, buying up large tracts of surrounding property and building a community modeled on the northern idea of the self-contained mill town. The cemetery was laid out on a few acres of undulating ground just east of the great mill. It was land left over after the church and the school and the housing were finished, full of little knolls and not much good for anything else.

Leila found someone to care for her children—James was already twelve and William was ten, old enough to help out a good deal—and she went to work as a machine operator at Net and Twine. The middle children, Annie and Harmon, were eight and six; only the twins, Huey and Louie, weren't old enough to do anything for themselves. They were barely a year old when their father died.

Huey and Louie grew up in the intimacy typical of twins; even after they left home and went to work they stayed together, living on Leyden Hill near the Blue Mountain Mill. When Huey married Lucille Meads in 1931, the twins were separated for the first time. Louie decided soon after to leave Alabama and head west. Huey and

Lucille moved into one of the dozens of identical small houses on the hill built and rented out by the company to its employees. The little front porch and the two rooms inside were all in a straight line; they were called shotgun houses—whether because the house was long and narrow like a gun barrel, or because you could fire a shotgun through the front door and hit the back wall, no one was sure.

Lucille had been working since she was thirteen, so the time she took off when they decided to have a baby was like a rare vacation. Their anticipation built with Lucille's pregnancy during late 1931, but it ended with the stillbirth of a child the next spring. They buried their first child down the hill in Edgemont Cemetery, which was slowly filling up with the cheap, small headstones of mill workers and their families. The permit cost them $7.50.

Huey and Lucille Frazier spent that summer, in the third year of the Great Depression, recovering from the shock of their loss. Slowly their determination to have a child reemerged from the gloom, and by fall it was confirmed: Lucille was pregnant again. They had reason to be prepared for twins: In addition to Huey's twinship, there was a history of double births on Lucille's side of the family as well. And there was another omen: Huey and his twin had been born under the sign of Gemini, the constellation named by the Greeks for the hero twins Castor and Pollux, and Lucille was due to give birth during the same period. The baby arrived on June 4, 1933, five days after Huey's birthday and a little more than twenty-four hours from the middle of Gemini's reign, but it was a solitary, and healthy, daughter. They named her Audrey Marie, but for all the use she ever got out of her first name, they might as well have done without it.

For the first few years, Huey worked at the mill, now called the Linen Thread Company, and Lucille stayed home and took care of the baby. Whether it was the experience of losing a child, or simply concern about supporting a large family, nobody knew, but Huey and Lucille never had another child. They wanted to do everything they could for the one they had, and from the time she was a small girl, little Marie always got what she wanted.

Huey was a sweet-natured man, loved by children and adults alike, but the older people soon noticed that he wasn't very reliable. He was thin and seemed sickly. Work was scarce then, and it was rare to see an adult make much of illness, but there were many days when Huey stayed home from the mill and rested in bed. He came to miss his twin brother, and at times he would disappear for long stretches. It was said that he went to visit Louie and his family in Tyler, Texas, near Dallas. Later, after Louie moved to Utah, the story got around that Huey came home from work one day, took most of the family's small savings out of the bank, and set off for the West, returning two or three months later as if it were the most natural thing in the world to hop a bus and disappear for a season. There were whispers that Huey and Lucille were periodically in trouble with creditors, and at least once they moved because of problems paying the rent in Blue Mountain, although they later moved back to be near their jobs.

The burden of supporting the family fell on Lucille, who soon went back to work at Linen Thread. She, or Huey when he was around, would drop Marie off at her Grandmother Susie Meads' house before work and pick her up later. Three of Lucille's four brothers and sisters lived nearby—her married sisters, Margaret Key and Cathleen McCullars, and her brother, Jim—and they all pitched in to help out. When she was old enough to tag along, Marie joined a pack of cousins who played among the headstones in Edgemont Cemetery and picked blackberries and huckleberries in the woods nearby. Uncle Jim's wife, Evelyn, took care of Marie and the others until Marie started school, but Evelyn was only fifteen and seemed part of the gang. The one constant was Lucille's mother, Grandma Susie Meads, who became a substitute mother for Marie through much of her youth.

Marie and Robbie McCullars were the only girls in the group of cousins. As the youngest, Marie became something of a pet to the boys. She had her father's sweet temper and winning personality, but there was steel in her, too. Lucille and Huey had taught their daughter to expect things her own way. Robbie had particular reason to be impressed with her little cousin's ferocity. When Marie was about five years old, Robbie caught the measles and was forced to stay home from school. While she was in bed recovering, her mother brought a sweet cake as a treat. Marie demanded a share, and when Robbie refused, the little girl insisted. Rebuffed again, Marie threw herself at her cousin. As they struggled, she bit Robbie fiercely on the stomach, leaving toothmarks that took months to disappear.

It hardly seemed to matter what Marie did, though. A delicate, pretty girl with a lively, affectionate manner, she got away with things that would not be permitted to anyone else. Robbie and her brothers fought constantly, in the noisy battles of self-assertion common to large families, but the boys always seemed ready to surrender to Marie. They coddled and petted her, and when she put her foot down—insisting that she had seen a snake as big as a tree, or demanding a ride on Charlie McCullars' shoulders—they would give in, allowing the pretty child a tyranny that no one else could command.

Perhaps there were the seeds here of what happened later, of the evil and deceit that the adult Marie carried among those who were closest to her, but no one saw them at the time. The people around her saw a pretty girl, an only child, fortunate in the love and attention of her parents, cared for by relatives who treated her like their own, surrounded by other children who awarded her their tolerant affection.

In 1939 Marie was old enough to start school, joining the others at Blue Mountain Elementary, next door to the mill where her parents worked. Her cousin Robbie, who was four years older, played an important role in Marie's life. She may have been the first in a lifelong series of peers against whom Marie defined herself, now by opposition, now by emulation. Robbie McCullars would pick up a newspaper one day in adulthood and find that Marie had done the latter, had stolen Robbie's name and pieces of her life to make a new story for herself, but in childhood it was their differences that were dominant. Growing up in the company of three brothers, Robbie was developing into a rough, sporting youngster, considered a tomboy by adult and child alike. That was probably a good thing, because with four children and only one income, the McCullars family never had much money left over for pretty dresses or other extras. Robbie wore her brothers' hand-me-downs as much as possible, and her mother, Cathleen, sewed whatever else she needed.

The contrast with her cousin was striking. Marie was dainty and ladylike from the first, and her dresses were bought at the store. In the fourth grade Marie became fascinated by tap dancing, and soon Lucille had arranged for her to begin taking lessons. Lucille was still at the mill when her daughter finished a lesson, so Marie would come back to the McCullars' house afterward, proudly wearing her brand-new, black patent-leather tap shoes with the bows on the top. Robbie and her mother and whoever else was around would gather respectfully in the front room. Marie would step onto the hearth of the fireplace and show them what she had learned that day, reveling in the swirl of her skirt and the clatter of the metal taps against the rough stones.

As Marie's parents responded to her every wish, buying her a doll, a purse, a blouse, a hat, a new bookbag, the disparity between her possessions and those of her cousin Robbie became more and more apparent. Finally, a friend of Robbie's parents whom the child knew as Aunt Sally noticed the contrast and took pity on her. When Sally came to visit after that, she often made it a point to bring a doll or a piece of clothing to even things up a bit. Marie was a sweet child, but everybody thought she was terribly spoiled.

The Fraziers managed to hire a black woman—they knew her as Aunt Florence—to help out around the house from time to time. Their food seemed a little bit above everybody else's, too. Lucille always kept a nice selection of fruit—apples, oranges, pears, and others that were less common in the rural Alabama of the time—and varied the family's diet with beefsteaks and other expensive cuts. Robbie McCullars ate her first lamb chop at Marie's house, and the fact that it sickened her, beginning a lifelong revulsion to lamb, did not keep her from reporting on the experience at home. After Robbie spoke admiringly to her mother several times about the food at the Fraziers', describing her discoveries and asking for things that her family couldn't afford, Cathleen McCullars became annoyed and ordered her daughter not to go there anymore. Of course, she didn't mean it, but the incident added to Robbie's sense that Marie and her parents lived on a different level from her own household. She envied them a little, but their way of living seemed unhealthy, too, as if they were breaking the rules that everybody else followed.

The McCullars children were leaders in the fights and other mischief that naturally developed, and often Marie and the others were drawn in. Responsibility for disciplining Marie fell to her grandmother, Susie Meads. Years later, when Marie began weaving fantasies about an oppressive childhood darkened by cruel punishment inflicted by her grandparents, nobody who had known her as a child could remember anything more serious than an occasional spanking from Mom Meads, or being forced to sit quietly in a chair for a little while.

By the time Marie finished elementary school, Blue Mountain had been incorporated as a separate town and was sending its older children on to the rural school in Alexandria. Lucille wanted something better for her daughter, so the Fraziers moved the five miles down to Anniston, and Marie started at Quintard Junior High School. For a time, Marie stayed in frequent contact with her relatives and friends in Blue Mountain, taking the bus out to visit after school, or on a Saturday morning, but Robbie eloped with a boy she had met at Fort McClellan, and soon Marie was more involved with new friends and activities at Quintard. She was friendly with girls, but before long most of her time was taken up by boys. At first she was close to Donnie Frazier, a distant cousin her own age, but soon she was being monopolized by older boys. She was the kind of fourteen-year-old that high-school boys search for among the incoming freshmen, those few girls with a radiant, new-grown sexual presence that makes them seem almost a different species from boys their own age.

A muscular, square-jawed tenth-grader named Calvin Robertson was one of the first town boys to notice Marie Frazier. Over the years, the memory of the pretty, brown-haired newcomer waving to him from her porch took on a powerful, almost intoxicating sweetness that grew rather than faded with time. Calvin was compact and handsome, with the kind of looks that should match up neatly with a seventh-grade beauty queen, but his infatuation with Marie Frazier accentuated his gentle, patient nature, making him quiet and self-effacing in her presence. He found it impossible to assert himself when he was challenged for her attention, and after Frank Hilley came into Marie's life, Calvin simply seemed to fade away.

More than three decades later, when he was a successful executive with a large trucking company in San Francisco, comfortable in a long, stable marriage, the father of three grown children and grandfather of four, the memory of his inaction filled Calvin Robertson with regret, and the chance to see Marie Frazier again seemed like a chance at redemption. By then, however, she had learned to control and exploit the sensuality he had watched first emerging in the girl on the porch, and she would use it mercilessly against him.

Marie and Frank Hilley went to a movie on a double date with Frank's friend Charles Lecroy, and soon Marie and Frank were going steady. No one who saw them together doubted that they would one day be married. At home, Frank announced proudly that he was bringing his girlfriend over to meet the family. He ordered his sister Freeda, three years younger than Marie and still a tomboy, to put on a dress for the occasion. Their mother, Carrie, obligingly plaited Freeda's hair. Freeda was impressed from the first with the femininity and friendly self-confidence of her brother's girl.

Freeda's older sister, Jewell, was the same age as Marie, but they never became friends. Freeda, on the other hand, happily tagged along on dates with her older brother and his glamorous girlfriend, sitting contentedly with them at the movies, or riding in the back of the Hilley family car as Frank drove out to the lake for a swim. Frank and Marie didn't seem to mind taking Freeda along, and she was never bothered by thoughts that she might be an intruder. Afterward she would bring her mother innocent, enthusiastic reports of everything "the lovebirds" had done. The lives of Freeda and her mother were to remain intertwined with the fate of Marie Frazier through darker, dangerous times ahead.

Marie was in the eighth grade when Grandma Susie Meads became sick late in 1947. The illness was soon diagnosed as cancer, and she took to her bed in the little house at Blue Mountain that she rented from the mill company for $2.50 a week. Her children and grandchildren in Blue Mountain gathered around to take care of her, and Lucille and Marie would come out from Anniston to lend a hand. They plumped the pillows to make her comfortable, combed the creamy white hair she was so proud of, and sat by the bedside to divert her with news of their lives.

Propped up in the brown-painted iron bedstead, her frail hands looking bleached and still against the colorful handmade quilt, Grandma Susie, the woman who had crossed the space of a generation to become like a mother to Marie Frazier, called forth her memories. And though she would not be there to see it, she spoke, too, of what was to come. Sometimes her mind wandered, but one day she told Robbie, now happily settled with the soldier from Fort McClellan, that the baby she was soon to bear would be a girl, born after a difficult delivery, and that she did not expect to see her great-granddaughter. Another day she spoke about the early years of her marriage, living on a farm in southern Alabama, before any of the children now surrounding her had been born. Again her mind was drawn to the bringing of new life, and to the tragedy that nests within the miracle. She described the wrenching experience of giving birth to three children who had died, two of them twins. The living children, now adults, were amazed at this hidden piece of family history. One version of the story that survived with her descendants many years later had one twin dying at birth and the other succumbing within the year, but Susie's husband, Thomas Paul Meads, told other family members that the twin had been born with Margaret, the oldest child. It had been a boy, he said, and had died at birth.

Margaret Meads Key would live long enough to see her niece Marie pluck odd threads from this fabric of family history and weave for herself the story of a new life. Marie took an overheard tale, a commonplace of southern country life, a minor injury, even the given names of her grandfather and her cousin, and created from them a mad fantasy of neglect and menace amid lavish wealth, of tragic loss and brave perseverance. She would make of her life a thrilling adventure, and she would re-create herself as its heroine.

She was not to put the final flourishes to this revised biography for more than three decades, but there were signs even in her high-school years that some mechanism of dissatisfaction, some imagined grievance, was already beginning to work at the edges of Marie Frazier's reality. She told Freeda Hilley, who had not met her until Marie was approaching high school, that she had been neglected as a child. By the time she spoke of it she was back living with her parents in Anniston, but the memories were still strong, and the hurt burned within her. Her parents had abandoned her to the care of her grandmother, Marie said. Sometimes she had waited for them to arrive at Grandma Susie's and take her back, her heart sinking finally with the realization that they were not coming, that they did not want her with them. Often they left her with Grandma Susie, even on weekends.

At Anniston High School Marie joined the Commercial Club, a group that brought together the "business women of the future," as the yearbook put it; in those preliberation days this meant girls developing their secretarial skills. In the club's yearbook picture in her sophomore year, Marie placed herself in the front row, but she seemed to have been caught unaware by the photographer, eyes half closed, mouth open a little too wide, shoulders twisted at an unbecoming angle to the camera. That would not happen again. In several class and club pictures from her junior and senior years—she also joined the Future Teachers of America—Marie's neat sweaters, smoothly arranged skirts, and carefully rolled bobby socks set her off from all but a few of her classmates. Each time, she arranged to place herself in the front row, and each time she sat erect, legs pulled up decorously to the side, her smile perfectly calibrated to combine good spirits and dignity. She seemed firmly in control of the way she was perceived by others.

There is only one of these yearbook pictures in which Marie Frazier did not place herself in the front row. Rachel Knight was the brightest star of Anniston High School's class of 1951. She was chosen for the National Honor Society, won election as a class officer, and was voted "Sweetest Girl" among the seniors. Her classmates selected her as Class Queen, pairing her in a "coronation" ceremony with the King, George Keech, the handsome captain of the football team. Rachel Knight was the kind of girl whose classmates remember her in middle age with longing for the simplicity and innocence of high-school years, when a few people made the possibility of goodness seem real.

Rachel Knight had been chosen as a leader in the clubs Marie Frazier joined, elected secretary of the FTA Club in her senior year, secretary of the Commercial Club as a junior and president as a senior. And each time a picture was taken, of twenty girls in a club or eighty students in a class grouping, Marie Frazier worked her way to the side of Rachel Knight, bathing herself in the aura of the Class Queen. The physical likeness was established—Marie had given up the pleated skirt and the shoulder-length mass of hair from junior high school for a look that made her virtually a double for Rachel Knight. Now it was as if by keeping close to Rachel—sitting by her side, joining the same clubs, seeking out her company—Marie might absorb some of the qualities of this special person. Perhaps Marie could somehow re-create herself, take on some part of Rachel's identity, enter into a kind of twinship with this girl, who was blessed with the affection and respect that Marie already felt to be missing in her own life.

Her connection to Rachel Knight did not end with high school. When it did end, this devotion to another, better self, it was with a tragic finality that would foreshadow later events in Marie's life.

After high school, Rachel Knight moved away from Anniston. Marie, married now to Frank Hilley and the mother of two children, would go to visit her old friend, sometimes taking Carol, who was in elementary school. The little girl thought Rachel Knight looked just like her mother. On one visit, Carol was puzzled by something her mother's friend was wearing on her head. It was like a helmet, but soft and strange. Later Marie told her daughter what it was: Rachel had been operated on for a brain tumor.

Marie did everything she could to help, going regularly to sit with her old friend, caring for her, supporting her, standing by as she slowly lost strength until at last she died. Marie Hilley had forged a kind of psychic twinship for herself with Rachel Knight, only the first of many she would find and invent throughout her life. And now, without knowing it, she had rehearsed for the second part of the cycle, the loss of the twin she had created.

These events were more than two decades in the future, when Rachel Knight died, however, and even well after that time there was little sign that Marie's life would hold any but the ordinary kinds of drama.

Frank Hilley had gone into the Navy soon after graduating from high school. It was the period between the end of World War II and the beginning of the Korean War. He finished boot camp and shipped out for Guam. Near the end of Marie's junior year in high school he came home to Anniston on leave.

One Monday night during the leave—on May Day of 1950—Frank and Marie went to the wedding of Eldon Williams, a friend of Frank's. Whether they had planned it in advance or were just reacting to the example of Eldon and Dorothy, no one was quite sure, but the following Monday night, Marie and Frank returned to the same Anniston church for their own wedding.

Marie went back with Frank to Long Beach, California, where he was stationed, but soon she came home and got a job as secretary to an attorney. Later she remembered using her first paycheck to buy a sewing machine for her mother, paying for it in installments. For her father, she bought the first new suit he had ever owned.

On leave once more at the beginning of 1952 before a new duty assignment at the Boston Navy Yard, Frank came home again. Marie went back to Boston with him that winter, and in the spring they learned that she was pregnant. When Frank got out of the Navy they returned to Anniston to be near their families and raise the son who was born later in the year, but Marie often reminisced about the cold weather, imagining herself in the living room on a winter day, sitting by the window with a book, watching the snow fall.

The hometown they came back to had the peaceful, sleepy aura of a typical small southern city in those early years of the Eisenhower administration. Anniston had been established after the Civil War by a bold capitalist named Noble, who organized it to exploit the rich red seams of iron ore that lay beneath the virgin forests on the surrounding hills.

By 1883 Noble and his family had created the embryo of a model city, with a broad, central boulevard lined by trees, a neat grid of macadamized streets with stone gutters and curbs, and a growing economy based on the production of cast iron and the manufacture of a diverse mix of machinery and other items, including great iron wheels for railroad cars. A corps of farm laborers worked the outlying land, also part of the Nobles' sixty-five square miles, to supply the community's food. The first issue of the Anniston newspaper that year carried a recipe for a spray to kill a mysterious worm that was threatening the crops: one pound of arsenic and two pounds of salt boiled for an hour in five gallons of water. Arsenic was as common as dirt in a farm and foundry town at the beginning of Anniston's first century, and while it would virtually disappear from common use in the next hundred years, there would be just enough around to figure prominently in the story of Audrey Marie Hilley.

The investors had assembled a population of more than three thousand for their private town, much of it handpicked by Sam Noble himself, and the county had a newly installed Prohibition law.

"The results here are wonderful," the mayor of Anniston exulted three months after the banishment of "King Alcohol."

"The change to bright and happy faces of the women, the cheerful looks of the men, the marked increase in purchases of fine furniture and other home comforts make one feel that a little heaven on earth has been started at Anniston." It was time, the founders decided, to open the town to the public and begin recouping their investment.

By the time Marie and Frank Hilley settled down to raise their own family, Calhoun was still a dry county, and a thriving welter of illegal juke joints and honky-tonks had made it famous for a riotous nightlife. For several years Anniston topped the national list of cities its size in homicides and assaults, mostly the product of Saturday-night disagreements among men and women without "bright and happy faces" or "cheerful looks." This seemed to have little to do with people like the Hilleys, however, white people who owned their homes in pleasant neighborhoods, separated from the blacks and poor whites and their segregated drunkenness.

Anniston's cast-iron industry had evolved into a thriving concentration of foundries that made the city one of the nation's largest producers of the pipe that carried wastes from toilet and sewer. Frank Hilley went to work as a helper in the shipping department at

Standard Foundry, under old Mr. Pitts. It seemed a good time to be going to work in a foundry, joining a prosperous industry that dominated the city, but the development of polyvinyl chloride—the plastic known as PVC—had already prefigured the virtual extinction of iron pipe; two decades later, coincidence would link a major step in this decline to Frank Hilley's own life. Marie, her skill as a secretary increasing steadily, left her job with the attorney and went to work at the Alabama Gas Company.

The Hilleys settled into a comfortable circle of friends, based mostly on Frank's friendships from high-school years. Three or four couples gathered every Saturday night for penny poker and beer, though it was mostly the men who did the drinking. They taught the women to play pinochle, which they had learned in the Navy. Several times a week Frank would meet his friends at the Elks Club for beers after work before going home for dinner. He didn't seem to drink much in those early years—two or three beers, maybe—and it had little effect beyond making him more cheerful.

After several years the old foreman, Mr. Pitts, died and Frank was promoted to head the shipping department. Eager to improve his position further, Frank attended night courses at Jacksonville State University for several years. Marie took some time off from the gas company when Mike was small, but she soon returned to work. She was a fast, efficient secretary and soon earned a reputation for reliability.

In public the Hilleys presented the picture of a model family. Marie was an attractive woman who took great care with her appearance. She always seemed to have put a little extra effort into her wardrobe, and her hair looked fresh from the beauty parlor. Frank was quieter but consistently friendly, a slim, pleasant-looking man with reddish-brown hair and a face that always seemed close to a smile, but there was a shadow of sadness there, too.

There was no outward sign here of the horror that awaited the Hilleys a few years ahead, but beneath the calm surface of their life, there were small currents of potential trouble. Friends noticed that Marie had a penchant for spending money. The high-school girl's habit of dressing neatly and carefully was becoming in her twenties a desire always to have dresses in the latest styles. She refused to buy any but the most costly clothes, and among her friends or in a group at work, she was known for her sense of style and the glossy look of her outfits.

Soon after they were married, the Hilleys had bought a small house. They anticipated moving to something larger when they could afford it, but Marie wasn't satisfied with the house, even for a short time. She decided that it had to be remodeled. She asked Rose White, a friend who had studied interior decorating, to take over the job. There was no one else in their crowd, couples in their late twenties and early thirties with small children, who would even have considered hiring a decorator, much less spending so much money on new furniture, wallpaper, carpeting, and drapes. The whole thing seemed extravagant to people who knew Marie.

Marie's enthusiasm for redecorating may have been reinforced by her interest in Rose and Buddy White. Of the several couples included in the poker parties and outings to the state park, the Whites stood out. Buddy had been a star football player at Anniston High School a few years before Marie graduated, and Rose had been a popular high-school beauty like Marie's friend Rachel Knight. The other men in the group had graduated from high school and worked at modest jobs—driving a bread route, selling used cars, working at the foundry—and earned modest incomes. Rose was one of the few who had gone on to college, at the University of Alabama, and Buddy was a teacher and football coach. But most significant to Marie Hilley was the wealth Rose stood to inherit from her father, who was building a sizable fortune in real estate.

The Whites' home was a gift from Rose's father, one that was to be followed by a number of other properties of all kinds over the years. It was larger than the houses of the other couples in the group, with better furniture and more elaborate furnishings. After Rose and Buddy invited the Hilleys over to eat homemade pizza one weekend, Marie seemed to swell with pleasure. She described the evening in detail to other members of the group, speaking with admiration of the Whites' house and possessions and taste and wit. Magnifying her connection with the Whites by talking about it, Marie seemed to be seeking status by association, trying to absorb for herself what she admired in them, like a primitive tribesman eating the heart of a brave warrior.

It never seemed to occur to Marie that her gushy admiration of the Whites implied that she thought them superior to the others in the group, including the ones who were forced to listen to her praise them so often and so excessively. But Marie couldn't help it. The glow of beauty and popularity and success that enveloped Rose and

Buddy, their education and status, and most of all the aura of wealth that surrounded them—these things were coming to exert a powerful attraction over Marie Hilley. Feeding her hunger, if only by association, far outweighed the importance of other people's feelings. It was a small but significant thing, this willingness to sacrifice the feelings of friends to her pursuit of the association with the Whites. She would inflict far greater damage as the need grew more insistent and as she required more elaborate prizes to satisfy it.

Marie was the same way about her car as she was about the other symbols of wealth and status, things like houses and clothes. Frank had modest tastes. He didn't want to drive a good car to the foundry, in any case; the fallout from the smokestacks would peel the paint off a car parked regularly in the lot. But Marie always seemed determined to have a new car, or a bigger car. Part of the problem, it seemed, was that Frank could never refuse his wife anything.

"Anything that she wanted, he'd give it to her," one old friend said. "It didn't make any difference, whether he could afford it or couldn't afford it, she got it." Even with Marie's salary, it seemed to their friends that the Hilleys might be getting in over their heads.

"Damn," Frank said to a friend once, "Marie can spend more money than anyone. She can sure spend more money than I can make." But he smiled as he said it, and the friend was sure that if they didn't have a penny and Marie said to him, "Frank, I need a thousand dollars," Frank would find some way to get it for her and wouldn't ask questions.

When their children were small, Dorothy Williams, who had married Frank's old friend Eldon the week before the Hilleys' wedding, became a close friend of Marie's. Each morning she hurried to get her children bathed and fed and back in bed for their naps before Marie would call. She looked forward to the chance to talk about their families and people they knew. Marie could be very sharp-tongued about people she thought were foolish or stupid. And she always seemed to be buying something.

"Guess what Mother bought for Mike and Carol Saturday," Marie would say on a Monday morning and describe an expensive collection of sweaters or a new bicycle Lucille had paid for. These purchases were so frequent and often expensive that Dorothy began to wonder whether Lucille Hilley, who was still working at a low-paying job in the mill, could afford them. Later, as Marie's tastes and interests began to assemble themselves into a pattern of constant shopping and spending, like the nonstop feeding of a shark, Dorothy was suddenly struck with a suspicion that hardened into a certainty: These were not Lucille's purchases, but Marie's.

Yet why would she lie about something like that? Dorothy wondered. Marie was too proud of these purchases, and of her own possessions, to hide them out of modesty. The only explanation Dorothy Williams could think of seemed strange and incongruous: Marie was hiding her purchases from Frank. Dorothy was dying to know what was going on, but it wasn't the sort of thing you could just ask somebody, so she never learned the answer.

3

The All-American Family

It seemed to those who knew them that the Hilleys were blessed. They were happy, attractive, and successful in every way that meant anything to a middle-class Anniston family of the time.

Their son, Michael, was born in 1953, and just when it seemed he was to be an only child, a daughter came along seven years later. Marie, who had chosen to be known by her middle name, was determined to pass it on. They named the little girl Carol Marie.

Frank never seemed much interested in organized religion, but Marie made sure Mike and Carol attended Sunday school and church every week over at Northside Baptist. At Mike's Little League baseball games, the family would arrive together. The parents made a handsome couple, comfortable and courteous with each other and open to outsiders. The children were polite and well-behaved.

Frank would rise from the bleachers and move around, uncomfortable staying in one place for long, occasionally returning to sit near Marie and Carol for a few minutes, then heading off to join the men by the fence behind the backstop. Marie was outgoing and easy to talk to, always ready to make cheerful conversation with the parents of Mike's teammates. The mother of one boy, after seeing them at games for several years, came to think of them as an ideal family, handsome, cheerful, calm, and untroubled, free of blemish, a family that could be held up as an example for others. The term "All-American" came immediately to mind. And of all the parents present, the teammate's mother thought, Marie Hilley was the one you would look for in the stands when you arrived at the game, the one you could consider as a friend.

Like his mother before him, Mike Hilley stayed with his grandmother while his parents were at work. Once he had started school, Mike would go to Carrie Hilley's home when school let out and wait for his father to pick him up after work. They would go on together to Alabama Gas to pick up Marie. One day soon after Mike had started school, his mother got in the car, and after greeting him, she turned to talk with his father. She was telling him something about the gas company, and she said that that day at work they had "fired" her. Mike didn't understand the word and he was worried for his mother until his parents explained what had happened: She had lost her job.

Mike couldn't know it, but there was real cause for concern in the incident. His mother told her sister-in-law Freeda what had happened at Alabama Gas. She had gotten into a disagreement with a woman who worked in the office, Marie said. The woman was not doing her job well and interfering with Marie's effectiveness, so she had spoken to her in hopes of bringing about some improvement. Instead, the woman turned against Marie. She had worked at the gas company a long time and had formed many alliances. Her friends joined her in ostracizing Marie.

"It's terrible," she told Freeda. "They just won't have anything to do with me."

She was outnumbered, Marie said; management had been left with no choice. They had to ask her to leave. It all seemed unfortunate, Freeda thought, but those things happen. She sympathized with Marie.

It was not until Freeda looked back on the incident a decade later that she realized it had been only the first in a repeating pattern. Marie would begin on a new job by quickly making friends with her fellow workers, impressing everyone in the office with her pleasant personality and exceptional competence.

"Then something would happen and she would end up being alone," Freeda recalled later. "She would think things that weren't really the way it was. She would think people were doing things against her, trying to hurt her in some way, and she would drop her relationship with them."

After leaving the gas company she soon found another job. That was part of the pattern, too. Her disagreements were always with the people immediately around her, usually other women in clerical positions, but her performance always brought her excellent references from the people above her. The list of men who employed her as secretary sounded like a *Who's Who* of the Anniston power structure. They included Harold Musk of the First National Bank, James Standridge of the city Water Works and Sewer Board, Walter Clinton of Clinton Controls, Clare Draper of Jenkins Manufacturing, and Harold Dillard, the owner of Advance Construction.

Her relationships with several of these men crossed over from the professional to the personal. After Marie's father, Huey Frazier, died in 1965, Freeda thought Harold Dillard became like a second father, a confidant, to Marie. His company, Advance Construction, had been an important local employer for decades. It had become a major manufacturer of uniforms, with large contracts from the military services. Dillard was an older man, well connected in the business community, a board member of a major bank and several large corporations, and more than once he helped Marie to find a job. He would play another role later in the drama of Marie Hilley's life, and it would cost him dearly.

By the 1960s Frank had been promoted to foreman and placed in charge of a large group of men. He was known as a fixture at the after-work Elks Club gatherings, where a large amount of beer was consumed in a short period before most of the men headed home for supper. The men who drank with Frank Hilley regularly thought of him as a man who kept things under control. He might drink a few beers, but you'd never know it to talk to him. His quiet, friendly manner rarely seemed to change much, and he kept his problems to himself. But one engineer who worked with Frank at the foundry, a teetotaler himself, saw it differently. He thought Frank was overdoing the drinking; he had developed a reputation as a man who had to have a six-pack after work before he could go home.

Friday night at the Elks Club was Ladies' Night. The club was decorated for dinner, and the all-male enclave was turned into a supper club for couples. As their children grew older, the Hilleys' poker dates became less frequent and their socializing shifted to the club. One night Marie took Mike to meet Frank for dinner at the club. Mike thought his father was behaving strangely, with an exaggerated cheerfulness he hadn't seen before. It soon became obvious, even to the young boy, that his father had been drinking since leaving work, and it was affecting his behavior. Mike could see that his mother was furious. His parents made a halfhearted effort to postpone the conflict, but their anger kept pushing through the cloak of polite reserve they were trying to throw over it. Soon they were arguing openly.

When they left the club, Mike waited with his father while Marie went to get the car. As they stood in front of the club, Frank was suddenly overtaken by nausea. He bent to retch in the bushes at the side of the entrance. Mike looked up to see his mother approaching at the wheel of the family car. His father had seen her also. The boy watched in horror as his father stepped from the curb and lay down in front of the car.

"Come on!" Frank shouted. "Run me over! Put me out of my misery!" He spread his arms, inviting the blow that would release him from his torment.

Someone stepped down from the curb and wrestled Frank Hilley to the sidewalk. As his father was being pulled to safety, it seemed to Mike that his mother was accelerating the car toward the spot where she saw Frank lying.

Incidents like this gave Mike a glimpse at an early age of a distance between his parents that few others saw. Frank had been promoted to supervise a whole floor at the foundry. There was hardly a man under or over him, black or white, who didn't think Frank Hilley was a good man and a good worker, fair-minded and even-tempered, always friendly, but even his closest friends never felt they knew what was going on inside him. Frank himself often said, "Boy, if I could put my thoughts into words a little better, I could write a great book." If he had strong feelings—passions and ambitions, fears and worries—he kept them to himself.

The tension between his parents left a space that Mike learned to fit into. As a disciplinarian, his mother was inconsistent. At one of the poker parties, with the children gathered in a bedroom playing, Mike punched Robert Williams, who was two years younger. Robert's screaming brought Dorothy Williams to investigate.

"Mike did that? Oh, no," Marie said, when Dorothy told her what had happened. Marie maintained a haughty disbelief that Mike could have acted badly; she refused to discipline him.

By the time he was twelve, Mike knew he could defy her and get away with it. Once when she became exasperated and slapped him, Mike shouted at her, "If you want to hurt me, you gotta hit harder than that!" She threatened to tell his father, but when Frank came home from work and she failed to mention it, Mike knew that he had viewed the slow collapse of their relationship from yet another angle.

He also knew he had found a zone of immunity for himself in the household. He learned to put up a barrier, maintaining an emotional distance from his parents and keeping his activities to himself. It was a psychological stance that would give him partial protection in a few years from the whirlwind of destruction his mother was to unleash upon the household.

Carol was another story. From things he overheard later, Mike came to believe his mother had never wanted another child. Friends noticed that Marie behaved as if she was crazy about Mike, especially when he was young, ready to tolerate whatever he might do. It was never like that with Carol, as if Marie had a higher standard for her daughter.

Mike had been raised in his early years by his mother, before she went back to work full-time. Like Marie herself, Carol spent her early youth largely in the care of her grandmothers. She thought of Carrie Hilley, not her parents, as the chief disciplinarian of her first years, one who did not hesitate to administer a spanking when she thought it was needed. Later, Marie's mother, Lucille Frazier, came to live with her daughter's family after Huey died. She shared a room with Carol, and they became close. Lucille had no taste for discipline.

Carol grew up in a neighborhood of boys, playing baseball, basketball, and tackle football, and although she was small, she always felt she was as good as any of the boys. In the early years her closest friend was her cousin Lisa, the daughter of her father's sister Freeda. The two girls stayed with their Grandmother Carrie while their mothers worked.

Carol had a hard time in school almost from the first. Anniston schools were going through the process of desegregation, tensions were high, and Carol was a pugnacious child. Marie sent her to a Catholic school for a few years, which were more peaceful, but when she returned to the public schools, the pattern continued. Carol recalled walking in the hall at Anniston High School one day when a tall black girl blocked her passage. As Carol moved to pass on the other side, the girl stepped across to obstruct her again.

"Get your black ass out of my way," Carol said.

"Don't you shout at me, you white bitch," came the reply.

The two girls pushed at each other before Carol stepped to the side and walked on. As Carol proceeded to her classroom, she looked back to see the girl walking in the same direction. Carol was barely five feet tall and weighed less than a hundred pounds. As she realized the powerful-looking girl was stalking her, Carol felt her knees begin shaking, but she was determined not to be intimidated. Inside Carol's classroom, the girl closed in, but Carol's friend Tracy, who was also black, quickly saw what was happening and intervened.

"Carol, come on over here," she called out, glaring at the other girl. She stepped between Carol and her pursuer. After a few moments of tense confrontation, Carol's antagonist turned and walked out of the room.

Carol's rebellious attitude had appeared first in confrontations with her mother. From an early age she regularly defied Marie, sometimes throwing a tantrum in public or at a family gathering in order to get her way. As she got older, the conflict intensified, and Marie never seemed to know what to do about it. When she was at a peak of exasperation, near tears, she would clutch her heart.

"I can't take any more of this!" Marie would cry. "You're going to kill me!" She would rush to find her "heart medication." Returning with the bottle, she would swallow a pill to summon the children's guilt, then ostentatiously calm herself, in an attempt to bring their misbehavior to a halt.

Frank's sister Freeda thought her sister-in-law should just take Carol over her knee and spank her, but Marie seemed incapable of it. She ended by alternating ineffective attempts at strictness with occasional permissiveness.

"Marie would just try every way in the world to give her what she wanted, to make her happy," Freeda recalled later, "but Carol was really crying out for her mother to say no to her sometimes, and she never would." Frank Hilley was capable of administering a spanking when it was called for, and the children were more respectful of their father. With Carol in particular, he was affectionate but firm. She learned that her mother was the one to approach when she wanted something.

"Carol knew that she would get her way with her mother if she had these little tantrums," Freeda observed. "Marie would get so nervous and upset that she would give in to Carol about a lot of things, she would try to pacify her."

The most coveted object of Carol's preteen years was a motorcycle. She asked for one, then begged, but her father refused. When her cousin Lisa, who was only a few months older, was given a motorcycle, Carol redoubled her efforts.

"Mom, look, Freeda bought one for Lisa," she begged. "I just want one like that, just to ride here and there, not to go anywhere in particular, just in the neighborhood." Frank Hilley was adamant, but Carol launched a campaign of persuasion and finally her mother and grandmother took her to the shop and bought the motorcycle. Frank Hilley was furious when he found out.

Lisa outgrew her motorcycle and turned to more traditional, feminine pursuits, but Carol's pleasure in her little dirt bike didn't seem to fade, and she continued to prefer wearing jeans long after her mother thought she should be making a transition like her cousin's. Freeda had been divorced and living in a house behind her parents' home on Moore Avenue in Anniston when the time came for Lisa to attend the Cooper School. The student body at Cooper was almost entirely black, and Freeda didn't want her daughter going there, so she moved out to Weaver, a few miles away. She had another motive, though. The two cousins had been spending their free hours together at the home of their grandmother, Carrie Hilley, all through grammar school. Freeda wanted to separate Lisa from the daily influence of Carol. Carol still preferred jeans to dresses and never showed any interest in wearing makeup. She was already beginning to get into fights at school and was giving signs of a general rebelliousness. Most of all, Freeda felt Marie was too permissive, letting Carol come and go almost at will.

Lisa fit easily into her new school, making friends quickly and playing an active part in school activities. She was a pretty, lively girl, and a good student as well, earning selection as a member of the National Honor Society. She became a drum majorette and was chosen to head the squad. Her classmates elected her Homecoming Queen, and later they named her Senior Class Beauty. Her beauty, her popularity, and the honors she won made Lisa seem a reincarnation of the high-school friend Marie had admired so deeply, Rachel Knight. Marie had sought repeatedly to fill some great void created in her childhood, first through her association with Rachel, and later with Rose White, whom she had asked to redecorate her home. Perhaps she sensed some magical possibility of change for herself through a greater closeness to these special people.

Now those opportunities were past, but life had presented another chance, in the form of her daughter, Carol. Like all children, she offered her mother the opportunity to rewrite her own history, to relive her own youth through her daughter in an improved version.

And there was Lisa, a perfect model of the possibility, creating for Freeda the chance at a vicarious experience of those sweet years of innocent popularity and achievement, an experience uncannily similar to the one Marie had so long coveted for herself.

"Why can't you be more like Lisa?" Mike remembered his mother saying to Carol. But Carol, headstrong and energetic, was not cooperating.

Carol recalled later that she had her first sexual experience at fourteen, and it was with a girl. Carol couldn't remember her mother ever commenting or asking about her sex life directly, but Marie did ask her a question once that seemed related to what happened later.

"Carol," she asked, "why are you always out with girls? You never go out with boys."

"I do go out with guys," Carol said, and mumbled some vague explanation, but the real answer was that even when the girls were out with other girls, they were often with boys. When their parents knew they were going to be with boys, they were required to come home earlier, so the girls would meet at each other's homes and then go to join the boys at the drive-in or the movies. But that wasn't something a girl would confess to her mother.

When she looked back on it, Carol thought that her mother's question might have been inspired by a suspicion about her sexuality, and the issue became an important part of the explanation for what Marie did to her daughter later. But at the time Marie seemed to accept Carol's noncommittal response. She wasn't the type to get any more specific about the subject of sex, even if she were suspicious, and of course Carol wouldn't have told her if she had asked. Carol did have boyfriends, too, but she would be finished with high school and well experienced in intimacy with women before she had sexual relations with a man for the first time.

Whether such suspicion was a factor or not, Marie's unhappiness with her daughter seemed to deepen. Incapable of influencing Carol in any other way, Marie was reduced to nagging. It had little effect. Relations worsened. At the same time, Frank and Carol seemed especially close. Perhaps it was in compensation for the growing gulf between Marie and her daughter during Carol's early teens. Frank took Carol fishing and sometimes invited her to join him for a round of golf, which he had taken up in the past few years as he moved up in management at the foundry. He seemed amused by Carol's spirited, physical nature, and he had gotten over the incident with the motorcycle.

"This is my little girl who likes motorcycles," he would say affectionately, introducing her to his friends.

This closeness between her husband and her daughter was like a barb in Marie Hilley's flesh. She often felt they were joining together against her, that Frank was taking sides with Carol. Her resentment found other outlets as well. Frank's visits to the Elks Club were becoming more of an issue between them, occasionally provoking bitter arguments. Marie complained to Freeda that Frank was drinking too much, and she was angry that he was spending so much time away from home. He went to the club regularly to be with friends and watch football and baseball games on television. Mike Hilley came to understand that his father was also playing poker at the club for small stakes.

Occasionally, in spite of her resentment, Marie would have to drive down to the club to pick him up, and sometimes she would take Carol along. Carol speculated later that her father may have been reluctant to drive because he felt he had drunk too much, though she never saw him obviously out of control. Sometimes Marie would send Carol in to get her father and the child would be allowed to go into the back room to tell him Marie was ready to drive him home. But at other times the men at the bar would prevent her from going inside, sending someone instead to tell Frank that his daughter was there. Carol wondered what secret activity the men might be involved in—a high-stakes card game was one guess—but she never found out why the back room was sometimes barred to her.

At other times, Marie would drop Frank off at the club and go to the home of Harold Dillard, owner of Advance Construction and her employer for a number of years. He owned a large home with a swimming pool.

When Carol was young, Marie took her along, and several times she invited Dorothy Williams to join them. There were other signs that Marie's relations with her employers went beyond the usual. Dorothy was amazed when Marie called her up one day to say that Leroy Tunis, a local business executive who was a friend of Marie's, had bought Carol a pony. And Marie showed her sister-in-law, Freeda, a pair of diamond earrings that she said Harold Dillard had bought for her as a present. If Frank was concerned about Marie's receiving such a lavish gift from an employer, he didn't show it. He laughed when Marie showed off the earrings. He knew these men. Dillard, Tunis, and other business friends of Marie's had been to dinner at the Hilleys' from time to time.

But there were other activities of his wife's that Frank Hilley did not know about. Her penchant for spending money had been building. Her mother, Lucille, who was living with Marie and Frank, was a willing accomplice. Frank didn't like the idea of being in debt, and occasionally he would become worried about their spending. He would notice that Marie had made a large purchase of clothing.

"Marie, this has got to stop," he would say, but he didn't like conflict and he didn't have the heart to challenge his wife for long. He must have sensed, too, that it wouldn't make any difference.

When Freeda proudly told her sister-in-law about a blouse she had bought at a cut-price store, Marie was aghast.

"You go there?" she asked, putting on an exaggerated expression of shock. "I wouldn't go shopping in a cheap place like that."

Wakefield's was the most expensive clothing store in Anniston, a place where elegant women, the wives of professional men and business executives, browsed at their leisure along aisles of costly garments. A middle-aged woman, a longtime saleslady at Wakefield's, described Marie Hilley as one of her best customers.

As the balances of Marie's accounts at Wakefield's and other stores mounted, she rented a post-office box to receive the bills. Frank Hilley never saw them. He had no idea how much money was owed in his name, but by 1973 a partial accounting showed that Marie and her mother owed money at a dozen stores, banks, and finance companies. Their creditors included the kind of small loan companies that serve as a last resort for people who have borrowed up to their limit somewhere else and need money fast.

In the fall of 1974 Marie walked into the office of the Universal Credit Corporation in Anniston, a reputable firm specializing in auto loans. Frank had borrowed $2,000 there in 1966 to buy Marie her first new car, a light-blue, two-door, hardtop Mustang. He had gone back every year or two for a new loan to buy a car, making each payment exactly on time with never a delay, never a problem. In 1971 he had borrowed three thousand dollars to buy a two-year-old Buick. When it was paid off in the fall of 1973, Frank Hilley had returned to Universal Credit. He was not there for a new car loan, he said; he wanted to borrow five hundred dollars against the Buick for a year. He had never done that before, but his credit rating was impeccable and the loan was made. For the first time, Marie Hilley signed for the loan, too. As before, the money was paid back exactly on schedule.

Now, within days of the last payment, Marie Hilley appeared alone at the office of Universal Credit. She wanted to borrow another five hundred dollars against the Buick, she said. No, Frank's name would not be on this one, she would take care of it herself. Marie had never taken a loan on her own name, but Universal's credit manager didn't have to look in the files to know that the Hilleys had accumulated twenty years of satisfactory accounts. He approved the loan. Marie asked to have the address on their account changed from the house on McClellan Boulevard to a box at the post office. Soon she was borrowing money at Gold Key Financial Services, another loan company in Anniston. Again she used the post-office address.

Anniston had a population of more than twenty-five thousand, but it operated in many ways like a smaller town. Soon bits of news about the Hilleys were leaking into circulation. In twenty years of selling cars, Frank's old friend Eldon Williams had gotten to know loan officers at the banks and credit companies. He was chatting about sports one day with the credit manager of an Anniston store when the man abruptly changed the subject.

"What's going on with Frank Hilley?" the man asked.

"What do you mean?" Williams wondered.

"His wife owes us money and we're not getting paid," the man said. Later, Williams heard similar news from someone else. He had lost regular contact with Frank after getting sick and cutting back on his social life several years before, so he never had a chance to find out directly from Frank what was going on, but Williams was puzzled. It didn't sound like his old friend at all. He could have no way of knowing that it was one more small sign that life was starting to close in on Marie Hilley.

The idea that she was unloved had run like a black thread through Marie Hilley's life. As far back as her adolescent conversations with Freeda, Marie had complained that her parents did not care about her. Now the same fear recurred, this time with her own family.

Carol had reached an age where she was confident and stubborn enough to stand up to her older brother. Marie had no tolerance for their bitter arguments. When she intervened they would sense her vulnerability. Like participants in a domestic quarrel turning on a policeman, the two sharp-tongued children would join in attacking her.

"Nobody loves me around here!" she would cry in the traditional complaint of the mother who feels she is taken for granted, but with Marie Hilley the roots of this anguish ran deeper. She repeated the complaint to Freeda from time to time and sometimes she included her husband as well.

"He doesn't care about me," she would say. "He leaves me alone all the time, he goes down to the Elks and drinks. He's ruining his health, and he just doesn't care about me. Nobody cares about me. Frank doesn't care, Mike doesn't care, and Carol doesn't care."

And she would lapse into a bout of self-pity. Freeda had come to share Marie's concern about Frank's drinking, but he was good about calling his wife to let her know where he was, and he always came home to Marie at a reasonable hour, not like some men. Her sister-in-law obviously needed someone to talk to—about her problems at home, about her conflicts at work—so Freeda listened, but really, she thought, Marie didn't have that much to complain about. It could have been a lot worse. The fact was that Marie Hilley's sense of grievance had a depth and intensity that raised it out of the ordinary, but that was another sign that nobody could read at the time it appeared.

Freeda put some of the blame for Marie's problems at home on the fact that Marie's mother, Lucille, was living with them. It could be a difficult situation, having an extra person in a household. Marie sometimes got into arguments with her mother, usually over nothing at all, it seemed. Frank would be thrown into the position of mediator, if only to restore peace to the household. Freeda thought her brother was sometimes nicer to Lucille than her own daughter was.

Marie had always enjoyed reading, but now she seemed more and more to be submerged in a book. It was as if she could enter the world within the pages, retreating from her surroundings, using it as a way to escape from the things that were troubling her in everyday life. She often bought hardcover books, mostly romantic novels by writers like Taylor Caldwell, Thomas B. Costain, Mary Stewart, and R. F. Delderfield, but there were mysteries, too, and Faulkner and Fitzgerald. Finally they had begun to take up every bit of available space in the house, and she decided to get rid of some. There were close to 150 books on the neat, handwritten list she offered to the Anniston Public Library.

Her books provided a stable, manageable environment amid the change that was surrounding her. Mike had lived at home for a year while he started at Gadsden Junior College. In 1972 he went to live on campus for his sophomore year. It would prove to be an escape for Mike, but his departure left Carol alone to face her mother's increasingly erratic attentions.

There seemed to be no middle ground for Marie where Carol was concerned. There were times when Marie seemed to live in her own world, going off by herself in the evening or on the weekend. Aunt Freeda would come by with Lisa on a Saturday to pick up Carol and take the girls to the roller-skating rink or a movie. Marie never went along. At other times she would take a sudden interest in what Carol was doing, wanting to know every detail of who she was seeing and where she was going with her friends.

Perhaps Marie was hoping Sonya Gibson would be a more wholesome companion than some of Carol's friends her own age. She was three years younger than Carol, a pretty, blue-eyed brunette who was active in the Brownies and had finished second in a school beauty contest. After she and Carol met at church and found that they liked each other, Marie would call Sonya's mother and invite Sonya over. They lived about a mile from the Hilleys, and Marie would volunteer to drive over and pick Sonya up. Sonya spent time at the Hilleys' house over Christmas of 1973, taking some meals there. There was no sign of any problem until Sonya got what seemed to be a mild bout of flu in early February. Two days later she sickened suddenly, unable to walk, with a high fever and vomiting, stomach pain, and a bluish tint to her lips and fingernails. Her mother took Sonya to the Army Hospital at Fort McClellan, where doctors soon decided her condition was too serious to be treated locally. They called for a helicopter ambulance to take her to Children's Hospital in Birmingham, but it was too late. Sonya Gibson died in the helicopter before it reached Birmingham.

A routine autopsy identified the cause of the child's death as severe viral illness leading to an inflammation of the heart lining, but Sonya's mother never fully understood or accepted the explanation.

Sonya had hardly been sick a day in her life. How could she be taken away so suddenly, without any warning? Sonya's mother died without an answer, but the question lived on, later to become a poignant footnote to the story of Marie Hilley.

Marie was entering her forties, but everybody said she looked fifteen years younger, and she seemed to grow more attractive with maturity. There was nothing special about her features individually, which probably had something to do with the fact that photographs rarely captured the essence of her, but she had a powerful effect on people. Women noticed her eyes, which took on the color of whatever she was wearing—now gold, now green, now gray. Her gaze was direct, as if she could see inside a person, and in a way, it was true. She seemed to fit herself quickly, instinctively, to the empty space in a person's expectations, like a cat curling up on a crowded bookshelf. She was sure of herself, free of the petty fears and hesitations that made other people self-conscious or shy. She was often funny, with a quip or a frank comment about other people's idiosyncrasies, and she was capable of quick compassion for the suffering of others. She couldn't sustain this kind of uncomplicated friendliness—in the longer run her own urgencies pressed forward for attention and made her curt, suspicious, even brutal—but people who were meeting her for the first time found her magnetic, and those among them who never spent much time with her at close quarters in these later years continued to think of her ever after as an exceptional person—brilliant, sympathetic, witty, even charismatic.

That was true of everyone who met her, but there was no question that these qualities worked most powerfully with men. As she matured, the fresh sexual presence that had drawn high-school boys to the ninth-grade girl rounded into a powerful sensuality. She seemed to put it on and wear it as easily as perfume. For a woman there was no promise in this aura of Marie's; it was merely something to be noticed. But for a man, she gave off a heady whiff of possibility, a hint that for the right man, at the right time, she might be available. Where a woman would come in time to see the sharp edges and the tough core underneath it, men were often dazzled by the aura of sexual energy that surrounded her. And there were some who never saw anything more until it was too late.

One of these was Walter Clinton.

Clinton was a powerful man, well known in Anniston business circles. He had graduated from Auburn University in electrical engineering and gone to work at the Union Foundry, overseeing the electronic equipment that controlled the heating and pouring of metal into the molds. But he had been restless working for someone else. After a few years he left to start his own company. Clinton Controls had built up a healthy business selling control equipment to large industries, including some customers making the PVC pipe that was putting Anniston's foundries out of business.

As his company continued growing, Clinton decided he needed an executive secretary, someone he could trust to manage his business affairs. The salary was good enough to stimulate Marie Hilley's interest, and the job seemed to offer a new challenge. She was still working for her old friend Harold Dillard at Advance Construction, but the new job seemed like a good opportunity for her, a healthy change of scenery, and they parted amicably.

Walter Clinton was over six feet, still solid and attractive in middle age, with thick black hair and the confident air of an entrepreneur who had taken risks and seen them pay off. He was not a man to hang back when he wanted something. Marie's work placed her in intimate contact with him, often for long hours.

Frank Hilley, in spite of his willingness to remain ignorant about his wife's activities, must have sensed the danger in this situation, but he was preoccupied with his own career. Many employees at the foundries had been losing their jobs as companies closed and those remaining were consolidated, but Frank Hilley continued to move ahead. He had been promoted again, to assistant superintendent, bringing him across the line into the upper layer of management at the foundry.

Frank's new position put him in contact with salesmen from the foundry's suppliers. He had been a longtime fan of the Auburn University football team. Usually he had been satisfied to watch the games on television, but now the salesmen often gave him tickets. He was generous with the tickets, frequently taking fellow workers from the foundry. At Thanksgiving of 1974, though, he kept two tickets for himself. Mike was coming to visit with his in-laws, and Frank wanted to take Mike's father-in-law down to the big game Thanksgiving night between Auburn and the University of Alabama.

After two years at Gadsden Junior College, Mike had gone on to

Jacksonville State University, where his father had taken night courses twenty years before, but he had not been satisfied. After one semester he had transferred to Atlanta Christian College, and now he was on his way to becoming a minister. At college he had met and married Teri Henderson. Her father's name was Everett, but everybody called him Happy.

Happy Henderson didn't know Frank Hilley very well, but it was obvious as they began the drive to Auburn for the game that something was troubling Frank. Frank was not a large man, several inches under six feet, and at forty-five, in contrast to his wife, he looked older than his years. His reddish hair had thinned, and deepening lines of worry etched his face. At Teri and Mike's wedding, Happy had found him friendly and relaxed. Now he seemed tense, as if rather than sitting at the wheel of his own car he were in some strange place with unfamiliar people. When at last he spoke, the words seemed almost to leap out, powered by some force long held in tension.

"I really need to talk to somebody," Frank said. "It's real difficult." He reached for a cigarette.

Henderson was taken aback. In the short time he had known Frank Hilley, he had never heard him speak about his troubles. It just wasn't like him, and Henderson didn't know what to say. While Frank was lighting the cigarette, Henderson tried to think how to respond. Nothing came to mind. Frank took a few puffs on the cigarette before he spoke again.

"Marie and her mother just can't get along together," he said. "They're always fussin' at each other."

He described some of the arguments the two women had gotten into over petty household matters. Frank was clearly a man who was disturbed by conflict of any kind. He had always tried to avoid situations where there might be disagreement or raised voices. But the disputes between his wife and his mother-in-law had forced him into the role of peacemaker. It was role that made him uncomfortable.

"I get along better with Lucille than Marie does," Frank said. "She just gets on Marie's nerves, I guess." He was lighting another cigarette.

If anything, Frank's nervousness had increased. It seemed as if the talk about Marie and Lucille had been only an introduction, Henderson thought. Frank seemed to have something more on his mind.

"Maybe Marie ought to see a doctor," Frank said. He didn't go on for a minute. Henderson's first thought was that Marie might have cancer. How was that related to her problems with Lucille? Maybe she was worrying about her health. A lot of people are afraid of cancer. Marie's father, Huey Frazier, had died of cancer in 1965. But Frank didn't explain what he meant about the doctor. It was only later, too late, that Happy Henderson realized Frank must have been thinking of a psychiatrist. It just wasn't something you'd associate with Frank Hilley.

The conversation was making Happy increasingly uncomfortable, but Frank hadn't finished yet.

"There's something I want to tell you," he said, "but I don't want it to get around."

In spite of himself, Henderson felt something inside pulling him back. He wanted to be helpful, but he wasn't sure he was ready to hear about the serious personal problems of Frank Hilley.

Perhaps Frank Hilley sensed this hesitation in Henderson's manner.

"I really need to talk to somebody," Frank said, as if he were trying to go back and start the conversation again.

The words came slowly, as if he were forcing them through a thick wall of restraint. Happy Henderson was a compassionate man, and Frank's muted cry for help moved him. But he had his own habit of reserve.

"A minister is always a good person to talk to," he said. He knew as soon as he spoke that the idea would be no help to Frank Hilley. Frank's face showed his disappointment.

"I kind of got turned against the church," Frank said softly.

It was clear that the conversation had reached a dead end, and they moved on to other things. Later, after Thanksgiving dinner, Happy and Frank were alone together again. Frank still seemed worried, and Happy was determined to give him a chance to speak, but the moment seemed to have passed.

Frank's worries persisted, and they continued to force their way to the surface from time to time. The following spring, he tried again to speak of them. Mike and Teri were living in East Point, on the outskirts of Atlanta, while Mike went to Atlanta Christian College. It was only about an hour and a half from Anniston, and Mike drove over on Saturday to play golf with his father whenever he got a chance. Frank had become an enthusiastic player, and they enjoyed the chance to be together. Frank would take several cans of beer along in his golf bag. He seemed to talk more easily after he had drunk a couple of them. One Saturday afternoon on the golf course, Frank's manner turned serious.

"You know, Mike," he began, "things aren't so great at home these days."

Mike wondered what his father was getting at. He had observed the tension between his parents long ago but had come to take it for granted. It had been two years since he moved out and nowadays he only caught glimpses of the strain. It wasn't something he liked to dwell on, anyway. As a boy he had learned the trick of letting these things pass through his mind without leaving painful scars of memory. It was almost as if he wasn't aware of them unless something forced him to think about them.

"Your mother and I aren't really getting along that well," Frank went on. It obviously pained him to talk about it, but he seemed determined to go on.

"We're going through a rough time," Frank continued. "With you gone and Carol growing up, things are changing."

Certainly this was true, Mike knew, and he could see how the changes might be disrupting life for his parents, but once again Frank Hilley stopped short of telling the full story of his worries. Mike was left feeling that his father's concern was the kind that all couples face as marriage passes through its phases. It was uncomfortable, Mike thought, but temporary.

And it is easy to imagine that for a long time Frank Hilley still felt that way himself, that he passed only slowly from the gentle routine of long domestic habit, first into pained but tolerant acceptance of his wife's increasingly erratic behavior and then into a state of growing alarm. A man does not easily come to see menace in the eye of a woman he has lived with for twenty years. And yet, beneath the calm surface of Frank Hilley's temperament, something dark was moving fitfully.

Sometime in the fall of 1974, at about the time Marie was opening her personal account at Universal Credit, Eldon Williams ran into Frank Hilley on the street in Anniston. Williams had been laid up for a long time with pancreas problems, and he and Dorothy had gotten out of regular touch with Frank and Marie. Williams thought his old friend looked a little wan.

"Frank," he asked, "are you feeling all right?"

"Oh, I'm not so bad," Frank replied. "I keep running this fever. I get a fever and then it'll go away, then I get a fever again, and it'll go away again." It was annoying because the doctor couldn't seem to figure out what was causing it.

Williams recalled an occasion a few months before when he had gone by to visit and Frank had a headache so bad that tears were forming in his eyes. Frank had said it was his hay fever. Eldon urged his friend to see a specialist about the fevers. It was probably nothing, but they were reaching an age where symptoms like that could worry a man.

Perhaps something like that was in the back of Frank's mind, too. A friend of Frank's learned that sometime in the spring of 1975 Frank had spoken to Marie in an offhand way about something he had been giving some thought to.

"I wonder how much it costs to bury a person," he said.

"Oh, I don't know. Probably at least five thousand dollars," she was said to have answered.

And Frank Hilley took out a burial policy on himself, according to this friend, for five thousand dollars.

Perhaps it was the routine housekeeping of a man just passing the age of forty-five, rounding the corner into middle age and thinking about the next stages of life, but Frank certainly had thoughts of mortality on his mind. His sister Freeda remembered him saying more than once, "If anything ever happens to me, Marie's gonna be a wealthy woman."

And maybe, like the worries that Frank Hilley seemed to carry with him constantly in these months, the burden he had already tried twice to share with others, these thoughts of death were anything but routine. Maybe it was all part of an awareness that was just starting to take shape on the edge of his consciousness, moving fast but never visible until it was full upon him, like the shadow of a high cloud.

The next time Frank Hilley spoke of his worries, he left no room for illusion. In early May, Mike's grandmother, Lucille Frazier, called from Anniston to chat with him. Teri was a few months pregnant, and Lucille mentioned that Frank was planning to drive over to East Point the next weekend to bring her some maternity clothes. He also had something he wanted to discuss with Mike.

"What does he want to talk about?" Mike asked.

"Oh, I don't know," Lucille said. "I expect he'll tell you when he sees you."

During that week, Mike wondered vaguely what his father wanted to take up with him, but he was too busy to think about it much. He satisfied himself with the thought that he would find out on Saturday. But Friday night Marie called to say that Frank was sick and wouldn't be coming over the next day. He had been having stomach problems, coming home early from work every once in a while, and he had gotten sick the day after they had all eaten together at the Red Lobster in East Point a few weeks before. This looked like more of the same.

It was a few weeks later before Mike had a chance to drive over to Anniston again. They had been on the course at Pine Hills for several hours when Mike realized that his father had not brought up anything out of the ordinary.

"Granny said you wanted to talk to me about something," he said.

Frank stared at him for a few moments before saying anything. The words came haltingly at first, as if he were wondering whether to speak at all.

"I don't know what I'm gonna do," he said finally. Mike remained silent, for fear of breaking the delicate mood that allowed his father to speak. After a moment, Frank went on.

"Something's happened," he said. "I just don't know what I'm gonna do about it."

"What is that?" Mike asked.

"You know me and your mother have not been getting along lately," he said.

Mike's memory went back to their earlier conversations on the golf course. His father must still be concerned about their marriage, Mike thought. But he was completely unprepared for what came next.

"I got sick one day at work and came home early," he resumed. Each word was like a separate declaration. Frank paused so long it seemed he had decided not to go on. Finally he spoke.

"Your mother was in bed with Walter Clinton."

Mike was stunned. He tried to picture the scene, the house, the bedroom, his father walking in, but his mind wouldn't accept it. Even ordinary intimacies between one's parents were hard enough to imagine. But this, it was beyond the limits of reality.

And yet it was real. Frank was talking softly about coming home to a quiet house, walking back to the bedroom to lie down, and slowly realizing that his wife was there, the initial surprise at finding

49

her home so early on a weekday afternoon being overtaken by the understanding that there was someone else present, that it was a man, it was her boss, Walter Clinton.

He had stood, stunned and mute, for several moments, trying to absorb the meaning of the scene, before turning and walking out of the house and driving away.

Things hadn't been so good between them before that, he said, but since then they'd been pretty rough. They hadn't talked about it much. What was there to say? They hadn't talked at all, hardly. Of course he had seen things over the years, knew about her men friends, but he wasn't a suspicious person. They had their disagreements, especially lately, but nothing like this. Everything was shattered.

Mike felt faintly guilty, like a child who had been eavesdropping on a conversation between adults. A part of him wanted to know more: What had Walter Clinton said? How long had it been going on? Was it still continuing? And what was his father going to do about it? But another part of him didn't want to know anything, wished his father hadn't told him in the first place. All those years he had learned to avoid knowing things at home, to keep his distance, a boy protecting himself from the painful world of adults. It was too late to change.

They finished playing in the early afternoon and went home. Frank changed his clothes and went off to the Elks Club. They parted with an agreement to play again the next week. Mike headed back for East Point.

Until events forced Mike to struggle back through his memories, looking for an offhand remark here, a bit of evidence there, some pattern that would explain what happened next, he hardly thought again of the incident with Walter Clinton and never spoke of it to anyone, even Teri—she was innocent and it would upset her terribly. He pushed it far back to a dim place in his consciousness. Eventually this day on the golf course with his father blended into the hazy picture of the many pleasant hours they had enjoyed together.

The following Friday, his mother called.

"I don't think your father's going to be able to play golf tomorrow," she said. "He hasn't been feeling so good. He came home early from work today."

Frank had vomited several times and was suffering from diarrhea.

During the week he had gotten sick at work, breaking out in a sweat. There were always rumors around the foundry that powerful chemicals and wastes from the casting process were threatening the health of the workers. Some of the men had speculated that the drinking water had been causing Frank's periodic bouts of illness. They had put in a new cooling pond at the north end of the property near the old machine shop building. Maybe cutting oils and cleaning fluids from the machine shop's waste had leaked into the cooling pond, or maybe it was the cooling water, somehow trickling back into the ground and finding its way to the water supply. None of this made much sense, since nobody else was sick, but Frank had been carrying his own water from home, just in case.

He was feeling better now, Marie said, but was still weak and tired. He had been planning to take some vacation days the next week; it would be a good chance for him to rest and recover his strength. The Standard Foundry was closing and a lot of men were losing their jobs, but Frank would be going back after his week off. He would be transferring to the Union Foundry, the last survivor of half a dozen major plants.

Mike felt there was no cause for alarm. His father had experienced these minor stomach problems and felt a little sluggish at times over the last year—it seemed he was constantly taking Alka-Seltzer—but he had always been basically healthy. This sounded like another bout of stomach flu. But over the next week his mother called almost every day with a report on Frank's health. He had been awake with chills and fever Friday night. They called Dr. Jones, and he recommended fluids and aspirin. When he had not improved by Monday, they went in to the doctor's office. The fever was gone but Frank was still vomiting and his abdomen was tender. Dr. Jones diagnosed it as a routine viral stomachache and prescribed Kaopectate for the diarrhea and Maalox for gas. There was still nothing ominous in it.

Frank continued to feel nauseated on Wednesday. Dr. Jones suggested over the phone that he try eating small amounts of food every thirty minutes to stabilize his digestive system. When there was still no improvement the following day, Dr. Jones prescribed Pridonal, an antispasmodic used to treat patients with ulcers. On Thursday night Frank awoke with a stuffy nose that was making it difficult for him to breathe. Earlier he had been showing signs of disorientation. As he reached for a nasal spray on the bedside table, his hand closed instead around a spray can of Bactine, a disinfectant for cuts and insect bites. In his confusion, he shot a heavy mist of the disinfectant over his nose and face. The skin began to burn, and he was jittery and unable to sleep.

It was still dark Friday morning when Marie called Mike again. There was alarm in her voice.

"I took your dad to the hospital," she said. "I found him in the yard at three-thirty this morning, wandering around in his underwear." She had awakened to see that he was not in bed. When she couldn't find him she walked out on the porch and saw him wandering aimlessly. "Where is the car?" he had asked. He didn't seem to recognize her. There was fear in her voice as she described the scene.

"The doctor can't seem to do anything for him. If he doesn't get well, he's going to die."

Mike was shocked at his mother's words. "'He's going to die?'" Mike thought. "Dad's hardly even been sick."

"He's never been in the hospital," he said to Teri. "I can't even remember him going to the dentist." They decided to drive to Anniston right away.

Frank was sharing the hospital room with a man who was recovering from surgery. Mike and Teri were startled when they walked in. It was as if something had sucked the substance out of him in the two weeks since Mike had seen him. His skin had taken on a yellow color so vivid that it seemed grotesque, a color that didn't belong on a human being. His movements were slow and he seemed weak. After visiting for a few hours, Mike and Teri went to wash up and get something to eat. When they came back, Frank was gone. He had been moved up to the fourth floor, placed in isolation. At last they had a diagnosis: He was suffering from infectious hepatitis.

It was a relief to know what was wrong. Now they could begin some effective treatment. Dr. Jones prescribed diet and medication to cope with the liver malfunction associated with hepatitis. Later in the day, Marie encouraged Mike and Teri to go back to the house and rest. She would stay with Frank and come home later that night.

On Saturday morning there was no sign of improvement. One minute he was taking part in the conversation with his visitors, looking wan but responding normally. The next minute his attention would wander. He seemed to drift away, his eyes open but his mind somehow turned off. When he looked up again it was as if he had just realized for the first time that there were others in the room with him.

By Saturday afternoon, Marie seemed exhausted. Mike urged her to go home and rest. He would stay with his father. She agreed; she had been up with Frank night and day, she said, ever since he had gotten sick, more than a week now. She would come back after supper.

When Marie had gone, they chatted for a while; Frank drifted in and out of lucidity. Suddenly he sat up in bed and reached across the front of his hospital gown, as if pulling a ballpoint pen out of a shirt pocket. The gown had no pocket. As an assistant superintendent at the foundry he had been responsible for processing the layoffs of other workers. He took a corner of the bedsheet in one hand and moved his imaginary pen across it. He wrote methodically for a moment.

"This is the third pink slip this month," he said.

Mike didn't know how to respond. Abruptly Frank seemed to regain awareness of the room and his son sitting next to the bed.

"What am I . . . ?" Frank started to speak, then semed overcome. He looked around the room, as if trying to find something solid to fix on. He turned back to his son. There were tears in his eyes.

"Am I going crazy?" he pleaded.

Mike was still at a loss for something to say. He had always thought of his father as steady, reliable, in control of things. Seeing him so helpless was like being a child again, lying in bed and feeling an earthquake move the house.

"Well, don't worry about it right now." Mike fumbled out the words. "Just relax and take it easy."

Frank continued to alternate periods of clarity with eerie charades. He and Mike discussed the professional basketball playoffs for a few minutes, the kind of conversation they might have had while walking on the golf course. Then, after a pause, Frank held up an imaginary newspaper and read the headlines aloud. His voice tailed off and he looked at Mike.

"What am I doing?" he asked plaintively.

Frank repeatedly felt the need to go to the bathroom, but when he started to get out of bed, he was unable to keep his balance. Mike helped him make his way back and forth, supporting his father's weight.

When Frank's sister Freeda came in for a visit, he stared at her with a wild look in his eyes; it was clear that he didn't recognize her.

Freeda was upset at the deterioration of Frank's condition. After finishing work Thursday at the Anniston Army Depot, she had driven to her house to pick up her mother, Carrie Hilley, and then gone over to visit Frank at home. When they arrived, he was sitting up in bed, rubbing the crook of his left arm. He looked discouraged. Freeda went to sit by him on the bed.

"Dr. Jones has told Marie she'll have to learn to give me shots at home," he said to his sister.

They had a neighbor, Doris Ford, who was a nurse. She had volunteered to teach Marie how to give an injection. That was unusual, Freeda thought. She took his arm and rubbed it gently. There was a red spot in the bend of the arm. She was shocked by what Frank said next.

"Freeda," he went on, "I'm sicker than I've ever been in my life. If something isn't done for me, I'm not going to be here long."

Marie stood at the foot of the bed, looking at them. She had a strange expression on her face. Freeda couldn't tell if it was concern about Frank's condition, or something else. Marie complained that Dr. Jones couldn't figure out what was wrong with Frank. She had phoned several times and left messages, she said, but the doctor wasn't returning her calls. Frank seemed restless, so after several more minutes of intermittent conversation, Freeda and Carrie had left, promising to return the next day. Now he was in the hospital. It had been only forty-eight hours, but Frank seemed much worse.

Freeda couldn't stay. She was working a late shift at the Army Depot. In the hospital lobby, Freeda and Carrie ran into the pastor of their church. He inquired politely about their business at the hospital. As Freeda told him about her brother's illness and his failure to recognize her, the minister heard the anxiety in her tone.

"That doesn't sound like anything to worry about," he said in a gentle voice. "Nobody dies from hepatitis nowadays."

Freeda was reassured by the thought. A minister would have been around hospitals enough to know what he was talking about.

By evening, only Marie and Mike were left in the room with Frank. Mike had to be back in East Point for Sunday services in the morning; at about nine o'clock he decided to return to his parents' house and get some sleep before driving back with Teri early in the morning. On the way back to the house he began feeling uneasy about leaving his mother alone at the hospital. He lay in bed for a few minutes before turning to Teri.

"I've had a very rough time getting him back and forth to the bathroom all day," he said, "and I'm not sure Mother can handle it by herself."

He had also been concerned throughout the day about the performance of the hospital staff. Dr. Jones had told him to call a nurse if blood appeared in his father's vomit; when Mike did try to signal for the staff, it had taken close to an hour before a nurse came. When he had left the hospital there seemed to be only one or two nurses on night duty.

"Maybe I better go back up there," he said to Teri. She agreed.

Marie was still sitting just inside the door when he arrived. It was around ten-thirty. Mike explained why he had come back, and they settled into a routine. Helping Frank to the bathroom had become more difficult; he had weakened further. Mike had to lift him from the bed and stay with him in the bathroom, as if he were a child. The process was complicated by the need to move the intravenous feeding equipment, with its needle stuck into Frank's arm and taped to the skin. The night passed quietly in this way, with Mike or Marie making an occasional trip down the hall to the soft-drink machine.

Mike was still concerned about getting back to East Point in time for Sunday services, but he didn't want to leave his mother alone in the hospital room. They arranged that he would go pick up his grandmothers, Lucille Frazier and Carrie Hilley, so Marie would have some help with Frank. When the three returned, it was four-thirty in the morning. Marie was asleep in her chair by the door. Mike's first thought was that something about the scene was wrong. The fan was riffling the sheet on the bed, but there was a peculiar stillness about his father. He turned to Marie, who opened her eyes and looked up as he spoke.

"I don't think Dad's breathing."

Mike hurried to the nurses' station. The hospital still seemed deserted, and there was only a single nurse there. By the time he had spoken to her and rushed back to his father, however, the room seemed to be full of hospital personnel. It was too late. Frank Hilley was dead.

Freeda arrived soon after, and then a doctor, who examined Frank. As the doctor turned away from the body to officially pronounce Frank Hilley dead, Freeda was struck by the expression on Marie's face. She had moved to stand at the head of the bed, and she was looking down at her husband. Her face reflected pure, stark dismay. Freeda was struck by the intense, focused power of emotion on her sister-in-law's face, but there was more, and it would come back to haunt her again and again as time went by. Carrie Hilley, the mother of Frank and Freeda, had seen it, too, and she and Freeda would come to speak of it often, though that was much later. Such feeling as they saw on Marie's face should not have been surprising in a woman whose husband had just died, but what struck Freeda about it was the fact that she had known Marie close to thirty years and she had never seen anything like it, never the power of emotion, nor the vulnerability, nor the picture of Marie's soul that seemed to be visible in that moment for anyone to see. It spoke of a self that Marie had never shown to anyone. This was a Marie Hilley that Freeda did not know.

Frank Hilley, age forty-five, was only one of several people who died in Anniston on Sunday, May 25, 1975, and it was only much later that his passing came to seem extraordinary. But there were several small circumstances that added uneasiness to grief for the family, friends, and neighbors of Frank Hilley.

Frank's mother, Carrie Hilley, was not a terribly emotional woman, but she could not rest. It was more than just the grief of losing her only son. Why should someone die like that, so fast, with no time to get ready, no time for anyone to get ready? It all seemed so strange. And Freeda had said no one ever died of hepatitis. Carrie phoned to ask Dr. Jones more about Frank's illness, but he didn't have much to say, certainly nothing that could explain what happened. It seemed to Carrie after a few minutes that he didn't want to talk about it anymore.

Carol Hilley seemed bewildered. Only fifteen years old, she had grown especially close to her father in the past few years, even as she had become more estranged from her mother, and she had had no time to prepare for his going. One day she had returned from school to find him home early, feeling slightly sick—"nothing serious," they said—and then, almost before she had a chance to realize he was really ill, he was gone.

Several of Frank's friends—those who didn't see him frequently, like the Williamses and Charles Lecroy—wondered why they hadn't even heard he was sick. Frank had died without a chance for a final visit, a leave-taking. Marie explained that things had happened too fast, that they had never realized how sick he was until it was too late, but that wasn't much help.

Mike's father-in-law, Happy Henderson, remembered a conversation with Frank a couple of years before. The Hendersons had come up from Florida to attend their son-in-law's ordination at Indian Oaks Christian Church in Anniston. Mike had preached the sermon during the service. Afterward, Happy and Frank had stood together for a moment by the road outside the church. It was the first time Frank had been to church in a long while.

"Wasn't he terrific?" Frank had said. Happy Henderson agreed that his son-in-law had done an impressive job.

"I can't think of anybody I'd rather have preach the sermon at my funeral," Frank said.

It had seemed a somber note at a happy time, and Henderson had never spoken of it to anyone. After Mike Hilley called with word of Frank's death, Henderson thought again of the conversation and told Mike what his father had said. Mike preached at his father's funeral, and again at the graveside service. Happy Henderson was left to reflect on the irony of a man so rarely in church and seeming, in his age and health, so far from death, giving thought to a funeral that then followed so soon, so shockingly soon.

The official finding that Frank Hilley had died from infectious hepatitis brought county health inspectors hurrying out to the Union Foundry. The foundry used water from both the city's lines and its own well; either could have been a source of Frank Hilley's infection. But repeated tests turned up no trace of the bacteria. That didn't stop the rumors, which continued to swirl among the men at the foundry, as if they sought to invent a real danger to replace the anxiety of the threatening unknown.

4

Disintegration

Frank Hilley died early Sunday morning. Tuesday he was buried at Forestlawn Gardens, a spacious, attractively landscaped cemetery. It was only a few miles across town from the sparse, hilly Edgemont Cemetery of Marie's childhood, but it seemed to be in another world. On Thursday Marie applied for Frank's life insurance.

In the strange series of events that surrounded Marie Hilley after her husband's death in 1975, there is one theme that emerges again and again: money and its uses. Certainly finances are a matter of concern for any new widow, for any person, so there was nothing surprising in that. And Marie's natural secretiveness kept hidden much of what was happening, or enabled her to reveal a little to many people but a lot to almost no one, so that at the time nothing seemed amiss. It is only in retrospect, and then only by patiently assembling a thousand separate bits of evidence and observation, that we see the specter of madness slowly emerging from the shadows.

Frank Hilley's life insurance came to a little more than thirty thousand dollars. There may have been another several thousand dollars in veterans' insurance. Social Security survivor's benefits came to about $5,000 a year. By many people's standards that would not have been enough to fulfill Frank Hilley's prophecy that Marie would be "a wealthy woman," but to a forty-two-year-old widow with a steady job and no extraordinary expenses, it was a big pool of ready cash and a sizable supplement to a secretary's salary of around $225 a week.

The mortgage on the house and money owed on Frank's credit accounts were paid off by life insurance on the loans. Just before Frank died, Marie fell behind in the payments on the loan account she had started on her own at Universal Credit. A regular fifty-one-dollar installment was due in the first week of May, three weeks before Frank Hilley was to die, but Marie did not make the payment. Could she have anticipated a windfall? Within a week of receiving the check on Frank's insurance she had paid off the balance on the account.

That fall, she bought a new Oldsmobile, a white, two-door hard-top Cutlass Saloon with an eight-cylinder engine. Frank had favored General Motors cars, too. She paid cash.

Marie's pleasure in shopping for expensive clothes was not muted by Frank's death. On the contrary, it seemed to intensify, and she set about running up her account at Wakefield's and at Hudson's, another clothing store in town. She bought a jade-and-diamond necklace with matching earrings, and she spent freely at furniture stores downtown and the little housewares and gift shops in the malls out toward Fort McClellan and the Army Supply Depot. Even in the grocery store she picked out the most expensive specialty foods. Much of her spending was on herself, but she was generous with others, too. Freeda noticed—reflecting, perhaps, that it was her brother's death that had made it possible—that Marie bought her mother a diamond ring soon after Frank died. She often took Lucille with her on a shopping spree, including her mother's choices among the purchases.

Her children came in for their share of the largess, too. Whenever Mike called home, Carol would list off the things—a stereo, a bicycle, furniture for her room—Marie had bought her lately. As soon as she was ready to drive, her mother bought her a new 1976 Honda. She was constantly offering to buy things for Mike and Teri, who were not long married and setting up their first household.

The phone rang one day at Mike and Teri's house in East Point, near Atlanta, less than a year after Frank died. It was Marie.

"Are y'all going to be home later on today?" she asked.

"Yeh. Why?" Mike asked.

"Oh, nothing, I've just got something coming for you, and I want you to be there."

Delivery men showed up later that day with a washing machine. They had to take the frame off the door to fit it in, and the only place where there was space for it in the small apartment was the bathroom, but it remained in Mike and Teri's household long after everything else about their relationship to Marie had changed completely and irrevocably.

"Honey, you shouldn't be buying your clothes at Kmart," Marie said to Teri. "It doesn't look right for Mike's wife to be going out there." She insisted on taking Teri to the expensive stores where she shopped. The clothes Marie bought for her only made Teri uncomfortable.

"I'm afraid to wear them," Teri said, "they cost so much. I'm afraid I'll get a stain on them." She was only half joking.

Mike knew how she felt. There was something desperate in many of Marie's purchases. What seemed to be generosity on her part was often undercut by the feeling that she was driven more by her own need—for affection? for a feeling of usefulness?—than by the wishes of the recipient. She insisted on taking Mike to Wakefield's, picking out suits for him to try on. Normally Mike bought his clothes at J. C. Penney and Sears. He didn't wear a suit except on Sunday, and he didn't feel he needed more than he had. The need all seemed to be on his mother's side, and he ended up with several new suits hanging in his closet. Mike was shocked to find out later that they cost three hundred dollars or more. It made him uncomfortable. Just as unsettling was the feeling that somehow his mother expected something in return, though she never made it clear what that might be.

If Marie's financial situation was temporarily made easier, even luxurious, by Frank's death, there were signs over the next year that other aspects of her life were not so comfortable. The week after Frank died, Marie's mother found a lump in her breast. It was diagnosed as cancer, and she soon began treatments.

Carol was growing up, expecting greater freedom, but instead of relaxing her control, Marie became more possessive, trying to oversee Carol's social activities and choice of friends. She was ready to buy her daughter things, even a new car, but not to let her move on to a life of her own. Carol's defiance of curfew hours and other forms of resistance led to more frequent conflict, and without Frank to deflect some of the hostility, their arguments became more bitter.

"She's making my life unbearable," Marie complained to Mike on the phone. "I don't know what to do with her. I try, I do everything I can for her, and she just goes right ahead and does what she pleases."

His mother was trapped in a tragic cycle of failure with Carol,

Mike reflected. Carol's need was for emotional support and guidance, but her mother was incapable of providing these things. Instead, she gave what she could: she indulged Carol's material demands. Carol accepted the things her mother bought her, but they left her empty, and she became ever more resentful at her mother's failure to help her in the way she most needed. Marie, who felt she was doing what she could for her daughter, saw the resentment as ingratitude. And relations between them became constantly more tense and combative.

Marie felt helpless, she recalled later:

"I realized that somewhere along the way, [Carol] had moved into [her] own world, and I felt more alone than I've ever felt. I didn't know how to reach [her]."

Life had been "peaceful and predictable," Marie said. Now it was spinning out of control.

She complained to anyone who would listen, reaching out for sympathy. Marie had always been a favorite niece of her father's twin brother, Louie. Louie thought of her as "a sweet girl," cheerful and considerate. She regularly called Louie and his wife, Ailene, in Florida, where they had moved after he retired. Marie had stayed in touch with Ailene Frazier following Louie's death. Now Ailene was surprised at Marie's tone as she talked about the situation at home.

"Nobody loves me," Marie told her. "The whole family is against me."

Ailene figured Marie was going through a difficult period of adjustment to her husband's death. Ailene knew how traumatic that could be, but Marie would get over it in time, she thought.

Marie came to confide increasingly in Freeda in the months after Frank died, and their friendship took on a new closeness. They had shared the loss of Frank, and now Freeda sensed that her sister-in-law needed someone to talk to. They got together regularly for coffee, especially after Freeda was divorced, and they exchanged the little favors that single parents need from time to time. They even exchanged clothes—Marie's weight fluctuated widely, and she seemed to tire of things quickly—and Freeda often received a blouse or dress that looked as if it had never been worn.

Marie's troubles were not confined to her family. She confided to Freeda that she was having trouble at work. She had left Clinton Controls—she found the job dull, Marie said, but Freeda sensed that there had been other problems, possibly the kind of friction with

61

other women that had plagued her before. Now she was working at Sturm, Wallace, and Whitlow, the most prestigious law firm in the city, but she still seemed unsatisfied. She was secretary to Arthur Sturm, the senior partner, but she complained that he was "a crude little man" and she seemed perpetually on the verge of quitting.

Mike Hilley was concerned about his mother, too. She called him often in East Point, and she always seemed upset about something. Lucille was weakened by her struggle with cancer and needed a lot of physical and emotional support. Marie herself seemed overwhelmed sometimes. Since Frank died she had complained often of feeling isolated. She was easily disturbed by small things. She had received a series of nuisance phone calls, someone calling and hanging up without speaking, she said. One day she had come home from work to find drawers pulled out in the kitchen and a teapot broken. Mike did what he could to help, but the problems were constant and it was a three-hour round trip to Anniston from the Atlanta suburbs.

When he was invited to serve as assistant pastor at Indian Oaks, the church in Anniston where he had been ordained, it seemed the perfect answer. The idea of getting some experience while serving his first ministry in his hometown was attractive. Teri would be able to help take care of Lucille. Perhaps Mike might be able to help his mother stabilize her life. He accepted.

Marie invited them to move in with her and Carol and Lucille. Teri had gotten sick right after the funeral and stayed with Marie in Anniston to recuperate, while Mike went back for final exams at Atlanta Christian College. It was easy for Mike to join them there. The house on McClellan Boulevard had plenty of room for all of them, Mike and Teri could save some money on housing, and it would be convenient for Teri to help with Lucille. The idea of reestablishing the family unit, three generations under one roof, sounded attractive. Mike and Teri accepted the invitation.

It soon became obvious that their ideal vision of the family was not going to be realized. Mike was no more comfortable living with his mother's authority than he had been as a boy. Rather than blending together as one family, the household simmered with conflict. Mike and Teri had established their own routines, Marie and her household had theirs, and the two didn't fit together. After several months of constant tension, Mike and Teri gave up and went looking for an apartment. When they told Marie they were planning to move out, she was upset.

"I need you here," she said. "You know what it's been like for me since your father died, and then Granny got sick."

"We're not going far," Mike told her, "and Teri will be right here to help with Granny."

Marie switched directions, trying to play on their guilt and sense of duty:

"I've been here when you needed help, and now you're going to leave me."

But they were determined and she couldn't change their minds. The stage was set for the appearance of a new element in the story of Marie Hilley: fire.

The night before they were to leave, Teri and Mike were at church, where he was preaching the Sunday evening service. Carol was out with friends. A neighbor spotted smoke coming from the house and called the fire department.

"Her mother's sick in bed!" someone shouted to the fire fighters as the trucks pulled up. "She must be in there!"

Firemen were preparing to rush into the house to search for Lucille Hilley when Marie drove up. Lucille was in the car with her.

"We went for a ride," Marie said. There was little flame, but heavy smoke caused extensive damage. Marie, Lucille, and Carol couldn't possibly stay there. They moved into the new apartment with Mike and Teri, delaying the separation.

It was never clear how the fire had started. Marie blamed it on a heating and air-conditioning unit installed by the gas company, and she filed a lawsuit against them. As the suit progressed, Marie was slipping ever deeper into a quagmire of lies and deception, until finally the suit failed.

Repairs, cleanup, and repainting took close to a month. At last Marie prepared to move back into her house. One evening, again when no one was home, fire broke out in the apartment next to Mike and Teri's. The flames were confined next door, but the heavy smoke drifted through the building and saturated Mike and Teri's apartment. They had no choice but to move back in with Marie. It was almost as if she had planned it, to keep them close. But they were determined to have a home of their own, and soon they put down a deposit with Jerry Ray, the landlord of a small apartment complex not far from Mike's church.

It is easy to imagine the flames that sprang up wherever Marie went over the next two years as the outward manifestations of the fires burning ever hotter within her. The sequence of fire-related incidents was interrupted for a few months after Mike and Teri moved out the second time. Their departure eased the tension in the household somewhat, but Marie was still under strain. Nothing she tried with Carol seemed to work out right, and her mother was requiring more care. Lucille's breast had been removed, but it was clear that the cancer had established itself, and her condition was deteriorating quickly. She wanted to stay at home, so the family took care of her as well as they could. After Christmas of 1976 she was in pain and required frequent medication. Doris Ford, the neighbor who was a nurse, gave the injections a few times when it was necessary. She also showed Marie how to give her mother the shots when no one else was available. The whole family contributed in the last weeks, before Lucille Frazier died in early January.

Several months later, Marie called Lieutenant Gary Carroll at the Anniston Police Department to complain that she had been smelling gas fumes in her house for several weeks. An officer investigated but found no sign of a leak. Doris Ford told someone about the same time that the gas on her outdoor grill had been turned up all the way and she had smelled it outside. If there was a connection between these events and Marie's suit against the gas company, nobody noticed it.

A month later Marie discovered a fire in her hall closet just before four o'clock one morning. The police investigated and found no sign of a break-in. There was little damage.

Forty-eight hours later, Doris Ford returned from a short trip to discover that there had been a fire in her hall closet. It had burned itself out. Doris felt lucky. If it had gotten started from that central location, the house could easily have burned down. There was no sign of forced entry, and nothing was missing. Doris had given a key to Marie Hilley in case of emergency, but Marie said she had not been in the house and had seen nothing unusual.

Though he had not met her, Lieutenant Carroll had become familiar with Marie Hilley over the previous months. Carroll was one of two supervisors under the captain of detectives. Ordinarily he wouldn't have taken a direct interest in something like a report of gas fumes; he would have left it to one of the detectives under his supervision. But Marie Hilley was getting to be something special.

She seemed to be experiencing more than her share of difficulties. Going back over the reports, Carroll found that the problem with the gas fumes was the fourth involving Mrs. Hilley in just three months. In March she had reported a burglary in which jewelry, two guns, and a hair dryer had been stolen. A short time later she had arrived home after dark to find the light in her kitchen being turned on and off; when she returned with the police, no one was there. And just a few weeks after that, she had reported receiving nuisance phone calls and a threatening note.

Gary Carroll is a tall, quiet man, serious about his work, and widely regarded around the police station and courthouse as a first-rate detective. He decided to investigate the note himself.

In the practiced way of an experienced detective, Carroll looked around the house as he introduced himself to Marie Hilley. One of the first things he noticed was a Bible on the end table. The furniture looked new, and everything appeared to be well cared-for. There was a collection of expensive-looking glass objects—a clown, a crystal sphere, a cat, and others—carefully arranged on a shelf. Mrs. Hilley was neat and well-spoken, a widow with a son who was a minister in town, a teen-age daughter at home, and no man in the house.

"May I offer you some coffee?" she asked.

Carroll didn't like coffee and never drank it, but he was impressed by her courtesy. It was rare for anyone to make that kind of thoughtful gesture to a cop. Most people with a complaint to make were too preoccupied with their own worries.

Marie Hilley appeared to be genuinely concerned. There was real fear in her voice as she talked about the threat, the feeling that somebody was out to get her. She reported that she had come back from shopping and found a piece from an envelope tacked to the screen door at the rear of the house. The front of the envelope had been torn away and the note was scrawled on the outside of the remainder. The writing, in blocky, quarter-inch letters, looked like that of a child, or an adult using his off-hand.

The message read, "You are going to be sorry if you don't move."

There was no clear lead to follow. Mrs. Hilley had no idea who could be harassing her. That only magnified her fear, she said. Carroll examined the note and sent it to be processed for fingerprints. Nothing turned up. In the normal course of business the file was eventually sent down to Central Records.

There was no reason for Gary Carroll to think he would ever see that piece of envelope again, but two years later he would have reason to remember it and retrieve the dusty file on Marie Hilley from the archives of the Anniston Police Department. By then he knew a good deal more about her—he had spent enough time talking with her and thinking about her that he thought of her familiarly as Marie—and he examined the note with a fresh eye. This time he found a faint impression on the inner surface of the envelope back, where the typing of the address had come through from the missing front.

Rubbing lightly with the side of a pencil point, Carroll brought up the address:

"Miss Carol Hilley, 2905 McClellan Blvd., Anniston, Ala. 36202."

It would have been interesting to know the source of the envelope when Marie first presented it to him, but Carroll was forced to admit to himself that it probably wouldn't have made much difference in the case. Too much was below the surface, out of sight and beyond anyone's control.

No sign of this was present in his first contacts with Marie Hilley, though, and no hint that her case would become the most challenging he had ever faced, at times approaching an obsession. He did notice that during the several months when Mrs. Hilley was lodging her series of complaints, a neighbor, Doris Ford, had also called in with similar problems—a noise in the backyard, window screens cut out—but nobody could find a connection. Things soon became more complicated, however.

Over the months, many different officers had investigated and studied complaints at Marie Hilley's house on McClellan Boulevard. One of them was Billy Atherton, an officer in his late thirties. Atherton was a rather ordinary-looking man except for a pink heartshaped birthmark on the back of his right hand. He had just been divorced for the second time, and practically everyone in the Anniston Police Department thought he knew the reason: Billy Atherton pursued sex constantly, without hesitation or discrimination. He said it himself, he said it often, and he never seemed embarrassed about it: "I'll take whatever I can find." As far as anyone could tell, that was Billy Atherton's motto.

As Atherton told the story later, several officers on the evening shift were sitting in the station doing paperwork when someone called with a prowler complaint. The cars on the road were tied up and the dispatcher needed an officer to make the run. The caller was a Marie Hilley, out on McClellan.

"Bet you'd like that one, Billy," somebody said.

"Now, why would you say that?" Atherton replied. He was on his guard, expecting to hear that the complainant was a particularly troublesome or eccentric "repeater."

"Damn good-looking woman," the other officer said.

"That's right," someone else said, and described a complaint he had taken from her a few weeks before.

Atherton still suspected they were pulling a practical joke on him, but he had been at the paperwork long enough.

"What the hell," he said, "I'll go."

Atherton was pleasantly surprised to find that Marie Hilley was what they had said, a small, well-built, nice-looking woman, widowed a couple of years, who appeared to be in her early thirties. He made a point of listening sympathetically and offering reassurance. Soon she was asking specifically for him when she called in with a complaint during the night shift. After a couple of visits, Atherton started to get a distinct feeling that she was interested in more than his investigative skills.

One day, as Atherton told it later, he was at her house in response to a call—something about a prowler looking in the bedroom window. They sat at her kitchen table while he wrote out the report.

"I don't know what I'd do without you, Billy," she said, and leaned forward to put her hand on his knee. She looked directly into his eyes.

"I'm so alone, and I need a man to help me," she went on, and as she spoke, Marie Hilley slid her hand up his leg until the end of her finger touched his penis through the cloth of his trousers.

Atherton was already involved with several women at the time, but it wasn't every day that you got such a direct invitation, and he had never been one to pass up an opportunity. Billy Atherton began seeing Marie Hilley in his off-duty hours and soon they were sleeping together.

Atherton liked the comely widow, and he thought of her as a "sweet lady, a caring, loving mother" to her daughter. Though there was no special emotion between Atherton and Marie, he was glad to have her on his list. She called the station often; most of the time it was during the night shift. Once, after consecutive prowler incidents, they even staked out her house for several nights, two detectives in an unmarked car, but nothing turned up. A few times her daughter, Carol, corroborated her complaints, but Atherton noticed that some of them seemed strange or nonsensical. He told himself she was just using them as a pretext to get him out to her house. He was happy to play along with her.

The death from cancer of Marie's mother, Lucille Frazier, in January 1977 seemed to give rise to a new series of strange events surrounding Marie. But that was only in retrospect. At the time, no one saw the connection.

Something was affecting Teri Hilley's health. When she had gotten sick the day after Frank died, she had assumed it was the morning sickness. She was in her fourth month, and she had been nauseated on waking up for a few weeks. Her appetite had disappeared.

Marie had come into Teri's room that Monday morning to see why she was still in bed. Marie's grief, only twenty-four hours old, didn't prevent her from being concerned about her daughter-in-law.

"What's the matter, honey?" she asked Teri.

"Oh, it's just the morning sickness, I guess," Teri had answered.

"But you've got to eat something. You've got to keep your strength up."

"But I'm sick. I just don't feel like it."

"Don't be silly. I'm going to bring you some soup. It'll taste good."

There was finality in Marie's tone. She was putting an end to the discussion. She reappeared a little later with a bowl of potato soup, thick and fragrant.

"Now, you eat this. It'll do you good. You need all the good food you can get. It's an important time."

And Teri was surprised at how good the soup tasted. Maybe Marie was right, she thought, maybe this was the way to deal with the morning sickness.

But within an hour she was feeling nauseated again, and soon she developed pains in the stomach and legs. She began to vomit and couldn't keep anything in her stomach, even liquids. The pains became cramps and it felt as if her body was tying up in knots. Marie took her to the hospital and she was placed on intravenous feeding to stop the dehydration. They were concerned that whatever was causing her symptoms might threaten the baby.

The doctor wondered if Teri had gotten hepatitis from Frank. He wanted to give her gamma globulin for protection, but asked her to consult the obstetrician who had been taking care of her in East Point. Marie volunteered to make the call, and returned to say that he had approved the injection. When Teri went back to East Point for an examination a few months later, she mentioned the injection to the gynecologist.

"I told them not to give you that shot," he said.

"My mother-in-law said you told her it was okay," Teri said.

"Your mother-in-law called me and I told her you shouldn't have the injection at that point. She was going to tell the doctors there."

Teri was puzzled by the discrepancy. Marie must have misunderstood, she thought, and dismissed the incident from her mind. It was another of those routine happenings that would later prove to be unforgettable, haunting reminders of peril.

Afterward Teri had seemed to recover a bit, and her fear for the baby eased. But within a few days of going home to Marie's she got sick again, and this time she was hemorrhaging. She returned to the hospital, but it was too late. The baby was lost in a miscarriage.

Mike joined Teri at Marie's house and began work at Indian Oaks Christian Church. Teri was staying in bed, trying to recover her strength. Her appetite had still not returned to normal. One of the few things that appealed to her was soup, especially Marie's vegetable soup with tomatoes, potatoes, and beets. Marie often served Teri in bed, while the others ate at the table.

Several weeks after the miscarriage, Teri became sick one evening. Within ten minutes, she was suffering intense nausea. She was breathing rapidly and couldn't seem to get enough air; she was hyperventilating. She vomited repeatedly, uncontrollably, and soon she was stricken with sharp pains in the abdomen. Mike wanted to take her to the hospital, but she resisted; she had almost never been sick before, and she didn't want to give in to her symptoms. She spent a sleepless night. By midmorning she was delirious, and Mike became alarmed. She was so weak they had to carry her to the ambulance. This time she was in the hospital more than a week; she needed intravenous feeding.

Teri Hilley was in the hospital four different times while she and Mike were living with her mother-in-law. An old friend teased her, "You were never sick until you got married, Teri. Maybe marriage doesn't agree with you."

It was true that these episodes coincided with the period soon after their marriage, when Teri and Mike moved to Anniston, but except for the joke, nobody made anything of the connection at the time.

It was the same way with other quirks that started appearing in Marie's behavior: She was Marie Hilley, a bereaved and proper widow, a generous and loving mother, a bright and charismatic friend and confidante. Against the background of what she had been and seemed still to be, the changes that escaped her talent for concealment seemed insignificant or temporary.

The fire and smoke damage had been repaired and Marie and Carol had moved back into the house on McClellan when the radio warned of a storm moving toward the Anniston area one day during the tornado season. Freeda and her daughter, Lisa, were living in a trailer park and became worried about what a high wind might do to their mobile home. When the wind picked up force in midafternoon, they called to ask if they could spend the night with Marie and Carol.

Carol invited Lisa to share her bedroom. Marie had taken to sleeping on the couch, which struck Freeda as strange. She settled down on another couch, across the room from Marie. A light sleeper, Freeda suddenly found herself awake without knowing what had brought her out of sleep. It was still well before dawn, pitch-black outside. Across the living room, the door to the bathroom was slightly ajar and the light was on, but there was no sign of activity. Marie's place on the couch was empty.

"Is everything all right?" The words framed in Freeda's throat, but she caught herself before speaking them. Something strange in the scene stopped her. It was the extraordinary stillness, a complete absence of movement, of sound. What was Marie doing in there?

Minute after minute went by without change. Freeda was mesmerized: The eeriness of the scene pressed on her. She felt she should avoid any movement or sound of her own, even stop her breathing, to match the stillness that seemed to flow from the bathroom, almost like something you could touch.

Freeda imagined Marie standing motionless before the mirror. She pictured her sister-in-law's gaze, those piercing eyes locked onto their own image, searching for a self she could trust, transfixed by the image of herself searching. Freeda saw again the almost supernatural power and intensity of feeling on Marie's face at that moment in the hospital when she had heard the doctor pronounce Frank Hilley dead. Now it was fear that kept Freeda from moving. The minutes had drawn out. Was it an hour? More? Less? She had lost all sense of time.

Finally the light was snapped off and Marie emerged. She seemed to be in a trance. The darkness and the sense that she had been eavesdropping on some private ritual still kept Freeda from speaking as Marie settled down on the couch. It kept her, too, from ever mentioning later what she had seen, but the eerie strangeness of the scene lingered in her mind.

Carol Hilley also stole a glimpse into the mysterious double world of Marie Hilley that summer after Lucille Frazier died, and it was as bizarre, and finally unfathomable, as any of the bizarre and unfathomable happenings that came to view wherever Marie Hilley went.

School was out and Carol was at loose ends, unsure what to do with herself, not strongly drawn to anything, drifting through the house from day to day. Poking around in the china cabinet one afternoon, she opened a drawer where there should have been only napkins and tablecloths, and found a letter. She thought at first it was something her mother had written. It wouldn't be so bad to read it, she thought, and even after she found it was addressed to her mother, curiosity drew her on. She read the letter.

It was from a woman whose name Carol didn't recognize, but she described herself as an aunt of Marie's. Now that your mother is gone, it said, and your father and most of your close relatives, there is something I think you should know about, before everybody who could tell you has passed on: You were born with an identical twin, a sister.

Your father, Huey Frazier, was a twin, the letter went on, and he believed that being raised with his brother Louie had caused him great unhappiness throughout his life. He was not willing to inflict the same unhappiness on his daughters. Soon after they were born, he gave one of the babies to a relative in Texas. The baby's name was Mandy, and she had lived her whole life there. In recent years her husband had been killed in an auto accident.

Lucille had been sick before the birth and unconscious for some days afterward, so she was not aware what had happened. She awoke to the news that she had given birth to a single daughter, who was named Marie. Huey insisted on keeping the story secret, the letter said, for fear of Lucille's reaction. The writer had noticed an unhappiness in Marie's life as a child and had wondered if she somehow sensed the loss of her other self. Now that she was older, and those who had sealed and kept the secret were dead, perhaps it might help her in some way if she knew the truth.

Carol was stunned. She read the letter over several times, and as she did, fear crept over her, a fear she could not explain. She called a friend, Laura, to come and share it with her. When they finally put the letter back in the drawer, arranging the table linens to look untouched, Carol felt guilty at having read it, and overwhelmed by the magnitude of a secret she was not meant to share. Like Freeda, she clutched her share of her mother's mystery to herself. She had never asked her mother about the letter, and eventually the memory slipped away.

It was revived only when Carol heard six years later of the separate life her mother had built for herself as a fugitive, and the past she had invented to explain herself to new acquaintances. The idea of the twin, the second self, was always an important part of those inventions, and Marie had been ingenious in creating documentation for her fantasies, notes and letters that gave substance to her fears or told parts of her story. They were like fragments of an autobiography, except they recounted a life not as it had been, but as she wished it had been.

And this story was so improbable, Carol reflected—Lucille's ignorance of the twin's existence was especially hard to accept. As far as Carol was aware, nobody who had known her mother as a child remembered any particular unhappiness, or any reason for unhappiness. Besides, Marie's Aunt Margaret, Lucille's sister, said later that there was nothing to the story of the twin. She would know, wouldn't she? The letter must have been another of Marie's creations.

And yet, and yet . . . the letter, as Carol remembered it, was not in Marie's handwriting, that distinctive, neat, flowing script, nor was it in the kind of blocky, childlike scrawl produced by using the off-hand. Where had it come from? Carol would never achieve certainty on that question, but to outsiders looking back, the letter came to seem just another in a series of strange events set in motion by Marie Hilley.

Marie continued her calls to the police department during these months after her mother died. Half a dozen officers responded to her calls, though she often asked for Billy Atherton, but after she phoned Lieutenant Carroll about the gas fumes, he continued to work on her case. After the first few calls it was obvious that she liked him, and they became friends. She always offered him coffee, and he always politely declined. The incident with the threatening note remained unsolved, and the nuisance phone calls were continuing.

Carroll was to be the first person who formed a coherent suspicion about Marie Hilley's behavior, and it was the phone calls that did it.

At first the calls seemed to be just another way in which somebody was trying to frighten her. The phone would ring, she said, and when she picked it up, no one was there. This had happened several times, and it was very upsetting. The detective asked the phone company to put a trace on her line. She reported several incidents of minor harassment over the next few weeks—flowerpots turned upside down, a pound of hamburger disappearing from the kitchen counter near the screen door—but no phone calls. The tracing equipment was removed from her line.

In the meantime, however, Doris Ford filed a complaint: She had been receiving nuisance phone calls. They had started six months before, she said. The phone company had suggested she keep a log. In the last month she had received thirty-two calls. Lieutenant Carroll contacted the phone company and asked them to put a trace on Doris Ford's line. The calls stopped, and after several weeks, the trace was suspended. In July, soon afterward, the calls resumed. Carroll had the trace reinstated.

Within a week, Marie Hilley called. She had moved to an apartment on Marguerite Avenue. She had kept her new phone unlisted, but the night before, she had received a call from someone who did not speak but breathed heavily into the phone.

"Who knows your new phone number, Marie?" Carroll wanted to know.

"Nobody, Gary. Only Carol and Mike, and Doris Ford." The detective suggested she keep a log of any further calls.

It was getting to the point where Carroll was surprised if two days went by and he didn't hear from Marie Hilley, but this time she didn't call for almost three weeks. When she did, she mentioned that she had received five more phone calls, but she had something more pressing to report. The night before, she had been at the Wash World Coin Laundry on Quintard Boulevard. When she turned out of the parking lot heading for home, a large, dark car pulled in behind her. As she stopped for the boulevard traffic lights, then made a series of turns, it became clear: They were following her. She was terrified, but she decided to try to elude them. She put on her right-hand directional signal and then turned left. Eventually she slipped away from the pursuers and made her way home.

Carroll scratched his head. The more he heard from Marie Hilley, the less there was to get a hold on. This latest story had a feeling of never-never land to it. Later that day, a call from the phone company sounded another warning bell in Carroll's mind.

The trace on Doris Ford's line had finally paid off. She had reported no-voice calls two days in a row, early in the morning. The phone company's security department had checked the call-tracing records. One was from a man she had experienced problems with before. The other, placed at 4:46 A.M., came from Jenkins Manufacturing Company. Marie Hilley worked at Jenkins Manufacturing. Carroll called Marie Hilley.

"Marie, we got a trace on a call to Doris Ford last week," he said.

"Who was it, Gary?" she responded. She sounded genuinely curious. She and Doris had talked about the phone calls they had been receiving, and the other incidents that had plagued them in the half a year since Marie's burglary and the removal of the window screen from Doris's utility room.

"We traced the number, Marie, and the call came from Jenkins Manufacturing."

"You think it's somebody at Jenkins?" she asked. There was no sign of surprise or shock in her voice.

"You work out there, Marie. Do you know anything about this?"

"I don't know anything about it. How would I know anything?"

Carroll kept his thoughts to himself. There was only the beginning of a suspicion in his mind, and she was such an intelligent, self-confident woman, the picture of a proper matron. Her denial was very convincing.

Three days later she was on the phone.

"I got four more calls, Gary," she said.

Here we go again, he thought. He offered to get the trace put back on her line.

A few days after that, she phoned to report another three calls. Finally, Carroll thought, we ought to get something. He contacted the phone company security people to get the information on the calls.

It was several days before he reached Marie Hilley. The calls had all been traced to an Arthur Dozier, he told her.

"That's Sandy," she said. She sounded excited. Sandy Dozier was a friend of Carol's.

"I've had problems with Sandy," Marie said. "That must be it."

They discussed Sandy Dozier for a while. The detective had

considered the possibility that the calls might be directed against Carol, but this was the first indication that there might be something to it. He was left with the impression that Sandy Dozier was close to Marie's daughter, Carol, perhaps closer than Marie liked. Sandy lived with her parents. The detective said he would go and talk to them about the phone calls.

When Carroll visited the Doziers the next day, they were puzzled, but they agreed to talk with their daughter about the phone calls.

Maybe that'll finish this thing, Carroll thought on the way back to the station. And though she was still seeing Billy Atherton, there was a six-week break in Marie Hilley's official contacts with the police. But it was only an interruption, not an ending. And Gary Carroll's involvement with Marie Hilley had barely started.

It was now two years since Frank Hilley had died. In the spring of 1977, Mike and Teri were preparing to leave Anniston for a new ministry at the First Christian Church in Pompano Beach, Florida, when Marie came to ask Mike for a favor. She wanted to get a loan from a bank, she said, but they had turned her down. It was terrible the way they discriminated against single women. A bank officer had told her that because she was widow, she would have to get someone to cosign her loan. Would he take a loan with her?

How could she need money, Mike wondered, with the insurance and her salary? She was always talking about the things she would buy, and she took every opportunity to mention how much something had cost, but now she was vague about what the money was for. But she was his mother, and she needed a hand. That was good enough for him. She couldn't get enough from one bank, so they ended up taking two loans, for a total of eight hundred dollars.

The loans weren't enough. A year after buying the Oldsmobile, she had refinanced it for forty-five hundred dollars. Now, less than a year after that, she was falling behind on the payments.

Mike had bought a Chevrolet Chevette the year before and was getting ready to trade it on a Chevy Nova. Could I buy the Chevette from you? Marie wanted to know. Mike wondered why his mother would give up her Oldsmobile for the little Chevy. She talked about gas efficiency and how the car fit her better, but as they talked, Mike gradually suspected that there was something else, something she didn't want to say: She needed the money. He had never thought of her that way. He had seen the same picture of his mother that she presented to outsiders: a comfortable widow with high-class taste and no concern for what things cost. You can have the Chevette, he told her, just take over the payments.

Marie sold the Oldsmobile for three thousand dollars and changed over to the smaller Chevette. At the time the little car was merely a subtle, and mostly unnoticed, symbol of Marie's deteriorating circumstances. But the transaction was also the first of a series involving cars that became a strange reflection of Marie's inner turmoil.

Mike and Teri were relieved when their time in Anniston was over. Being around Marie for a year had been exhausting. And the Florida position called for a more active ministry, just what Mike had wanted. Marie didn't want them to go, but she took their departure more gracefully than she had when they moved to the apartment. She wanted to buy them a new set of living-room furniture, but Mike and Teri couldn't see how she would be able to afford it. They refused. When she insisted and they still refused, she compromised. They would take her old furniture and she would buy a new set for herself. She even went down to Pompano Beach to help them look for a place to live. When she left they invited her to come back for a visit later in the year.

At the last minute, their landlord, Jerry Ray, had refused to give back their deposit on the apartment. They were breaking their lease, he claimed, and they were not entitled to have the money back. He was adamant. In the last-minute rush of preparation for the move, they didn't have time to pursue the matter. They had given up on ever seeing the money again when Marie offered to talk to the landlord about it. A few days after she got back to Anniston, she sent them Jerry Ray's check for the full deposit. A few weeks later, she phoned.

"Guess what?" she said excitedly. "You are not going to believe this." What news could have aroused her so? they wondered.

"Somebody shot Jerry Ray in the head," Marie said.

It was bizarre, Teri and Mike thought, that someone they had known, their own landlord, should die that way, murdered, but they thought nothing more of it at the time. The incident came back to mind only later, when they wondered how well Marie had known the landlord. How had she been able to get the money back, when Ray had been so definite in refusing them? It was an FBI agent, questioning them, who ignited the speculation, when he mentioned that Ray had been known as a professional gambler. Perhaps this could help to explain something that continued to puzzle everybody, even those who knew Marie Hilley's compulsion to spend money: How *did* she get through all that money—Frank's insurance, her salary, the money from the sale of Lucille's house after she died, later the proceeds from the sale of the house on McClellan—in such a short time?

Mike recalled how much his mother had seemed to enjoy talking about people she knew who were involved in gambling—"It's big-time gambling," she would say, "big time," savoring the words, something seductive in them—and the debts they had run up. And Mike wondered now if what had seemed a fascination was something more, a heightened attention as she gauged his reaction, wondering whether to tell him something about herself, or even a combination of fear and excitement in talking about herself disguised as these "big-time gamblers."

In November Marie took them up on the invitation to visit, and she returned in December to celebrate Christmas with Mike and Teri and Teri's parents in Orlando. But it was uncomfortable being with her. She was obviously agitated.

"I've got to get away from Anniston," she told Teri one day. "I need a change of scene. I want to start over, make a new life."

It sounded as if she felt that Frank's death had ended a chapter in her life. She had sold the house after they left.

"I don't need all that space anymore, now that you're all gone," she said.

She was also concerned about Carol. She was about to graduate from high school. She was drifting, without plans for the future. Marie didn't seem to like the people her daughter was spending time with. No matter how Marie tried, every effort she made to talk seriously with Carol ended in bitter confrontation. Maybe if she could get Carol to a new place, things would improve. She talked with Mike and Teri about the possibility of moving to Florida.

"If Carol would come down here with me, I'd move in a heartbeat," she said.

Marie had other reasons to be restless. Back in Anniston, her money problems continued—the money from the sale of her house had been like a Band-Aid on a hemorrhage—and her relations with the police department were coming to a head.

Marie and Carol called Mike one night from Anniston.

"Somebody stole Carol's Honda from the shopping mall and set it on fire up on top of the mountain," Marie said.

Mike wondered why anyone would have stolen the Honda. Carol had been in an accident and the car had been heavily damaged. It was still running, but it looked like a wreck. Carol, who had never been very good at keeping a secret, later told Mike what had happened. She and Marie had taken the car to a remote part of town, pushed a rag into the gas tank, and burned it for the insurance money.

Within days, Marie called Billy Atherton to report another wave of no-voice phone calls. The tracing equipment was still on the line, and Lieutenant Carroll quickly got a list of the callers. He phoned Marie Hilley.

"Two of them were from a John O. Key, Marie," he told her.

"That's my uncle, he's called Sammy Key, and my Aunt Margaret," she said. Margaret Frazier Key was one of the sisters of Marie's mother, Lucille. She had taken care of Marie when she was a child while Lucille worked in the mill. They had been close ever since. Margaret had called last night.

The other call was from Charlie Dyer, a boyfriend of Carol's. There was nothing wrong with that call, either. But Marie continued to claim that the call at 5:14 P.M., which the records showed as coming from the Keys' telephone, had been a caller who held the phone but wouldn't speak.

"I got that call shortly before the one from Margaret," she insisted. Carroll agreed to check it again with the phone company. He called Marie again a little later.

"Marie, I checked it," the detective told her, "and they said there was no call forty-five minutes before that and forty-five minutes after."

"There was a call, Gary, there was," she repeated. "They just made a mistake."

The discrepancies in the situation were making Carroll increasingly uneasy.

"Marie, we've tried and tried with this thing, and when we put the trace on, the calls stop, and when we take it off, they start up again. What's going on there, Marie?"

"It's probably somebody connected with the phone company, someone who knows when there's a trace on the line," she said. She had had some problems with a neighbor in Anniston who worked for the phone company, she said.

It all sounded improbable to Lieutenant Carroll, but he was a thorough man, and duty required him to make one last effort. He called the phone company and asked about their security procedures. All tracing investigations were handled from the Birmingham office, they said. That was sixty miles away. Nobody in Anniston could know what was going on.

When he called Marie with this last piece of news, she was adamant. There must be some other explanation, she said, but when he pressed her, she couldn't think of one. It must have been clear to Marie that the flimsiness of her story was growing more and more serious. She never reported another nuisance phone call.

Carroll was careful by nature and experienced enough to know it was safest in the long run to play it by the book, so he ignored the urge to tell her what he was thinking. The case was still unfinished, however, and he couldn't resist the temptation to make one last try at getting some explanation. He went to see Doris Ford. Maybe she knew something about what was going on with Marie, or at least had some hunch that might support his own.

When he arrived at Doris Ford's house to talk with her, Carroll found that she was still nervous about the calls she had received herself. He didn't like loose ends, and on top of that, he had become friendly with her in the course of investigating her complaints. It bothered him that she was still upset. Carroll was uncomfortable talking about his suspicions without final proof, but in addition to pursuing the investigation he wanted to put her mind at ease about the threat. He outlined the sequence of events for her, the series of complaints from Marie, the way the calls had stopped when the tracer was put on the line and started again as soon as it was taken off. He reminded her of the call she had received from Jenkins Manufacturing, where Marie worked.

She listened calmly to his recitation of the facts. She didn't seem to have anything to add. Finally Carroll decided to be explicit about it.

"Doris," he said, "I think Marie is responsible for all this."

She looked at him calmly. His statement hadn't produced the effect he might have hoped. In fact, it hadn't seemed to produce any effect at all. She wasn't shocked at what he had said, and she seemed willing to consider the possibility that it might be Marie, but she didn't commit herself one way or the other.

Well, the detective thought, she's been a neighbor and friend to

Marie for a long time. Maybe she's just being loyal. But as far as Carroll was concerned, the case of the phone calls was closed.

That didn't mean that Marie Hilley had no contact with the police over the next few months, though. She called to report that she had been followed home again one evening, this time by a man in a tan Buick or Cadillac. A few months after that, someone broke out the windshield of the Chevy. Carol reported that it had happened while the car was parked at the high school.

By the summer of 1978, Marie seemed at loose ends again. She had left her job as executive secretary to Arthur Sturm at the law firm. She had worked there less than a year. She told Mike that Sturm had propositioned her.

"I refused, and he took his pants off right there in the office," she said. "Right in front of me." Sturm and the law firm's personnel officer later told an investigator that Marie Hilley had had difficulty getting along with the other employees.

Marie was ready for the new start she had talked about to Mike and Teri. The day after Carol's graduation they headed for Pompano Beach. They would stay with Mike and Teri while they looked for work and thought about making the move permanent.

Marie was short of money and needed some help buying "a few things" to get settled, so Mike loaned her his VISA card. He was shocked when six hundred dollars' worth of bills came in, but she said she would pay him back when she got on her feet.

At least Mike and Teri had no problems with credit. They had even received a MasterCard in the mail that they hadn't requested. They rarely used credit cards, so they just threw it in a drawer. Mike and Teri weren't sophisticated in money matters; maybe, somewhere in the back of their minds, they thought they should keep the extra card in case of an emergency someday. They never noticed when it disappeared from the drawer.

The problem with Marie wasn't just the money. The atmosphere soon became even worse than during her previous visit. Teri was pregnant and they had banned smoking in the house. Carol kept defying the ban and running afoul of Mike.

"Why do you need to have all these rules?" she challenged him one day.

He explained their reasons, but it didn't seem to make much difference, and the tension deepened, Marie often joining in the criticism of Carol. Marie soon got a job, working in the office of a chain of convenience markets. There was a position available in her office that she wanted Carol to take, but Carol wasn't interested.

"I don't want to sit in an office all day, Momma," she said, and her mother couldn't—or wouldn't—force her to do it. That didn't stop Marie from calling her daughter "lazy," and the two of them argued constantly. Marie was fed up.

Mike and Teri's baby was born at the end of May, and soon after, Teri's parents came down from Orlando to visit. They found a different Marie from the one they had known before. She wasn't around much, and when she was, she stayed most of the time in her room at the back of the house. When she did come out she was moody and withdrawn. Always an avid reader, she seemed preoccupied with strange stories of hauntings and disappearances, and she talked about the house catching fire in Anniston.

She joined them for lunch only once while they were there. It was a tense meal. Marie and Carol were arguing. It was as if nobody else were present. After some particularly tense exchange with Carol, Marie finally turned to them.

"I don't know what I'm going to do with her," she said. "Frank just spoiled her to death."

Happy Henderson knew that had been true, and it struck him that Marie was trying to compete with the memory of Frank, desperately attempting to win Carol's affection, but she was using material things to do it. Her strategy was obviously not working. If Marie bore any love for her daughter, it had gotten twisted into an urge to control her.

"I am going to make her go to trade school for a year," Marie wrote to Freeda and Lisa back in Anniston, "just so that she will know how to do something. After that, if she wants to go to college, that will be o.k. with me, but she has no idea what she wants to do, and I am not going to let her waste the time and money playing around for a year to find out. She needs to know how to do something."

Marie drew a sharp contrast between her daughter's lack of direction and her niece's industriousness. "Lisa," she wrote, "if you were down here, I could put you to work for me, starting salary $150/week. They offered the job to Carol, but she couldn't do it. Staying in an office all day would be more than she could handle."

Her daughter was eighteen years old, but Marie was still trying hard to regulate her behavior. Carol had committed herself to go to camp for a few weeks, but when the time came, she had changed her mind.

"She doesn't want to go," Marie said, "and I really hate to force her, but she has to learn that when she makes a commitment, she has to do what she promises."

Marie offered occasionally to do things around the house. Several times she helped out with the baby so Teri could get a rest, or made soup and tea for them when everybody was too tired to cook, but she wasn't around much. She got back late from work most nights, and every Tuesday they dropped her off after dinner at a hotel in Pompano Beach. She said she had picked up some extra work helping out with the bookkeeping there. An FBI agent told them later that there was gambling at the hotel, and they thought Marie might have been involved, but there was no hint of it at the time.

Teri had been healthy since they left Anniston, but now she became sick again. This time the doctor said it was her kidneys. Once again, she was supposed to rest and watch her diet. With Mike busy getting established in his new church and the baby to take care of, the young couple was relieved when Marie decided to go back to Anniston. She just wasn't ready to make a permanent move to Florida.

Marie Hilley had other things on her mind besides living arrangements. She needed more insurance. In January and February she had taken out life insurance, twenty-five thousand dollars on herself and fourteen thousand dollars on Carol. Now she started a family group policy with another company. The policy included insurance for personal and residential losses due to fire, and there were also burial payments and cancer coverage, but the main parts were life insurance. Carol was beneficiary of twenty-five thousand dollars' worth of coverage on Marie, and Marie was beneficiary of twenty-five thousand dollars' insurance on the lives of each of her children, Carol and Mike. Carol was now covered for close to forty thousand dollars.

Back home, Marie and Carol moved in with Freeda temporarily. Marie's mother-in-law, Carrie Hilley, was living there, too. She had left her house on Moore Avenue to join her daughter, but she wasn't happy. She wanted to go back to her own home. She asked Marie and Carol to come live there with her. They could help pay for the food and utilities and stay there rent-free. Marie accepted. She was nearing the bottom of her financial slide, and she needed any help she could find.

She got a job at Dresser Industries, not far from Carrie's house, and went shopping for a car. The best she could do was a seven-year-old Toyota Corolla; they wanted five hundred dollars for it. Fearing that her credit record would not stand up, she persuaded Freeda's 19-year-old daughter, Lisa Duke, to cosign a note at Universal Credit. Certainly they would make the loan; the old man who owned the company, Mr. Darnton, had played golf with Frank for years.

When she didn't hear from them for several days, Marie called. Darnton sounded embarrassed.

"I'm sorry Mrs. Hilley," he said, "we can't help you. You're already overloaded."

He didn't go into detail, but it was cut and dried. He had the figures in front of him. She had borrowed over four thousand dollars from two of the high-rate loan companies a year before, and she still owed close to three thousand dollars. She was a month behind on one of the accounts, two months on the other. They hadn't gone any further with the credit check, hadn't needed to. That was enough. What was going on with Frank Hilley's widow?

Marie was still unable to sleep in a bed. When they asked why, she would say something vague about memories of Frank, but nobody ever quite understood what she meant. It was just a quirk. She used the couch at Carrie's, with a sleeping bag and a pillow.

Freeda had just arrived at the Army Depot, where she worked as a secretary, when the phone rang. It was Marie. She sounded close to tears.

"Freeda, something has happened," she began.

Freeda felt a sudden flush of dread. It was her mother, something had happened to Carrie! Her fear jumped another level at Marie's next words.

"There's been a fire."

"What happened, Marie? What happened?"

The question seemed to cut through Marie's obsession with her own problems.

"Everybody's all right. Nobody was hurt."

Freeda relaxed a bit. Marie's attention returned to her own perspective.

"Oh, Freeda, Carol and your mother are mad at me. They won't even talk to me."

Under Freeda's prodding, she told the story. Marie had been getting ready for work. Carol was awakened by the faint smell of smoke. By the time she was fully awake, the house was filling up with smoke. She raced to wake up her grandmother Carrie and get her out of the house. Marie had called the fire department from next door. The firemen said it had started in a sleeping bag on the washing machine.

Freeda had been concerned about her mother moving back into the Moore Avenue house. Partly to ease her own mind, she had put in smoke detectors.

"Marie, what happened to the fire alarms?" she asked. "Didn't they go off?"

"I took the batteries out," she said.

"What?" Freeda could hardly believe she had heard correctly.

"It kept going off." Marie sounded embarrassed.

Freeda talked with her mother and Carol about it. She could see why they were upset with Marie. She had taken the batteries out while they were at church on Sunday and hadn't mentioned it afterward. The alarms kept going off, she said, and it was bothering her.

It was Marie's sleeping bag that burned, the one she ordinarily used on the couch. She said she had gotten hot in the night and put it on the washing machine, using only a sheet. Somehow the sleeping bag had caught fire and smoldered, but the bag's insulation had kept it from bursting into flames. They were lucky they hadn't burned up.

It was only one of several odd incidents plaguing them at Moore Avenue. Thinking about the sleeping bag, Carrie remembered that she had found a wad of partly burned paper towel in the kitchen trash can a week earlier. Later the wire to the window fan was cut, and after that the kitchen phone cord was cut. They were the same kind of peculiar annoyances that had sprung up around Marie at her house on McClellan Boulevard the year before, but Carrie didn't know about the earlier incidents. If Carol made a connection, she wasn't saying.

From a distance it seems that some evil fury, long bound up and held back, was already emerging from the shadows, and surely someone must have caught a glimpse of menace. But evil came to

Marie Hilley's household dressed in the innocent guise of daily life or routine mischance, and there was nothing at the time to join the small events that were slowly undermining the remaining foundations of Marie Hilley's family.

Carrie called her granddaughter from the living room one day.

"Carol, come here." There was tension in her voice. Carol rushed in to find Carrie holding the cushion from the couch where Marie had been sleeping. Carrie had been straightening up the living room. She pointed wordlessly to the couch. A length of nylon rope lay where the cushion had been. Next to it was a thick iron crowbar.

"What's it doing there?" Carol asked, fearing as she spoke that she knew the answer.

"I don't know, I just found it here," Carrie said. "I'm gonna move it."

"Go ahead," Carol encouraged her. Better to have it out of sight somewhere. Carrie took the rope and crowbar away.

The next day when Carol came home from work, her grandmother was waiting for her.

"Come here," Carrie said. "I want to show you something."

She walked to the couch and pulled away the cushion. The crowbar lay where it had been the day before. They stared at it together for several moments before Carrie replaced the cushion on the couch. Marie had found the crowbar and put it back, they knew, but what did it mean? What compulsion, what bizarre demon, was taunting Marie Hilley with a vision of fear, and how had that vision become so real that she needed the comfort of heavy, cold steel to protect herself?

There were no answers. Marie said nothing, and nothing her daughter and mother-in-law could think of to say made any sense. They never spoke of it again.

Marie was in the habit of coming home for lunch around noon, and she and Carrie often ate together. Lisa Duke often came, too, arriving a little before one o'clock to grab a sandwich and then sit down with her grandmother to watch a soap opera.

At home one evening, Lisa mentioned to her mother that Carrie had missed most of the soap opera that day. She had been back and forth to the bathroom, throwing up her lunch. Freeda was not overly concerned, but when it happened again a little later, she began to worry about her mother. Carrie was getting to an age when little things could grow to be big things, and she had never had any problem with her stomach before. The nausea came back a few times, but it didn't turn into anything serious, as far as they could tell. It was only later that Freeda and Lisa thought they had an explanation, and then they couldn't prove it. They would have been too late by then, in any case.

5

Money and Love

Marie's money problems were steadily worsening. It was a little more than three years since Frank had died. She had spent the proceeds from his life insurance; eventually she sold the house, and soon that money was gone, too. Her debts had far outrun her salary, and she had exhausted her borrowing power. She had used up her credit, first through loans at her bank, then by borrowing to the limit on a bank charge card. She had tried Universal Credit Corporation and been turned down. She was behind on her accounts with at least three of the small loan companies in Anniston. Finally, she had drawn on members of her family, first Mike and Teri, then her niece, Lisa Duke. In late 1978, she turned in a new direction.

Marie had remained close with the builder Harold Dillard, her "second father," since the days when she had gone up to his house on the East Side to sit by the swimming pool. She confided to Freeda that Harold was giving her outside work in the evenings as a way to make some extra money. During the period when she lived with Freeda, Marie had gone out with Harold several times. He drove by to pick her up but never came in. She was going to his house to do secretarial work, Marie said. Apparently she was paid in cash. She liked to show Freeda or the children a thick roll of bills, with a fifty- or hundred-dollar bill on the outside, and talk about how well she was doing with her extra work. Mike remembered one evening when she unrolled a wad and ostentatiously counted off the hundred-dollar bills, eight of them, savoring the crisp snap of each bill as she flicked the end of the roll.

But Marie was looking for more than eight hundred dollars. She had turned loose the demons, and now she had reached the point where she couldn't escape them by herself. She needed access to a lot of money, and she needed help. She needed a man to rescue her, and Harold Dillard was a prime candidate, rich, vulnerable, and trusting. The fact that he was married didn't keep her from trying, and a letter she wrote him near the end displays her extraordinary skill at manipulating the emotions of others.

She was writing to say "a special good-bye to a very special person," she told him. "You have been such an important part of my life for so long."

Dillard had known about her relationship with a man named John. Now she was preparing to go away with him.

"It doesn't seem possible that I may never see you again," she said to Dillard, "but nothing is permanent."

"I feel very lucky to have someone like John," she said. "I love his kindness, gentleness, and I respond to his love for me. It won't be the wild, passionate love I felt for someone else, but I will be happy and content. . . .

"I want a relationship, with a good man, that will be permanent. The relationship you and I had would probably have been too much for both of us, on a permanent basis, but I had to stop wishing for that a long time ago. I will never stop being in love with you. . . ."

Again she reminded him of the passion they had shared: "John will never know the woman you knew. Not even Frank knew that woman, because I've never responded to anyone the way I did to you."

For all her admission that she and Dillard would never be together, in spite of her professions of love for the new man, the letter sounds more like a last attempt to pry Dillard loose from his marriage than a farewell:

"If I could have had a choice, it would have been you," she wrote. "There will always be a part of me that will never belong to anyone but you."

She recalled that he had told her once, thinking about the power of his love for her and the barrier between them, that "they write books about people like us." He could write a book like that, Dillard had said wistfully, because he had lived it.

"Every time I think of this," Marie wrote him, "I wonder how you would end it."

It is a touching letter, and it is written with great skill. The cool grace of Marie's neat handwriting contrasts with the uncontrollable feeling it expresses for Harold Dillard. Each statement of quiet affection for the new man, John, is contrasted with the wild passion she feels for Dillard, and each scene of a tranquil but dull future with John is undercut by a memory of the lascivious abandon she has shared with Dillard.

The letter foreshadows the sadness of a parting that she has reluctantly come to see as inevitable. If she cannot have real love with Dillard, she will have to settle for the stolid loyalty that John offers. The letter throbs with the tension of a love that cannot be lived out, and it hints at the possibility that perhaps, just perhaps, it may not be too late for Dillard to come to her rescue. And she closes with a subtle challenge: "I wonder how you would end it?"

Marie was a fine writer, and she must have been proud of her letter to Dillard, because she wrote virtually the same letter to Calvin Robertson.

Life had separated Calvin Robertson from Marie Hilley, but it could never steal his memories of the pretty thirteen-year-old who had waved to him from her back porch. He had done well in life, moving up steadily to a managerial position in the home office of a nationwide freight-hauling company based in San Francisco. He had been married for thirty years and had three grown children. Two of them lived in the suburbs across the bay, and he got to see his four grandchildren regularly. He had passed the age of fifty in good health, and everything about his life made him seem invulnerable to passion or impulse. But Marie Hilley knew better.

Calvin Robertson may not have been obvious about it, but he didn't have to be. Marie Hilley had a genius for knowing what other people needed, and if she wanted to give it to them, she was a genius at that, too. Robertson's parents still lived in Anniston, so he came to visit every year or two, leaving his wife, Josie, at home, and he couldn't turn a corner on the streets of Anniston without hoping for a glimpse of Marie Hilley.

Over the years he had wondered again and again how he could have given up so easily when Frank Hilley came along to pursue the fourteen-year-old Marie Frazier. He had never showed resentment or disappointment, and he had stayed in occasional contact with Marie and Frank and with Marie's parents. He was a religious man, and he found some peace by telling himself that control of events had not been in his hands. God had prepared other plans for Marie and Frank, he wrote to Marie, plans that had no place for Calvin.

Now Marie Hilley had plans, but she couldn't carry them out by herself. She needed someone like Calvin Robertson, and she knew, with an uncanny certainty, how to get him. She told him she had cancer.

Over dinner at a restaurant in Anniston before Thanksgiving of 1978, Marie flashed Robertson glimpses of the dazzling young girl, bursting with new sensuality, who had lived in his memory for three decades. Then, cold and steady as a high priest in a rite of sacrifice, she reached down inside him and took a grip on his heart.

Calvin was shaken by Marie's overtures, and by the rush of fresh emotion they inspired in him. In his letters he became again the adolescent who had first glimpsed Marie Frazier on the porch, innocent and full of awe at his good fortune. He was astonished at the depth of his feelings, Calvin mused. It was more than her beauty alone, he told Marie, something unnamable and irresistible that drew him to her.

And then she told him about her visit to the doctor.

"The X rays showed spots on my lungs," she said. She was by turns brave and helpless. Don't let it make you sad, she told him, I can beat this thing. But it's so hard, trying to do everything by myself. And the treatments are so expensive. Oh, how I wish you could be by my side, she told him, the power of her need glistening in her eyes.

Calvin was stricken at the news, and yet he was deeply grateful that she had chosen him to call on for help. She was giving him a chance to redeem his youthful failure, to erase the regret that had hung like mist in a corner of his heart all these years.

Back in San Francisco a few days later, he mailed Marie a check for three thousand dollars. He was praying for her constantly, Calvin told her. He had no thought for himself, only for her well-being. His only Thanksgiving prayer was to be by her side, he wrote. He was in a hurry to get the note and check in the mail. He didn't have time to put on the yellow happy-face stickers that decorated his other letters to Marie Hilley.

She wrote back, and they talked on the phone, and she told him how much she loved him and how grateful she was for his love and support, and she tightened her hold on his emotions and swung him this way and that.

"I know we can't be together," she told him, brave in her

self-denial, "but as long as we have what we feel for each other and it doesn't hurt anyone, we can be glad we have at least this."

"And I know," she said, "that if I ever needed you by my side, you would do everything possible to be there with me."

You are absolutely right, he wrote back. If you ever needed me beside you for any reason, I would move heaven and earth to come to you.

Could Calvin Robertson have considered even for a moment that Marie would soon call in this promise?

He was delighted even at the sound of her voice, disappointed only that circumstances prevented him from speaking to her regularly in order to offer her his affection, cheer her up, reassure her that things would come out right. He was amazed at the joy and ease he felt with her. He could share with her his deepest feelings, think of her as a friend. He could open his heart to Marie in a way that was not possible with anyone else, even his wife.

Josie Robertson wrote to Marie when she heard about the cancer. She had been thinking about Marie and praying for her, Josie said, and she and Calvin were both glad that Marie had felt she could turn to Calvin in her time of need. He had been giving her regular reports of his phone conversations with Marie, Josie told her, and when it seemed to her that too much time had passed without contact, she urged Calvin to give Marie a call. She hoped Marie would come to visit them in San Francisco.

Marie was like a jailer with a prisoner, alternating gentleness with reprimand, good news with bad, to establish control over Calvin's moods, making him ever more dependent on her. He sent her a Christmas present, a sweater from Iceland. She raised the possibility of accepting the invitation to visit San Francisco, then pulled back: She had to go to Atlanta for cancer treatments. She upbraided him for an innocent remark about the letters he had sent her, and when he called her at the office and asked her if she loved him, she would not reassure him. And, oh, yes, she was going out to dinner with someone the next weekend, she told him.

He was plunged into anxiety, like an adolescent feeling love for the first time, and jealousy, too: when she went away he would feel physically sick, wondering where she was, worrying about whether she would meet someone else, fearing that she would lose interest in Calvin.

Now he was desolate at having wounded her with his offhand

remark. He had wanted only to worship her, he wrote; instead, he had injured her. In his imagination he threw himself to his knees before her and begged forgiveness.

He recorded a letter to her on a cassette, and he sent her two telegrams at Dresser Industries, and a week later she called him at the office. All was forgiven, of course she loved him; if only they could be together.

His heart leaped. He was like a child in a thunderstorm. His letters bounded wildly from despair to joy, to exultation. If only he had the opportunity, he wrote Marie, he would delight in pampering her. It was not merely lust that drove him, he assured her. He imagined a happy domestic scene in which he would pamper Carol as well.

Was her message getting through to him? Could her campaign be nearing success? Calvin's declarations of his feelings took on added warmth.

Their love was a precious chance to view again a fantasy lost in their youth, he wrote Marie. But the vision alone was not enough. If only it could become a reality, he exclaimed wistfully.

He was planning another trip to Anniston, he told her, sometime in the next couple of months. His anticipation of the trip spilled out with his joy at her forgiveness in a confused jumble of words. He offered himself completely, as a lover, a confidant, whatever she might want or need. Then, his confidence restored by her approval, he turned sly. He would hold her hand if that was all she wanted, but he would prefer to hold more of her. He would not be so easily satisfied.

They set the date, a month away. The next week, she put a ban on letters between them. They could not keep on like this, she said. Robertson reluctantly agreed. He had no choice.

In the first week of February, she called him. Exciting news! She had been back to the doctor for an examination. The shadows on the X rays were gone.

Calvin whispered his thanks to God. His prayers had been answered.

But there was more news. She was going to get married.

Calvin was stunned. How could that be? What would happen to their love? It was too sudden, all this news at once, he couldn't take it in. Of course he would still come to see her at the end of the month. He had to see her. They would have a chance to talk then.

But Calvin couldn't wait. He wrote to her immediately. He

begged her forgiveness for violating the ban on letters, but he had been driven to express his joy at her deliverance from the threat of illness. And he had also needed to express his shock at hearing her "other news." He looked forward to her meeting him at the Atlanta airport in two weeks. He had questions that could only be asked in person.

Robertson could not bring himself to be specific about her impending marriage, referring to it only as "the other news." Marie had led him blind, step by step, into a quicksand of emotion—abject apology for violating the ban, joy at her recovery, desolation at the loss of her, all in a single moment. He was flayed, vulnerable, set up for her final moves. She prepared to spring the trap.

Marie wrote to him the same day, their letters crossing in the mail. She adopted the trite, overdramatized tone of a soap opera, to match Calvin's naive sentimentality.

"My Dearest," she began, once again all warmth and affection, "Let's lift the ban on letters. I, too, know what it is to feel lonely in a crowd, but only since 'you.' Oh, God, how I love you. There is no way I can stop—if you were different—maybe—but you are so kind and gentle—it isn't possible for me not to love you—which brings me to John Romans."

Here he was, the same mysterious "John" who had arisen to challenge Harold Dillard. Now he had a last name, and it was uncannily like that of John Homan, the man who would later come to play such an important and mystifying role in Marie Hilley's life. Yet it was still a year before the date she and John Homan later claimed they met in Fort Lauderdale.

But of course Calvin Robertson had no way of knowing any of this. In any case, he was concerned with another side of her relationship with this man she was planning to marry.

On the phone, Calvin had wanted to know if she loved John.

"I can't be anything but honest with you," she answered in her letter, and quoted part of a poem:

> The night has a thousand eyes,
> The day has only one.
> With the setting of the sun,
> The day is done.

The mind has a thousand eyes,
The heart has only one.
The light of a lifetime dies,
When love is done.

"No, My Darling," she went on, "I'm not in love with John." Her description of John echoed the one she had written to Harold Dillard:

"He is a very easy person to be with; he, too, is kind and gentle. He will be very good to me, and to Carol. I will be content, but not happy the way I would be with you. But I have to make a life for myself. I can't spend the rest of it just on the edge of yours." Here it was again, the reluctant conclusion that a parting was now inevitable, and as with Harold Dillard, she followed by painting a picture of the inferior existence, stable but devoid of passion, that she would share with John:

"I won't be the happiest person in the world, but neither will I be unhappy. Since I can't have you, I can settle for what I will have with John, and I don't feel I'm cheating him. He knows that I'm not in love with him, but he does know that I admire and respect him. . . ."

Now she anticipates the terrible tension of a great love that she and Calvin will never be able to live out:

"We will both belong to someone else, and probably our paths will never cross again. You will always be there in my heart. You will always be near me, no matter where I am. I will always reach across the miles and take your hand, kiss you good night and say to you, 'I love you my darling—for always.' "

And then, at last, comes the tantalizing offer of hope, the hint that her mind can be changed, that it is not too late for their love to be redeemed:

"Calvin, I don't know if I'm doing the right thing in marrying John. Not when I want you so, but I'm doing it to get me out of your life."

And finally, a reminder of sensual delights: "I wish I knew the words to say so that you could know how much I love you. I want to hold you close to me, so close that we are one person. I want to kiss you, to hold your hand, to hear your voice, to take care of you. I want to say to you, 'I'm here Sweetheart, I'll always be here for you, for whatever reason you want.'"

She had told him her lungs had cleared up, but she could not resist one more chance to reinforce his pity and love for her: "Please love me, and keep me in your prayers. God has heard you—and it had to be you, no one else knows how ill I am, and I've never asked him to let me get well. I love you, for always."

Marriage or no marriage, nothing would affect their plans for his visit to Anniston, she assured him—of course, he was coming to see his family, Calvin had written her earlier, but there was no question that the chief object of his visit was the visit with Marie, his lover. Yes, Marie concluded her letter, they must have their time together: "We have to have that much." She would meet him at the airport in Atlanta.

"Fifteen more days"—her passion must have leaped off the page at him—"how will I ever be able to wait that long!"

The itinerary of their time together resembles the joyous rounds of a couple about to be married. Robertson went out to see Carrie Hilley, Marie's mother-in-law, and they visited with Carol and her friend Cynthia. The couple drove down to Florida to stay a few days with Mike and Teri. Mike had a church in Merritt Island, near Cape Canaveral, 165 miles up the coast from his former home in Pompano Beach.

Mike had thought of Calvin as an old schoolmate of his mother's and a friend of the family, not as somebody who might be her lover. Still, there had been a lot of changes in his mother's life since Frank died, so it wasn't a great shock when she casually dropped a bit of news into a conversation one evening:

"Calvin wants me to marry him, Mike."

That put Calvin in a different light, Mike thought. It could take a little getting used to. And what about the practical difficulties?

"Isn't he married, Mom?"

"Oh, he's got that all worked out," she said, dismissing the problem with a little backhanded gesture of the fingers.

"What do you think I ought to do?" she wanted to know.

As a minister, Mike was in the business of giving advice, often on matters similar to this, but he had never felt he could take that role with his mother.

"Whatever makes you happy, Mom," he said. It was as close as he could come to being noncommittal while still offering the support of a son to his mother.

It was only after Marie and Calvin left for Anniston that the idea of intimacy between them became real to Mike and Teri. They had left behind a shower cap and a towel from a motel they had stayed in on the way down to Florida.

Back in Anniston, Marie and Calvin took a few solemn moments to visit the graves of Marie's parents, Huey and Lucille Frazier. The Fraziers were buried out at Forestlawn Gardens, just a few feet from Frank Hilley's grave. Robertson had liked Lucille, had even imagined what it would have been like, if life had turned them in a different direction, to live with Marie and her mother, providing for Lucille as his mother-in-law. They would have had fun together, he told Marie.

Now he stood before the grave of Huey and Lucille Frazier, hypnotized by a vision of the passionate intimacy Marie was laying before him, and he whispered to the spirits of her parents, "I love your daughter."

They visited with Robertson's mother at her house on Rosewood Lane, making little effort to conceal their relationship. Afterward, when she was alone with her son, the old woman took an early opportunity to speak to him about it. She fixed him with her watery stare and spoke as if she were describing the weather. Her words bespoke a mother's pride in the admiration her son evoked from others. Marie was still in love with him, she told Calvin. He was startled at the announcement, but she was unfazed. She had seen it in the way Marie gazed at him, she told her son. And not only that, she went on, bad eyes or no, she could see that Calvin felt the same way about Marie.

She was blissfully oblivious to the significance of her discovery, to what it might mean in her son's life, and she couldn't resist elaborating on what she had seen of his infatuation.

Calvin Robertson was like a man dreaming in the sun, drifting backward in his rowboat toward a waterfall. He was an uncomplicated soul—he had once written to Marie that God had made him gentle and patient as a boy and he had remained that way all his life. All unknowing, he was coming to a moment when he would have to make a decision that would affect his life for ever after.

But it was not Marie Hilley's style to let Calvin relax with his dream. And perhaps also, the tension as she neared the critical moment, with uncontrollable forces closing in on her from all sides, a last chance at escape shimmering so near at hand, was having its effect on her. She snapped at him for some slight—she had done it before, over an offhand remark he thought was humorous—and afterward she would not grant him forgiveness.

Calvin was due to go back to San Francisco in three days. He could not understand the source of her anger. He was devastated. After she went to work the next morning he raced to the Western Union office in Anniston and sent her a telegram at her office, two miles away. He was being punished for something he had not done, Calvin told her in abbreviated telegram language, yet he still worshiped her. Must she allow their visit to end on this tragic note?

Now she was doubly annoyed with him. He had sent her a telegram at work. He had done it twice before, from San Francisco, and she had told him not to do it again. The people at work made too much of it. She piled indictment on indictment, and he poured contrition after contrition.

And then, she forgave him once more. There would be one last chance to tantalize, to mesmerize, to bring him to her side. She would drive him down to Birmingham for his flight home.

For more than a week afterward he could not bring himself to write to her about their last hours together, and then he sat for minute after minute, trying one approach, then another, before beginning to set down his thoughts.

It had been a harrowing experience, those moments at the airport, a shattering decision. He compared it with his decision to volunteer for hazardous night patrol duty in Korea, knowing that he could be picked out in an enemy sniper's sights at any moment, wondering whether to risk his life.

At the airport, she had parked the car and gone inside with him. There was time to spare and he could not face leaving her. He walked with her back to the parking lot. He stood, suspended, for the last moments. And then, finally, he turned away.

It had been almost impossible for him to turn away, he wrote. It had been so disturbing an experience that his mind had erased all memory of those moments. On the plane he had sat staring out the window, tears blurring his vision of the night sky.

Still, he was grateful for what she had given him, he told her. She had made him feel manly, desired. He apologized once more for having angered her. And he declared his devotion yet again; it was undiminished by anything that had happened. He had knelt and prayed for her, weeping with emotion, each day since arriving home.

He knew he had offended her at times, but that should not obscure the real depth of his feeling for her, he said. His language taking on a biblical ring, he reaffirmed his commitment: If God asked him whether he was willing to give up his life for Marie, Calvin assured her, he would not hesitate to offer himself up. His love for her would never die.

He added a postscript: Josie was now aware of how strong his feelings were for Marie.

It would have been merciful now for Marie to end her contact with him, but that was not her way. And though he would not, could not, leave his life in California and come to her side, he was devoted to her. He remained loyal and willing, ready, still, to answer her call. He was an asset, to be hoarded for a time of need, to be used when the moment was ripe, and she would not forfeit that, no matter what the cost to him. She had not finished with Calvin Robertson yet.

But now she was occupied with other matters. She had told Calvin in January that Carol was sick, but the illness had passed and Carol had forgotten about it. In the spring of 1979, Carol got sick again.

Marie phoned Uncle Louie's widow, Ailene, in Florida. In their last conversations, Marie had talked again about how nobody loved her, and she had told Ailene about Carol's illness. Now Marie had bad news. They had received the results of the tests on Carol.

"It's leukemia, Ailene," Marie told her. Ailene was shocked. Marie was such a good, sweet girl, Louie had always favored her, and she was having such a hard time, first Frank, now this. And Ailene felt a wave of pity for Carol.

"I've made an appointment for her at the Mayo Clinic, up in Minnesota," Marie told her. She wasn't satisfied with the treatment Carol was getting from the local doctors. She wanted the best for her daughter. It would be expensive, but that didn't matter.

"I have some property down in Florida, in Pompano Beach," Marie told her. "Mike's selling it for me. He's going to send me the money. It may take a while, though, and I've got to get Carol up there right away for the treatment."

Ailene could hear that Marie was going to need money to tide her over. She offered to lend her a few thousand dollars. Marie was grateful.

"I'll pay you right back as soon as Mike gets the property taken care of," she said. Ailene was glad Louie had left her in a position to help out; she just hoped Marie could hold up through all her troubles.

Mike was also concerned about his mother. There was so much going on, the bank loans unpaid, the stock still not cashed in, and she couldn't seem to get things straightened out. When she said she wanted to come down for another visit, he was relieved. It would give her a little break, and maybe they could talk things out. They arranged that Mike would meet her at the Orlando airport. Her flight would arrive at eleven-thirty at night.

As Mike walked into the airport he thought he heard his name being called on the public-address system. He stood still to listen more carefully.

"Mr. Mike Hilley, message for Mr. Mike Hilley, please pick up the courtesy phone." What now? he wondered.

It was a message from his mother. She had been driving down to Birmingham to get the plane. She had been run off the highway by two men, who grabbed her purse and cut her arm with a knife. The cut was not serious. She was calling from a phone booth, waiting for the police.

Mike wasn't sure quite what to do. He drove home and called Carrie's house. Carrie hadn't heard from Marie. He decided to try to locate her. Over the next few hours he called the state police and sheriff's departments all around the Birmingham area. None had heard of the incident. At about 5:00 A.M. he called Carrie's again. The phone rang but he couldn't seem to get through. He tried twice more, but there seemed to be something wrong with the line. He finally gave up and fell into bed, exhausted.

When he woke up late in the morning he called again. Carrie answered the phone. She seemed confused. Marie had come back from the airport saying somebody had tried to run her off the road, Carrie told him.

"She said, 'They tried to take my purse away from me. Look what they did.'" Marie had showed them some scratches on her arm. The purse hung on its strap, undamaged.

Marie had gone to sit by the phone. She had still been there when Carrie returned to bed, as if she were expecting a call. Carrie heard the phone ring a couple of times during the night, and it sounded as if Marie picked it up. But there was no conversation.

"What's she doing, Mike?" Carrie wanted to know.

I wish I knew, Mike thought, but he didn't say that to Carrie. He didn't want to worry his grandmother. She was sick, and she depended on Marie to help run the household. She had to live with Marie. Mike was noncommittal, but he was determined to do something. His mother needed help. The next weekend he flew to Atlanta, rented a car, and drove to Anniston.

They sat at the table after supper. Carol had gone out. When Carrie got up to go watch television, Mike tried to turn the conversation toward his concerns.

"What's going on, Mom?" he asked gently. As a boy he had built a wall to protect himself from her erratic moods and her attempts to control him. Even now, he felt little warmth for her. It was only a sense of duty that brought him to her.

"What do you mean?" she responded. "Nothing's going on."

She was immediately on the defensive. It was in her voice, and he could see it in her posture, the quick straightening of her back.

He was determined to continue. He reminded her of the loan payments, the money problems, the constant struggle with Carol. He didn't mention the airport incident. It had been strange and upsetting, but he had no idea what had actually happened. She had repeated her vague explanation. He would only offend her by showing that he didn't take her story at face value.

"Oh, that's nothing," she said, waving it away like a fly on a fruit salad. The money from the stock would take care of everything, she said. And she had gotten Carol a car to make up for the Honda. Everything was fine.

He had tried for so long to find a way to deal with her. It might even be part of the reason he had chosen the ministry for a career. It was a way to understand the cruel things that people—parents and children, families—did to each other, to learn how to help them, finally to get control of these situations. Could there be an element of self-defense in his choice of a career? He was determined to do his best with her, at least this once, no matter how hard she was going to make it for him.

"Mom, you've been under a lot of pressure since Dad died," he began. That seemed to ease the atmosphere a little. She nodded agreement and looked at him, curious about what he was leading up to.

"Have you ever thought of getting an evaluation?" he asked. He was speaking as softly as he could, trying to keep any sense of a challenge out of his voice. She didn't seem to understand what he meant. His own studies in the ministry had been leading him toward psychology and counseling.

"You know, a psychiatric evaluation," he said. It sounded so stark like that, the word "psychiatric." He started to say something to soften it, about the pressures of being alone, of trying to do everything for herself after years of marriage, but it was too late.

"There's nothing wrong with me." She hammered out the words, glaring at him. He couldn't find anything to say. "I don't need any help," she added. She hit hard on the word "need." She got up from the table and left the room.

The next day she was still cool toward him, but she had a favor to ask. If he was going into town, would he pick up the license plates for Carol's MG? The dealer was getting them for her.

At Bama Auto Sales, Mike asked about the plates. They hadn't come in yet. "Hey," the salesman asked as he was leaving, "when's your mother going to pay for the car?" What do you mean? Mike asked. She had been expecting some money to come in a few days, she had told them. They had let her have the car on her promise to bring the money down as soon as she got it. "I don't know anything about it," Mike told the salesman. She's still trading on Dad's reputation, Mike thought. Frank had always been able to buy a car on his word and work out the financing afterward.

Mike was frustrated when he left for the Birmingham airport. He couldn't do anything for her if she wouldn't talk to him. He really just ought to give up.

It wasn't the first time he had decided to back away from the edge of the whirlpool that was forming around his mother, and it was not to be the last. But each time he had been lured from his resolve, and now the events began that would draw him closer and closer to the deadly center of her life.

Early in the year, Mike had tired of the Chevy Nova he had bought after turning the Chevette over to his mother. He had experienced a series of mechanical problems with it, one after another, and he was planning to trade it in. When he had mentioned his plans to his mother, just making conversation, she had asked to buy it from him. He told her in detail about the problems the car had caused him, but she was insistent.

"I've got a good mechanic here," she said. "He'll take care of it for me." Mike was reluctant, but she would not rest until he agreed to turn the car over to her. As he had done with the Chevette, he let her take over the payments.

Back in Merritt Island, Mike received another of the telephone calls that little by little, like spotlights in a dark theater, opened the hidden side of Marie Hilley's life to her son's view. This time it was a collection officer from the Birmingham office of GMAC, the financing company of General Motors.

"Mr. Hilley," the impersonal voice said, "you haven't made a payment since January."

Mike was puzzled at first. A payment on what? he wondered. The collection agent explained: It was the Nova he had bought twenty months before.

"We've had a hard time tracking you down," he said. "You moved from Anniston to Florida." There was accusation in the man's voice.

Mike explained that he had turned the car over to his mother and that she had agreed to make the payments. When they hung up, he called Marie. She was noncommittal. She had sold the car, she said, traded it in on a Ford Torino. She didn't know what the problem was.

"I'm coming up there and we're going to straighten this out," he said, "once and for all."

At first thought, it is a strange association, the automobile and this small, delicate woman who, according to her family, drove a car from the time she was old enough but never held a driver's license—she couldn't pass the eye test, she told them. In the four years after her husband died, Marie Hilley displayed a passionate concern for cars, buying them, trading them, borrowing to finance them. No sooner did she acquire a new one than she was talking about the next one, a car for herself, a car for Carol, a car for Mike. She possessed a dozen cars in that time, more or less.

Yet in all this, the automobile meant to Marie Hilley very much what it means to all Americans. It was both a necessity of daily life and a measure of status, an object to be admired, to be coveted, to be bought, owned, and discarded. It was, most of all, an icon, something to be manipulated in a financial ritual. As her dealings became more and more desperate, hardly a week seemed to pass without a new transaction. It is a measure of the endurance of Frank Hilley's good reputation and of Marie's own talent for concealment that she was able to carry on for so long. Finally, however, the façade was cracking.

It was the middle of the week, but Mike couldn't bear to wait. On Thursday afternoon, he flew to Atlanta once again and drove to Anniston.

The MG Marie had "bought" for Carol was gone. In its place there was a yellow Buick Cutlass. The Nova was gone, too. Marie said she had sold it to a car lot on Quintard Boulevard. She was vague about where she had gotten the Ford and the Cutlass. Mike checked with the car lot. They had given her twenty-six hundred dollars for the Nova and she had promised to bring them the title. She hadn't delivered it yet.

Mike was at the end of his patience. GMAC was chasing him for more than two thousand dollars. He confronted her at dinnertime.

"They're after me, Mom," he said. "What are we going to do?" He was almost pleading with her, asking not just for a solution but also for some explanation, an answer that would rescue his belief in her as a parent, someone to be trusted and relied upon.

"Well, Harold said he'd give me the money," she responded.

Mike remembered Harold Dillard, the owner of Advance Construction. Why Dillard would give her the money, Mike had no idea, but at this point it didn't really matter. Anything to get this settled, he thought.

"All right," he said, "let's go get it."

"Not tonight," she said. "we can't do it now. I'll get it tomorrow."

Mike was reluctant to wait another minute, but he didn't seem to have much choice.

"Okay, but first thing tomorrow we're gonna go and get the money and settle this thing once and for all."

A night's sleep did nothing to soften his sense of urgency. At twenty-six, Mike was a pleasant man, with his father's light brown hair, soft features, and easygoing manner. Like his father, he was inclined to keep his feelings to himself, but this episode with his mother was turning him inside out. She had made her problems into his problems, forcing him to try to help her solve them. In the process she was bringing him face to face once again with the fear and distrust, mixed with love, that he had felt for her as a child.

Mike awoke early. He was too agitated to eat breakfast. He sipped distractedly at a cup of coffee. His mother didn't seem to feel the same pressure he did, but he finally got her into the car. She drove downtown, toward Harold Dillard's office in the Anniston Bank and

Trust Building. Mike was preoccupied, eager to have things settled, when he became aware that she had passed the turnoff for the bank.

"Where are you going, Mom?" he asked.

"To Harold's office."

"You just missed the turn. His office is in the bank building."

"Oh, no," she said, "that's his old office. He's moved."

They finally pulled up in front of another office building.

"I'll go find him," she said, and disappeared inside the building. She was gone several minutes before she returned to the car. She looked disappointed.

"He's not there," she told him.

"Well, where is he?" Mike asked her. "Where else would he be?" He knew Dillard was involved in a number of businesses and boards.

"They don't know," she said. "They don't expect him back until Monday." She wanted to leave it over the weekend. "We shouldn't bother him on the weekend," she said, but Mike was adamant. It was time to get things settled.

They spent the rest of the morning driving from one of Dillard's enterprises to another. They stopped periodically at a phone booth, where Marie tried to reach Dillard's wife at home to find out where he had gone. It was a hot day and their tempers grew ever shorter. Finally, at midmorning, they gave up.

She didn't need Harold's money, Marie said. She would be getting the money from Frank's stock, she told Mike, trying to reassure him. Her statement had the opposite effect.

"You've been talking about that for months," Mike replied. Impatience had all but destroyed his soft-spoken manner. He seized on the idea of the stock money.

"Where is the money?" he demanded.

"The bank is taking care of it," she said. She was taken aback by the force of his question.

"Which bank?"

"The bank downtown," she said. His persistence seemed to throw her into confusion.

"Which bank?" He wasn't going to let her off the hook.

"Anniston National," she replied finally. They were pulling into the driveway.

"Okay, that's it. Right after we eat we're going down to the bank and we're going to get this straightened out."

She couldn't seem to think of anything to say. It was so unlike him to be so assertive with her. She seemed dazed.

They arrived home in a haze of anger and accusation. Marie felt he was pressing her too hard. She was treating his insistence as an insult. Mike took a seat at the table in the kitchen. The heat and the emotional turmoil had destroyed his appetite for food, but he gulped a glass of Kool-Aid and asked for more.

He had come up from Florida just to deal with the money due on the Nova, and he was determined not to let his mother wriggle out of it before they got it resolved. She was obviously avoiding further discussion, wandering in and out of the kitchen.

Suddenly his stomach was gripped in a spasm. He hardly recognized it at first; he hadn't been sick, even with an upset stomach, in ten years. In the next minute, he was struck by a wave of nausea. He vomited repeatedly for an hour, until he felt as if he had been wrung out. His mother was sympathetic. When the nausea failed to subside, she drove him to the Anniston Medical Clinic. Dr. Donald, who had been seeing Carol, was on duty. He gave Mike an injection for the nausea and told him to rest.

Mike started to feel drowsy on the way back to Carrie's house. By the time they arrived, his eyes were so heavy he couldn't keep them open. He fell into a drugged sleep.

It was dark when he woke up and at first he couldn't figure out where he was. As he staggered out of the bedroom to see who was around, the events of the morning came back to him. His mother had sidestepped him again! What was she up to? His eyes fell on a purse resting on the table next to her bed. He had never pried into her business before, but he was tempted. Maybe it would offer some clue, some way to understand what she was doing. He walked to the table and opened the purse.

The hard, metallic surface was incongruous among the soft, delicate items that inhabit a woman's handbag. Mike had little experience with guns. He reached for it carefully, as if it might go off before he could touch it. It seemed small and somehow feminine, qualities that were incompatible with the lethal possibilities of the revolver's cylinder and its neat round of bullet chambers. Mike put the gun back in the purse and replaced it on the table. The mystery of his mother had taken on a new, more menacing, dimension. Although he knew no one was in the house, Mike tiptoed back to his room. He soon returned to a dreamless, artificial sleep that lasted through the rest of the night.

The next morning his mother was in high spirits.

"I've got the money," she said. "I sold the car."

Mike was confused. "What car?" he wanted to know.

"The Cutlass," she answered.

"But that's Carol's car."

"Oh, she doesn't care. She doesn't need it." His mother seemed to think that this announcement settled everything. "I'll send them a check," she added, with the manner of a judge bringing down his gavel.

Mike wasn't satisfied. He had struggled this far to get things settled. He wasn't about to leave it to her to take the final steps.

"You give me the money and I'll send it to them," he said.

"Then let's drive it over there," she said.

Mike's thoughts skipped back to his discovery of the night before. He had almost forgotten about the gun amid the discussion of Carol's Oldsmobile and the payments on the Nova. Now he pondered the image of the little revolver. He couldn't imagine his mother using the gun. That would be so direct and violent, not her style at all. But the drive to Birmingham included long, isolated stretches of highway, and he wasn't so sure what she'd do anymore. He wanted to settle the matter as quickly as possible, but they didn't have to deliver the check by hand. He phoned GMAC to tell them he was taking care of the payment, then went to the bank with his mother to get a cashier's check, which he mailed immediately.

As he drove back to Atlanta, Mike thought about what had happened. His mother had told him about some more strange phone calls; now it was some man demanding money. Carol was sick again, with stomach problems and tonsillitis and fever; she had looked emaciated, Mike thought, and the doctors still couldn't figure out what was wrong with her. His mother still talked about the money from the stock, but it seemed increasingly unlikely that she was ever going to sell it, if it even existed. It would have been nice, he reflected, to have some help with these plane trips back and forth from Florida, and the debts she had run up for him. But he had given up expecting the ten thousand dollars. What would happen next? he wondered.

He didn't have to wait long to find out. His mother called the next week. It was the phone calls, she said. The man had called again.

Mike heard fear and helplessness in her tone, but the sound of her voice seemed to come at him through a filter. She had pushed him too far and had finally killed his capacity for sympathy. He had reverted to his childhood habit of turning his mind off.

She was talking about his father's gambling. The caller was a man who spoke in a menacing whisper. She couldn't recognize the voice. He had threatened her if she didn't pay up, and he had also threatened to hurt Carol. Frank had run up tremendous debts in the last year or so before he died. It didn't make sense, Mike thought, but his impulse to tell her so was erased by a great fatigue that seemed to fall over him like a cloak.

"Mom . . ." He tried to interrupt her, but she seemed determined to keep talking, as if her words could become a barrier between her and any challenge or disbelief he might express. He kept trying, until at last she stopped.

"I can't do anything for you," he said. "I can't do anything." She kept bringing her problems to him, but she wouldn't trust him to help her. He knew the months of worry and confusion were in his voice. She must have heard it, too. She remained silent.

"Why are you telling me all this?" he asked. "Call the FBI. They're the ones that deal with extortion. Call them up and tell them about it."

"Well, I really don't know if I could do that," she said.

"My God, Mother!" he shouted. "This is tearing my life apart." He hadn't wanted it to go this far, but he couldn't stop. "If you don't tell me what's going on, I'm going to hang up the phone and I don't want you to ever call me again."

The outburst stunned both of them. There was a silence before she spoke. She seemed subdued. She was trying to explain about the phone calls. She must know that wasn't what he meant, but she was starting to describe the caller's whisper again. He interrupted her.

"Call the FBI," he said. He was calmer now. His tone was flat. "Call the FBI. If you don't call them, I will."

"All right," she said simply. "I'll call them."

They talked a few minutes more, attempting to ease the tension out of the space between them, before hanging up. Mike tried for the rest of the day to get the conversation out of his mind, but he couldn't. He was still a little chastened by his anger, but as he calmed down, his skepticism, compounded of boyhood defenses and the experience of recent months, returned to full strength. She would never call the FBI, he thought, she would just let the situation go on and on, and she would call him up and complain about it, and he would never stop feeling frustrated and angry. And nobody would ever find out what was really going on with her.

He called her back the next day. Yes, she said, she had called the FBI. She had told them the whole story, and they were going to investigate. Mike wasn't convinced. It had been too easy. He called the FBI office in Anniston. Yes, the agent said, he had talked to Mrs. Hilley, and the case was under investigation. There wasn't much satisfaction in this little victory, Mike reflected, but maybe the FBI could figure her out. He certainly wasn't getting anywhere himself.

As it turned out, even experienced FBI agents were left shaking their heads over Marie Hilley's extortion case. Amid the looming tragedy of Marie's life, the story in retrospect has a slapstick, Keystone Kops quality to it.

Frank Hilley had been a habitual gambler, Marie told the federal agents, and his losses had mounted into the thousands of dollars. The caller, she said, seemed to know a lot about Frank and about her, but she had no idea who it was. He had told her that Frank owed him personally close to ten thousand dollars, and he expected to be paid. She had responded that she thought a debt was a debt and should be paid. Besides, she told the police, she wanted to protect her late husband's memory. She had been making payments ranging from several hundred to a thousand dollars at a time, but this time he had gotten greedy: He wanted five thousand dollars, and she couldn't afford it. He had threatened her before, but now he had gone too far: If she didn't pay, he would hurt her daughter, Carol.

The FBI called in the Anniston Police Department, and Gary Carroll's reaction was immediate.

"That's a farce," he told the agent. "That's just Marie again."

Lieutenant Carroll described his experiences with Marie Hilley, the ghostly intruders, and the phone calls that stopped whenever there was a trace on the line. The federal agent was bemused by Carroll's recitation, but they both knew they had no choice: They had to treat the extortion case seriously.

Half a dozen law-enforcement officers gathered at the Anniston Police Department the morning of the drop. When a question arose about what evidence they needed to make an extortion case, they called in Joe Hubbard, the young assistant district attorney for Calhoun County. Hubbard and FBI agent Larry Sylvester were meeting Marie Hilley for the first time, but it was only a beginning. They were to join Gary Carroll as key characters in the unfolding drama of Marie Hilley over the next several years.

The caller had instructed her to put the money in an envelope, Marie told them, and place it in the dog food section of the Winn-Dixie supermarket on Twelfth Street, across from Sears, Roebuck. He had told her to put it behind the Alpo. "The Alpo?" somebody asked, holding back a grin. She didn't see the humor in it. "Yes, the Alpo," she said.

Carroll put together an envelope with several hundred dollars wrapped around enough paper to make it look at a glance like five thousand dollars. He sprinkled the package with "thief powder," the invisible dust that turns into a purple stain on contact with the moisture of the hands, and sealed it.

At the supermarket, the officers took their places. Carroll and Hubbard sat in a car half a block down the street, with a view of the front door and most of the parking lot, their car radio tuned to pick up transmissions from inside. A woman officer posed as a shopper, with a walkie-talkie concealed in her purse. Sylvester, wearing Bermuda shorts and a T-shirt, tried to make himself inconspicuous within view of the dogfood. Other officers covered the front door from the parking lot. When they were ready, Marie entered the store, placed the envelope behind a row of Alpo cans, and left. The officers settled down to wait.

Several people walked through the dog food section, one or two pausing to take a bag or cans from the shelves, but none of them seemed to be anything but ordinary shoppers. A large, middle-aged man with dark hair entered the aisle from the opposite end and walked toward the dog food. He was wearing a suit and tie. He wasn't the type of person most likely to turn up for grocery shopping on a weekday morning. He was carrying a package of toilet paper. He seemed hesitant, stopping briefly to examine a product on the shelf and then putting it back. There was something furtive in his glance, and the officers tensed for action.

He walked to the dog food section. After a final look up and down the aisle, he stepped over to the area where the bags and cans of Alpo were lined up. He moved in close and seemed to be examining the packages and the surrounding shelves, but he made no move to reach for the envelope. He looked up, seeming confused, then stooped over and reached in behind the bags of Alpo on the bottom shelf. A woman pushing a shopping cart entered the row from the other end. He raised his head and saw her coming toward him. A flush spread over his face. He stood up and walked away.

Sylvester was sure the man had been looking for the envelope, but for some reason he hadn't been able to find it. And since he hadn't picked it up, they had no grounds to stop him. The man walked to the checkout area, paid for the toilet paper, and left.

"You won't believe who was just poking around in the dog food," the woman officer whispered into the walkie-talkie. She had recognized the man, a prominent Anniston businessman, and she was sure the others would, too.

The man was Walter Clinton, the owner of Clinton Controls, Marie Hilley's former employer and lover, the man Frank Hilley had found in bed with his wife. As it happened, Gary Carroll knew Walter Clinton; he had been a friend of Carroll's father. Though there was nothing more to the case, Carroll was curious. He had enough experience with Marie Hilley to suspect that things were not what they seemed. A week later he dropped by to see Walter Clinton.

Clinton was shocked to hear that he had been observed in the store. What were you doing there? Carroll asked him. The story Clinton told was a mirror image of Marie Hilley's, but seen in a distorting glass. A woman had called him, speaking in a whisper, and claimed that she had papers that would be useful to him. Clinton claimed he had not recognized the voice and had no idea who she was, but he had been involved for several years in a lawsuit with a former customer. The papers she described sounded as if they would help him make his case. The woman had said she would hand them over to him. He claimed there had been no mention of money. She had set up the exchange at the grocery store.

He had looked where she told him, Clinton said, behind the Alpo, but he had been unable to find the papers. He was blind in one eye, he told Carroll, from a childhood accident. He had trouble with his depth perception.

Even in retrospect, no one was sure what the purpose was of this elaborately staged incident. Was it to establish a source of the insidious attack that was slowly destroying Carol? Marie had made a point of calling the FBI office to say that she might be hard to contact in the next few weeks.

"I won't be around much," she had said. "My daughter is in and out of the hospital and they don't know what's wrong with her."

Or was it intended to create an explanation for the disappearance of Marie's money? Whatever it was, within a few weeks, events made the extortion case into nothing more than a bizarre footnote to the story of Marie Hilley.

6

A Lost Child

At nineteen, Carol Hilley was a tiny girl, just an inch or two over five feet, weighing a little more than a hundred pounds with all her clothes on and heavy shoes, but she was quick to stand up for her rights, and she was still willing, as she had been in high school, to fight rather than back down from anybody. It was hard to see the look of either parent in her narrow face, but her mother's energy showed in quick bursts of speech that contrasted with her southern accent and laconic style. Her shoulder-length brown hair was shaped in a layered cut that softened her sharp features and gave her a pretty, girlish look. She had surprisingly long fingers, and she was capable of great gentleness and delicacy with a sick puppy, but she liked to affect a tough style, with ungrammatical country speech and fluent vulgarity.

She still had the changeability of an adolescent, bold and sure one minute, hesitant and confused the next. If it came down to action, something like riding a motorcycle or hitting a softball, she always knew what to do. When she talked about herself, the example she used was revealing, reflecting the bravado of her street-smart side:

"If I was planning to do something," she told somebody, trying to summarize her personality, "like rob a bank, I could plan it out real good, and I might get away with it, and then I could find a great hiding place for the money, nobody would ever find it." But that was in her fantasy life, and few people knew about that side of her. What others saw in her was something quite different.

"My friends'll tell you I got no confidence in myself," she said, "and they're right in a way." If it came down to where talking was important, she'd never get anywhere, she said, and she couldn't tell a good lie if her life depended on it. "I just can't look somebody in the eye and tell them something that isn't true."

For all her pose of toughness, she was basically an innocent, and in spite of the fierce resistance she would raise time after time against her mother's powerful attempts to control her, Carol was still very much a child, trusting and vulnerable. Those were the qualities that now put her life in danger.

Marie had followed through on her statement to Freeda that she would make Carol go to trade school so she could learn a skill. She had tried a semester at the State Technical School in Anniston, thinking she might do something in nursing or cosmetology, but it hadn't worked out. Now she was going up to Jacksonville State University, still living at home. She wasn't quite sure why, or what she wanted to do with it, but she was majoring in law enforcement.

In April, Charlie Dyer, who was a year behind her at Anniston High School, invited her to the junior-senior prom; it would be their third year in a row at the prom together. After the dance a group of the graduates went out to the Ramada Inn in Oxford, ten miles away, where Charlie and Ed Dailey had rented two rooms so they could continue the party. Carol drank a Tom Collins, then several more, and later she joined most of the others in smoking marijuana. Suddenly she was struck by a wave of nausea.

"Don't get sick, girl," she told herself, gritting her teeth, "not in front of your friends," and she fought off the feeling. Charlie took her home at about four in the morning. She was still feeling slightly sick.

When she woke up to go to Sunday school the next morning, the feeling had intensified. She assumed it was the effects of the drinking and the pot, on top of a steak she had eaten before the prom at a restaurant in Birmingham. She set off for church, thinking it would go away.

As she sat in class at First Christian, the nausea struck again. It was like a blow in the stomach. She quickly got up and walked from the room. In the parking lot she felt a little better, so she got in the car and drove for a few minutes. She found herself in front of the Faith Temple Christian Center, where she had attended services a few times. She decided to try again, choosing a seat at the back of the sanctuary so she could get away easily if she had to. Soon the sick feeling welled up again. By the time she got to the parking lot, she was overwhelmed by nausea. Before she could reach the car, she threw up violently.

On the way home, she stopped for a Coke at McDonald's. Again she felt a little better. Now that she had gotten it out of her system, she thought, maybe the sickness would pass. She didn't want to have to tell her mother about it. She would know immediately it was from partying, and that would give her an opening to jump on Carol again about her friends and social life and lack of direction.

She arrived home at Carrie's house to find her mother just coming out the door. Carrie had been taken to the emergency room at the Regional Medical Center; they assumed it was some complication of the cancer or her medication. Carol turned around and went with her mother. At the hospital, Carol became nauseated again and had to run from the waiting room to throw up. When she returned, her face was pale and drawn. It was obvious something was wrong, and she was forced to tell Marie that she was sick. When the vomiting continued through the rest of the afternoon, Marie drove her back to the emergency room. It seemed as if they had spent the whole day there.

The emergency room doctor took a sample of Carol's blood and gave her a shot. It seemed to work, and by the next morning she was feeling better. It was a day out of her life, but everything was back to normal.

The next Sunday, she got sick again. Marie insisted on taking her back to the emergency room at the Regional Medical Center. Along with the nausea and vomiting, this time she had severe pains in her abdomen. The doctor on duty had her admitted to the hospital for tests.

Carol was feeling terrible. The pains made it seem worse than just an upset stomach. When she talked to the doctor and he asked about her family's medical history, it reminded her of her father, how suddenly death had come, and she was frightened. But X rays and lab tests showed nothing abnormal in her kidneys and liver. By late Monday her symptoms had disappeared, and she was discharged on Tuesday.

The following day, she was back. The vomiting, racking and uncontrollable, had resumed soon after she got home, and with it the intense stomach pains. This time they used a tube to pump out her stomach, to rest her digestive system while they did more tests. The testing took five days, but nothing turned up. Once more, she was released from the hospital. There was still no diagnosis, but at least she was out of the hospital, Carol thought, and she was free of the vomiting and pain again. It was a relief.

The illness, or something, seemed to be affecting her mother, Carol thought. There seemed to be money problems, and she knew, too, that it was hard on her mother, taking Carol back and forth to the hospital. Her mother was obviously worrying a lot about what could be making her sick, but it didn't appear to reduce the tension between them. It felt like the only time her mother eased up on her was when she was really sick. As soon as she recovered a little, Marie would go on at her about something. It seemed to Carol sometimes that her mother was just trying to provoke her.

One evening at dinner, her mother said something vague about their going out together. Carol said she had a date.

"You don't ever want to go anywhere with me," Marie complained. "You act like you're ashamed to be with me."

"I'm not ashamed to be with you," Carol replied. "I just want to do other things sometimes."

"And when I want to go somewhere," Marie responded, "you're always too busy."

"Mother, that's not true," Carol answered. "I just want to go out with my friends once in a while." Carol was sensitive on that point. She was nurturing a new relationship, one with a kind of love and gentle affection that she had never experienced before. The feelings seemed especially fragile and private, not like the relationships she had with boys in high school, and she had kept it a secret from her mother, trying to protect it. Of course, she had been spending a lot of time on it.

The color was rising in her mother's face.

"That's all you want to do," Marie yelled at her, "ruining your health, running around all night, taking drugs . . . !"

Carol exploded. She had a short temper; it seemed her mother was never satisfied until Carol blew up.

"Sure I smoke a little pot!" she shouted. "Big deal! Everybody does it! So what? What do you care?"

When they were at home together, it seemed, they never did anything anyway. When she wasn't nagging at Carol, Marie sat for hours with her nose in a book.

Freeda happened to be at the house one day when Charlie Dyer came by and Carol wasn't at home. Marie let him in, but her face was creased in a disgusted look and her greeting was an unintelligible mumble.

"Is Carol here?" he asked.

"You'd know better than I would," Marie answered, glaring at him for a long moment before turning her back. The boy seemed startled.

"Is she coming back?" he asked.

Marie walked out of the room, ignoring the question. Charlie stood by the door for several moments, befuddled, trying to decide whether to wait for Carol or leave. He had started to turn toward the door when Marie came back into the room. She began talking to him, but it sounded more like an interrogation.

Marie questioned Charlie for several moments about things he and Carol had done together recently. The boy confined his answers to a polite "Yes, ma'am" or "No, ma'am," but he was obviously puzzled and uncomfortable.

"You're not what she needs," Marie concluded. "You can't give her what she needs."

"I guess I'd better be going now," he said nervously, and made his escape.

Marie never spoke to Carol about Charlie, but she was very specific about Rick Turner. She just didn't like him.

"Why not, Mom?" Carol begged her. "What's wrong with him?" She couldn't understand it. They were just friends, and he had never done anything wrong.

"I just don't like him, that's all," Marie said, and Carol never could figure it out.

Freeda's daughter Lisa came home one day to say that she had stopped by to see Carol, but she hadn't been there and Lisa had ended up visiting with Marie. Marie took her out to Dresser Industries, where she worked, and introduced her around the office, talking about the honors Lisa had won in school and the success she was having at her job. Marie had never taken Carol to work with her.

Freeda felt sorry for Carol. She and Lisa were cousins, they were close in age and physically similar, and they had been raised together until Freeda moved out to Weaver to get away from the Anniston schools. The temptation was there to compare them, and Marie had never tried very hard to resist. She had often held up Lisa, the blond honor student and cheerleader, as an example to her daughter, and her disappointment at the comparison was never far from the surface. Freeda liked Carol, and she knew her niece was simply a different kind of person from Lisa, more independent, unconventional, even rebellious. She would never have the same kind of success or popularity as Lisa. The comparison was stacked against her. Carol would never satisfy Marie.

But Freeda was most concerned about the effect the tension between Carol and Marie was having on her mother, Carrie. Sick as she was, Freeda thought, her mother was entitled to a little peace in her own house. This constant fussing between Marie and Carol was putting Carrie under a lot of extra stress.

Carrie was already upset with Marie, she told Freeda. It was the utility bills. Under their agreement, Marie was supposed to be taking care of the electric charges and paying a share of the phone bill. At lunch one day, Carrie had given Marie the bills, along with cash for her own share of the phone charges. Marie was to write checks for the total and mail the bills. The next month's bills had just come, and they showed that the previous charges hadn't been paid. Marie said she had misplaced the envelopes and forgotten about them, but Carrie was upset. She always paid her bills on time.

There were times when Carol felt her sickness was just part of the strange atmosphere around Carrie's house, as if the tension and anger were seeping into her blood vessels and digestive system. She had always been frightened by her Grandmother Hilley's house, ever since she could remember. As a child she had been sent occasionally to spend the night with her grandparents, and they always brought her into the bed with them. Lying there between the two old people, she thought it was the darkest place she had ever been, and she was never sure if the groaning, scratching sounds she heard deep in the night were menacing spirits under the bed or the snoring of her grandparents.

Now she was nineteen years old, but it still seemed especially dark in Carrie's house, and when she lay down to sleep, the memory of old fear was never far from the surface of her mind. She was grateful for the distant streetlight that cast a few weak rays into the corner of her room.

It was one of the days she had been sick, and perhaps the fever and dehydration cast their own eerie glow on what happened. She woke suddenly, completely alert in an instant, aware at the same moment that her mother was in the room. Marie stood perhaps ten feet from the bed, and she was completely motionless. At first Carol thought the scene too strange to be real and considered the possibility that she was dreaming. After a few minutes, Carol was able to separate the vision from the remnants of her dreaming, and when she knew it was real, a cold fear came over her. It was like the fear of the unknown menace that had gripped her as a child sleeping between her grandparents. The fact that this strange vision was her own mother only made the menace seem greater. Carol held herself still to avoid breaking the spell that seemed to grip her mother; long minutes later, Carol eased her head around to look again. Her mother was gone, leaving only a chilling sense of eerie mystery behind.

Carol associated some of the problems around the house with money. Mike had called from Florida. A loan officer from Anniston National Bank had finally reached him there. They had been trying to find him for months. The loan he had taken for five hundred dollars with his mother hadn't been paid off.

"What's going on, Mom?" he wanted to know.

She had gotten behind on the payments, she said. She had told the bank she was going to pay it off as soon as she cashed in Frank's Alucite stock. Alucite was an iron company in New York State, related somehow to the foundry where Frank had worked. Mike had first heard about the stock from his father. Marie said it was worth close to fifty thousand dollars now. That was the stock money they had been searching for the morning he got sick. Why had Marie taken so long to cash it in?

"They want their money, Mom," he said. "What am I supposed to tell them?"

"I'll take care of it," Marie responded. She sounded a little exasperated at the idea that the bank would be so insistent over such a small amount. She would have preferred to keep the stock and collect the dividends, but she finally agreed to go ahead and sell it. She would give Carol and Mike ten thousand dollars each and use the rest for the household.

"Can I do what I want with my part of the money?" Carol asked her at dinner. Marie was showing her a large, official-looking certificate of Alucite, Inc., a division of the Warnimock Iron Company. The top of the certificate was decorated with engraved drawings of figures wearing robes.

"Well, I guess," Marie answered, "but what are you going to do with it?"

Carol had dreamed of another car, a sleek, powerful Chevy Camaro.

"I'm gonna get me a Z28," Carol said, and she described the car to her mother, excited by the vision. She had loved and coveted the Camaros but had never thought she might be able to afford one. She could hardly contain her anticipation.

"When are we gonna get the money, Mom?" she wanted to know.

"Oh, we'll get it soon," Marie told her. "I'll tell them to get right on it."

There was hardly a day when Carol didn't think of the car. She was feeling weak and sick a lot of the time, and the thought of driving fast with the radio playing loudly, free and powerful, gave her something to look forward to. She waited as long as she could before asking her mother about it again.

"When's the money coming, Mom?"

"We can't get it right now," she answered. It was something to do with trading in the certificates.

"Well, how long is it gonna be?" Carol was getting impatient.

"Oh, it won't be long," Marie said. "They have to do the paperwork." She look distracted, as if there were other, more important things she wanted to concentrate on.

The next time Carol asked, she was more insistent.

"How long, Mom? What takes so long?"

"It'll be here in four weeks," she said.

"That's how long it'll take to get the car. Can I go down and order the car, Mom? Please, Mom?"

Marie was reluctant, but Carol kept after her, pleading and insisting until she agreed to a compromise.

"All right," she said. "let me do it, I'll order it for you." Carol gave her the details: a white car with a blue stripe, blue interior, radio and cassette player, white walls. The car would use up almost all of Carol's ten thousand dollars. Marie made note of everything Carol wanted. The next day Marie reported that she had called around to the Chevy dealers in the area. Pierson Chevrolet over in Gadsden had a car coming in that was just what Carol wanted. It would be arriving in a week or two. By then they ought to have the money.

Carol was ecstatic. It was like having a lover, the excitement constantly just below the surface of everything she did, her thoughts leaping to the car any time something else wasn't occupying her completely, again and again throughout the day. The wait seemed endless, but at last the car arrived. All through breakfast, Carol could feel the excitement in her stomach.

As they got into Marie's car for the forty-minute drive, the feeling inside her turned suddenly into queasiness. Within minutes she was seized by a violent urge to throw up. Marie pulled the car to the side of the road, but Carol was already leaning out the window, convulsed. When there was a break in the retching she started to get out of the car to get some air, but she was too weak to open the door, and the pain in her stomach held her, bent forward, in her seat.

Marie looked concerned. She reached out her hand.

"We'd better get you home, honey," she said.

"No, Mom," Carol cried, "I want to go get the car!" She was desperate.

"You can't go down there in that condition," Marie said. "There'll be plenty of time for that. Let's get you home to bed, get your strength back."

Carol pleaded, crying, furious that the sickness had interfered with her dream, but Marie was adamant.

At home the nausea continued, and Carol had to admit to her mother that she was also having another of the headaches that had bothered her periodically for several months. They had been getting more severe in the past few days. It was time to see a doctor again, but Marie didn't want to go back to the Regional Medical Center. They hadn't done anything for Carol the last time; there was no reason to think they could now. She drove to the Anniston Medical Clinic, where Carol was given an appointment with Dr. Donald.

Dr. Donald couldn't find anything obviously wrong with Carol.

"Everything looks normal," he told her.

Carol was concerned about the headaches. The doctor had gathered, from a few things she said, that relations had been strained between Carol and her mother for several months.

"You can get headaches from tension," he told her. She didn't have much to say in response, but that seemed to make her feel a little better about it. In the next week she developed a rash on her legs, but the headaches had stopped; her stomach was a little queasy, but she hadn't experienced any vomiting or serious nausea since her last visit to Dr. Donald.

He was reassuring when he talked to Carol and Marie again: All the tests had come back with normal results. It didn't look like anything to worry about. He gave Carol some medication, but she was to use it only if the headaches came back.

It was a relief to feel better, Carol thought. Now they could go get the Camaro. Except for the queasiness in her stomach, she felt fine.

But on the drive to Gadsden a few days later, she started feeling sicker.

"We'll stop and get some medicine," Marie said. She came out of the drugstore with a large bottle of Maalox. The doctor had recommended it for Carol's indigestion. They didn't have a spoon or cup. Her mother produced an empty plastic Tylenol bottle for Carol to drink from. When Marie poured the Maalox into the smaller bottle, it fizzed up; that must be the powder from the Tylenol tablets, Carol thought. She drank the Maalox. It burned going down her throat. She had never felt that before, but at first it seemed to be settling her stomach.

In Gadsden she couldn't pretend anymore. "Pull over!" she shouted, and as her mother drove into a parking lot, Carol threw up. When there was a break in the spasms that were wracking her body, she spoke.

"Let's go get it," she said. She was bent over from the pain.

"We can't go get any car," Marie answered, watching her as the spasms began again. "I'm taking you home. You're sick."

"I want to go on and get the car," Carol managed to gasp.

"Don't be silly," her mother replied. "You couldn't drive it home even if we did go get it."

Carol had to admit that what her mother said was true. If she was going to be sick like this and never know if she was going to get better, what good was it all, anyway?

At home, lying in bed, weak and confused from the loss of fluids, Carol was struck by a frightening thought: This kept happening when they went to get the car. I wonder if she's doing this, making me sick somehow, because she doesn't want to tell me there isn't any car? The thought had hardly crossed her mind before she pushed it away. This is my mother, my own mother, and anyway, it doesn't make any sense. Carol grasped for some clarity in the feverish muddle of thoughts that swam through her mind: Mother didn't even have to tell me there was a car in the first place if there wasn't going to be one. She wouldn't have to put herself in that position. Carol let the thought wash over her with its comforting warmth, and, relaxing finally, she fell asleep.

When Marie told her, days later, that the stock money had been held up again, Carol was still in bed, suffering through another attack. They would have to cancel the order for the car, her mother said.

Carol was too weak and discouraged to be angry. The periods of sickness were running together now; there was hardly a day when she felt right. Worst of all, she was losing the ability even to imagine herself being healthy again.

"I don't care," she said. "I don't want the car. I'll take the money and I don't want no car." All she wanted was to feel good again. Her mother seemed to take pity on her.

"I'll make it up to you," she told Carol. "I'll get you a car." Within days she brought home an MG. Carol loved the little English sports car, but she was too sick to use it much. And as for the stock money, that sounded like a fantasy, too. She was tempted to say so, but her mother was so defensive and irritable.

If I told her that, she'd just get mad, Carol thought. Her mother would think Carol was accusing her of lying, and she wasn't doing that; she wouldn't do that to her mother. She was just tired, tired of waiting, tired of the disappointment, tired of the whole thing. All the pleasure and excitement had gone. She wouldn't let herself get interested again. It wasn't worth it anymore. And she was increasingly preoccupied with her health.

Carol's last visit to Dr. Donald had been devastating. The tonsillitis and fever just wouldn't go away, and she had pain throughout her body. The tests kept coming back negative. They couldn't find anything wrong with her. Dr. Donald prescribed Ampicillin for infection and Tylenol for pain, but the next day she was back.

The physical symptoms were not the worst part of what was happening to her. Each time she started to think she was getting better, the sickness came back. It had been like this for close to four months now. Just when she was getting her hopes up, they were crushed again. She had been taking summer courses, but she couldn't keep up, and her life seemed to be falling apart. Even when she felt a little better, she couldn't make a date for the next weekend; she couldn't be sure she was going to stay well. She felt as if the world was closing in on her.

Carol was depressed and anxious, her mother told the doctor. Carol cried at the least provocation and lost her temper easily. After leaving the doctor's office the previous day, Marie said, Carol had gotten furious at her with no provocation. She had screamed and cursed at her.

Dr. Donald had done everything he could. Perhaps there was

some psychological explanation. He told them he wanted Carol to see a psychiatrist. He would make an appointment for Carol and let them know.

Afterward, Carol exploded.

"I ain't going to no damn psychiatrist!" she shouted. "I ain't crazy! I want to know what's wrong with me! I want to get better!" She broke down in tears. What's the point of living if it's gonna be like this? she thought.

But she had to admit there was something wrong. She was growing steadily weaker and she couldn't get free of the pains for more than a day or two at a time. Her mother insisted on taking her to the clinic again. Carol reluctantly gave in.

She was examined by a doctor she had never seen before. He was concerned at her recitation of the symptoms and admitted her to the Regional Medical Center. It was her third time there in two and a half months. A week of tests turned up only minor indications of abnormality in her pancreas and liver. Dr. Hixon, who was overseeing the treatment, thought these could be due to errors in the lab, and she should be retested. He was impressed with the interest showed by Carol's mother. She spent a lot of time with her daughter and wanted to know all about the progress of the tests and treatment. By the end of the week, Carol was feeling better. When they released her she was determined never to see a doctor again. She never went back to Dr. Hixon for the follow-up tests.

Her mother's close attention and the many hours they were spending together had been making Carol feel confined. She had talked with her mother about wanting to get out on her own. She was nineteen, old enough to have her own place. Marie decided now that it was time to do something about it. She rented a two-bedroom duplex apartment on Christine Avenue and took Carol to Moss Furniture, where they spend a little over two thousand dollars on furnishings. The salespeople at Moss knew Marie. She had shopped there often. They were glad to accept her check for the total.

The purchase seemed like an ordinary transaction, but it was to be a fateful event for Marie Hilley. Like the first pebble in an avalanche, Marie Hilley's signature on the check to Moss Furniture set in motion forces that would finally overwhelm her. But now those forces were in a race with the evil energy of her nature, and desperation was driving her ever faster toward a deadly conclusion.

On August 8, Marie wrote another check that would come to

seem like more than a small strip of paper. The amount was $123.64. She sent it to the Liberty National Life Insurance Company in Birmingham, to cover the two twenty-five-thousand-dollar policies she had taken out a year before: One policy insured herself, with Carol as beneficiary, the other insured Carol and Mike, with Marie as beneficiary. The check was late. It was meant to cover the two months ending August 31, a bit more than three weeks ahead.

The same week, Marie Hilley walked into the lobby of Commercial National Bank in Anniston. She approached the window of the head teller, Margaret Cleghorn. Marie Hilley did not have an account at Commercial National, but Mrs. Cleghorn recognized her. She had been head teller for twenty-two years and knew most of the people around town, one way or another.

After a few moments of small talk, Mrs. Hilley announced that she would like to open two accounts, one for herself, one for her daughter, Carol. Marie had been down in Florida with her son, Mike—"He's got a church down there, now," she said—and Mrs. Cleghorn recalled Marie telling her that her son was a minister. She had owned a house in Florida, Marie said, and Mike had just sold it for her. The check for thirty thousand dollars would be arriving any day now. When it came, she would buy a certificate of deposit with it.

In the meantime, she had a check on her account in Florida that she'd like to deposit to start the two accounts. Mrs. Cleghorn took her across the lobby to New Accounts and introduced her to the woman at the desk. In a few minutes Marie was back with the check on her account in Pompano Beach for forty-five hundred dollars. She took two hundred dollars in cash and deposited the rest. No need to wait for the check to clear. They knew she was good for it.

Marie wanted to know what she should do about the thirty thousand dollars.

"I'll be away for a few days, Marie," Mrs. Cleghorn told her. "You just have your bank send it to the care of Mrs. Ann Flannagan. I'll tell her to be expecting it and what to do with it."

When she returned to her desk the following Tuesday, Mrs. Cleghorn found a note from Marie Hilley:

Margaret,
   Thanks for holding these checks until my checks clear. I'll see you Monday. Mike is sending the $10,000 in a certified cashier's check.
                                                          Thanks.
                                                          Marie Hilley

Attached to the note were checks to Moss Furniture Company for $2,002.98 and $158.95. Marie's first attempt to pay for the new furniture hadn't worked. She was trying again.

Marie Hilley had never owned a house in Florida (though several years and two identities later, she would create a bizarre echo of this theme), and the only ten-thousand-dollar check Mike Hilley had ever heard of was the one his mother had promised him from the sale of the iron company stock. He had given up on ever seeing that money, and he had tried to separate himself psychologically from his mother, but he could not escape the reach of her desperate manipulations.

Mike and Teri had never used the MasterCard, but every month they received a statement. After finding the first few blank, they assumed it was the automatic monthly work of a computer. They had gotten in the habit of setting them aside unopened, or throwing them out. Suddenly they were getting letters threatening legal action. There must be some mistake, they thought; the letter claimed they owed several hundred dollars. It was no mistake, and it didn't take them long to figure out who was responsible. Somehow, Marie had gotten hold of the card. Mike remembered throwing it casually into a drawer.

But that wasn't all. The credit manager telephoned from Moss Furniture in Anniston. "Where is your mother?" the caller asked. "How should I know?" Mike replied. "She's in Anniston." "She's not at Dresser Industries anymore and we can't find her," the caller said. "She bought some furniture and her check was returned by the bank." Mike brought this phone call to mind later when he thought about the way his mother had changed her address again and again after Frank died: Was it six, seven, eight different residences in four years?

"Why call me?" Mike asked. "She told us you were holding her money and you were sending her a big check from her account in Florida," was the reply. "I don't even have any money of my own in a bank in Florida," Mike told him, "let alone her money."

Mike called his mother, but he hardly had enough strength left to be indignant. It was like helplessly watching an airplane spiraling out of control toward the ground. He told her to stop using the credit card. She said she had needed it, and if he'd just let her use it for a while . . . He couldn't listen. It had to catch up with her sometime, and it had to be soon. But how?

There was a week and a half left in August, a week and a half left on the insurance policies. It was four months since the night of the junior-senior prom, and Carol was still weighed down by illness. Marie had taken firmer control over Carol's movements, insisting that she needed a quieter life and more rest if she was to get better. At Carol's new apartment on Christine Avenue, Marie seemed to be around a lot of the time, even during working hours. She was employed only part time at Dresser, or maybe she had stopped working, Carol wasn't sure. Marie hardly did anything but read. Soon Marie seemed to be living with Carol, and little by little she brought her things over. Carol's bid for independence had come to nothing.

Carol's Aunt Freeda and her Grandmother Carrie wanted to visit, but it was difficult to arrange a time with Marie. She always had some good reason why it would be inconvenient—the furniture was being delivered, or she was taking Carol to the doctor, or Carol needed more rest—but underneath it all they slowly got the feeling that she wanted to keep Carol to herself. Marie especially discouraged anyone from visiting when she was not there with Carol.

Early in the year Carol had become friendly with Eve Cole, the young teacher of her Sunday school class at the First Christian Church. The friendship quickly transcended ordinary relations between teacher and pupil. Eve had been born without arms; she managed her handicap as a routine part of life, but perhaps Carol, set apart from others by her persistent illness, found some echo of her condition in Eve's experience.

In spite of Marie's resistance, Eve had been a faithful visitor during Carol's repeated attacks of sickness. Eve's husband, Ron, had dropped her off at the apartment after lunch one afternoon. As she sat and tried to talk with Carol, Eve could see that her friend was increasingly distracted. Carol had been in and out of the bathroom. Now she lay face down on the couch, shifting restlessly from one position to another, trying to get comfortable.

"Mom," she called out finally, "it's hurting, Mom!" Marie came into the room. Carol was near tears.

"I can't wait for four hours to go by," she said. She had just taken her medication a short time before. "You got to give me something. I can't stand it."

Marie was sympathetic. She seemed to consider the situation for a moment.

"Okay, honey," she said. "I'm going to go and get something for you. I'll be right back."

Marie was gone for several minutes before returning to the room. She was carrying a syringe.

"We can do it ourselves and save having to go to the clinic," she said.

Eve was sitting on the floor in front of the couch. Marie stepped past her to Carol's side.

"This will help with the nausea," she said to her daughter. They struggled for a moment to pull Carol's jeans and underpants down, exposing her buttock. Eve didn't want to watch the needle go into her friend's flesh; she looked away. She heard a small yelp of pain as the needle went in. When she looked back, Carol was pulling her pants back up.

"Dr. Donald gave me permission to give Carol shots at home," Marie said.

It didn't seem to do much good. When Ron came to pick Eve up, Carol was still nauseated, lying uncomfortably on the couch.

When she returned home after doing errands with her mother the next day, Carol noticed a new and ominous symptom: She had to struggle to climb the three steps up to the door of the apartment, and when she reached the top her legs were heavy with fatigue. When she finally slumped into a chair, exhausted, she felt a numbness in her toes, and there was a tingling sensation in the tips of her fingers. It was frightening, as if little by little some outside force was taking over her body.

It was no good pretending, her mother said. She needed to see a doctor. They wouldn't go back to the Anniston Medical Clinic. They hadn't gotten any help there. There was a specialist in internal medicine just down the street from the apartment, a Dr. Warren Sarrell. Marie drove the few blocks and helped Carol into the office.

Dr. Sarrell was alarmed at the girl's condition. She was painfully thin and badly dehydrated. She ought to be hospitalized, he told them. Carol broke down. There were months of failed effort and crushed hopes in her voice. She was taking courses at the college, trying to keep up, she had been sick for months now, it seemed like forever, she had already missed so much, she didn't want to go in the hospital again.

Marie left Carol to talk with the doctor privately. Carol didn't want to go to the hospital. Could they try something else? Dr.

Sarrell was reluctant, but he couldn't hospitalize a patient against her will. He prescribed Thorazine tablets for the nausea and vomiting.

At home that night, Carol felt as if all her strength had been drained like air from a motorcycle tire. The medication wasn't doing her any good, wouldn't ever do any good, all the doctor could think of was putting her in the hospital, and that wouldn't do any good, either. It hadn't made her better the other three times. Why would it help now? She had held out against going into the hospital, and now that she had won, she was too weak to do anything with her freedom. They couldn't figure out what was wrong with her, and they never would. It would go on like this forever. It would be better not to be here at all. If it was going to end like this anyway, why not get it over with? A bottle of medicine caught her eye. Why not? She could kill herself. It would save everybody a lot of time and trouble. She opened the bottle and poured a bunch of tablets into her hand. It was the Tylenol they had given her at the clinic. She swallowed several tablets in a gulp. What the hell, might as well take a couple more. If the pills didn't kill her, maybe they would make her feel better. Soon she drifted into sleep.

She woke up the next day feeling terrible. As she remembered taking the pills, a realization slowly came to her: She couldn't even commit suicide. She was beyond caring, even about that. When her mother said they should go back to Dr. Sarrell, she offered no resistance.

If anything, Carol seemed in worse condition than the day before. There was no question that she should be in the hospital. Once again she checked in at the Regional Medical Center. It was to be her fourth stay there, and her last.

Dr. Sarrell set about trying to establish a firm diagnosis. The physical symptoms continued as before. She had lost fifteen pounds from her usual 105. But as the week went by, the test results remained inconclusive. There was no physical cause for her illness, they told her.

Now Carol noticed that the questions the doctors and nurses were asking seemed different from before, more probing, more personal. It was as if they thought she was making herself sick. "Anorexia nervosa," somebody said; they thought that might be it. The typical anorexia patient was a girl in her late teens, like Carol, psychologically disturbed, and so obsessed with her weight that she starved herself.

Had they all turned against her? Carol wondered. It made her angry. She wasn't starving herself; it was the nausea that kept her from eating most of the time, and the fits of vomiting that kept her from digesting what food she could get down. There was nothing wrong with her mind, it was her damn body that needed help. But if the doctors couldn't help her, if that was the best they could do, what hope was there?

Marie sat for long hours at Carol's bedside, absorbed in her reading, looking up occasionally to chat. Even when she was forced to leave the room while Carol was undergoing examination or testing, or when there was a break in visiting hours, it seemed she rarely left the hospital. She would go off to sit in the lobby waiting area, returning as soon as Carol was free again. As far as Carol could tell, her mother didn't seem to have much of a life outside the hospital room. She wasn't going to work; Carol assumed her mother was taking a leave from Dresser Industries to be with her.

Marie seemed to want to help, but there wasn't much she could do. She satisfied herself with bringing in food. Because of their suspicions about anorexia, the doctors and nurses were glad to see Carol eat anything at all; they encouraged Marie to bring in whatever her daughter asked for. Pizza was what she wanted, and Marie was happy to get it for her. She even brought in jars of baby food, thinking it would be easier to digest, but Carol didn't show much enthusiasm for it.

Carol didn't have much enthusiasm for anything. As the days passed and her hope for some diagnosis dwindled, she became increasingly depressed.

"If this keeps up, I might as well end it all," she told Dr. Sarrell. He knew she had tried already, and though the attempt had seemed halfhearted, it had to be taken seriously. She had been there a week and there was nothing more they could do for her, the doctor told Carol; he wanted to refer her to a doctor in Birmingham.

He met privately again with Marie Hilley. They weren't having any success finding a cause for the physical symptoms. Possibly a psychiatrist could help Carol, he said; there might be a psychological component to her problems. He would call ahead and make an appointment for them.

Marie drove Carol directly from the hospital to the office of Dr. John Elmore in Birmingham. During the ninety-minute drive, Carol was too depressed to protest. By nightfall she was in Carraway Methodist Hospital.

It was a strange place, Carol thought, more like a jail with beds than a hospital. While she was getting settled in her room, a nurse went through her things. At the bottom of a change purse inside Carol's handbag, the nurse found a small, hand-rolled cigarette.

"This looks like marijuana," she said to Carol.

"Let me see it," Carol said. She didn't recall having any pot in her purse, but there was no question that it was a joint, dried and crackly with age. She laughed.

"That's probably been in there a couple of years," Carol said. "I forgot it was there." The nurse looked at her intently; she did not seem amused.

They also confiscated her matches; to get a light for a cigarette, she had to walk down the hall and ask the nurses. When Marie brought Carol her radio later in the week, it took three days to get it in; security procedures, somebody said. Marie sympathized with her daughter. The rules were ridiculous, she said. She smuggled in a cigarette lighter for Carol, hidden inside a box of cookies.

The hospital was very strict about contact with the outside world. They discouraged visitors, and there was no phone in Carol's room. Making a call required another long walk to the nurses' station, where it was hard to get any privacy. They wouldn't even let you dial the number yourself.

Carol claimed later that she never understood why security was so tight, why they locked the doors at both ends of the floor. Certainly her alertness was dulled by illness and discouragement. Carraway looked like all the other hospitals she had been in, and except for the annoying but minor intrusions on her freedom, her floor was like all the other floors. Carol never realized that her mother had let them place her in a psychiatric ward, and she never knew that Dr. Elmore was a psychiatrist.

Marie Hilley was moving Carol around like a piece on a chessboard. To her daughter and the world, she showed the face of a loving, concerned mother; behind this mask, the hot pulse of murder quickened steadily. Now Marie Hilley was pushing her deadly double game toward its cruel conclusion.

In her first days at Carraway, Carol was examined by the psychiatrist, a psychologist, a psychiatric social worker, a neurologist, and a blood specialist. The nurses, too, observed her and made notes of what they saw.

The physical symptoms weren't many, but they were distinct. There was a history of repeated stomach distress and vomiting attacks. Carol had lost a good deal of weight and some of her strength. There was a tingling numbness in her hands and feet. Some of her reflexes were dulled, and she had lost part of the sensation on the bottoms of her feet. She moved awkwardly, with a jerky step. There was some sign of anemia. And that was about it. It didn't add up to much, the doctors thought. The best guess was some nutritional problem. They started her on daily injections of Vitamin B_{12}.

But it was the psychological aspects of the case that were getting the most attention. In interviews with the doctor and psychiatric social worker, the patient's mother described her daughter's mental state.

Carol's personality has changed over the past several months, Mrs. Hilley told them. She's terribly short-tempered, and she overreacts to every situation. She throws tantrums, screams and yells, without any reason. At other times she gets depressed easily, over nothing, and sometimes she just sits and stares.

In the period before all this happened, she was extremely busy and active, much more than usual, almost frenzied, Marie went on, but she's become withdrawn, quiet. I've been awfully worried about her. She's dropped a lot of her friends completely and rarely sees the others; she's unpleasant with them, she seems to want to argue, and sometimes when people try to see her she's rude to them. She's restless and changeable: Just a couple of months ago she broke up with a boy she'd been going with for two years, and then right away she took up steadily with someone new. And she's been using marijuana; she told me she had been smoking with her friends.

Carol has shown self-destructive tendencies, her mother told them. Several times she said she wanted to die, Marie went on, and you know she tried to kill herself with the Tylenol. She even wrote a note to her father, who is dead; I found the note in her things. She told him she wished she could die.

That period after her father's death, four years ago, was especially traumatic for Carol, Marie continued. She had a normal upbringing and the family was always close. Her father was a supervisor at the foundry, and I've worked for many years at Dresser Industries.

Carol used to be self-confident, sociable, and she had plenty of friends. She had asthma as a child and kidney infections around the age of twelve, but otherwise she's been healthy, although always petite and thin. Then her father died, and the next year her grandmother passed away, and her brother left home, and it just seemed to change her.

Marie's account was cleverly composed to divert attention from Carol's physical symptoms and from their true cause. There was a good deal of truth in what she told them. Carol had been angry and short-tempered lately, depressed and even suicidal. It was a logical enough reaction to the physical agony, the utter disruption of her work and social life, month after month of frustration with doctors who couldn't even control her symptoms consistently, much less figure out the cause. And all of it tangled in the erratic behavior of her mother, Marie's unkept promises, her wildly swinging moods, the secretive manner, and the unexplained comings and goings.

Marie's little lies and revisions of the truth—Carol's letter to Frank had been written shortly after his death, four years before; Marie had worked at Dresser less than a year, and recently she had been fired—only reinforced the cruel masquerade that lay behind them, Marie's own pretense of motherly concern and earnest puzzlement.

Carol unknowingly reinforced the picture Marie was painting of her as still immature at nineteen, an adolescent who had steadily lost control of her life. Carol's conscience had been bothering her. The doctors were trying to find out what was wrong with her, but she hadn't told them about smoking marijuana. Actually, she had been smoking less lately; there had been a scare about Paraquat, a poison the government was spraying on the marijuana plants to kill them in the fields. There were rumors of people dying after smoking grass from the poisoned plants.

Carol had talked with Charlie Dyer and Lydia Allen about how much she should tell the doctors; they had both smoked with her a number of times. They agreed that she ought to say something, just in case, especially after the nurse found the joint in her purse. Carol summoned up her courage and told Dr. Elmore: She had smoked grass quite heavily until the scare. Could the marijuana or the Paraquat have anything to do with her illness?

She had finally gotten it off her chest, Carol thought, and it was an anticlimax. Dr. Elmore didn't seem terribly impressed.

The confession did contribute to the overall picture of Carol's erratic behavior that Marie had been helping to create. After reviewing all the tests, Dr. Elmore prescribed a tranquilizer and antidepressant medication, along with vitamin injections to help her regain her strength. It was really just a way of buying time while they looked at her more closely.

Within days the nausea and vomiting had eased again. The improvement only made Carol more restless. When were they going to let her out? They couldn't let her go, came the answer, until she had gained some weight back and could walk out of the hospital without help. There had to be some sign that she was getting better. They had to figure out what was wrong with her.

They were all over her with their testing and their questions, endless questions, and they all kept asking the same things.

They probed her about marijuana and about other drugs, and she wasn't sure they believed her when she told them the truth, that she was scared of hard drugs.

And they asked her about sex. "Have you ever had sexual intercourse with a man? Who was on top? Who was on the bottom?" "What has that got to do with it?" Carol wanted to know. "We need to know everything we can to help us figure out what's wrong," was the answer. I don't get it, Carol thought, but she gave her reluctant cooperation.

"Did you ever have sex with a woman?" one of the psychologists asked her. Carol instinctively lied:

"No, of course not," she said. "What do you think I am, crazy?" Carol had no idea of the irony in her question.

She did sense that they thought she was causing her own problems somehow, that they were blaming her for what was happening to her.

"What do you think might be causing this?" a psychiatric social worker asked her.

"How would I know?" Carol responded. "That's what the doctors have been trying to find out for five months."

"Is there anything that might be bothering you, something inside?"

They were only trying to be helpful, Carol thought. As long as they were asking her, and she was getting a chance to talk without her mother listening in, she might as well try to tell them.

"The only thing I can think of that could possibly be bothering me enough to do this . . ." Carol began. This is ridiculous, she thought. She looked directly at the social worker: ". . . which it's not," she added emphatically, pausing to make sure her disbelief had registered before she went on, "is that Mother is in some kind of trouble. Money trouble, I think."

At last, Carol thought, it's out. I wonder what they'll think of that? The interviewer asked a few questions and said she would check into it. They went on to other subjects.

But now an event took place that pushed the drama of Carol Hilley and her mother into its final phase. Marie's checks to Moss Furniture to outfit Carol's new apartment had bounced again at Commercial National Bank. The ten-thousand-dollar check from her Florida account that she had promised Mike would send to the bank had never appeared. While the furniture company was trying to locate Marie, she had cashed other checks. The total was more than five thousand dollars. Finally the bank had filed charges. For several days the police had been going through the legal steps leading to an arrest warrant. The charge was to be "obtaining money by false pretense."

Carol was starved for news of her friends. She had been in the hospital a week and she felt she was sealed off, losing contact with her ordinary life. Her room was at the end of the corridor, as far from the nurses' station as it could be, but ordinarily she wouldn't even have thought twice about walking down to use the phone. It was amazing how her perspective had changed, she thought, as she shuffled haltingly along the corridor, staying close to the wall for the extra support. She leaned against the counter as the nurse dialed Lydia Allen's number and handed her the phone.

"Hi," Carol said when Lydia picked up the phone. "It's me."

"Where are you?" Lydia asked. There was a note of excitement in her voice.

"What do you mean, where am I?" Carol responded. "I'm here in the damn hospital, just where I've been for a week. Where do you think I am?"

"What about your mother?"

"What *about* my mother? What's going on? What are all the questions?"

"Don't you know?" Lydia waited for Carol to say something. She couldn't seem to believe that Carol had no idea what she was talking about. Why is everybody treating me like this? Carol thought. They act like I'm crazy. Finally Lydia relented.

"She's been arrested," Lydia told her. "It's all over the radio and the newspaper."

Carol found that she wasn't terribly surprised at the news. I wonder why? she thought.

"What for?" she asked, hearing a flatness in her voice as she spoke.

"Something to do with bad checks," Lydia said. She had noticed the peculiar tone of her friend's voice. She mistook it for secretiveness. "C'mon, Carol, what's going on?" She sounded annoyed at being denied the details.

"I don't *know* what's going on!" Carol cried. "I'm stuck here in the damn hospital and she don't tell me nothing!" She was near tears.

"Okay, okay," Lydia said. "I'm sorry. I didn't mean to upset you. I just thought you'd know. She's with you all the time."

"Well, I don't, so that's it," Carol said.

Marie was back a few hours later. She walked into the room and greeted Carol as if nothing had happened.

"What's going on, Mom?" Carol pleaded. Something kept her from approaching the subject directly.

"What do you mean, 'What's going on?' " Marie responded. She was acting surprised. Carol hesitated. Could there be some mistake? This was her mother. A person's mother didn't get arrested.

"I heard you got arrested," Carol said.

"How did you hear about that?"

"I heard. Somebody told me. Is it true? Did you get arrested?"

"It was nothing."

"What do you mean, 'nothing'?"

"It was just a mistake. It's all over." Now she seemed more annoyed than injured or angry. Her attitude seemed to say that this was just a passing incident of no significance, like a parking ticket, that it meant nothing to her, and that Carol was not to take it seriously. But Carol was not ready to let it drop.

"What kind of a mistake?"

"Oh, it was just some checks." She made that little waving gesture of hers, dismissing the subject. "It's all straightened out now."

"Well, what happened?" Carol couldn't let it drop.

Marie turned the annoyed look on Carol. "It was a mistake. I took care of it. It's all done." The subject was closed, her tone said. She didn't want to discuss it further.

7

Suspicion

In spite of the expectant dread he had lived with for months, Mike Hilley was also shaken by the news of his mother's arrest. He had tried so many times to help her, without success. The frustration and anger had become overwhelming; he had surrendered to a numb fatalism that distanced and protected him from his mother. Something terrible would happen eventually, he had thought, but there was nothing he could do about it. But now that his fear had become real, it was surprising how easily his defenses were destroyed.

Mike had more reason than anyone else to expect his mother to get into financial trouble. He might have been relieved to have his suspicions confirmed, to know that it wasn't just in his imagination. But it wasn't that simple. She was still his mother, no matter what happened, and maybe he hadn't tried hard enough to help her. Had he given up too easily? Maybe he should have seen it coming sooner. And what should he do now? The arrest had released a tidal wave of guilt and uncertainty that Mike had held back for months, plunging him into confusion. He decided to go to Anniston.

The arrest had an equally powerful impact on Carrie Hilley, Mike's grandmother, but it led her thoughts in a different direction. Once again, she relived the death of her son, Frank, four years before, her inability to do anything about it, the horror of seeing him slip away, like a person falling in a dream.

"Mike," she said as they sat in her living room, "do you remember when your daddy died?" They had talked and talked about Marie's arrest, about her money problems and what they ought to do next, never fully coming to grips with what was happening. She was changing the subject.

"Did you ever know anything about your mother giving him an injection while he was home sick that week before he died?" she asked.

"I've never heard anything about it," Mike said. "Why?"

She told him about going to visit Frank a couple of days before he went into the hospital and finding him rubbing a red spot on his arm.

"He told Freeda that Marie was going to have to give him some shots," Carrie said. She had never been able to accept the way her son had died, so fast, and from hepatitis, a disease they said nobody ever died from, and the doctors so helpless to do anything for him.

Afterward, Mike kept thinking back to what his grandmother had said about her son's death. "It just never seemed right," Carrie had told him. Mike recalled his father's agitation in those last weeks, so unusual in that quiet, easygoing man. He thought of the many times Frank had seemed to want to say something, until finally, that day on the golf course, he had shared his brutal secret, describing his discovery of Marie and Walter Clinton in bed. And the scene, which Mike had been incapable of absorbing at the time, which he had pushed to the edge of his consciousness, came back to him in a rush.

The memories only deepened his confusion. As a child, he had hardened himself against his mother in self-defense, painfully building a wall against her to make himself room to grow. In recent months he had reacted to her erratic behavior and his own frustration by reinforcing that boyhood wall, abandoning her to whatever fate she might bring upon herself.

Of course she had been playing fast and loose with money and she had gotten herself arrested for it. But did that have anything to do with his father's death? And was it fair at a time like this, was it right for him to turn away from his mother, entertaining suspicions, pulling back when she needed him more than ever?

Back home in Florida, Mike carried on the regular duties of his ministry, but he was like a man walking in his sleep. The questions kept forcing their way back into his awareness. He and Teri went over and over them without coming to any resolution. After several days, Teri called her father in Orlando. It was close to midnight.

"Daddy, can we come over and talk to you all?" she asked. "Mike is terribly upset about all this, and he just doesn't know what to do."

Happy Henderson had felt his son-in-law's unease in earlier phone calls. He had quickly sensed the direction that Mike's worry and doubt were taking, but it had been obvious that Mike was finding it

137

difficult to acknowledge his suspicions. Happy had maintained a diplomatic reserve so far, but now Mike's painful state of indecision seemed to call for a new approach. When Mike and Teri arrived and they sat down to talk, Happy was ready.

"Mike," he said softly, "are you suspicious that your mom killed your dad?"

Mike looked up at his father-in-law. Happy Henderson knew immediately that he had said the right thing. He thought he had never seen a look of such intense gratitude and relief.

"Yes." Mike breathed the word in a sigh.

They began discussing what Mike should do. As they talked through the night, it gradually became clear to Mike. He would have to separate his love and loyalty to his mother from his suspicion and the obligation to see justice done. It would be like holding some things in one hand, some in the other. And he would have to take action.

The next morning he phoned the coroner's office in Anniston. Could the diagnosis of infectious hepatitis be consistent with something else? he asked. Could it have been poison? That was certainly possible in theory, he was told. Mike described his grandmother's account of the red spot on Frank Hilley's arm that could have been caused by a needle, and he repeated Frank's remark about Marie learning to give him injections. If there was a question about what killed Frank Hilley, could they dig up the body and find out? That might be possible, was the answer, but there certainly wasn't enough evidence to justify such a step at this time.

"It sounds like kind of a wild story to me," the coroner said. But keep in touch, Mike was told, and let us know if you find anything more.

It was discouraging to be turned away so lightly, like a child asking a question of an impatient parent, but now that he had started, Mike wasn't about to let the matter drop. He began trying to piece together the remnants of memory, the scraps of evidence, the odd bits of suspicion that family members had always dismissed over the years and months. Now he had begun to feel an urgency about his quest for understanding. His suspicions were still vague, however, and he could not yet see that his sister's life was at stake.

It was not only in Marie Hilley's family that her arrest began stripping away illusions that had long protected her. The news got around the police station quickly, and it made Billy Atherton nervous. He went in to see Gary Carroll immediately.

"Gary, I don't think I ought to have anything to do with Marie Hilley any more," he said.

"What's the problem?" Carroll wanted to know.

Atherton described his relationship with Marie.

"I flattered myself," Atherton confessed. He smiled ruefully. "I thought she kept making all those complaints because she wanted to see me. I guess there was more to it than that."

It would be a bit longer before Atherton was to find out how much more, but that was enough for Carroll. The arrest put Marie Hilley in a whole new light. He agreed that Atherton should keep his distance from the case, and from Marie, too.

The charge on which she was arrested was perfectly symbolic of Marie Hilley's life, which by now had shrunk to little more than a web of false pretense. She had begun by needing money, and she had set in motion a series of intrigues to get it. As they failed one by one, she had become increasingly desperate. Rather than bringing her back to reality, the failures had expanded her need into an obsession. Driven onward, she had lost contact with any sense of restraint or the reality surrounding her. No scheme was too hopeless for her now, no act too destructive.

Over the next several days she scurried from bank to insurance company to bank, trying to shore up the collapsing foundation of her deception. Her check to continue the insurance policy that included Carol had been returned by the bank. At the Birmingham office of Liberty National Insurance Company, she delivered a new check for $380.26, written on an account at First National Bank of Anniston, to reinstate the coverage from the beginning of September, six days before. She closed the bank account in Florida that had figured in the scheme that led to her arrest. She was still writing checks on another new account, at Citibank in Anniston, but that account was already overdrawn.

Marie stepped up her covert attack against Carol in a deadly counterpoint to her financial manipulations. First there were the pills. There were two of them—small, round, orange ones—and Carol didn't recognize them as anything she had taken before. She was feeling especially weak and discouraged, and her mother said they would help. She took them, and nothing happened. In retrospect they seemed like a trial run for what came next, and maybe

139

they were just to get her used to taking medicine from her mother again.

A day or so later, sitting by the bedside, Marie told Carol about the little girl. Carol had sunk back into the pattern of alternating fury at the doctors who were keeping her against her will and despair at the futility of her situation. Her mother's story seemed to offer some possibility of hope. In the hospital waiting room, Marie said, she had run into the mother of a girl who had the same problem as Carol.

"Her mother gave her this medication," Marie said, "and it worked. It helped her legs."

Carol was silent. Could anything help? she wondered.

"I asked Doris about it," her mother went on. "Maybe we should try it."

Doris Ford was their neighbor, a registered nurse. Carol gave a noncommittal grunt. It doesn't matter one way or the other, she thought, I've got nothing to lose.

It was some time later—the days ran together and time had become featureless, without landmarks—and Carol had forgotten about the conversation, when her mother walked into the room one evening with a cheerful greeting. She bustled around for a moment, establishing her presence.

"I've got something for you," she said finally. She paused expectantly, but she didn't seem to need a response. "The medication."

Carol wasn't sure what her mother was talking about. She was speaking in a quiet voice, as if she were telling Carol a secret, and she kept glancing at the door. Doris Ford had told someone about Carol at the clinic where she worked, Marie was saying, and they had gotten the medicine for Carol. Doris said it was all right, it was from a reliable company, and it might help with the numbness in Carol's legs. Marie glanced at the door again, leaned forward, and lowered her voice so that it was just above a whisper.

"We mustn't say anything about this or Doris will lose her job," Marie said. Carol was having trouble taking it seriously. She didn't respond.

"Okay?" Marie was waiting for agreement. Carol thought it hardly seemed worth bothering with. At last she summoned the energy to nod. Her mother didn't seem satisfied.

"You promise?" she asked. "You won't tell anybody about the shots or the medication?"

"Yeh, okay," Carol said, and looked away.

"All right, turn over, honey, and I'll give you a shot."

Carol rolled onto her stomach. As her mother stood over her, something prompted Carol to speak.

"Let me see it," she said.

"What?" Her mother seemed surprised.

"Let me see it. I want to see what it looks like."

Marie held the syringe in front of Carol's face. It was filled with a cloudy, whitish liquid. After a few moments, Carol turned her head back into the pillow. Her mother gently pinched off a section of flesh on her buttock; Carol had lost so much weight that there was hardly anything to take a grip on. Her mother inserted the needle and slowly squeezed the liquid into Carol's system.

Carol whimpered softly. The pain was excruciating, worse than for any injection she had ever received. But there was nothing she could do. It was just one more assault, to be endured like the rest.

Over the next few days, Carol watched for some improvement. There were small signs, but nothing obvious. She had been telling the doctors and nurses that she was feeling better, but it was a lie; her appetite had not recovered. She was still having great difficulty walking, and the numbness was affecting her lower legs. If anything, it was moving up toward her knees. When her mother offered to give her another injection, Carol agreed. Maybe more of the medication was needed to have an effect.

Marie took the syringe from her purse while Carol prepared herself. A few moments passed and nothing happened. Carol looked back at her mother.

"I'm not sure you ought to have the whole thing," her mother said. She looked apprehensive.

"I'll just give you half of it," she said at last.

She pressed the needle into Carol's buttock. When she had finished, some of the liquid remained in the syringe.

They chatted idly for a little while. Marie kept looking at Carol. Finally she seemed to reach a decision. It had been a half hour or more since the injection.

"Maybe we ought to go ahead with the rest of it," she said.

She retrieved the syringe from her purse. Carol obediently turned once again onto her stomach. Everybody in the hospital had been giving her shots, she thought. One more wasn't going to make a lot of difference. Her mother emptied the syringe into Carol's body.

There was no immediate sign of improvement, but somehow Carol continued to look for some indication that the shots were making a difference. It was hope that made Carol break her pledge of silence.

When they told her there was a phone call, she staggered down to the nurses' station, leaning on a nurse, and hugging the wall for support. If anything, she was even more helpless, but maybe that had something to do with being in the hospital all this time. The call was from Eve Cole.

"How're you doing?" Eve asked.

Carol told her about all the interviews and examinations and blood tests and how none of it had produced any improvement. Without any sign of hope, it was a gloomy picture. Carol needed something positive to talk about.

"What about your legs?" Eve asked.

"Mom gave me some shots," Carol said. "They're supposed to help my legs."

"She gave you shots?" Eve said. She remembered the injection Marie had given Carol in the apartment on Christine Avenue not quite a month before.

Carol told Eve how her mother had acquired the medication for the injections from the clinic where Doris Ford worked.

"I'm not supposed to tell anyone," Carol said. "It's supposed to be a secret. Doris might get in trouble if they found out."

They talked about the need for secrecy a bit more, then went on to other things. Eve was worried about her friend. She and her husband, Ron, had made the drive to Birmingham to visit Carol earlier in her stay in Carraway Methodist Hospital. Carol had looked pathetic—shrunken and weak.

After they hung up, Eve mulled over what Carol had told her about the shots. When she had seen Marie give Carol the injection before, it had seemed a little unusual, but nothing special. Most of the time you couldn't get a doctor to make a house call for anything, much less a minor matter like giving an injection. But in the hospital it was different. Why would Marie need to give Carol injections in the hospital?

Of course, it was impossible to think that a mother would do anything to harm her daughter, but Marie had done some strange things. Eve had heard how she had kept Freeda and Carrie from visiting Carol out at Christine Avenue. Freeda and her mother were starved for some word of Carol. Eve worked at the Anniston Army Depot, where Freeda was also employed, and she had taken it on herself to call Freeda when she had any news about how her niece was doing.

The Army Depot, a manufacturing and storage dump for military materiel, sat on a reservation that occupied thirty square miles just west of Anniston. Eve phoned Freeda from her desk.

She told Freeda about the continuing deterioration of Carol's condition. Freeda was shocked. It had been more than three weeks since she had received any news of Carol.

Eve hesitated before going on, but she had made the decision.

"Carol says Marie has been giving her shots," Eve said.

Freeda asked for the details. As Eve recounted Carol's description of the injections, Freeda thought of her mother's suspicions and the day they had visited Frank just before he died. Carrie had been talking to Freeda about her memories lately, uneasily recalling Frank's decline and voicing her worries about Carol. Freeda had been upset about their inability to visit Carol, but she hadn't put much stock in her mother's restlessness. Just the other day, Freeda had been telling a friend at work about Carol's illness and Marie's strange behavior.

"Do you think that Marie might be doing this?" the friend had said. Freeda had been taken aback.

"Oh, no," she had answered, "she wouldn't do anything like that."

Now Eve's revelations were like a sunrise, slowly pouring new light over things Freeda hadn't seen clearly before.

There was a note of concern in Eve's voice as she finished her account.

"I don't want to accuse anyone of anything," she said. And she felt guilty about disclosing something Carol had told her in confidence. But she felt she had to tell someone.

"She's getting sicker every day," Eve said. "She can hardly walk. What's going on?"

Freeda talked it over with Carrie that evening. They decided to call Mike in Florida.

"Mike, something's going on over there with Marie and Carol," Freeda told him.

Mike's first reaction was irritation. Freeda had been calling him about all the problems with Marie, as if she expected him to solve them. He had felt helpless in the face of his mother's endless manipulations. He was a victim, too, but Freeda didn't seem to understand that. Her expectations had been contributing to his feelings of guilt and inadequacy. She was going on about a conversation with Eve Cole when suddenly something she was saying cut through the defenses he had been putting up.

"Eve says Marie's giving Carol injections."

Injections! Mike recalled what his grandmother had told him about the incident in Frank Hilley's bedroom, and Marie's comment about giving her husband shots. Freeda described Marie's strange behavior after she moved Carol into the new apartment, how she had treated her daughter like a prisoner. What was she hiding from?

Since his discussion with Happy Henderson and his call to the coroner, Mike had been trying to put the pieces together, but he had felt no sense of urgency about it. Now, suddenly, with the news of Eve's discovery, everything had changed.

If all these events were somehow tied together—his mother's strange behavior over the past months, even years, and all the money problems, and his father's illness, and now Carol's shocking deterioration—Mike could barely bring himself to face the conclusion, but there was no running from it. If all these events flowed from the same source, Carol was in terrible danger.

He had to be sure, Mike thought. There had been so many lies, so much misunderstanding, constant tension in the family; nothing could be taken at face value. He phoned Carol in the hospital. The arrangements at Carraway Methodist Hospital were ridiculous. He was forced to wait, with the long-distance line open, while Carol was notified and made the long trip down the hall to the nurses' station.

Mike concealed his impatience while he asked Carol how she was getting along. She was obsessed with the idea of getting out of the hospital. Finally Mike found an opening in the conversation.

"Carol, is Mother giving you injections?" he asked her.

"No, why?" There had been a pause, almost imperceptible, before she answered. There had been a hollow note in her voice, something he remembered from their childhood, when she would try to put something over on their mother.

"Carol," he said, making his voice stern, "do you promise me, do you swear, that Mother has not given you an injection?"

There was no answer. Freeda had said that Marie had sworn Carol to secrecy.

"Carol, did Mother give you a shot?"

"Yes, she did," Carol said at last. She sounded relieved at giving up the lie. She recounted the details for Mike, but she was more interested in the possibility of getting out of the hospital.

"Mom said she'd take me out of here," Carol said. "She promised." She was expecting to be home in a day or two.

Mike didn't tell her what he was thinking. The coroner hadn't taken him seriously, but now there was more evidence. It was one thing to talk about doubts and suspicions with members of the family; it would be something quite different to take these matters directly to Carol's doctor. It would amount to an accusation. What if it turned out to be a mistake? He caught himself. What if the suspicions were correct and he did nothing? He thought of Carol, the advancing paralysis, her struggle with despair. Mike picked up the phone for one more call. He had to try to stop his mother from snatching Carol away again. The only safe place for Carol was in the hospital.

Marie had moved to the Holiday Inn out by the airport in Birmingham. Living in a motel could be expensive, but she shouldn't have to stay there too much longer. Things were obviously coming to a climax.

Her final attempts at manipulation contained a strange combination of cool calculation and desperate fantasy. She had contacted an agent at Liberty National Insurance Company, arranging to send another premium for the policy that covered Carol and Mike; unlike the last payment, this one did not include the premium for Marie's own policy. With her check for $132.98, written on the account at First National Bank of Anniston, she enclosed a note on Holiday Inn stationery:

> Ray,
> I will pay two months until I get settled. I haven't closed the post office box yet, so any mail can go there. Good luck to you.
>
> Marie Hilley

But she had closed the account at First National, a month before. Had she forgotten, or did she still harbor some hope that the check might slip through, or was it just the momentum of her frenzied search for the answer to a question no one had asked?

And what of her pose as a responsible Anniston matron, living temporarily at a motel while making arrangements to "get settled" in Birmingham? She was like a defeated chess master madly pushing pawns around the board long after the opponent has left the hall. The insurance company had already received her previous check back from the bank, marked "Account Closed." They didn't even bother to submit the new check.

But Marie had at least one more move to try, one more asset to bring into play. It was Calvin Robertson's blind love and loyalty of more than thirty years, and his inability to see through the hazy illusion of a dream remembered from childhood.

"I know," she had written to Calvin in California nine months before, teasing out his promise of devotion, "that if I ever needed you by my side, you would do everything possible to be there with me."

He had sent her three thousand dollars to help with the cancer treatment she had told him she needed. And he had responded by affirming his devotion: she had only to call on him and he would overcome any obstacle to race to her aid.

Here was the hope of a magic carpet to carry her away from the tangled ruin she had made of her life. Once again, Marie called Calvin Robertson.

Dr. Elmore was puzzled by the course of Carol's illness. The nausea and vomiting had gone away early in her stay and she claimed to be eating, but she had continued to lose weight. Now she was down to eighty-one pounds. The medication and counseling had seemed to improve her frame of mind at first, but lately she had been moody and uncooperative, snapping at the psychiatric social worker and the nurses, insisting that they let her out of the hospital.

The medical personnel had developed the impression that the mother was part of the problem; Carol's emotional state seemed to deteriorate after her mother spent time with her. Dr. Elmore had talked with Mrs. Hilley, trying to find out more about her relationship with Carol, but the discussion had been inconclusive.

And then there had been the phone calls. Someone had talked to an aunt of Carol's who was full of questions and ominous fears, and a man who said he was Carol Hilley's brother had called to ask if Mrs. Hilley could be giving her daughter injections. It was hard to figure out what all this meant, but it didn't make the diagnosis any easier. And each day, the situation seemed to become more muddled.

Finally Dr. Elmore had asked Mrs. Hilley not to visit her daughter for a while, thinking that maybe it would help them sort things out. Marie had resisted the idea but finally agreed. They had put up a "No Visitors" sign.

Now the nurses reported that Carol had fallen down in the hallway yesterday, trying to walk to the nurses' station for something. She had lain alone on the floor for several minutes, unable to regain her feet, before they found her. Mrs. Hilley had been upset with the nurses, complaining about the staff's "neglect" of her daughter, claiming that Carol had been injured in the fall and threatening to take her out of the hospital.

When Dr. Elmore had talked to Carol this morning, she hadn't seemed upset about the incident. She was cheerful, looking forward to seeing her friends again. Apparently her mother had promised to take her home. She claimed to be feeling much better, but when he asked her to walk for him she was unsteady on her feet and could barely move without support. She wasn't in any shape to go anywhere, Dr. Elmore told himself. If he had anything to say about it, she was staying right where she was until they got some improvement in her condition.

But now Mrs. Hilley was on the phone again, pleading for permission to visit her daughter.

"I have to see her, Doctor," she was saying. "I have this lump in my breast and I'm going to have it removed. I'm going into the hospital the day after tomorrow, and I want to see my daughter before I go."

It was the first he had heard of her surgery. She was trying to appeal to his emotions, but he remained firm. He persuaded her to call his office for an appointment to come see him later in the day. They could talk further then.

When the receptionist showed her into the office, Mrs. Hilley could hardly contain herself.

"Carol can barely walk and she isn't getting any better," she said, "and then she falls down in the hall and hurts her foot and the nurses don't even notice. Not just once, several times." The nurses had told Dr. Elmore that Carol had fallen twice. He tried to calm the woman, but she wouldn't be pacified. She seemed obsessed with the picture of her daughter lying in the hallway, crippled and alone.

"She was lying there, helpless, and nobody did anything for her. What kind of a hospital is this? I don't want her in a place where nobody cares about her. I'm going into the hospital and I'm not going to leave her down here by herself. I'll take her to the Mayo Clinic, or Ochsner in New Orleans, someplace where they can give her some help."

"Mrs. Hilley," Dr. Elmore said, speaking carefully, "I thought we had an agreement. Yesterday you said you'd leave her here with us. You were going to stop visiting her for a while, give us a chance to try and get her well. Today you're saying you want to take her away. Is there something going on here that I'm not aware of?"

"I'm just not happy with the care she's getting down here," Marie told him. "She's so sick, and she's been sick for so long, and nobody's doing anything for her. Her legs are just getting worse."

Dr. Elmore was no more pleased with Carol's progress than her mother was. The neurologist had checked her again that morning and found that the neuropathy—the deterioration in her nervous system—had progressed to an alarming degree. As Dr. Elmore discussed the situation with Mrs. Hilley, she seemed to be leaning again toward leaving Carol in the hospital. He wanted to be sure she understood his conditions.

"If she stays," he said, "I'm still going to insist that you not come to see her for a few days."

That appeared to swing her back in the other direction again.

"In that case," she responded. "I'm not going to leave her here. I'll get her admitted in Anniston until I can take her to Mayo or Ochsner."

But she didn't seem ready to leave it at that. It was as if she were negotiating for something. Was she angling for visiting rights? She had changed her plans repeatedly. This seemed to be more of the same. What is going on here? Dr. Elmore wondered. She was complaining about the difficulty of figuring out what was wrong with Carol.

"What could be causing this?" she asked. "What are the possibilities?"

"Well," he said, "with a neuropathy like this, there are a lot of things that could be responsible. Things like malnutrition, vitamin deficiency, lead or some other metal poisoning, and so on. Lots of things could be doing it."

Carol Hilley was alternating between fury and utter despair. She had been through the whole range of emotions over the past few months, but this was the absolute bottom. That morning they had told her she couldn't see her mother anymore. During her three weeks at Carraway, Carol had sunk deeper and deeper into a frightening sense of isolation. The phone calls and visits had slowly decreased until she felt as if nobody knew she was alive. It was like being a prisoner in solitary confinement. She wasn't even allowed to go down to the lobby any more.

The hospital personnel weren't any help. They wouldn't let her go until they figured out what was wrong with her, but they didn't have any more idea than when she came in three weeks ago. They all thought she was crazy. She had come to loathe the place and hate the people. Her mother had become Carol's only contact with reality, her only hope of escape. And yesterday she had finally promised to take her home. Carol had felt liberated. She had been thinking about her room, her own things at home, getting back to her friends.

And now, suddenly, cruelly, they had taken it all away. They were telling her she wouldn't be allowed to see her mother at all. It was as if they had opened the door of her cell, waited until she had started to move toward the daylight, and then slammed it shut in her face.

Late in the afternoon, her mother appeared.

"Come on," she said. "We're getting you out of here."

Carol could hardly believe the sudden reversal. Her mother bustled about, packing Carol's things. A nurse came to help, but it was obvious that they were leaving against the judgment of the doctors and other hospital personnel. They put Carol's clothes on; it was like dressing a Raggedy Ann doll. She had become virtually helpless.

They stopped for a pizza on the way to the motel. Marie had to throw Carol's arm across her shoulder and support her daughter's weight with an arm around her waist. Carol swung her legs in front of her one at a time, shifting her weight haltingly from side to side. She had the floppy, jerking gait of a badly managed puppet. Even so, it was a treat for her, eating pizza, basking in her new freedom.

Afterward, they took a taxi out to the Holiday Inn near the airport. Marie talked about going into the hospital in Anniston for the operation on her breast.

"I'm getting a car," she told Carol. "The man I'm buying it from

149

is going to come and pick us up in the morning and take us back there to get it. I'll just write him a check and we'll go home."

Carol awoke the next morning eager to pick up the car and start the ninety-minute drive to Anniston. She was stunned when her mother said she had changed her mind.

"We're not going home until we find out what's wrong with you," Marie said.

Carol exploded. "You told me we were going home! You promised me!"

"I want to know why you can't walk!" her mother shouted back. "You're going to the hospital until we find out."

Carol raged and cried, refusing to go back into the hospital. Her mother tried to calm her. Finally she stepped up close to the crippled girl.

"Shut up!" she cried. "Shut up!" And she slapped Carol hard across the face.

The blow seemed to startle both of them, and they quieted down. Carol submitted sullenly as they rode across town to the University of Alabama Hospital. She sat quietly in the emergency room through the long wait for a doctor.

At last they were taken into an examining room. It all seemed so familiar, Carol thought, the questions about when and how she had first been sick and what she felt, the prodding and poking and lifting and tapping of her limbs. And the usual conversations between her mother and the medical personnel, and the discussions between nurses and doctors, so much of it out of her hearing, half whispered, with nods and glances at Carol, as if they were trying to keep Carol a secret from herself, as if nobody seemed to care what she thought. And then, slowly, for the first time since she had gone to the emergency room the day after the junior-senior prom way back in April, a sympathetic face emerged from the crowd of cold medical authorities. It was a woman doctor, and she seemed like a merciful angel, Carol thought. It was as if she had been sent specially to take care of Carol.

"I need to talk to you," she said. She arranged to take Carol back to an X-ray room, saying she wanted to examine the foot injury Carol had suffered in the fall at Carraway Hospital. Carol heard sympathy and understanding in the doctor's voice, and she dared to believe that the X ray was merely an excuse to get her away from her mother and give her a chance to tell her side of things. It was as if she knew about Carol and her mother in advance.

"What's going on?" the doctor asked in a kindly voice once they were safely settled in the X-ray room.

"God, I'm so glad somebody finally wants to listen to me!" Carol cried. "They've been thinking I was crazy over there for the past three weeks, and I'm not crazy. Here I am again, and all I want to do is go home. I want to go home to my grandmother's house."

The doctor said something about Carol's mother.

"Listen," Carol responded, "I don't know what she's been telling them, but they all think I'm crazy. I'm not crazy. Something's keeping me from walking, and it ain't in my head."

Once again Carol told her story, the frustrating, infuriating, and finally crushing series of events she had described so many times, but now she was telling it her way, ending with the hurried departure from Carraway Hospital against the wishes of the medical staff, and as the doctor gently questioned and guided her through the recitation, Carol slowly came to a most amazing conclusion: This time, at last, a doctor believed her.

Other physicians were called in, including a young neurologist named Brian Thompson. The examination revealed the full extent of her muscular and neurological damage. She was wasted and bony, like a famine victim in some underdeveloped country. The feeling was gone from her feet and legs, she was virtually paralyzed below the knees, and her hands were almost useless. They wanted to keep her in the hospital for further examination, and her mother agreed.

"We're going to find out what's wrong with you," the woman doctor told Carol, and for the first time in months, she dared to believe it might be true. At least now there was one person who didn't think she was crazy. They took her upstairs to her room. It was almost time for lunch.

Dr. Thompson was puzzled by Carol Hilley.

He had been called to the emergency room after preliminary examination indicated there might be nerve problems. Thompson was just beginning his residency in neurology at University Hospital. He was still extremely careful with his notes, drawing and labeling diagrams to show where the patient had lost sensation and motor control in her legs and hands, things a more experienced physician might have managed with a few scribbled code words and numbers. He had found extensive neurological breakdown.

Mrs. Hilley had hovered nearby while he was examining her daughter. They had come over directly from Carraway Methodist Hospital. Mrs. Hilley implied that she had been dissatisfied with the treatment there.

Dr. Thompson was curious about Carol Hilley's treatment at Carraway. He had worked there for two years as an intern until coming to University Hospital a short time before. He phoned Carraway and talked to a physician there. Carol Hilley had been treated on the psychiatric floor, but what Thompson heard only deepened the mystery about what was wrong with his new patient. They had never reached a satisfactory diagnosis at Carraway. Mrs. Hilley had been upset about a fall Carol had taken in the hallway. She had removed her daughter from the hospital against the recommendation of the medical staff. And there had been nonmedical complications, changes of plans by the mother, and phone calls from family members.

Dr. Thompson's initial diagnosis was peripheral neuropathy—nerve damage affecting the hands and legs. It was acting both on sensory nerves, which carry information to the brain, and motor nerves, which carry impulses from the brain that control the movement of the muscles.

But that didn't say what was causing the problems. The first thing to do was make sure she didn't have Guillain-Barré syndrome. It was a rare disease, affecting no more than thirty people a year in the whole state, but the early symptoms were like Carol Hilley's, and it could lead to breathing problems and death by suffocation. He made arrangements for testing of her lung function. They also got permission to do a spinal tap.

Carol was obsessed with the idea of getting out of the hospital. Once she was confined in the hospital room, surrounded again by the familiar paraphernalia of medical routine, fixed solidly in the web of nurses and schedules and rules, she had lost the mild optimism inspired by the sympathy of the woman doctor. Once again her whole world had collapsed around the single thought of escaping.

Her mother hovered, sitting in her chair, reading, getting up to move things or straighten up, sitting again. It seemed as if they had been together almost constantly for months, until all of Carol's hopes and thoughts had become focused on her mother. She could no longer move around on her own, or dress herself, or manage even the most routine tasks of everyday life without help. Even if they let her out now, she wouldn't be able to get herself home to Anniston. Her mother held absolute power over her. If she were to escape from the hospital, it would be through her mother's action. Only her mother could do it. No one else could help.

A movement in the hallway caught Carol's eye. Through the open doorway she saw a man with a beard. He was checking the room number, looking from side to side. There was another man with him. The bearded man stepped into the doorway. Marie looked up at him.

"Audrey Marie Hilley?" he asked. It sounded peculiar. She never used the name Audrey.

"Yes," she said.

"Could you step out here a minute, please?" The words were polite, but his tone made clear that she had no choice. He watched intently, slowly backing out of the room as Marie stood up and stepped toward the doorway. She looked back at Carol.

"I'll be right back," she said.

A few minutes later she came into the room. The bearded man stood just outside the door, shifting restlessly from one foot to the other.

"I have to go to Anniston," Marie said.

"What for?" Carol asked. She felt panic spreading over her. She was going to be left by herself.

"They want me to go," her mother said. "It's something about that car." Carol thought of the car her mother had been planning to buy that morning. It seemed so long ago now.

"They say it was a stolen car," Marie continued.

If her mother left her, there would be no one to help, no one to argue for her, to help her get out, to take her away from the hospital. She would be abandoned, alone in the world. Her anguish and fear escaped in a cry of protest.

"No, Mother!" she screamed. "You can't leave me here!"

Through her sobbing she heard her mother trying to calm her, promising to return soon. And then she was gone.

Even now, with the last remnants of her schemes hanging in tatters around her, Marie's obsession with concealment had remained at full force. She had succeeded in hiding from her daughter the fact that the two men were detectives from the Birmingham Police Department, acting on a warrant from Anniston. She had been arrested.

There was a new charge growing from the same checks to Moss Furniture that had figured in her previous arrest, on the bank's complaint, for obtaining money by false pretense. This time a complaint by the furniture store brought a charge of issuing worthless checks. And there was another charge, contempt of court. Marie had been released on the earlier charge pending a hearing. She had simply failed to show up at court in Anniston for the hearing.

The bearded detective called the Anniston police to tell them that the warrant had been executed and they could come to get the prisoner. It was too late in the day to pick her up; they would come for her in the morning.

Marie Hilley spent the night in the Birmingham city jail.

Even in the first words of the phone call, Freeda could hear the hysteria just below the surface of her niece's voice. It had been a long day at work, but Carol's anguish cut through the fatigue. Two men had come to her room to take Marie away; Carol was confused about what was happening. She was obsessed with one idea: She wanted to get out of the hospital. She begged Freeda to help her. Freeda agreed to drive to Birmingham right away.

In the car, Freeda went over the events of the past few days with her husband, Charles, and Eve Cole. Mike had talked to the doctor at Carraway, and when they heard Marie was getting ready to move Carol again, he had called the nurses' station on her floor.

"She'll probably try to smuggle her out," Mike had told the nurses. Freeda had called, too, hoping to get them to stop her. It was too late. Marie had just checked Carol out the previous night as if it were a motel, and there was nothing anybody could do about it.

Now Marie was in custody, at least temporarily, and yet she had succeeded. Carol was a fugitive from a place where they had treated her as if she were insane, isolated in a new place where nobody knew of her past or the bizarre pattern of her mother's behavior, helpless and alone.

They had been talking about it for days now, Freeda and Charles, Freeda's daughter, Lisa, her mother, Carrie, now Eve Cole, and over and over in the phone calls with Mike. All the talking had made it more real, made it easier to consider Marie in a new way. But it was still too big to accept all at once.

Freeda remembered shedding her tomboy ease, dressing up specially to meet the pretty fourteen-year-old her brother was bringing home to meet his family three decades before. It was hard, almost impossible, to reconcile that memory with the obsessed and frightening woman who had hovered over a hospital room in Birmingham. Freeda had come to fear a confrontation with Marie; she had not seen her sister-in-law for several months. She prayed that Marie, with her almost superhuman powers of deception, would not have found a way to return to Carol's side by the time they arrived.

And yet there was too much that could not be explained, too much pain and too much destruction over these past months and years, to let fear or timidity hold her back any longer. Freeda still couldn't put a name on the danger, but she felt it looming closer, like a great ship running through the night without lights, and it was bearing down on Carol. Somebody had to be warned.

At the hospital, Freeda was driven by the need to tell somebody what she suspected. She set aside the urge to go directly to comfort Carol.

"I want to see Carol Hilley's doctor," she told the receptionist.

It was Dr. Brian Thompson, Freeda was told. They were in luck. The young intern happened to be in the hospital; he was on call.

Dr. Thompson had been trying to get some sleep, catching up for the long cycle of on-call service, but he quickly became alert as Freeda began the story. Her account wandered and doubled back on itself. Freeda could hardly reconstruct for herself the steady accumulation of small events that had led her from love and trust to curiosity, to doubt, and finally to suspicion; it seemed almost impossible to make it seem real to someone who had not experienced it. She tried to concentrate on the injections, and her growing fear that Marie had somehow been trying to harm her daughter, but Freeda was left with the feeling that the doctor didn't quite believe her. Dr. Thompson listened patiently to Freeda's account, but her fears seemed to be confirmed when finally he spoke:

"It sounds like something you'd see on a soap opera," he said.

As he questioned her and she added details, however, it became clear that Dr. Thompson was taking her fears seriously. When they had finished, he headed off to examine Carol again.

Now all thoughts of Guillain-Barré syndrome and other forms of nerve disease were gone from his mind. The kind of nerve malfunction Carol Hilley was suffering from could also be caused by heavy metals, like lead, mercury, and arsenic. If the injections had anything to do with Carol's condition, the likely culprit was arsenic. Once in the bloodstream, arsenic could be carried throughout the body, causing nausea, diarrhea, and other gastrointestinal symptoms, simultaneously attacking the nervous system, beginning at the periphery—the hands and feet—and moving toward the center of the body.

Some of the poison could be excreted over time, but the rest remained in the body, forming compounds that were stored in the bones, skin, and hair. These deposits could be identified by complex, time-consuming laboratory testing of samples taken from the patient. But there was a faster way of checking for arsenic poisoning, based on the fact that it could also be deposited in the fingernails and toenails. The arsenic compound eliminated the pink pigment from the fingernail, creating a whitish line across the width of the nail. The deposits, which were named Aldridge-Mees' lines after their discoverers, started about six weeks after the arsenic entered the body.

Carol was surprised by the doctor's arrival. It was getting close to bedtime. Responding to his request, she held out her hands for inspection, like a nursery school child getting her hand-washing checked.

Dr. Thompson looked at the fingernails, then examined her toes. The telltale white line ran evenly across every nail.

The lines could also be caused by thallium, which was used in insecticide, but Carol showed no sign of the hair loss that went with thallium poisoning. Another cause of the lines was isoniazid, a medication used against tuberculosis; that, too, could be eliminated in this case. The diagnosis was solid: Carol Hilley was suffering from arsenic poisoning.

He questioned her about how she had felt in the past day or two. The sole effective treatment for arsenic poisoning, the young doctor recalled, works only if it is given within twenty-four hours of the body's exposure. There would be no treatment for the poison that had left its residue in Carol's nervous system and showed up in her fingernails and toenails, but if she had received a new dose, its effects could be softened.

But Carol had not taken any medication except what she had received in the hospital, and she reported none of the nausea or vomiting that would give a preliminary sign of poisoning. Treatment would be a waste of time.

The tests of Carol's urine and hair could begin tomorrow. One thing could not wait: Dr. Thompson ordered Carol moved to a room on the eleventh floor. Only authorized visitors would be told of the new location. Her mother would have no further contact with Carol Hilley.

Freeda followed along with Charles and Eve as the nurses moved Carol upstairs. Carol was still upset and distracted, on the edge of tears. As they made ready to leave, Carol burst into tears.

"Don't leave me!" she cried. "I don't know what's going on. I'm scared. I don't want to be alone."

They made arrangements for Freeda to stay overnight. She was filled with sympathy for her niece. Carol looked so small and helpless, weeping uncontrollably, cut off from the world like a battered child whose pain is intensified by the confusion of her continuing, instinctive love for the mother who has brutalized her.

Freeda settled down for the night. At last, she thought, Carol is safe from Marie.

8

Discovery

"Mike, your mother's been arrested again."

It was Marie's Aunt Margaret, calling from Blue Mountain, outside Anniston. She sounded more puzzled than upset. It was bad checks again, she said, and Marie was in jail over in Birmingham. What should they do?

Mike was still pondering that question when the phone rang again. Probably somebody else telling him the news.

"Mike, it's me." Carol's voice sounded thin and a little hoarse.

"Mike," she went on, "I've got arsenic poisoning."

For Mike it was like seeing a film of a building demolition running backward, all the pieces flying into place to form a whole, solid structure. Three years of questions, doubts, and contradictions, the minor discrepancies and major incongruities of his mother's behavior and his sister's decline fell into place around the words "arsenic poisoning."

After they had finished talking, Mike thought back over the long series of puzzling events. So much that had been mysterious would make sense now, in the new light of what Carol had told him. He thought again of his phone call to the coroner's office. It would still sound like a "wild story," as they had said, but now it would sound like a true one. The coroner had told him to get in touch if he learned anything new. Mike picked up the phone.

He reminded the coroner of the earlier phone call.

"My sister Carol's got arsenic poisoning," Mike told him. When Mike had finished outlining what he knew, the coroner asked him to put it in a letter. Mike was concerned; he didn't want to be in the position of attacking his mother.

"Regardless of what a mother does," Mike said, "there's always that question they'll ask: How could you do that to your own mother?" He asked that the letter be kept confidential.

The coroner was reassuring. Mike felt satisfied that the letter would be used for internal purposes only. He agreed to set his thoughts down on paper.

It would be a help to him, as well, Mike thought. He felt the need to review the events that had dominated his life for so long, to reorganize his understanding of them. As he typed, all the confusion and hesitation, the love and concern for his mother, the anger at her deceit, and the growing fear of what she might do materialized on the paper before him. When he had finished, he sat back in his chair and looked over the three single-spaced sheets. The key words leaped off the page:

"It is my belief that she probably injected my dad with arsenic as she has apparently done to my sister."

Mike sealed the letter and mailed it to the coroner's office.

Gary Carroll had watched the events surrounding Marie Hilley with a degree of detachment. Officers from the department had picked her up in Birmingham the day before and brought her to the city jail to wait for trial on the bad-check and contempt charges. The section Carroll commanded wouldn't be involved directly. Any investigation work would be handled by the other half of the detective force; her crimes involved property, not people.

She had let her financial situation get out of hand. All those strange incidents—the prowlers and the phone calls, the burglaries and the fires—must be related to her money problems somehow. Carroll hadn't had anything to do with Marie since that crazy extortion case with the FBI guys and the Alpo in the Winn-Dixie supermarket. That was two months ago. Well, he thought, the property guys would figure it out.

The detective had been in the department for twelve years. He had seen a lot of people get into problems with money. If it weren't for money and sex, he'd be out of a job. But Marie had seemed different. She was so well-spoken, nice to be around. With all the complaints she had filed, Carroll had made a lot of visits to her house and they had spent many hours on the telephone. He was a quiet man, with a deep reserve, but she was easy to talk to. Over time their conversations had sometimes gone beyond police business; in spite of her arrest and his discussion with Billy Atherton, Carroll still felt friendly toward Marie. Obviously, though, there was a lot he didn't know about her.

Carroll kept his pride to himself, but he was pleased with his career in police work. He had taken a few courses in police science during his early years in the department, but he had never gotten a degree. Even so, he had worked his way up to lieutenant, one of two under the captain in command of the shift, and Carroll enjoyed the challenge of overseeing investigation of crimes against persons, everything from assault and rape and child abuse to robbery, kidnapping, and homicide. And his rank also meant the best of the shift assignments; he could look forward to starting a free weekend in a few hours.

His thoughts were interrupted by the telephone. It was Ralph Phillips.

"Gary," the coroner said, "I've had a call from Marie Hilley's son, Mike. His sister, Carol, is in the hospital over in Birmingham. He says the doctors found arsenic in her system. He thinks his mother did it. And Gary, he thinks his mother poisoned his father, too."

Suddenly thoughts of a weekend's break from the job didn't seem so enticing to Carroll anymore.

The situation was tragic, a sincere man being so completely duped, flying all the way across the country, but it was also so absurd that Mike Hilley had difficulty suppressing laughter when he realized what had happened to Calvin Robertson. When the phone rang, Mike was still struggling to assimilate all the events of the few days since Carol's call about the arsenic. There was a hesitation in Calvin's voice, like that of a man who is ready to believe he has turned up a day early for an appointment.

"Mike, where's your mother?" Calvin asked.

"What do you mean, where is she?" Mike asked.

"I'm here at the airport in Atlanta. She was supposed to meet me. She didn't show up."

Mike hesitated, anticipating the effect the news would have on Calvin. There was no gentle way to put it.

"I hate to tell you this, Calvin. She was arrested the day before yesterday."

There was a long silence. Mike imagined Calvin's jaw dropping in a cartoon caricature of surprise. Calvin had no idea of that side of Marie Hilley, Mike reflected. Distance and his idealistic love had made it possible for her to keep her façade of virtuous dependability intact in his eyes.

She had called him at his office a week or two earlier and talked of suicide, Calvin told a reporter later. He had tried to help her, to talk her out of it, but he hadn't felt he was getting through to her. He had finally offered to fly to Atlanta, he said, and she had agreed to meet him at the airport.

As long as he had come this far, Calvin decided to go on to Anniston to see if there was anything he could do. And to figure out what was going on.

It was time, Gary Carroll thought.

Over the past few days he had done everything necessary to get the investigation started, interviewing Carol and the doctors, gathering specimens from Carol for the state laboratory, collecting copies of Frank Hilley's medical records.

His visit with Carol at the hospital in Birmingham had made a deep impression on the detective. The cruelty of what her mother had done was apparent in Carol's clawed hands and her halting movement. A nurse had brought in Carol's lunch while he was there; it had taken her forty-five minutes to feed herself.

Gary Carroll didn't seem the type to dwell on a young woman's problems. He didn't talk a lot, and when he did open up, he never seemed in a hurry to part with his thoughts, letting them out in a way that made each one seem a solemn statement of personal principle. He was over six feet tall, with large, powerful-looking hands, and he moved in the same studied way he talked. He had a pleasant face, a little short of handsome, and his reddish-blond hair and slightly florid complexion gave an impression of vigor. He could have passed for the kind of old-time hero known as "strong and silent," updated with a standard-issue cop's moustache.

The detective's exterior could seem forbidding, and people were always surprised to learn that he was a gentle and habitually sympathetic man. He had grown up in Anniston, where his father had owned a jewelry store for forty years. After high school Gary had worked in the store for a while before serving his time in the Army and joining the police department. Gary and his brother still owned the store. The brother managed it full-time, but Gary spent several hours each week helping out with the accounting and other paperwork. It was another paradox to those who didn't know the detective well, as if it had turned out that John Wayne played the flute in his spare time. At thirty-six, only eight years from retirement, he was already wondering what he could do after detective work that would be as interesting.

The natural sympathy Carroll had originally felt for Marie had turned into puzzlement after the Alpo extortion fiasco. The leftover feelings from that time had made it difficult at first to look at her as just another suspect in a murder case. Now his visit with Carol Hilley had made the case real. The tests had confirmed that her hair contained measurable amounts of arsenic. The detective had read Frank Hilley's records to one of the state toxicologists over the phone; he had told Carroll that Frank's history also showed the classic symptoms of arsenic poisoning. The case was taking shape.

Now it was time to talk to Marie Hilley.

Carroll signed her out of the city jail. She looked small and wan. They didn't talk much on the way back to the police station. In Carroll's office, she sat down without waiting to be told. Leonard Remer, who was known as "Buzz," the captain in charge of detectives, joined them.

After starting the tape recorder and explaining her rights, Carroll questioned Marie for a few minutes about the illness leading up to Frank Hilley's death in 1975. She described the scene in the hospital when they discovered Frank had died. She had been sitting at the bedside, napping in the chair, when Mike returned, bringing his two grandmothers, Lucille Frazier and Carrie Hilley, to relieve her.

"I woke up when they came back in," she said. "He couldn't have been asleep"—it was a slip of the tongue; she corrected herself—"or dead more than just two or three minutes."

Carroll moved on to the death of Marie's mother, Lucille Frazier, in January 1977, a year and eight months after Frank. Marie described the discovery of a lump in Lucille's breast, leading up to a mastectomy.

"Did they prescribe any kind of medication for her?" the detective asked. Toward the end the doctor had put her on morphine, Marie answered. Doris Ford, the neighbor who was a nurse, administered the injections.

"At any time during the time your mother was ill or at any time, did you give your mother any shots?" he asked. It was a routine question, prompted by the suspicions of Mike and Freeda about injections. Marie's answer took Carroll by surprise.

"I gave her some morphine when Doris was not there during the day," she said.

"You gave her some morphine?" he responded.

"Uh-huh," she replied. "I wouldn't give them unless Doris just couldn't be there; but she was there for most of Mother's shots." Marie had given the shots two or three times, she said, making the injection in her mother's hip, as Doris did.

Another potential victim! Her daughter, her husband, now her mother. They'd have to find out more about what happened to Lucille Frazier.

The detective asked her a few questions about the death of her father, then switched abruptly to Carol's illness. Marie described her daughter's nausea after the junior-senior prom, then named off the series of doctors and hospitals they had tried, looking for help. She recalled how the numbness in Carol's hands and feet had worried her, leading to her decision to take Carol out of Carraway Methodist Hospital:

"Well, it just got progressively worse. So I told Dr. Elmore last Tuesday that I couldn't see improvement, so I was going to take her out of Carraway. He said, 'You'll do it against medical advice.' And I said, 'Well, I have to take her somewhere else.' I was going to take her to Ochsner Clinic in New Orleans, and I decided on Wednesday that I would take her to University and let a urologist look at her, on Wednesday—before I took her to New Orleans."

Carroll tried to focus in on her reason for taking Carol abruptly from Carraway. Dr. Elmore had told the detective about his discussion with Marie concerning the remaining possibilities they might explore in the next few days.

"Did they tell you that they were wanting to run some more tests before you checked her out?"

She was evasive. He persisted.

"But did they tell you that they didn't want her to go, at that particular time, because they wanted to run some more tests?"

Again she tried to evade the question: "I don't think he said it that way. He said that these doctors had run these tests before; these same doctors."

Carroll pressed on: "But did he tell you that he wanted to run some more tests and asked you not to let her go at this time?"

She fumbled momentarily, then said that a nurse had told her they were going to repeat a glucose tolerance test that Carol had already undergone "two or three times." Marie was implying that the hospital's lack of diagnostic imagination had caused her to give up on them. It would be hard to find the unnamed nurse to check on it.

"So I told them I wanted to take her somewhere else," she concluded weakly.

That seemed to be as far as that line of questioning could go for the moment. Carroll switched direction:

"Has anybody told you what was actually wrong with your daughter?"

"Yeah, they've told me."

"What?"

"That she had arsenic poisoning." Mike had been the one to tell her, she said.

"Do you have any idea how she got arsenic poisoning?" Carroll asked.

"I certainly do not."

"Have you ever given her any medication?"

"I gave her a shot of Phenergan that Dr.—" She interrupted herself, as if she thought she had misunderstood the question. "—oh, you mean what pills and—?"

"Well, any kind." He had started to go on with the same line of thought, but her admission had sunk in. "You said you gave her a shot of what?" The detective wanted a clear statement on the record.

Carol had received a shot of Phenergan, a nausea-suppressant, in the emergency room, Marie told him. Later, Dr. Donald had given Marie a syringe and a bottle with enough of the medication for two more injections, to administer at home if necessary. She had given Carol only one shot, in July, using half the bottle; she didn't use the rest because the nausea had stopped. Eve Cole had been present in the apartment when Marie gave Carol the injection. Like her discussion about tests with the unnamed nurse, the arrangements with Dr. Donald would be difficult to check. He had died a month earlier.

"So you had one syringe and you gave her one shot back in July?"

"Uh-huh," she agreed.

"Did you give her any more shots?"

"No."

"You haven't given her any more shots?" Again Carroll was insistent, making a record. Again she answered, "No."

Carroll asked her about the color of the liquid, and of some pills that Marie said Carol had received later with the same medication. Her memory, so precise about the details of hospitals and doctors, was not so strong on this point. There had been so much medication, she said.

He asked if she had given Carol any medication while she was in Carraway Hospital. She denied it. Then she remembered that she had given Carol some Thorazine tablets to help her sleep.

They talked about Marie's insurance policies for a few minutes, before the detective brought the questioning back to arsenic.

"And you have no idea as to how Carol got arsenic in her body?" he asked.

"I can't . . . I wouldn't even know where you get arsenic," she replied. "I don't know what it's in, where it comes from."

This time the detective was more insistent: "And you're telling me you never gave Carol a shot while she was in the Carraway Methodist Hospital over there, Marie?"

"No, I didn't."

"Marie, Marie," he cajoled her, "you gave her a shot over at Carraway Methodist." It was a flat statement. It seemed to break through the wall of denial.

"Okay, it was Phenergan." She had been caught in a lie, but she was matter-of-fact.

Carroll sensed success. He pressed forward: "No, that's not what you gave her, Marie."

"I didn't give her anything poisonous. I've never given her anything poisonous."

"Well, why did you lie about that?" She had said there was only one injection, the one at home. She evaded the question by answering a different one, one that he had not asked.

"Well, she was in the hospital, she was a little nauseated, and I did not want her to have to stay because she was vomiting."

The detective followed up, but she insisted that she had given Carol only the one shot of Phenergan in the hospital. Carroll changed direction, asking about the source of the medication. First she said she had gotten it from a doctor in Birmingham through his nurse, whose name she knew only as "Toots." Marie had been introduced to Toots by Toots's mother-in-law, whom she had met in the lobby of the hospital. The mother-in-law was the one who had delivered the medication in a syringe, ready to use.

The story had a spontaneous feeling to it, accumulating one detail at a time. Carroll asked her the mother-in-law's name.

"Mrs. . . . it was a Mrs. . . . ah, Hill." She described the woman's gray hair and blue eyes.

Carroll's response implied disbelief. It was a careless way to get medicine for her daughter, he went on, buying a syringeful of a substance she couldn't identify from a relative she had never met of a woman she hardly knew.

"Why did you not mention [it] to one of her doctors and ask them if they would give her something?"

"I did. I asked the Turkish doctor there. I said, 'If she gets sick, can she have something for nausea?' And he said, 'I'll take care of it.' So when she was—her stomach was hurting that night and I asked them and they never came down there to do anything. She fell and laid on the floor for ten minutes; that was the reason I took her out of the hospital. They let her fall five times the last three days she was up there. And she almost broke her foot the last time she fell, and I told Dr. Elmore that's why: They did not come and look after her."

Carroll directed the interview back to the medication.

"Marie, it's hard for me to believe that you would buy something like that and carry it up to—"

"It's hard for me to believe that I did it now," she broke in, "but I had grasped for straws this whole summer for Carol. You can ask anybody. I've taken her—I've called Doris Ford, I've asked everybody who to take her to, what to do for her. They couldn't find it here. I've had about fifteen doctors with her. And I was getting ready to make arrangements to take her to New Orleans or the Mayo Clinic. And I decided I would take her to the urologist at University Hospital to look at her. And that's why I took her over there and took her out of Carraway, because they say they're the best in the country. Now, if I was trying to hurt my daughter, I would be keeping her *away from* the hospital, I wouldn't be taking her *to* a hospital, not all summer long."

Lieutenant Carroll wasn't satisfied: "Didn't you give her two shots, Marie?"

"One in July and one in the hospital."

"No. Didn't you give her two shots in the hospital?"

"No. I gave her one."

"You gave her two."

"One. I gave her one shot."

"Marie?"

"No, Gary, I gave her one shot."

She was standing firm. Carroll tried another approach.

"Somebody has poisoned your daughter. I have been over there. The girl is pitiful, Marie." The detective had lain awake after his visit to the hospital, thinking about the case, and the image of the tiny, sad girl and her clawed hands had come back to him again and again.

"I know. . . ."

"I have been over there."

"I know."

"Somebody has put poison in that girl's system."

"I know that."

Carroll shifted direction again. "Somebody had to be close to her to give it to her," he said. He was trying to stimulate her sympathy, to make her see what he had seen when he visited Carol. "A stranger walking down the street didn't give it to her. Captain Remer didn't give it to her. Somebody close to her that she trusted and loved gave her that."

"Well, it was not me, Gary."

"And on more than one occasion, Marie. It wasn't an accidental thing." The doctors and toxicologists had said that Carol's symptoms were consistent with repeated doses of arsenic over a long period.

"Who would have the opportunity to give it to her that often?" Carroll continued, pressing her to recognize the unavoidable conclusion.

"I don't know," she replied. "She didn't eat every meal with us. She had very few meals at home, because she would eat at a different time. She was not there when we would eat." Marie had adjusted easily to the assumption that Carol might have received arsenic in her food, not solely by injection.

"There ought to be somebody fairly close to her," Carroll went on. "Does she date fairly regular?"

"Yeah. She was dating . . ." Marie paused, then corrected herself. "Well, she was going around, too, with a girl quite a lot"—Marie had introduced the issue of Carol's social life, which would cause a sensation at the trial, but it passed unnoticed at this point—"and she was dating this boy, and neither of them have seen her in Birmingham."

She was not going to face the subject unless he put it to her directly. Carroll abruptly asked the question that had been hanging over the discussion:

"Marie, did you give her this poison?"

"No, Gary. No, I don't even know where you would get poison." Her impatience showed momentarily in her choice of words: "And I wouldn't give the crap to my own daughter." She wouldn't ordinarily use a word like "crap" in a public situation.

"That's why I'm asking, Marie. Did you give it to your own daughter?"

"No, I didn't."

"That little girl I went over there to see the other day?"

"No, I did not give her that."

She was adamant. Carroll's questioning hovered near accusation, swooping in occasionally to challenge her with a direct question. She was passive, answering the questions without protest, volunteering little information or speculation about the poisoning, like a seabird riding out a storm. She seemed almost untouched by the reality of what had happened and by Carroll's attempts to press it upon her.

"She's been suffering from arsenic poisoning since April, right?" he asked.

"I don't know. That's what I've been trying to find out. That's why I've taken her to the hospitals and doctors, to find out what was wrong with her."

"Somebody's been poisoning your daughter since April?"

"Well, they tried it on me and my son, too." That was a new chapter in the story.

"How is that?"

She had been sick for about two weeks in the spring sometime, she said; her son, too. "Mike came here and stayed about three days and I had to take him to Dr. Donald. I vomited off and on for two weeks."

The detective turned the discussion back to Frank's death again. She reminded him that the autopsy had shown hepatitis as the cause of death. Carroll tried to get her to visualize her own position as a suspect:

"If he died of poisoning, who do you think could have poisoned him?"

"Well, I don't think Frank died from poison." She laughed. She was remarkably relaxed, fending off his questions with calm insistence. "I think it's just what the doctor said."

The detective returned to Carol's poisoning, reminding Marie how "pitiful" her daughter's condition was.

"Ever who poisoned that girl, I'm going to find them," he told her.

"I hope you will," she answered calmly.

"I know I am, and I have a feeling I'm getting pretty close. It had to be somebody that knew her well, somebody that had close association with her. Now, think about that." The telephone buzzed, shattering the escalation of verbal pressure he was trying to create. When the interruption was past, he asked her to name the people who would have been close enough to poison Carol. She began with herself, then named Carrie, Freeda, and a number of Carol's other relatives and friends.

"All right," Carroll said when she had run out of candidates, "out of that whole list of people you gave me, who would you pick as the one that you think most likely would be the one that could have done something like this?"

She resisted briefly, then gave in.

"Well, I know I'm number-one suspect." Her submission was brief. She rallied quickly: "I'm her mother. I mean, I should be the last suspect."

Carroll took her back over the injections again. Suddenly he introduced a new subject:

"Do you ever have mental lapses, times that you don't know what you're doing?" Mike and Freeda had talked of her sudden changes of mood, her capacity to seem like two different people at times. And her responses to his questions had seemed so detached, as if she were separate from the matters they were discussing.

She was unfazed. "I guess everybody does sometimes, don't they?"

"I don't know. I'm asking you if you ever had any."

"Yeah, I guess I have." It was the kind of lapse where you couldn't remember what you had done the day before, Marie told him. She had first experienced them after her mother died. Frank had died not long before.

"I just had so much on me," she recalled. "I just assume I was so burdened with responsibilities all of a sudden"—now she changed pronouns, as if to establish some distance between herself and the weakness she was discussing—"that you just don't remember what you did maybe last week or last. . . . I mean, you name some certain date, I can't remember. But I'm sure that I'm not the only person in the world that does that."

"Well, I'm sure of that," Carroll answered sympathetically. "You know I understand that. But I'm asking you, do you think it's possible that maybe this could have occurred and you gave your daughter something like this—"

She interrupted: "Oh, no. . . ."

"—and put arsenic in her?" he finished.

"I don't think I could have a mental lapse and do something like that, Gary." She was almost plaintive. He pursued the subject, asking whether some kind of "mental lapse" was at least a possibility.

"If it is, I'd sure like to get some help for me," she responded, "because—"

Carroll interrupted, seizing on the idea: "Marie, do you not think that you might need some help?"

"Yeah, I need some help, Gary." She seemed to be softening. Could this be the opening to some acceptance and admission of her guilt?

"You know it and I know it, right?" He was seeking confirmation, trying to establish the point in her mind.

"Yes, that's right."

"You do need some help. I understand, Marie, I know you've had a lot on your mind."

Something took hold of her suddenly, some instinct for denial that had been lulled momentarily, and she snatched back the admission she had just given him.

"But I'm not . . . not help; but I think everybody could use a psychiatrist now and then. But no, I don't mean a . . . no, I can't ever think that I would hurt my daughter." Once they released her from jail, she said, she was planning to see a psychiatrist, but though Carroll persisted, she repeatedly denied poisoning her daughter.

The detective talked about his concern for Carol and his sympathy for Marie. He had known her a long time, Carroll reminded Marie, and he had always tried to help her. Somebody had been poisoning Carol, somebody close to her.

"And I think, possibly . . ." Carroll started again: "Like I say, you might not consciously be doing it. You would be doing it subconsciously."

"How, Gary, could you do something like that?" She was exposed, vulnerable.

He started to answer: "Marie . . ."

She was crying. "I couldn't do that."

"Marie, people do it, honey." His tone was gentle.

She dug in again, refusing to go any further. "You don't poison your own children."

He tried to maintain the mood, but she gradually pulled back. "Don't you think there might be another side to you, Marie?" the detective asked.

"I hope not that kind of side." She was recovering her composure.

Carroll continued with the questioning, pushing closer to her inner reality: "But don't you think there could be?"

"I don't know, but I don't want there to be."

"Well, listen, Marie, I've talked to some people that know you fairly well. And they say that sometimes you act like two different people."

"Gary, I couldn't do that to Carol."

"I know the real you couldn't. . . ."

"Maybe some other person could do that to Carol."

"Marie?" It was a gentle prodding.

"I couldn't, Gary."

"Not the real you, but . . ."

"What's the real me, then?" She seemed actually to be asking for enlightenment, as if she expected him to offer an insight that would explain something she had never understood. "Do you think I'm crazy, Gary?"

"I didn't say that, Marie. But I do think you need—"

"A person would have to be crazy to do something like that. You know that."

"Well, do you think you're crazy?"

"I'm beginning to wonder, since I've been up here a week. But I don't think I'm that kind of crazy. Maybe other people can see something in me that I don't see myself." Once again she had flirted with an admission of responsibility and then pulled back at the last moment.

He pressed the idea that there might be another side to her that performed acts she would not do herself, but she continued to resist:

"Gary, I can't believe there is a side to me that could do that. Now, if a psychiatrist digs that out of me and says there are two people and I could do that, then I might accept it. But I cannot accept the fact that there is a side of me that could—"

Carroll interrupted: "Well, I am not a psychiatrist. All I know is what people that know you and have known you for a number of years . . . what has been told to me. Like I say—"

"Well, my son's told me something of the same thing, and I agreed with him that I would go to a psychiatrist when I get out. That's the first thing I would do."

She seemed so reasonable, it was difficult to concentrate on the suspicions that surrounded her, even though they hung over almost everything she had done for the past few months. After several minutes of other conversation, Carroll returned to the subject of her mental state:

"What was the first indication that you had that you needed some help?"

"Well, I had this feeling," she told him, "it's like you're sitting off but you're looking on at everybody, you know, nothing seemed real. That's what I mean, instead of 'mental lapse.' It's more like just nothing's real. Like this doesn't even seem real to me, right now. Being up there"—she meant the city jail—"doesn't seem real. It's just like I'm asleep and I'm going to wake up and everything's going to be okay."

"In other words, like you're in another dimension? And you're just seeing yourself act out what you—"

"That's right, and it's just, you know, like that's not me and, you know, I wake up afterwhile." She revised her estimate of when the spells had begun: They had not followed on the strains of her mother's death. It was while she was in Florida. That had been the summer of 1978, a year and a half after her mother died.

The detective was curious about her reports of prowlers and other incidents at her house: "Do you think that was all real to you, or do you think a—"

She interrupted him to answer. "Well, there was more people there than me when we were having that, so they heard them, too. No, that was . . . if I had been there alone, I'd say maybe so, but no, there were too many other people. My son, he was there a lot of times when it happened."

She had the air of someone enjoying a spell of leisurely and open-minded speculation with a friend about the eccentricities of a mutual acquaintance. He asked her about the fires, her suit against the gas company, the people following her car, the extortion episode. The night after the stakeout at the Winn-Dixie supermarket, the FBI agent involved in the case had received an anonymous phone call about the extortion plot. He had been convinced the voice was Marie's, but she had denied it at the time. She denied it now again, along with any responsibility for the other incidents.

Carroll turned the questioning to a motive for Carol's poisoning. He asked Marie about insurance again. She had let the policies on Carol and Mike lapse, she said. She had tried to keep her own policy in effect, but she had been unable to get back to Anniston to put money in the bank to cover the check, so her own policy had lapsed, too. "I didn't even worry about it anymore," she said.

The truth, which would not be placed on the record until four years later, was quite the opposite. The last check, which she had sent to the agent with her note to "Ray" just nine days before, was meant to cover the family policy that included Carol.

They talked for a few minutes more, but the interview ended without any dramatic revelations. She had acknowledged experiencing those spells; they could have something to do with mental illness. She had admitted to giving Carol two shots, after lying at first, but she had stubbornly refused to go further. That admission would come back to haunt her, but as the interview ended, all Carroll had was several small mysteries to investigate: Toots and Mrs. Hill and the medication they had supplied. Dr. Donald's arrangements for Carol's injections at home, the insurance policies and bank accounts.

As for the larger questions about the death of Frank Hilley and the poisoning of Carol, Marie had not given him a single answer. If he were going to find out what had happened, he would have to go after the evidence on his own. Carroll had always respected Marie Hilley's intelligence and shrewdness when she had been a friendly acquaintance. Now he had come face to face with those same qualities in a resourceful and tireless adversary.

They didn't need Marie's permission to exhume Frank Hilley's body, but it made sense to ask anyway, to gauge her reaction. If she resisted, they could still go ahead without her.

Carroll and the coroner, Ralph Phillips, took the typewritten form over to the city jail. Marie was so cooperative it was almost disappointing. She put her neat signature on the line without any sign of reluctance. She was keeping to the stance she had maintained throughout her interview with the detective the day before, all puzzled curiosity about what might have happened to Carol and earnest willingness to do what she could to help. So much for any hope of guilty resistance.

With the formal exhumation order from the DA's office, Carroll set about making the arrangements. He could have a circus on his hands if they let it get out of control. At first, curiosity about the case had been confined to Anniston. It seemed as if everybody in town had known Marie Hilley; the city was humming with speculation. But at that point it had merely been a single case of attempted poisoning.

As suspicion had grown about the deaths of Lucille Frazier and Frank Hilley, reporters and television people from all over the South had started taking an interest. Word had gotten around that Marie's mother-in-law, Carrie Hilley, was sick, too. The idea was spreading that there might be something dramatic going on. Now there was growing pressure from the press for information about the case. Thinking ahead to any prosecution, the district attorney's office and the police had been trying to keep things under control. They didn't want to set themselves up to lose a case on grounds of prejudicial pretrial publicity. Carroll was working hard to keep the plans for the exhumation quiet.

When the detective arrived at Forestlawn Gardens, workers and the officials from the coroner's office were already there, with a truck and backhoe. They were not alone. The place seemed aswarm with media people. Reporters were rushing around, talking to the workmen and anybody else they could find, while photographers and television cameramen swiveled this way and that, arranging and shooting pictures. As the detective stood and watched, momentarily undecided about what to do, another television crew was arriving. When they saw Carroll, several reporters started moving toward him. It was a mess.

Carroll thought for a moment. The ground rules were set, he concluded; now his job was to continue to play by them. Somebody had leaked the word; at least he could try to establish order. The family was entitled to some privacy, too, if that were still possible. He radioed for uniformed officers to direct traffic and control the small mob of press and the spectators who were slowly gathering, attracted by the commotion.

When the press people had been moved far back from the area, the workmen approached the gravesite. It was located in a section of the cemetery called "The Garden of Devotion." They lifted the bronzed plaque Marie had arranged for her husband's grave. The name "Hilley" was set in large letters and flanked by open Bibles in raised relief. At one side was a small raised tablet with Frank's name and his dates "1929–1975." At the other side of the built-in flower vase was another tablet. It said, "Marie, 1933– ," with a blank space for the final date.

The backhoe moved in to unearth the casket. Water ran in streams from the heavy metal box as it rose slowly out of the hole. When they opened the lid, there was a collective flurry from the area where the press and spectators had been confined.

Carroll looked down into the metal casket as the lid was pried off the coffin inside. Even a professional felt a little flutter when a coffin was opened; there was the feeling that you were intruding on something sacred, interrupting something that should be eternal. Besides that, you never knew what you were going to find. The water that had been in the box was a bad sign; soaking could bring rapid deterioration.

But the first view of Frank Hilley was an anticlimax. The body was in fine shape. Except for spidery lines of fungus on the face, the features were almost those of a living person.

"Geez," somebody said, "I could have identified him in a lineup."

They moved the box to a small utility shed and left it to drain and dry out for a few minutes. Carroll glanced across at the trees opposite the shed. The lenses of a couple of cameras peered back at him. Some of the photographers had sneaked around through the woods to get closer. He wondered how long they had been there. Had they filmed the lifting of the casket from the ground? He sent a uniformed officer to herd them back with the others.

The coroner took a sample of the water and scraped some mud from the side of the coffin. There was often a small amount of arsenic, along with other metals, in ground water and soil. The state pathologist would compare these amounts with the levels of any arsenic found in the body tissues to determine whether the poison had been taken in before death or since the body had been in the ground. Finally, they loaded the body into a van and the coroner headed for the Department of Forensic Science in Birmingham.

As the uniformed officers drove off and Lieutenant Carroll headed for his car, he glanced back at the grave. Television crews and a little knot of photographers had gathered around the site. Some were shooting pictures of the grave, and others had gone over to photograph the shed where the body had been taken. There wouldn't be any way of keeping the case of Audrey Marie Hilley quiet from now on.

Carrie Hilley was dying, and everybody knew it. Her illness had been diagnosed as cancer, but Freeda found it hard to believe that Marie had nothing to do with it. The family had arranged for Marie to live at Carrie's house on Moore Avenue last year, thinking the arrangement would be good for both of them: Carrie had been sick and uneasy about living alone, and Marie and Carol had needed a place to live. And Marie's presence there had eased Freeda's concern for her mother and the feeling that she ought to do something herself to help out.

Now, looking back, the year had been like slow torture for Carrie. All those things that had seemed bad luck or peculiar but passing annoyances—the fire that broke out after Marie took the batteries out of the smoke alarms, then the almost identical fire next door at Doris Ford's house, the bills that never got paid, the tension over Marie's share of the expenses, the bitter arguing between Marie and Carol, the cut-off electrical cord left hanging from the socket—they had come one after another. Much of it still seemed mysterious, Freeda concluded, without purpose or motive, but everything had somehow grown out of a wild destructiveness in Marie.

The strain all that commotion had put on her mother, Freeda reflected, when she should have had a peaceful time, living quietly and saving her strength, that was unforgivable. And that wasn't the worst of it. Freeda thought back to that period when her daughter, Lisa, had been going over to keep her grandmother company after lunch and watch a soap opera with her. Marie would be on her way out, heading back to work, and Lisa would find her grandmother in the bathroom, throwing up the lunch she had just eaten with Marie. Carrie had never experienced stomach problems before living with Marie. And the symptoms, nausea and vomiting soon after eating, were the same ones Carol had gone through when she first got sick, symptoms that the doctors said were caused by swallowing arsenic.

Carol had been released from the hospital and had gotten her wish, moving back in with Freeda and Carrie and her cousin Lisa. The family was relieved to know that Carol was safe now, but it couldn't be doing Carrie any good to see her granddaughter all crippled up that way, and to live with the reminder of what had happened to her son.

Freeda joined Carrie and Lisa in the living room to watch the local news on television. They wouldn't be together much longer, Freeda thought sadly. Soon her mother would have to check into Stringfellow Hospital, where they had been treating her for the past several weeks.

Suddenly it came to Freeda what they were almost certainly about to see on the screen, and in the same moment she realized it was too late. There was a scene of a dump truck and some kind of big digging machine, and the announcer was talking about "the body of Frank Alfred Hilley" and "Forestlawn Gardens" and "exhume," and then there was a picture of the grave marker with "Hilley" spelled out in big letters. Freeda watched with horror as the open grave yawned before them on the screen. She turned to her mother, hoping that Carrie might somehow have missed the meaning of what they were seeing, but a quick glance told her at once that this was nothing but wishful thinking.

The image on the screen had etched a web of pain onto Carrie Hilley's face. She sat motionless. The silence seemed to have swollen around them. The coffin appeared. The lid opened slowly, and then it was gone. It took a moment to realize that the report had ended.

Carrie rose painfully from her chair. Staring straight ahead, she shuffled toward the stairs. The whisper of her slippers over the rug was the only sound in the room. She headed for bed.

Marie's arrest had released feelings within the family that had long been kept under cover. They were finding it impossible to untangle Marie's cruel influence from their relations with each other. Even as Marie sat in a cell at the Anniston city jail, the poison of her betrayal was still spreading among them.

Freeda's anger was compounded by her suspicions about Frank and about the illness of her mother. Freeda had gathered up some of

Marie's clothes from the things she had left at Carrie's house, but she made sure not to see Marie when she delivered them to the jail. Not like Marie's aunt, Margaret Key, who had been going down to visit Marie in jail. Margaret was a quiet, religious woman, living with her husband, Sammy, out in Blue Mountain, where she had grown up, still working every day at the textile mill. She was too good and innocent herself to see the evil in Marie, Freeda reflected, and it was like a stab to her heart each time she heard of Margaret visiting or phoning Marie.

It was the same with Mike. Freeda had called him in Florida during the summer, trying to tell him about all the strange goings-on with Marie, but Mike had kept himself apart. All he seemed to care about was money, Freeda thought, about Marie's financial problems and the money she owed him. "Mike, we've got to do something," she had said to him just before the arrest, but he had refused to come to Anniston to help; she had been left on her own. Now they needed him, but he was still worrying about money—how much he had spent traveling back and forth and whether he could afford the trip.

What was worse, he was trying to help Marie. Marie had phoned Carol one night from jail and said, "They have framed me." "Who are 'they'?" Carol had asked, and Marie had responded, "I can't tell you over the phone, but Mike knows who, and he is going to help me when I get out of here."

Mike had also written a letter to the judge, requesting psychiatric help for his mother. Calvin Robertson had gone over to visit her, and he seemed to believe in her, too. She could talk anybody into anything. They would claim she had psychological problems, Freeda thought, saying she didn't know what she was doing, and get her off scot-free. Freeda had talked with her sister, Jewell Phillips, who lived in Virginia, and she had agreed with Freeda. It would be just like Marie to wriggle out of this, the way she had always done in the past. She had to be stopped.

Freeda had driven over to Birmingham with her husband and Calvin Robertson a few days after Marie was arrested. At the Holiday Inn they had asked to see Marie's room. The clerk had refused to let them in until they paid the bill. Calvin put up the money and they gathered Marie's belongings. Freeda had looked through them, but there was nothing that seemed to help prove what had happened.

If it was like they said, Freeda thought, if Carol had been poisoned with arsenic, then the arsenic must be around somewhere. After lunch on Saturday, Freeda persuaded her husband and Lisa to drive over to Carrie's house on Moore Avenue with her.

Marie had kept her clothes and other belongings in a small back room next to the kitchen. There were clothes everywhere, neatly folded and stacked. A big chifforobe stood against one wall, and behind it a shelf in the corner held a lamp. Marie had the key to the chifforobe, but they found a bunch of spare keys and one of them opened the double door. More clothes hung on the bar, jammed from side to side, and boxes of papers rested beneath them.

Lisa sat on the floor and began going through the papers. Among the canceled checks and bank statements she found sealed envelopes with Carrie's utility and other bills inside. These were the payments Marie had volunteered to make for her mother-in-law while she was living there. They had never been mailed. Lisa was exploring them, announcing her finds to her mother and Charles, when suddenly Freeda cried out.

"Look at this!" she said.

Marie's black cosmetics case lay open on the shelf in the corner. Freeda reached inside and held up a small medicine bottle. The prescription label had the name of Dr. Jones, who had been Frank and Marie's family doctor. It read, "Take one tablet every day." The bottle was half full of liquid. It looked like water.

Freeda pulled the top off the bottle and sniffed at it. The liquid was odorless. They continued looking through the other items, but nothing of great interest turned up. After a while they closed the room and left.

The next day, after church, Freeda dropped the bottle off at the police station. The desk officer gave her an envelope and she addressed it, "Remer or Carroll." She asked for a piece of paper and wrote a note:

Found this bottle in Marie's jewelry box. It may not be anything but water, but needs to be checked.

The envelope was picked up by Buzz Remer, the captain of detectives, early Monday morning; he passed it on to Lieutenant Carroll a few hours later. Freeda's handwriting was remarkably similar to the neat, flowing script of her sister-in-law, Marie Hilley. The detective passed the bottle along to the state pathology lab at the

Department of Forensic Science in Birmingham and arranged an interview with Freeda after she finished work.

Since the state lab had confirmed the presence of arsenic a few days before in the hair samples the detective had taken from Carol Hilley, Carroll's thoughts had been turning to possible sources of the poison. Now Freeda's find and the interview had gotten him thinking about Marie's possessions. The next day he walked over to the jail and checked out Marie's purse from the locker where inmates' personal property was kept. A clerk had done a routine inventory of the contents when Marie was brought in on the bad-check charges, but now the detective had something specific to look for.

The purse was like a portable medicine chest. Carroll found four plastic medicine bottles; one was labeled "Murine for your eyes" and was half filled with liquid. The others looked like standard pill containers. Two of the containers were empty. There was also a package of Stanback, a headache remedy, containing three small packets of white powder. Carroll sealed it all in a large manila envelope and locked it in an evidence locker at the police station. The next morning he drove to Birmingham; he wanted to deliver the envelope personally to the state lab. That was one package he wasn't about to trust to anyone else's hands.

Carroll was on the scent now and he didn't want to quit. He went to see Carrie Hilley. Marie's mother-in-law had been admitted to Stringfellow Hospital a few days before and she didn't look well, but she was glad to help out. She signed a form giving them permission to search her house. Carroll went directly to Moore Avenue with Captain Remer. They gathered up some things that Freeda had overlooked: a wooden rack containing bottles of herbs and spices, a bottle of almond flavoring, a white glass bowl, and another medicine bottle. There were papers, too. The detectives picked out some documents concerned with insurance; they needed to focus on a possible motive as well as the method.

Freeda couldn't rest. Between doing her job and keeping things going at home, with responsibility for Carol added to the usual routines, it seemed Freeda never stopped running. But it wasn't just the physical strain. Freeda was losing her mother. Frank's exhumation had been a blow to Carrie, and she seemed to weaken visibly every day. Within a week she had gone into the hospital. With each visit, Freeda felt her mother growing more distant. Now they had exhumed Marie's mother, Lucille, and the police were saying that if she had been poisoned they would exhume Marie's father, Huey, who had been dead fourteen years. And the rumors were swirling around the autopsy of Frank.

Every day there seemed to be something new. It gave Freeda a helpless feeling, seeing all this happening and not being able to do anything about it.

There was one thing she could do, though. Finding the bottle in Marie's cosmetics case had given her a feeling of satisfaction. The police hadn't just laughed it off, or treated it like the work of some silly busybody. Lieutenant Carroll had taken her seriously, asked her a lot of questions about Marie's life and habits, and sent the bottle off to the state lab for analysis.

Freeda had been thinking about it for a week. They had gone through most of Marie's things over at Moore Avenue, but there were more, and they were right downstairs in Freeda's garage. Marie had dropped off a bunch of stuff from Carol's apartment before she moved to the motel in Birmingham, and the things they had collected at the motel with Calvin Robertson were there, too.

It was like rummaging through a yard sale, all the cast-off furnishings of a life, cooking utensils and games, paperbacks and magazines, clothes, a lamp. Lisa was poking through a stack of books when her mother reached into a box and lifted out a brown paper sack. There were bottles inside. She pulled them out one by one. Gerber's baby food. Three bottles. Freeda and Lisa had been the ones who suggested to Marie that she get some for Carol when she was in the hospital and couldn't keep her food down.

There was another bottle. Freeda held it up toward the light. She read from the label: "Cowley's Rat and Mouse Poison." "Manufactured by S. L. Cowley and Sons Manufacturing Co., Hugo, Oklahoma." She turned it over. The label listed the active ingredient. The word jumped out at her: "Arsenic trioxide, 1.5%." "Total arsenic, as elemental, all in water-soluble form, 1.14%."

Freeda raced upstairs with the sack. Carol was in her room. She was planning to start physical therapy soon, but she still looked emaciated; she couldn't weigh much more than eighty-five pounds. Freeda showed Carol the bottle and read the label to her. As Freeda watched her niece's reaction, she felt her own jubilation leaking away. Carol didn't have much to say. She had talked to a reporter a few days before about the charges against her mother. "I'm not going to believe it until it's proven," she had said. "I love her because she's my mom."

"If she did it," Carol had told the reporter, "she didn't realize what she was doing. My mother is not a bad person or anything. She's just been through a lot. She's had a lot on her since my dad died."

Now Carol seemed confused by all the bottles. Her mother had brought her baby food in the hospital to help her eat. Arsenic? Rat poison?

Gary Carroll's reaction when Freeda phoned was much more satisfying. This was worth breaking up a Sunday evening for. He would be right over.

Something was wrong. Usually in a situation like this the written reports from the state lab took several weeks, but you could get information informally before that. With the Hilley case, the Department of Forensic Science was measuring out the news in drops. Even the investigators were having trouble finding out what was going on. The DFS had issued the official report on the arsenic in the hair samples from Carol, but there hadn't been much news since. Except for the press conference.

The state officials had obviously become aware of the publicity value of the case. The DFS was playing an expanding role in criminal investigation throughout the state with the growing reliance on scientific evidence. They needed state appropriations to add the personnel and lab equipment required for an up-to-date operation. The Hilley case was the first with the potential to grab major headlines for the lab. They had called a press conference to announce the preliminary findings on Frank Hilley. The chief toxicologist had come over from Montgomery to hold the conference at the state crime lab at Jacksonville State University, just north of Anniston. That was when they had announced the presence of "significant amounts" of arsenic in Frank's body, but they were not ready to say if the poison had caused his death, and it was up to the investigators to determine if he had been murdered.

They had been ready to announce further findings ten days later, but then there had been a delay. The DFS announced that it had just acquired tissues from Frank Hilley's kidneys and liver. The organs had been removed for autopsy after his death in 1975, and he had been buried without them. The lab had been working with what was available, but these additional materials would make a more precise analysis possible. The kidneys and liver were organs that would tend to accumulate and concentrate any foreign substance that entered the body. And the findings could confirm or rule out the original diagnosis, that Frank Hilley had died of hepatitis, a liver disease, and kidney problems.

The Hilley case was starting to pay off for the DFS. In addition to stories speculating about the test results that went out almost every day across the state, not to mention the rest of the country, they got a long feature story about the lab in the *Anniston Star*. It quoted the district attorney, Bob Field, as saying the addition of toxicologists was "the biggest single improvement made in criminal investigation in Alabama in the last ten years." That couldn't hurt, come appropriations time.

Meanwhile, the tests were continuing. Preliminary analysis had turned up traces of arsenic in tissues from Lucille Frazier, but more detailed results would take longer. There was still no official word on whether the arsenic in Frank Hilley's system had killed him. Any indictment would have to wait.

Marie's bail had been set at ten thousand dollars on the charge of attempted murder and two thousand dollars on each of the charges related to the bad checks. She had been in jail several weeks when Mike Hilley received a phone call from Wilford Lane. Lane was an Anniston lawyer specializing in criminal cases. He had been starting to work with another lawyer named Bill Andrews on Marie's bad-check cases when the attempted-murder charge was brought against her.

Lane was calling to ask Mike to help his mother. Lane had a list of people Marie had said might be willing to put up bond for her. It would be better if the request didn't come directly from her, and it would be particularly effective if it came from her own son. Would Mike be willing to call them and ask for their help?

Mike was reluctant. The autopsies were still not completed, but he was sure he knew what they would show. He thought his mother should stay in jail. He had written as much in his letter to the judge a few weeks before, asking psychiatric help for his mother:

These charges against her at present are just a small part of the series of events over the past two or three years. After talking with her and having her live with us last summer, I am almost positive she has schizophrenic tendencies.

Beyond that, there were practical problems. Mike figured that with the debts his mother had left on his credit card, the loans she had involved him in, and the costs of traveling back and forth to Anniston over the past year or more—airline flights, rental cars, phone calls, and the rest—this affair had cost him close to ten thousand dollars. For a young family living on a minister's salary, that was a lot of money.

"I'm out of money," he told Will Lane. "I can't come up there. This thing has broke me."

In spite of his reluctance to help get his mother released, Mike would have liked to go to Anniston. He knew his grandmother Carrie was dying, and he wanted to see her. When Lane offered to send him a hundred dollars to help with the costs, he agreed to come and make the calls.

When he sat down in Anniston to start telephoning, Mike felt his earlier concerns taking over. He didn't want to see his mother out on the street, and along with this feeling he experienced something else: fear. If she had attacked his father and sister in this way, and maybe even his grandmothers, if his suspicions about the illnesses he and Teri had experienced around her were correct, what was to keep her from taking the next step? What would prevent her from coming after them again? Even worse, what about Matthew? He was sixteen months old. Last year, Marie had wanted to have her grandson with her for a while. When Mike and Teri had decided that he was too young to leave them, Marie had been offended. "I could just come and get him anytime, you know," she had said. He hadn't thought much of it at the time. Remembering the moment now, Mike felt a sudden chill. Now it sounded like a threat.

He had committed himself to making the calls, Mike thought, but he couldn't bring himself to ask people to put up the bail money. Instead, he found a way to tell each person he talked to that he thought it would be best if his mother were not turned loose. As far as he knew, none of the people he called had a lot of money; they couldn't afford to lose the bond if she took off. He told himself that it would be better for everybody if she were kept in jail, and besides, he hadn't actually promised Will Lane to ask them to help. He had merely said he would make the calls.

Mike wasn't the only one who thought Marie Hilley should stay in jail. Lieutenant Carroll heard from someone at the jail that Marie had been talking to a cellmate who was waiting for bail to be set. "If I ever get out on bail," Marie was quoted as saying, "I'm going to take off." Carroll passed the word to a bondsman and the district attorney's office. Everybody wanted to see her bail provisions revoked. The district attorney, Bob Field, recommended to Marie's lawyers that they have her examined by a psychiatrist and discourage her from making bail.

It was too late. Marie was released from jail on a Saturday evening. Five local residents had signed for the bond, guaranteeing a total of fourteen thousand dollars if she failed to show up for trial in three weeks. One of the signers was a prominent local businessman, another of Marie's former employers.

Here was one of the master strokes of a great con artist. Like all virtuosos of deception, Marie Hilley at work was a stranger to sentimentality. She never let the previous generosity or vulnerability of her target shield him from her need. And she always conserved her resources—the trust and gullibility of her quarry—with fastidious care. She was ingenious at covering her tracks so that the failure of one attempt should not destroy the confidence of its victim. One never knew when a fresh attempt to exploit that confidence might be necessary.

The businessman who came forward when Marie needed help with her bail was a man who had offered her employment, then his friendship, even the hospitality of his home. When she needed money, he had given her well-paying extra work. She had rewarded his generosity with deceit, seeking his financial help for her impending marriage to "John Romans," the scheme that failed with Calvin Robertson and Harold Dillard. When he wisely stood his distance, she had found a way to retain his confidence, even though the marriage never materialized. And even now, accused of attempted murder and fraud, she had kept his trust alive. He was ready to help again. He guaranteed ten thousand dollars of her bail. His faith in Marie Hilley would cost him heavily.

Mike Hilley was relieved to be back home in Florida with Teri.

The atmosphere in Anniston was overwhelming, with the terrible damage his mother had done to Carol, and his grandmother so near death, and the tensions in the family that had grown from the realization of Marie's treachery. It was like an earthquake, welling up from below the surface of everyday life, creating great new fissures in the foundations of the family, finding old fault lines and shifting the ground beneath them. Mike had been only twenty-two when his father died, and he had lived away from Marie since then. The family seemed to expect a lot from him, but he was still only in his middle twenties; there hadn't been much chance to grow into the role of an adult. There was so much happening to them all, but he felt helpless to do anything about it.

He had tried to be useful. He had asked his mother on the phone if she had her heart medication. She had said no, and he had volunteered to get it for her from Carrie's house on Moore Avenue. It would also be a chance to look at the papers Aunt Freeda had turned up. Freeda was so eager to see his mother punished, Mike thought, there was no telling what she might do if she got hold of sensitive documents.

It took him six hours to go through his mother's possessions. He started with the chifforobe in the small back room, then found a key to unlock a little shed out behind the house, where box after box of his mother's things had accumulated each time she moved. He had looked through some of the papers during a visit back in June. Now he examined them with greater care. There were unpaid bills, letters about a lawsuit, personal correspondence. There was a cassette tape he had heard about from Freeda. It was a declaration of love to Marie from Calvin Robertson. Freeda, Lisa, and Carol had already listened to the tape. One of them had said, "Wouldn't the press like to get ahold of this."

Somebody could have a field day with this stuff, Mike had thought. He had packed up the most sensitive items in a box and addressed it to himself in Merritt Island. He had never found the heart medicine, or any medicine bottles of any kind. He had gone home without feeling he had made much of an impact on things.

But Freeda and her sister, Jewell Phillips, seemed to feel differently. Jewell was on the phone from Anniston, it was one o'clock in the morning, and she was furious.

Jewell had come down from Virginia to be with her mother, Carrie, in her last days. The events surrounding Marie had reached their culmination at the same time, and Jewell was adopting her sister's view of things. There was a hard edge to her voice.

Mike later testified in court about the conversation: "Do you know that you've signed your mother's death warrant?" Jewell said.

Mike had no idea what she was talking about. It was a bizarre experience, being awakened by an angry phone call from his middle-aged aunt, hearing her talk to him like a pug-nosed hoodlum in a black-and-white gangster movie. She was outraged that Marie had been released.

"Why are you calling me about it?" Mike asked, still bewildered.

Jewell and Freeda had gotten wind of Will Lane's request and Mike's phone calls about bail for Marie. They believed Mike was responsible for the release of their brother's murderer. He couldn't talk them out of it. They weren't interested in listening. As Mike would later testify, Jewell brought the conversation to a stunning climax.

"Buzz and I are going over to Birmingham and find her, and we're gonna kill her." During her visit to Anniston, Jewell had been going out with Buzz Remer, the captain of detectives, Gary Carroll's superior officer.

It was frightening, Mike thought. She was so angry, threatening him as well as his mother. And he was exhausted, mentally and emotionally, by the whole thing.

"If you wanna kill me," he said at last, "come on. Just come on ahead and do it." It would almost be a relief, he thought. At the same time, the whole thing was ridiculous. He couldn't resist a parting shot.

"I know you two bozos from way back," he shouted, "and I doubt you could find your way out of Anniston, so don't give me that garbage!"

After they had hung up, he considered the threats. Could they possibly mean it? Mike wondered. Somebody should tell his mother, but he didn't know how to get in touch with her.

A few days later, she phoned Mike. She was in Birmingham. She hadn't lost her ability to start a conversation as if it were the most ordinary situation in the world and all the events of recent weeks mere petty annoyances to be routinely overcome. She was wondering if she could borrow his credit cards for a while. Mike was dumbstruck. It was so outrageous he could barely respond. She took his rejection of the idea with chatty indifference.

Her manner changed when Mike told her about the phone call from Jewell.

"This isn't the first time there's been a falling-out with Freeda and Jewell," she said. "I'm scared of those two."

She was trying to treat it as if it were just the continuation of a family spat, but she sounded more concerned than that. She questioned Mike about Jewell's threat to come find her, but he couldn't tell her anything more. They hadn't said when or where they would look for her. When he finished telling his mother everything he could about what Jewell had said, Marie seemed genuinely upset. After they had hung up, Mike realized he still didn't know exactly where his mother was in Birmingham.

Bill Andrews was getting more than he had expected when he agreed to work with Wilford Lane on the Marie Hilley case. First there had been the phone call to his office. It had been the voice of a middle-aged woman, completely incongruous with what she was saying to him.

"Are you the lawyer with Wilford Lane on the Marie Hilley case?" she asked. He told her that he was.

"You had better get off the case," she said.

"What?" He was taken by surprise.

"You better get off the case," she repeated, "or you'll be damn sorry."

Now Wilford had called him over to Birmingham to meet with Marie Hilley. They were moving her to a different motel. She had been threatened, too. Mike Hilley had warned Marie that her sister-in-law was threatening to come find her and kill her. Reporters were looking for her, too. She didn't want to talk to them, and the lawyers agreed it was best.

After lunch, Andrews and Lane checked her into the Rodeway Inn. They used the name Emily Stephens so no one could find her. It was the middle of the week. Lane arranged to meet Marie again at the motel on Sunday. That would leave them plenty of time to prepare for their opening appearance in court on the attempted-murder charge two weeks from the following Monday.

On Sunday afternoon, Andrews' phone rang. It was Wilford Lane. He was calling from the motel.

"Come on over here, Bill," he said. "She's gone."

Later that day, Carrie Hilley died at Stringfellow Hospital. She was seventy-one years old. She had been fighting cancer for several months, and family members said she had also suffered from diabetes and an ulcer. Physicians at the hospital said preliminary tests before her death had shown traces of arsenic in Mrs. Hilley's body. An autopsy was ordered.

9

The Search

The first reaction was not concern about the loss, about the things that were gone. It was a sense of having been violated, knowing that their private place had been invaded by an outsider. Margaret and Sammy Key were quiet people, soft-spoken creatures of routine, working near home in the mill at Blue Mountain, going to church, living peacefully. The car was gone, and someone had punched a pane of glass out of the back door with a brick and turned the knob to get in. It was like rape, much worse than the loss of an overnight bag and some clothes, even savings bonds and the car.

The note was frightening. It had been scribbled on the back of an envelope:

> Do not call the
> police. We will burn
> you out if you do.
> We found what we
> wanted and
> won't bother
> you again.

At the edge of the envelope there was a postscript: "Your car is in Gadsden."

By the time the police arrived and had a chance to put things together, the Keys were beginning to think differently. It must have been Marie. She had been discovered missing yesterday. All the missing clothes were Margaret's—dresses, sandals, slacks. Marie would need clothes, and since Margaret had been sick and lost weight, they were just about the same size. And the car: Marie wouldn't want to risk public transportation to get away from Anniston.

They told the police what they suspected. It was hard to decide whether it was better than being invaded by a stranger or much, much worse.

Marie's disappearance from the Rodeway Inn had looked like a kidnapping at first. The lawyers, Wilford Lane and Bill Andrews, had gone inside when the police from Homewood, a Birmingham suburb, opened her room. It looked as if the occupant had left in a hurry. The hanging rack and drawers were filled with her clothes. There was a row of paperbacks, romantic novels, on the chest. A curling iron and a row of cosmetics stood by the sink, a brown shoulder bag lay on the bed. In the bag were keys and lipstick and a set of Polaroid pictures, mostly of children. And there was a note lying on the table by the window. The curtains had been left open; anyone looking in from outside could read the note. It was scrawled on a small sheet of Rodeway Inn stationery:

> Lane—
>
> You led
> me straight
> to her—
> You will hear from
> me.

Lane told the police they had registered his client under the name Emily Stephens to avoid harassment by her family and the media. It looked as if there was no shortage of people with a grudge against her.

But there was more to the picture. There was no wallet in the purse, and all Marie's identification was missing. When the Anniston police were called in, they remembered the strange events surrounding Marie Hilley. There was still a note in the files that had been found on her back door in 1977. It said, "You are going to be sorry if you don't move." It was scratched on the back of an envelope, in the same style as the motel note.

And then the note had turned up at the Keys' house. To an untrained eye, it looked like the work of the same person who had written the one found at the motel. The l's and t's were written with the same symmetrical, two-legged loop, the a's were made from inverted v's, and both notes had the backward s's that children sometimes write when they are just learning to write, or that adults make when they use their off-hand for some reason. Nobody was taking the kidnapping story seriously any longer.

There was still another note that turned up the day Marie disappeared. Written on lined paper, it was a little neater than the others, but the style looked the same, with the distinctive t's and l's and the backward s's. It was addressed to Sergeant Don Williams, one of the detectives in the Anniston Police Department who had worked with Lieutenant Carroll on Marie Hilley's complaints, and it was related to the events of a year earlier. The punctuation was erratic and there was a repeated word, but the message was clear:

When its no fun to see her scared any more I will get the Hilley bitch Ill get her when and where shes not expecting me. You won't catch me. Then you can start watching the Ford bitch. You are a stupid cop. Nearly as stupid as the Hilleys and the Fords. After that, I have a few others on my list. You can start earning your pay.

The Homewood police turned the note over to the handwriting expert at the state Department of Forensic Science, along with the message from the motel room. His analysis showed that they had been written by the same person.

Several weeks after Marie Hilley fled, the tests on members of her family were completed. Carrie Hilley's body showed traces of arsenic, but the amounts were small. There was no way of telling whether the poison had been swallowed or injected, whether it had been put in her food or absorbed from water, where it occurred naturally. In any case, her death the day of her daughter-in-law's flight had been caused by cancer. There were no grounds for prosecution. And the death in 1977 of Lucille Frazier, Marie's mother, had also been due to natural causes.

Frank Hilley was another matter. He had been killed by arsenic; there was no question about it. The amounts were large. The poison had been taken a little at a time over a long period, with a massive dose near the end. On January 11, 1980, the Calhoun County grand jury indicted Audrey Marie Hilley for first-degree murder. It was almost two months since she had fled.

Following Marie's disappearance and throughout 1980, the investigation went ahead on two fronts, but neither of them was very productive. Soon after the arrest, Lieutenant Carroll worked on gathering evidence for the prosecution. Checking all the hardware stores and farm and garden outlets in Anniston, he located the one that sold the bottle of Cowley's Rat and Mouse Poison found with Marie's things; the cost marks on the label matched the code used at Miller Feed-Seed and Hardware. The store was one and a half blocks down Gurnee Avenue from Carroll's office at the Anniston Police Department.

But nobody at the store could remember selling the poison to Marie Hilley, and other leads were similarly fruitless. A search for the Mrs. Hill who Marie had said got her the medication from "Toots" for Carol's injection turned up nothing. And Dr. Donald, who Marie claimed authorized the injections, had died in August, a month before Marie's first arrest. Nothing is going to be simple on this case, Carroll thought. The more he searched, the more indication he found of Marie Hilley's genius for concealment and deception.

The other half of the job was the search for Marie herself, which entered repeated small cycles of rising hope and disappointing reality. There was no end to the leads. Carroll worked with Wayne Manis and other FBI agents to follow them out. Some seemed promising, and for a time they expected to locate their prey at any moment. The Army's Criminal Investigation Division reported a case of a man poisoned by his wife; there were some promising similarities to the Hilley poisonings, but nothing came of it.

More common were the people who thought they had been poisoned by a spouse or a neighbor. It seemed as if each time an article about the case appeared in a newspaper anywhere in the South, the phone calls came pouring in. Lieutenant Carroll was always polite, but few of the calls even seemed worth writing down.

Officially, it was the Keys' car that widened the search and brought the FBI in, that and the fact that Gary Carroll and the Calhoun County Sheriff's Department had exhausted all the leads in Alabama and nearby states. A woman arrested for waving a gun around in Lonoke, Arkansas, two weeks after Marie disappeared fit Marie Hilley's description very closely. She claimed she was from Anniston, Alabama, and the sheriff of Lonoke County told Gary Carroll that she looked exactly like the pictures of Marie he had sent out. But the fingerprints didn't match, and they had to let her go. Within a few days, calls and tips were coming from all over the South, but none of them was any better than the Arkansas lead.

The Keys' car had turned up at the bus station in Marietta, Georgia, outside of Atlanta, within a few days. It was in the same shape as when it was taken from the driveway. The police found no fingerprints. There was no clue to who had taken it or where it had been. But there was no question in anybody's mind that it was Marie Hilley's means of escape from Anniston, and it had crossed state lines. The district attorney officially requested that the FBI get a federal warrant for Audrey Marie Hilley.

Wayne Manis, an agent in the Anniston office of the FBI, was already aware of Marie Hilley from the newspapers and from talking shop with Gary Carroll. But nothing Manis had heard when he joined in the search indicated that she would turn out to be the most elusive fugitive he had ever pursued.

In Marietta, about ten miles northwest of Atlanta and a ninety-mile drive east of Anniston, Manis found a witness who remembered that the Keys' car had been parked by a light-skinned Negro man. Manis lost the trail there, but he picked it up again with a report from the chief of police in a small Georgia town a few hours by car west of Atlanta.

A woman had come to the police station with a sad story, the chief said. She had become friendly with a woman on the bus. Awakening from a nap, she discovered that the woman had gotten off sometime during the night. Her purse, with all her money, identification, and a valuable watch, was gone. The woman was personable and well-spoken, a cut above the lost souls who usually turned up at the police station, but she had nothing to fall back on. Her close relatives were either dead or estranged. There was no one she could call for help. After taking the report, the chief arranged lodging for her. The next day he took up a collection among the little town's merchants. With the small stake in hand, she got on the bus and left. From a picture, the chief identified the woman as Audrey Marie Hilley.

The bus had been headed eastward, toward Savannah, on the Atlantic coast of Georgia. In Savannah, the agents found a hotel where a woman answering Marie's description had registered soon after the bus arrived. After staying a few days at the hotel, she had left with a man. Available descriptions of her companion were vague.

If the identifications were all accurate, since leaving Anniston Marie had been heading steadily southward and eastward, toward Savannah. And there the trail ended again. This time there was no way to pick it up. She had vanished without a trace.

A search by the FBI is based on the assumption that a human personality has the permanence and solidity of sculpture. A person may flee a place, abandon contact with family and friends, and even change his appearance; it is rare that a fugitive maintains these breaks from his history without a slip, but some come close. Habits of movement and association are another matter. No attempt to suppress a lifetime's accumulation of habit can be successful forever.

With Marie Hilley, one key was her scrupulous attention to her appearance. Almost everybody the FBI agents interviewed had mentioned it, how neat she always seemed, how well dressed, almost a model of personal grooming, with no hair astray, no thread hanging from a seam.

The FBI sent circulars to beauty parlors throughout the country, in any town or city where someone thought she might have gone. Beauticians' magazines were asked to publish her picture. In southern Georgia, up into the Carolinas, and south to Florida, wherever there was some chance of picking up her trail, agents showed Marie's photograph in the fancier clothing stores and boutiques.

And she had been a faithful churchgoer, someone told Manis. She was most comfortable in the Church of Christ. Word went out and agents inquired at churches large and small, in scores of towns and cities throughout the Southeast.

Gradually tips came in from other places, clues pointed in new directions, and the search widened. Gary Carroll remembered Marie saying how much she liked Florida when she came back from her stay with Mike in 1978. Word filtered out of the city jail that she had told a cellmate she would go to California if she could get out. There was a bizarre lead that pointed to the Southwest: Marie had told a story about having a twin sister named Mandy who was given away at birth to relatives in Texas. Eventually there was some form of search activity in every state. There was still no sign of Audrey Marie Hilley.

All this investigation was standard stuff, going by the book, along with detailed descriptions teletyped throughout the Southeast, briefer bulletins sent to police agencies nationwide, circulars to the media, and the routine checks of credit applications and employment agencies. But Agent Manis was intrigued with the way Marie Hilley's trail had just seemed to evaporate over in Georgia. It was as if you were tracking a deer and it suddenly learned to fly. There was one thread to lift out of the tangle, though, and that was the identity of the man Marie had been seen with before she disappeared from the hotel in Savannah.

Back in Anniston, Manis sorted through the possibilities. He soon learned that there was no shortage of candidates. Next to the portrait of a churchgoing, Little League mother, another, fainter picture was emerging, like an image slowly forming on photographic paper in the darkroom developing fluid. One person said Marie Hilley liked nightclubs. Someone else implied that there must be some connection to gambling; possibly it involved her late husband, debts he had run up, a former landlord. These fragments were on the level of rumor, nothing that could be reinforced with solid fact, but through all the stories there was a theme that kept turning up, and this much was reliable: Men came to Marie Hilley like bears to spilled molasses, and she wasn't shy about returning their interest.

In fact, if Marie had enjoyed all the gaudy affairs that rumor painted, it would take half the investigators in the South a year's work to check all the leads and figure out if one of the gentlemen had taken a trip to Savannah at the critical moment. There were stories about a lawyer, several of the men she had worked for, a friend of her husband's, and half the officers on the Anniston police force.

Most of these tales seemed the kind of half-true but irrelevant and distracting trash that floats to the surface around any notorious crime, but there were a few kernels of useful information among them. One concerned Calvin Robertson, who had known Marie since childhood. The other involved her onetime employer Harold Dillard. As the investigators uncovered the story of Marie's relations with the two men, her disappearance no longer seemed the product of a spur-of-the-moment decision. She had been preparing the way for an escape.

Investigation cleared both Dillard and Robertson. Neither of them had known what Marie Hilley was up to; both were rueful and somewhat embarrassed at being so completely taken in. Both were married men with families; neither of them was eager to talk much about the case. Nevertheless, they provided the most interesting leads to emerge from the tangled story of Marie's romantic life.

She had spoken to both Dillard and Robertson about a man named

"John" who wanted to marry her. Their stories were remarkably similar; she had played both fish with the same tackle.

Another clue to the identity of "John" came from an unexpected source. Carol Hilley was gradually recovering her energy and emerging from the isolation her mother had forced her into. Carol recalled that her mother had spoken of a boyfriend who lived in Atlanta. He taught at a college there; he was a professor of Hebrew. Seemed like it was Emory University. His name? Carol remembered it as "John Ronin." After Calvin Robertson had sent a personalized glass coffee cup for each member of the family, Marie had asked him to get another one made up. Carol had found the cup, still unwrapped, in her mother's things at Freeda's. Engraved on it was the name "John." That was something to work with, Manis thought.

At Emory University there was no John Ronin, or Romans, or Roman to be found in the language department, or in the humanities faculty, or anywhere else in the university. But the hospital at Emory was where she had claimed she was going for cancer treatments when she got the three thousand dollars out of Calvin Robertson and his wife "to help pay the medical bills." Maybe there was something over there.

But at the hospital and medical school, the investigators came up empty once again. And this time there was no thread to pick up. The mysterious "John" would remain unknown, at least until something else emerged. If he even existed in the first place.

Long after Marie had fled, a last episode in her treachery remained to be played out. A few weeks after she failed to show up for trial, the Anniston court declared the fourteen thousand dollars in bail bonds on her forfeit. The money had been put up by friends; one of them was her former employer and friend, who was responsible for ten thousand dollars of the total. Over the following months he had been fighting forfeiture in the courts. The grounds were mainly technical. District Attorney Bob Field had called the friend's request for forgiveness of the debt "ridiculous."

"I don't know of any motion ever filed like this before," Field had said. Upset by Marie's flight and the publicity about her treachery, the friend asked Field not to comment publicly anymore, and the district attorney agreed.

It was not until mid-1981 that the court confirmed the forfeiture and demanded that the bonds be paid off. Marie's friend was forced to hand over the ten thousand dollars. A year and a half after Marie Hilley's disappearance, the last in her long history of betrayals was completed.

As the weeks became months and it began to seem that Marie would not be brought back soon to face trial, those who knew her tried to imagine where she might be, what she could be doing.

It seemed as if everybody in Anniston had known Marie Hilley, or had a relative who knew her well. The initial curiosity had been fed by the exhumations and the rumors of more poisonings: Had she really poisoned the police officers who investigated the strange events at her house? Stories about her sexual connections, which touched what seemed like half the important men in town, only intensified eagerness for the trial.

Rather than deflating the anticipation, Marie's disappearance raised it another several notches. She must really have something more to hide, the reasoning went, probably something that would blow the lid off the town if it got out.

A reporter found some Annistonians guessing that she was still in the area, hidden by friends. Others thought she must be living far away, with a new identity. Still others speculated that she was dead.

There was a lead from Marie's aunt in Florida, Ailene Frazier, who had loaned her niece several thousand dollars when Marie said she could not afford to take Carol to the Mayo Clinic. Mrs. Frazier said that her son had reported to the FBI sighting a woman in Las Vegas who he thought was Marie. Mrs. Frazier was skeptical, the newspaper related: "He says she had light hair and was very haggard-looking—too much so to be Marie," she said.

Among those closest to Marie, speculation was still more intense. Mike Hilley had received two phone calls that Sunday in November, the first telling him that his grandmother Carrie had died, another a little later saying his mother had disappeared. He had gone to Anniston for the funeral and ended up presiding over the ceremony. Carol's crippled condition joined with the memories of his father's funeral four years before, which Mike had also led, to infuse the occasion with an awareness of his mother's malevolent spirit. It was hard to shake the feeling that she was present.

Afterward Mike and Teri wondered about their own places in the ranks of victims. They sought out a doctor with their questions. He discovered signs of arsenic in their systems, but it was too late to say how much they had taken in. Mike and Teri found too much uncertainty in the answers; when Teri became pregnant again, they consulted another doctor. He only confirmed that they would never know for sure whether they had been poisoned. Still, it was impossible to put aside the thought that Marie had assaulted them both with arsenic and that she had played a role in the miscarriage of their first child. There was no easy way to understand that fact or to live with it. And when Mike thought about where his mother might be, it was always with a tinge of fear at the possibility that she was lurking within range, waiting for the right moment to attack again, perhaps this time making good her threat to touch them through their young son.

Mike told the FBI agents that there were four places he could imagine his mother taking refuge. Mike had found some of her correspondence with Calvin Robertson; one possibility was that she might go to San Francisco to continue trying to talk him into making a life with her. Also, she had liked Florida when she lived there with him and Teri, Mike said, and she might return. And she had often spoken in romantic terms about her time up North with Frank in the early years of their marriage, about the cold weather and the snow. Mike could picture her in a cold place—Colorado, perhaps—or somewhere way up North, near the Canadian border.

Carol was questioned, too, and she thought immediately of some cold place. She told Lieutenant Carroll that her mother had often talked about winter weather.

"Her dream of a place to be," Carol recalled, "was where it snowed all the time and she could stay in and read books."

Carol Hilley was slowly returning to an ordinary life. During the first months of her recovery she had stayed at Freeda's house, where she experienced a loving, stable environment for what seemed like the first time in years. At Christmas, with Freeda and her family, joined by her friend Eve Cole and Eve's husband, Carol had felt hopeful.

She had moved out of her aunt Freeda's house after a few months, pleased with her progress, eager to be on her own. But the first burst of optimism that had come with the release from uncertainty about what was causing her illness hadn't lasted. The routine of physical therapy was painful and tedious, full recovery came to seem distant or impossible, and many of her former friends fled from the notoriety that surrounded Carol now.

Carol had retained the suggestibility of a child. If she wasn't being wary and stubborn, she was too much the other way, gullible and easily persuaded. And now she was especially vulnerable. When the husband of Carol's former lover made advances to her, she finally yielded. For a moment, it seemed like a way to stay close to them both. Soon the husband was talking about making it into a sexual threesome with his wife.

Now Carol was coming to regret that she had given in to him in the first place. The reality was nothing like the innocent, hopeful dream. She turned down the idea of including the wife, and pulling her resolve together, told him she didn't think they should have sex again.

The husband, his scheme in collapse and suffering from belated guilt, confessed to his wife the brief affair with Carol. Choosing between her husband and her former lover, the wife was ready to believe him when he painted himself as a man seduced. The wife was furious at Carol, perhaps doubly so for the betrayal not only of her marriage but also of her continuing affection for Carol. The couple made the complete rejection of Carol a cornerstone of their reconciliation.

In May 1980, Carol made another attempt to take her life with an overdose of medication. Again the attempt seemed halfhearted, again she recovered. After a few days in the hospital, she emerged to a fresh start. This second suicide attempt seemed to mark the beginning of her true recovery.

She was living on her own, sharing an apartment with a woman friend in Anniston. The physical therapy seemed to take hold; she was recovering her strength and control of her limbs. Though her movement was still somewhat shaky, she no longer depended on her crutches. Her weight was around ninety pounds, still fifteen pounds less than normal, but she had returned to school at Jacksonville State University. She dropped her major in criminal justice.

"I don't want the responsibility of putting someone in jail," she said. "Besides, the hours are terrible." She changed to physical education.

Later in the summer, Carol agreed to talk with a reporter from a

Birmingham newspaper. Along with the recovery of her physical strength had come a change in her thinking about what had happened to her.

A few weeks after her mother's arrest, Carol had said, "I'm not going to believe it until it's proven. My mom is just a little mixed up. The mother that raised me and my brother wouldn't have done something like this."

Now, eight months later, Carol told the Birmingham reporter that she believed her mother was a paranoid schizophrenic. Carol had "no doubt," she said, that her mother had killed her father and had tried to kill Carol herself.

Following its usual assumptions, the FBI believed Marie Hilley might try to get in touch with a member of her family. Suspicion focused on Mike Hilley when he and Teri made what an investigator later told the newspapers was "an unplanned, unexplained" trip from their home in Merritt Island to Pompano Beach in the spring of 1981. His mother had lived with them in Pompano Beach for several months in 1978, and it was one of the places the searchers thought she might go.

Soon afterward, an agent questioned Mike about the "sudden" trip. It was very simple, Mike explained, and there was nothing sudden about it. He and Teri were about to move to Tennessee, where Mike was going to study for an advanced degree, a master's of divinity. Before leaving, they wanted to drive down to see some close friends from the time they had lived in Pompano Beach.

Mike was already worried about what his mother might do. Now he had another cause for anxiety. How did the FBI know about the trip in the first place? Mike came to believe that his telephone was tapped. Another legacy of his mother's intrigue.

A year later, Mike and Teri were coming to feel comfortably settled in Tennessee. The fears and anxieties in which Marie had enveloped them for so long were receding safely into the past, and Anniston seemed far away. Mike was studying for his master's degree at the Emmanuel School of Religion in Johnson City. They lived in a small house on a dark country road in Bristol, not far away.

One night in the fall, Mike heard a cry from the baby, their second son, nine months old. As Mike rose from bed to go check on the baby, he glanced out the window. Farther down the porch, he saw a figure silhouetted in the overhead light that hung near the front door.

The features were obscured, but it was definitely a woman. She seemed to be prying at the window frame of the baby's room, trying to pull it free. Beyond her, two men were standing out by the road, next to a white Chevy Nova.

Mike alerted Teri and moved quickly to the phone to call the sheriff. When he joined Teri in the baby's room moments later, the woman had moved off toward the front door. Teri had been watching as the woman walked along the porch.

"Mike," she whispered, "that looks like your mother."

Mike's fear of what his mother might do had slowly subsided, but it was barely dormant. He had been asked to identify photographs found in his mother's purse at the motel after she jumped bail. Most of them were family shots of Mike and Teri's first son, Matthew, Marie's grandson. Far from innocent, sentimental reminders, in the light of her threat to "come get him" the pictures seemed ominous. Little was needed to bring the fear back in full force.

Mike returned to the phone and called the sheriff back. There was no sign of help arriving.

"Listen," Mike said, his voice hard, "I called about ten minutes ago." The time had collapsed and Mike had no idea how long it had been, but he wanted it to sound as if he had been waiting a long time, and he wanted the sheriff to realize he was desperate.

"Now, if somebody's not here in about three minutes, you're gonna start pickin' up bodies out in the front yard." Mike didn't have a gun, but this temperate minister of the gospel wasn't sure he wouldn't use one if he did.

Suddenly the spotlight came on in the yard of the house across the street, throwing a bright beam over the street and the white car. A moment later the owner came out of his house. The woman moved quickly to the car and drove off with her two companions.

When the sheriff arrived a few minutes later, Mike related his suspicion about the identity of the intruder. Mike and Teri spent a nervous, agitated night. At eight o'clock in the morning a man appeared at the door. He was an FBI agent, carrying a photograph of Audrey Marie Hilley. After talking with Mike and Teri, he walked across the street. The Hilleys' neighbor positively identified the intruder as the woman in the photograph.

*   *   *

Audrey Marie Hilley now fell into the category of "long-term fugitive." The local office of the FBI requested that a full-scale psychological profile be produced by their Behavioral Sciences Unit at Quantico, Virginia. All the available information was submitted to the unit, which prepared an analysis of the fugitive's personality along with predictions about her behavior that might help in the search.

In October 1981, just short of two years after Marie's disappearance, the FBI decided to go public with what it knew. Audrey Marie Hilley had been the subject of one of the most intensive searches the FBI had conducted in the region for years. The agents had tracked down several hundred leads, but now all the clues had played out. It seemed certain that she had settled down somewhere. If she stayed put, the chances of finding her were slim. Maybe the publicity would spook her into some kind of action that would create new leads. The FBI agent talked to a reporter on the condition that his identity not be revealed.

The investigators believed Mrs. Hilley had some form of dual personality, or at least an extraordinary ability to change from one kind of behavior to another, adapting to her surroundings like a chameleon.

"She can be kind, laughing, considerate, and then brutal and hateful," the agent said. "We believe she is living in a world with make-believe friends and enemies."

In addition to the formal charges, the investigation had turned up suspicions about several other possible poisonings, dating back to the time when Mrs. Hilley was calling the Anniston Police Department frequently about mysterious incidents.

"One time, some investigators went to that house, and afterward they became sick," the agent said. "It's possible they had been given some type of poison."

"There was a family that lived next door to her for years," he went on. "The children were sick all the time, but doctors could never find out why those kids got sick. Anyway, this family eventually moves, and the kids get well in no time at all."

Urine tests had been ordered for anyone who might have been poisoned, but none of these suspicions had been validated.

Whatever personality she was using, the agent said, there were some things about her that could be predicted with confidence:

"It's likely she will be in a man's company, with a respectable job.

She will be in secretarial work; she is a perfectionist and wouldn't take a job that low-rates her."

"She'll be living a good life. She will be in a beauty shop at least twice a week. She always dressed nice and her appearance was pleasant. Always."

They knew a lot about her, the agent concluded, enough to catch her eventually. But if she did have two personalities, everything they were assuming might be irrelevant. In that case, he said, "It's the other personality, which we don't know, that we may be chasing."

The FBI didn't believe Mrs. Hilley was armed. Even so, the fugitive bulletins described her as "dangerous."

Unable to concentrate on her studies, Carol Hilley left school a second time. She was working at the Anniston Army Depot, where her Aunt Freeda had helped her join a special program for people with disabilities. She was a clerk in a warehouse. She talked vaguely of going back to school someday; this time she would study nursing. Although she still weighed less than ninety-five pounds, physically she was almost back to normal.

Her mother was rarely far from Carol's thoughts. There was the terrible mystery of her mother's assault: What could Carol possibly have done to provoke such anger? And there was the plague of questions: Where is she now? Is she even alive? Will they ever have a chance to see each other again, to heal the great wound to the love of mother and child?

In the summer of 1982, Carol heard about a woman at the Army Depot who was known as a psychic. Carol approached the woman and asked for help in finding her mother. The clairvoyant politely turned down the request; she was in the habit of conserving her gift. The rejection only reinforced Carol's determination. After two weeks of repeated requests, Carol succeeded in breaking down the woman's resistance. The psychic was drawn to the plight of this slight, almost childlike girl, touched by the desperate need she expressed. The woman would not invoke her own powers, but she would advise Carol on how to use the force of her own mind.

The clairvoyant spoke to Carol of the untapped powers of the unconscious mind, the abilities that lie unused beneath the surface of the brain's ordinary activity. She advised Carol to discipline herself to a sharp, diamond-hard concentration, to imagine her mother, to hold fast to the image, and to send her thoughts across the distance to her mother's mind. "The mind is powerful," she told Carol. "Think of her, and she will receive your message."

Carol attempted to carry out the clairvoyant's instructions. She sat alone and still, concentrating for long minutes on a telephone and the message "Mom, call me." It occurred to Carol that she had changed phones since her mother left; she visualized the telephone number at her new apartment. After several weeks, nothing had happened. She contacted the psychic again.

"I want you to do something more than this," Carol insisted. The woman was reluctant at first, but finally Carol's persistence and need broke through. She invited Carol to her house for a session.

The clairvoyant sat with Carol in the living room, a map of the United States spread out before them. The psychic concentrated, occasionally entering what seemed like a trance, and eventually pointed to the northern part of the country's midsection. Her finger homed in on Montana and the Dakotas, then gestured eastward. But there was a halfhearted quality to her conclusion.

"I'm not sure," she said, "but I do have a feeling about it." The psychic's finding was consistent with Carol's ideas about her mother's romantic attraction to cold weather. Back home, Carol pointed her thoughts to the northern tier of the Midwest, but the seer's lack of conviction undermined her concentration.

In late July, the psychic called Carol. Apparently Carol had aroused her sympathy, and she hoped to improve on her previous efforts. She was planning to consult the tarot cards that night and would be willing to include Carol's search among the questions she put. Carol was grateful and joined the party.

When Carol's turn came, the question was placed on the table and the cards were consulted: Will Carol ever see her mother again? The psychic read the answer from the play and fall of the cards' medieval images.

"You will see your mother between seven weeks and seven months from tonight," she intoned.

Carol was less impressed with the message than she might have hoped. Her initial enthusiasm about the psychic's powers had been blunted by the lengthening separation from her mother—she had fled in 1979, almost three years before—and by the repeated failures of the psychic's methods.

"If they don't find her by February," Carol thought on the way home, "I'll know this woman is a weirdo, just a big nothin'."

The third anniversary of Marie Hilley's disappearance was approaching. The reporter who had covered Marie's arrest and subsequent events for the *Anniston Star* had married and left the paper. The editor assigned a new reporter to update the story for the *Weekend* magazine.

If Marie is found, Lieutenant Gary Carroll told the reporter, it will be "just a matter of chance." Most fugitives are habitual offenders who use crime as a livelihood; they are caught when they commit crimes in a new place. But Marie Hilley didn't fit that pattern. She had no police record until the events that led to her flight.

"If she hadn't poisoned her daughter," Carroll went on, "we never would have known about her husband. That's a crime she would have gotten away with completely."

There had been numerous reports from local residents who thought they had seen her, the detective said. The previous Christmas, poinsettias had appeared on the graves of Marie Hilley's parents, Huey and Lucille Frazier. Freeda Adcock said no family member had left them. She believed Marie herself had been responsible.

Calvin Robertson had had a lot of time to reassess his idea of Marie Hilley since the day she had failed to keep their date at the Atlanta airport. In hindsight he was able to see things that she had concealed from him in all the years since their childhood. The FBI agents had talked to Robertson when they were compiling their psychological profile, but he didn't agree with all their conclusions.

"They believe Marie is a type of person who will try to contact her kids," he said. "I totally disagree with that, for one main reason: This woman can be totally indifferent. I can look back over thirty years of knowing her and say that. My personal opinion is that she could cut all ties to her family, to Anniston, to everybody. She could turn it on and off at will."

"She had a charm about her that was unbelievable," Robertson declared. "If they put Marie on the witness stand, the jury would find her not guilty. It was unbelievable how convincing she was. Marie could sell the proverbial refrigerator to an Eskimo." To those who knew the details of the story, Robertson sounded like a man with a garageful of refrigerators.

In the last year, Carol Hilley had taken another tentative step away from her mother. "I blamed myself for the trouble she was in, and it's not my fault," she said. But the bond between a mother and her child is not so easily broken, even by a twenty-two-year-old woman, even in such extraordinary circumstances, and she soon betrayed her new resolve.

"I haven't had a word from her," Carol said with regret. "Birthdays are kind of raunchy. Christmases are kind of bad."

"If she called me and told me where she was and asked would I come meet her, I'd go. I think that's what you call being an accessory to a crime, but I'd take that risk."

The reporter asked what Carol would do if her mother reappeared. In answer, the young woman did not describe her own response but speculated about how her mother would feel about Carol.

"She could either be really mad at me because I didn't die and got her in all this trouble, or she could miss me. If they bring her back, she will either be mad because they caught her, or all sympathetic, and I'll say, 'It's okay.' It doesn't take anything to win me over. . . . I can forgive real easy. I don't like for anybody to be mad at me."

"She wanted me dead for some reason," Carol said. "I tried to figure it out. I tried to. But it's so hopeless. It could be any one of so many things."

Carol still imagined her mother in a cold, snowy place. "I can't picture her in any big-name place," she said. "I don't think any of them have any idea where she is. The way I picture her . . . she would go to some rinky-dink little town where no one had ever heard of her."

"My mother has done it," Carol concluded. "She's outsmarted them."

Calvin Robertson wasn't so sure. Marie had a special ability to get along anywhere, "simply melt into society," as he put it. "It comes back to that charisma she has," he went on. But he was convinced she couldn't carry on that way forever.

"I think one of these years, they'll find her," he concluded. "She'll make a mistake. It's just a matter of time."

The interview was published a week before Christmas 1982.

Part Three

John Greenleaf Whittier
Homan III

10

The Family

The family's departure from Ohio when he was a young boy came to seem in John Homan's memory like an escape from Hell, and Florida took on the proportions of a Promised Land. That made his mother's death in Fort Lauderdale at an early age all the more shocking, a sudden, jolting end to a peaceful, sunlit time. The disintegration of the Homan family that followed, even his father's early death, had an inevitability about them, like the last act of a tragedy.

The Homans' particular tragedy was a version of a more common American story, the Decline of a Great Family. There was money on both sides, two wealthy families with Philadelphia roots. According to family legend, the first John Greenleaf Whittier Homan invented an insulating compound in the 1800s that played a great role in the development and proliferation of the electric motor over the next half century. The invention provided the family with a substantial and continuing income, and since it was named Homanite, it was also the source of a modest immortality.

The inventor's first son and namesake married the beautiful daughter of a family whose status and longevity led those in certain circles to refer to them as "the Wolls of Philadelphia." They are still referred to that way among the Homans, if nowhere else, and the residue of their reputation survives in the Homan branch as memories of a thriving mail-order business, the ownership of banks, and a mansion on the Main Line, Philadelphia's row of moneyed inner suburbs.

But Ann Woll's story had not begun with the Main Line. The first memories she recalled for her children were not of parents but of an Amish farm, where she thought of herself as primarily a houseworker and kitchen hand, everybody's child and nobody's. She told of being banished from the kitchen during the period of her menstruation, the special exclusion only intensifying the separateness she already felt. Taken in by the Wolls, she was raised as their daughter and given a coming-out party at the Waldorf-Astoria. The surviving version of this modern Cinderella tale culminates with Ann Woll's marriage before she was twenty to a son of the equally prominent Homan family.

The young Homans were a striking couple. She was graceful, quiet, still girlish, with brown hair flowing in a soft wave to her shoulders, a sweet face, and a clear, even gaze. He was three years older, handsome in the style of Clark Gable, a horseman and a pilot, a man who could afford and appreciate a powerful Stutz Bearcat automobile. An old photograph in the family's possession shows him posed in the attitude of a fearless African explorer, a thick, black snake draped around his neck.

The playboy years of John Greenleaf Whittier Homan, Jr., were short-lived, however, cut off by World War II. A graduate of Rollins College, with a start on an advanced engineering degree at M.I.T., he was drawn into scientific work for the war effort. Later the vague impression was left with the children that their father had been a valuable, high-level specialist for the Navy in electronics—radar, perhaps—and that he had contributed to projects of the highest importance for the war effort. His children recalled years later hearing that an incident in which their father repaired the ship's radar under fire had become the basis for a movie. Well into the 1950s, Mr. Homan would be called away from his growing family on special assignments that lasted several weeks or more. He left behind the understanding that the military value of his contributions had not ended with the war and that the children must help maintain the shroud of secrecy the work still required.

Nothing the elder John Homan did in civilian life ever quite measured up to his war work in seriousness or dignity. In Steubenville, Ohio, where his first child and namesake was born in 1947, he did some engineering work in the steel industry. Later he was an early dealer in television sets and opened a hobby shop.

John Greenleaf Whittier Homan III remembered the Steubenville of his first five years as a "disgusting place to live," a gritty, valley town blanketed in steel mill smog. That memory is no doubt colored by the asthma and assorted allergies that kept young John, already a sickly child, in a constant state of physical distress. By 1952, two daughters, Minnie and Greer, had been added to the family. Seeking relief for young John and sunshine for the whole family, the Homans moved that year to Fort Lauderdale.

The early years in Florida were idyllic, or at least grew to seem so in memory. Fort Lauderdale was still a small, easygoing place, a sunbaked southern seacoast town fading off to the west into pasture and great expanses of cattle range. In town, pressing up against the Atlantic Ocean, were pockets of the new prosperity, just beginning to swell with the current of postwar migration from the Midwest. The town's reputation as a refuge for winter-weary college students from the North was still of modest proportions, and there remained places along the bay where developers had not yet created the parallel peninsulas that would fulfill the dream of a waterside home in the sun for thousands of refugees. Pelicans and flamingos were as common as family dogs, and with a few hours' hunting a child could bring home enough blue crabs for a hearty dinner.

The Homans moved into a house on one of these man-made fingers of land off Las Olas Boulevard, where the new money was only beginning to spill over into a high-toned shopping district. Even from the start, their house stood out, the only two-story structure along a cul-de-sac flanked by low, two-bedroom dwellings painted in shades of white, pale yellow, and gray. The Homans' place looked as if it had been assembled by stacking up two "ranch-style" homes transported from a development up North. It was a gaudy bright yellow below, with a dark brown second story. It stood closer to the road than its neighbors, its aluminum combination windows presenting a discordant note on a street of sliding glass doors, open carports, and graceful palm trees.

In back, the Homans were more conventional, with a swimming pool set into a modest lawn that led down to the curbside canal. During the family's first five years in Florida, three more children were added, the last, Terry, ten years younger than John. A tide of six Homan children, their friends, and the family's two basset hounds, Joshua and Priscilla, ebbed and flowed through house, yard, and pool, creating a loose, friendly atmosphere and a constant hubbub of activity and small mishaps.

The elder John Homan, now coming to be known as Big John to distinguish him from his near-teenage son, presided over the action from a seat in the middle of the house at the dining-room table. He had never finished the degree at M.I.T. There were rumors among young John's friends that his father was partly trained as a nuclear physicist and that he "did some work" at the government's Oak Ridge labs. Other than that and some work for Kodak, he did not seem to make much use of his engineering training.

He was a good enough photographer to have his work published in a major camera magazine. Later, he designed and produced sophisticated ceramics in kilns he had built himself, outfitting the Mai Kai restaurant in Fort Lauderdale with attractive custom-made dinnerware. He created glazed statuary that he sold through a gift shop, and small ceramic animals that held a few shots of liquor, which he gave away as presents. But none of these activities seemed to hold his interest for long. He quit the ceramics business after the electric company protested that his six kilns were drawing too much current for a residential district. His priority was the children, and there was no urgency about money.

The Homans were never rich, but they were comfortable. The steady income, as the children came to understand it, was from Ann Woll Homan's side of the family. Big John's earnings, like his enthusiasms, were sporadic, and he had forfeited a large inheritance by refusing to make peace with a hated stepmother. Trust funds from the Wolls provided for the children, and another inheritance provided a modest supplement, along with Big John's occasional contributions. At Christmas the lawyers released extra money for gifts; one year they made a mistake and there were so many presents that nobody had time to wrap them. They were placed under the tree in piles, one pile for each of the six children.

It was only later, and through the eyes of others, that the children learned to think of their upbringing as unconventional. In their childhood, Big John was a fishing companion for his sons, an arbitrator of disputes, a ready source of a hug and kiss for a daughter. Friends of the children loved to hang around; there was always something going on at the Homans'. The atmosphere was cheerful and casual, with few rules. There was always music, with one of the girls playing the flute, John working at his clarinet, somebody else banging on the piano, Big John dabbling in half a dozen instruments. Big John was more like a good-natured older brother than a parent, always ready to work with his children's friends on a broken kite, help out with math homework, or hold long, confiding conversations. Young people felt that he respected kids. For a teenager, it was like talking to a friend who happened to be very smart, and Big John wasn't afraid to ask for advice, either, about running the house or problems with his own kids.

Within the universe of her husband's active and continuous presence, most visitors saw Ann Homan as a kind, likable, but secondary figure. Friends looked forward to the Homans' colorful cookout parties. A diverse mix of engineers and artists, Big John's business contacts, an accountant and a gallery owner, the children and their friends and the friends' parents came costumed to fit a theme—Chinese one time, luau the next. There was a loose, democratic atmosphere at the Homans' parties that younger children found heady and lively, older children thought adult and risqué, and neighbors considered "bohemian" and slightly disreputable.

At parties Ann Homan was friendly but rather detached. She seemed most comfortable with her own friends, several women nobody else seemed to know very well. Among them were a mannish, hard-drinking gardener named Stacia, and a very large woman named Judy, who took portrait photographs at Burdine's, a chic department store in neighboring Pompano Beach.

The children observed that their mother was given to spells of illness and depressed, sleepy moods. Later, as these times became more frequent and the children's understanding of the world increased, they learned to associate them with alcohol. Occasionally their mother would disappear for a few days; when she returned, nobody mentioned the absence, but it was understood that she had been on a binge.

Big John made an occasional attempt to bring things under control, but it was hopeless. Once he rampaged through the house, gathering up liquor bottles and pouring the contents down the sink in the kitchen. Mrs. Homan charged after him, ranting and scrabbling through cabinets in search of some overlooked treasure. Another time, a screaming argument ended with the slamming of windows and the sounds of adults running through the house and yard. The next day, Big John's gun was found at the bottom of the swimming pool, and there was a hole punched in the dining-room wall.

One night, after a dramatic argument, she appeared at the top of the stairs carrying a suitcase. Her beloved mink coat, which she had difficulty finding occasion to wear in the warm Florida climate, was thrown on over a housedress. While a little group of terrified children watched from below, Ann Homan staggered down the steps, crying, "This time I'm leaving and I'm not coming back!" As she reached the door, Big John parted the group of crying children, picked her up, and loaded her onto his shoulder. "You're not going anywhere," he told his wife, and carried her back up the stairs.

Young John was the one who seemed to feel most strongly the deep sadness beneath the sweet calm that Ann Homan showed the world. He was the oldest, he had been her only child for three years, he was her "big boy" and her helper with the other children. If only he could make her feel better. But there was nothing he could do. And each time something happened, it was a new failure for John.

Ann Homan's episodes, however upsetting to the children, always seemed brief and temporary. There was nothing in them to provide a warning of their mother's death. The day she entered the hospital, the younger children—Peter was nine; Todd, seven; and Terry, six—hardly noticed she was gone. The older children understood that she was checking in for treatment, something to do with ulcers, and that it would be brief. Afterward, they heard, it had been decided that instead of coming right home she would stay a little longer.

A high-school friend of John's, Tim Doherty, went one evening around dinnertime to Holy Cross Hospital, where Big John had been spending every spare moment with his wife. Carrying a container of coffee for his friend's father, Tim entered the room to find Mrs. Homan alone. Her husband had stepped out for a cigarette. As she recognized Tim and greeted him, he was shocked at her condition. She was forty-two, but she looked suddenly twenty years older. John had not said anything to indicate she was so sick. She was under intensive care, not permitted visitors. Apparently Big John had not told the children.

"How are you feeling?" Tim asked.

"Not too good," she replied, a terrible weakness in her voice.

At home a little later that evening, young John was getting the other five children ready for bed. At sixteen, he had taken on increasing responsibility during the periods of his mother's absence or illness. Greer was thirteen, Minnie two years less, and at times they resisted their older brother's authority.

Suddenly young John appeared in their bedroom, giving orders. "Get up, get up and get dressed." They ignored him, chatting happily, beginning to get settled for the night but not ready to bring things to an end. In a moment he was raging at them, half crying, half shouting:

"Get up, goddamn it, I told you to get up! Your mother's dead!"

The outburst was only young John's first reaction to the heavy weight of responsibility that would fall on his shoulders. "It was a disaster," he said years later of his mother's death. Solitary by nature, John now began the psychological flight that eventually led him away from his family and into the arms of Audrey Marie Hilley.

11

Young John

Big John Homan had talked to his children often about his attitude toward death and funerals:

"When you're dead, that's it," he told them. "No sense in other people going on about it, you're gone and you can't change anything." The only immortality he expected would be in his children's memories and achievements.

"Give people your respect while they're alive," Big John had told them. "Don't wait until they're dead. If you think I'm a nice guy, tell me now. It won't do me any good if you wait to say it over my ashes; I'm not gonna hear it. And if you want to be a hero, work on it today, every day; let it show in what you do and the way you treat people. Eulogies are glorious, but they're no practical help to anybody."

Now the family followed his precepts to the letter. Ann Homan was cremated. There was no funeral, no memorial service.

"It was like one day she left," Peter remembered years later, "and then there was no more Mom."

Big John labored bravely to maintain the warmth and unity of the family. He established "The Family Council," gathering the children, ranging from John, the sixteen-year-old assistant parent, to Todd and Terry, who were just starting school. Seated in his usual place at the dining-room table, Big John put family matters to a vote and encouraged the children to discuss problems and disputes. He made a special effort to keep up with everything the children were doing. Their friends, coming to visit, still ended up in long conversations with the Homans' father. Big John was so different from their own parents, always able to talk on their level.

But there were some matters that could not be overcome by affection and family solidarity. Money was chief among them. Mrs. Homan had died without a will. The trusts and inheritance, all in her name, were interrupted. Big John was forced to take a job at Broward Community College, teaching photography; on the side he attempted to build a clientele tutoring students in mathematics at eight dollars an hour. His absence only increased the need for young John's services as an assistant parent.

These pressures overlapped with difficulties John was having in school. Apart from playing the clarinet in the band, he hardly seemed involved in the high school. He had never been comfortable in the classroom. Though he had inherited some of his father's intelligence, John displayed no taste for applying it to his studies. He preferred mechanical things, work he could touch and see. In his teens he was learning to use the most complicated shop manuals to understand and rebuild an automobile engine, but such skills never carried over to school. He would not accept knowledge from another person.

John was spending a lot of time taking care of the other children. When he did get away, his social life revolved around cars. He always seemed to be in the midst of restoring an old English sports car with a friend. When they had a car running and $20 between them for gas and sandwiches, John and Tim Doherty would take off on a long weekend drive across Florida at a hundred miles an hour, stopping to fish or swim, sleeping on a beach at night.

Reserved to begin with, John found it easier to deal with engines than people. Ironically, as he spent more time working on cars, he developed "mechanic's acne," a skin condition aggravated by grease and shop chemicals; it caused welts on his face, hands, back, and arms. Along with his premature baldness, which began to appear around the time of his mother's death, the acne gave John yet another reason for a growing self-consciousness. He felt at ease with Tim's girlfriend, Karen Youngberg, just from being around the two of them, but he didn't seem to meet girls on his own.

With Ann Homan's death, relations between John and his father became more tense. Big John had hoped his son would make more of an effort in school and go on to college, pursuing a white-collar profession, possibly even something in the sciences. Perhaps because he had not realized his own potential, Big John made no secret of his expectations and of his disappointment at his son's failures in school.

After John's junior year at Fort Lauderdale High School, his father transferred John to a small private school in town, hoping that the personal attention would stimulate his academic interest and improve his record for college. But John was already drifting away from the course his father had plotted for him. He signed a contract to rebuild an old steam-driven tractor for a metalworking company. It was painstaking work, cleaning and reassembling the primitive engine, machining replacements for decayed parts. Chugging back and forth in front of the company's shop, the refurbished machine made an impressive publicity display.

There were bitter arguments between John and his father, including one in which John threw a punch and his father picked up a chair to threaten him. Yet John was not ready to give up trying to be what his father wanted. He started at Broward Community College in Fort Lauderdale, where his father was teaching, continuing to live at home and help with the younger children. At the college, John avoided his father's courses, but Big John's presence on campus only raised the pressure on his son.

At college, John became close with Karen Youngberg, Tim's girlfriend. There had been times during high school when Karen thought John was trying to win her away from his friend. She had not been much tempted. The advances behind Tim's back had made John seem sneaky, and she had thought him self-centered and socially awkward. There was nothing physically attractive about him; he was gaunt and slightly stooped, almost cadaverous, really, and his thinning black hair and sallow, mechanic's complexion made him look older and harder than his years. But his mother's death had seemed to make him gentler and a little more open. Perhaps, too, Karen thought later, her change of heart had been motivated by sympathy; talking about his mother, John had regularly broken into tears. At first he had even tried calling Karen by her middle name, Ann, but she had made him stop. It was a morbid reminder of his mother.

John didn't have the money for regular dates, but he and Karen enjoyed sitting over a cup of coffee at a college hangout or lounging under a tree on the campus, talking for hours at a time. When John had to stay home with his brothers and sisters, he and Karen talked on the phone and wrote letters; after a weekend's separation Karen might receive six or seven pages of John's cramped, extruded handwriting. The relationship developed into the first experience of physical intimacy for both of them. They fantasized about living on a boat, having six children, casting off and cruising whenever they felt like it. John gave her a cheap ring to wear until they could afford something better, and Karen told him she was happy with the ring and didn't need anything better.

For all the talk, John said little about his feelings. His mother's death had been an exception; once he had put that pain behind him, John kept his problems to himself. Still, it was obvious that things were not going well at home. His father needed help more than ever, but John had no gift for authority or the affection that softens it; his brothers and sisters often seemed willful and unruly. The atmosphere around the house had always been casual; now the clutter expanded. A bicycle and other toys ended up at the bottom of the swimming pool and stayed there for days, while palm fronds floated on the surface, harboring mosquitoes and turning the water green. Paint was peeling from the house, brush piled up in the front yard, the dogs ran loose, and the children seemed unsupervised much of the time. A court-appointed social worker came to inspect the "home environment"; there was anxiety over whether the children would be allowed to stay with their father. A neighbor must have called the Health Department; John was grounded for a week while they cleaned up and prepared for an inspector's visit.

Things were not going well at college, either. John's first thought was to quit, but he still wasn't ready to betray his father's hopes. He transferred to Miami-Dade Junior College, commuting the thirty-five miles to classes, for a little more distance and one more try.

John went to Mass with Karen and her father at Christmas of 1966. He never went to church on his own; it was as if he were making an effort to show Karen's father that he respected her beliefs. And then John just seemed to drift away. There was no big fight or argument, and John never said anything. He just stopped calling Karen. Too proud to question John directly, she visited Greer, who had become her friend, and found an opportunity to ask Big John. He was just as puzzled as Karen was, and he said John was acting differently toward him, too. Something was bothering young John, his father thought, but no one could get him to talk about it.

Over the next half year, John would drop by at Karen's every month or two and take her for a ride, acting as if there had never been anything more than a casual friendship between them. He seemed to need someone to talk to, Karen thought, but once they were together, he stuck resolutely to the casual and superficial.

It was like John to close himself off when he was having problems, to avoid the unpleasant subject, even to convince himself that it didn't exist. Things were still not going well for him at college. He had exhausted all the possibilities, from the public high school to the private academy, on to Broward Community College and Miami-Dade; there was nothing left to try, no way to succeed in school and fulfill his father's hopes. John saw no choice but to give up and flee. He quit college and was soon at work installing toilets and stabilizing equipment on pleasure boats. Later, on employment applications, under "College," John would write, "None."

As he was cutting his ties to Karen and separating himself from Big John's aspirations for him, John was also breaking loose from his responsibility for the family. Here, however, he had been replaced. Soon after the funeral, one of Ann Homan's friends, Judy, the department-store photographer, had become close to Big John. It was one of those matches that look ridiculous at first to everybody except the couple themselves. He was in his late forties, twenty-five years older than Judy; she was over six feet, taller than Big John by a couple of inches, big-hipped and flat-chested, and she weighed more than two hundred pounds. She wore loose clothes to camouflage her bulk, which had the opposite effect and made her look dowdy as well. But she was available when Big John needed help, and she seemed earnest about helping with the children. Eventually she and Big John were married, and she took over management of the trust-fund money that provided for the care of the younger children.

The Homan children understood that their stepmother was not their father's equal—one evening at the dinner table he launched into an extended critique of her grammar and Tennessee accent; she "talked like a farmer," Big John told her—but she did try to help. She replaced worn-out furniture and brought order to the house. It was Judy who took Peter to see a famous specialist in Houston when the teenager needed treatment of a congenital heart problem, and later she drove him to Montreal with John to see Expo 67. She bought the younger children's clothes and advised Greer and Minnie about boyfriends. She liked to repeat Big John's axiom that his children were his one claim on immortality. She adopted his view of the Homan family as a refuge against a complicated world crowded with unhappy people. She never saw how fragile the walls of that refuge were, how soon they would begin to crumble.

The Homans gathered at a Fort Lauderdale restaurant in May 1972 to celebrate Big John's fifty-fourth birthday. It was a surprise party and Big John was delighted, enjoying the attention of his young wife and six children, the "baby" now fifteen, the hardest years of child-rearing safely past. The celebration continued past midnight.

At home afterward, Greer and Minnie said good night to their father. Greer noticed that he answered, "Good-bye." She put it down to the effects of food and drink and the late hour. Lying in bed, she heard a jarring noise from below. She ran downstairs to find her father collapsed on the floor in the bathroom. Judy made Greer stay home with the younger children while she and John followed the ambulance to the hospital.

Later, Greer and Minnie took the younger children to join the others at the hospital, but they were too late to see their father. He had suffered a massive heart attack, the doctor said. He was dead. In the corridor, Peter broke down in tears. John became furious.

"Shape up!" he shouted at Peter. "You have the family to worry about. Stop that whimpering. You have to be a model for the little kids." John's own eyes remained dry throughout the night.

As he had when his mother died nine years before, John was playing the part of the oldest son, trying to take over the role of parent to the younger children. His cry to Peter had been an exhortation to himself. Judy had tried to take charge of getting Big John to the hospital and seeing to the children, but it was John who curled up in his father's big armchair in the living room and held Greer in his lap for the rest of the night, soothing her, getting up occasionally to comfort the younger children.

Judy had originally been more traditional than Big John in her views of death, but later she had taken up his attitude. Now she followed the same practical, unsentimental procedure he had carried out when Ann died. "Life has to go on," she said. "He would have wanted it that way." John Greenleaf Whittier Homan, Jr., was cremated; afterward, nobody knew what had happened to the ashes. There was no funeral or service, and no gravesite to visit.

John, too, tried to live by the precepts of Big John and to keep them alive for the other children. "We have to remember what Daddy taught us," he told them. "We're a family and we have to take care of each other, we have to stick together." Ironically, it was just at that moment, with the death of Big John, that the forces were let loose that would soon tear the remnants of the Homan family apart.

John brought no more talent or capacity to the role of Homan parent than he had displayed after his mother's death. He was no longer living at home, and for several months he had been going out with a woman named Linda. Like Karen Youngberg, she had been Tim Doherty's friend first, but John had stepped in and soon they were dating steadily. They shared an interest in music—John had moved on from the clarinet to the accordion and harmonica, she played the piano and organ—and Linda owned an old MG that John kept in good shape for her. She was a thin, boyish woman, as reserved as John, in sharp contrast to the plump, outgoing Karen.

The summer after Big John died, John and Linda were married. The couple made their home in a sailboat tied up at the Fort Lauderdale waterfront, living the dream that John had shared with Karen four years earlier.

Linda held a clerical job at an insurance company. John had been let go from Raritan Engineering, where he was installing toilets and stabilizing equipment on boats, and had set up his own business, Crown Marine. He continued the installation work, sold and serviced compressed air tools, and won an occasional contract to install decking and superstructure in the fiberglass hulls of small pleasure boats. John's brother Peter, who had gone to work selling subscriptions to *Grit* when his mother died and was a good enough student to get admitted to M.I.T., was exasperated when John turned down a large contract to build fenders for Texaco tank trucks. Peter thought the job could lead to long-term security, but John preferred the work he already knew how to do. Peter concluded that his brother was simply too timid to be successful; like their father, John lacked any ambition or plan for his life.

John Homan didn't need a plan in order to be secure. He had a substantial cushion. The principal in the trusts that Ann Woll Homan had held in her children's names was automatically turned over to them when they became twenty-one. When Greer came of age the same summer John was married, she was the third of the children to receive her inheritance. The sums, which included varying amounts of interest and other bequests, were between one hundred fifty thousand and two hundred thousand dollars each.

With his inheritance in 1978, John bought a Fiat roadster, then a

Marie Hilley's father, Huey Frazier (*right*), and his twin brother, Louie, about age four, around 1912.

The fact of her father's twinship provided the seed for Marie's fantasy about her own exiled twin, sent away because her father could not bear to see his children relive the unhappiness of his own youth. It also must have formed part of the inspiration for Robbi Homan's masquerade as her invented twin sister, Teri Martin.

Huey Frazier, Marie Hilley's father (and unidentified woman).

Marie's father, Huey Frazier, developed a reputation as a sweet-natured wanderer. Some said his occasional disappearances from Anniston were due to trips out West to visit his twin brother, Louie. His daughter incorporated the longing of separated twins into the fantasy autobiography she created while a fugitive from the law.

Marie Frazier, about age ten, with her mother, Lucille Frazier, in the early 1940s.

Marie was already showing the precocious beauty that won her the "Prettiest Girl" honors at Quintard Junior High School a few years later.

Marie Frazier at Quintard Junior High School, 1946.

Marie Hilley's powerful physical attraction began to appear at an early age. At thirteen, then Marie Frazier, she was voted the "Prettiest Girl" in her class at Quintard Junior High School. She posed for the yearbook against a 1941 Ford with the "Most Handsome Boy." It was about that time that she met Calvin Robertson, whose memory of her beauty made him her dupe more than thirty years later.

Marie Frazier, age thirteen, poses on a wall.

Marie Frazier, age thirteen, poses with a friend. Within a year she was going steady with Frank Hilley.

Marie Frazier poses with the Future Teachers of America at Anniston High School.

Marie (third from left, first row) *was always a neat, stylish dresser, and she worked hard to pose herself carefully in the front row of every group picture. She also managed to stay near Rachel Knight, the most popular girl in the class* (second from left, first row.)

Marie Frazier with Rachel Knight in the Anniston High School Commercial Club's yearbook picture.

FRAZIER, AUDREY MARIE—F.T.A. Club '50, '51; Commercial Club '50, '51; Student Council '47, '49.

It was almost as if Marie and Rachel Knight formed their own picture, separate from the rest of the Commercial Club, with Marie tucking herself in close behind Rachel's shoulder (second and third from right, seated on wall), apart from the rest of group. Rachel was the first of a series of doubles and alter egos that appeared in Marie Hilley's life, culminating with her masquerade as Teri Martin.

Yearbook pictures of Rachel Knight and Marie Frazier, senior year at Anniston High School.

KNIGHT, RACHEL DEAN—National Honor Society '50, '51, Officer '51; Class Officer '51, Annual Staff '48, '49, '50, '51. Business Manager '51; Commercial Club '50, '51, Officer '50, '51; F.T.A. Club '50, '51, Officer '51; Who's Who '51; Queen '51.

It was striking how Marie seemed to model herself on her admired friend, Rachel Knight, to the point where others sometimes had trouble telling them apart from a little distance. Rachel was elected to the National Honor Society, named "Sweetest Girl" in the class, and chosen Class Queen. She was one of four outstanding seniors whose pictures were singled out for placement at the head of the class in the 1951 yearbook.

Rachel Knight, Queen of the Class of 1951 at Anniston High School.

Rachel was paired with George Keech, captain of the football team, who was elected Class King.

Queen Rachel Knight

Marie Frazier and Frank Hilley.

Marie was fourteen, Frank eighteen, when they started going steady. A year or so later, Frank went in the Navy. They were married in 1950, while Frank was home on leave.

Frank Hilley, home on leave from the Navy, with his mother, Carrie, in late 1951.

Frank Hilley and Marie Frazier had been married the year before. This time she went back to live with him in Long Beach, California, where they discovered during the winter that she was pregnant with their first child. Frank's mother, Carrie Hilley, died in 1979, the same day her daughter-in-law was discovered missing from the motel room where she had been staying while out on bail. Police were never able to prove their suspicion that Marie Hilley had poisoned her mother-in-law.

Marie and Frank Hilley at Cheaha State Park near Anniston, about 1952.

Marie was nineteen, Frank was twenty-three, a year or so after they were married.

Marie Hilley in her thirties, around 1965.

Marie Hilley (*center*) in costume for a pageant.

Marie Frazier Hilley was born and raised in Anniston, where she was known as a model wife and mother, an efficient, reliable worker, and a participant in church and school activities, with a wild acquaintance among the wealthy and powerful men of the community. Anniston was unbelieving when the truth about her life was revealed.

Frank and Marie Hilley, with their daughter, Carol.

It was around Christmastime 1967. Carol was eight years old.

Carol Hilley and a friend at the beach. Carol never weighed much over a hundred pounds, even before she got sick.

The Hilley family, about 1971, four years before Frank died. *Left to right: Marie, Mike, Carol, and Frank.*

Carol Hilley and a prom date dressed for the junior-senior prom.

At first, Carol thought it was something she had eaten or drunk the night of the prom that was making her sick. It turned out to be the start of five months of mysterious, worsening illness that ended only with the arrest of her mother, Marie Hilley.

Detective Lieutenant Gary Carroll standing in front of the Hilleys' house on McClellan Boulevard.

The house where the Hilleys were living when Frank died in 1975 of what was diagnosed at the time as hepatitis. Lieutenant Carroll visited here several times, investigating the mysterious incidents that were plaguing the widowed Marie Hilley. Carroll, who didn't like coffee, always declined Marie's offer of a cup. Other officers, who had accepted Marie's hospitality while investigating her complaints, came down with stomach problems.

The grave of Frank Hilley at Forestlawn Gardens.

Marie buried her husband at Forestlawn in 1975. She had her own name inscribed (at right) on the plaque beside his, so she could be laid to rest next to him when the time came.

Four views of Marie Hilley.

Taken over the years, three views of Marie Hilley as the attractive, conventional housewife, and one (right) as a prisoner, under arrest for what the prosecutor called "the worst crime I can imagine."

Lucille Frazier, Marie's mother.

Marie's mother died in 1977, at the age of sixty-four. As with Marie's mother-in-law, Carrie Hilley, later events cast Lucille Frazier's death in a new light, but authorities were never able to substantiate their suspicions.

February 6, 1979

My Dearest:

Let's lift the ban on letters. I, too, know what it is to feel lonely in a crowd, but only since "you." Oh, God, how I love you. There is no way I can stop - if you were different - maybe. But you are so kind and gentle - it isn't possible for me not to love you - which brings me to John Romans.

No, My Darling, I'm not in love with John. He is a very easy person to be with; he, too, is kind and gentle; he will be very good to me, and to Carol. I will be content, but not happy the way I would be with you. But I have to make a life for myself - I can't spend the rest of it just on the edge of yours - Neither of us would be happy that way, and I refuse to mess up your life any longer. I've made you happy, but I've also

---

Letter from Marie Hilley to Calvin Robertson.

The mysterious "John Romans" appeared in a letter Marie wrote to Calvin Robertson early in 1979. She was reluctant to give up the passionate love they had shared, she told Calvin, but if she could not have a life with him, marrying John would be her second choice. A few months before, she had tried the same tactics with another lover, Harold Dillard, warning that she would have to marry "John." She was persuasive, but in the end neither man was willing to give up his wife for Marie. Eventually, a fugitive from justice, she met a man in Florida, moved to New Hampshire, and married him. His name was John Homan. Were the names just a coincidence, or did Marie and John Homan meet a year before they claimed?

John Homan's mother, the former Ann Woll.

The adopted daughter of a wealthy Philadelphia-area family, she married John Greenleaf Whittier Homan, Jr. Her early death left their son "young" John with heavy responsibilities at the age of sixteen for his five younger brothers and sisters and contributed to the breakup of the family several years later.

John Homan's father.

John Greenleaf Whittier Homan, Jr., at his fifty-fourth birthday party with his children. Later that evening, he collapsed at home and died. His loss was the final blow to the unity of the Homans.

The Marlow Grocery, Marlow, New Hampshire.

The commercial and social center of Marlow, the little town where Robbi and John Homan lived, with the post office at left, the store run by the Hammanns at right. Carol Hammann didn't know Robbi Homan very well, but she befriended Robbi's twin sister, Teri Martin. Carol was shocked when she learned the truth about the sisters.

The home of John and Robbi Homan off Route 10, a few miles north of the Marlow Grocery.

People who knew John Homan were surprised when Teri Martin showed up so soon after her twin sister's death, and even more surprised when she decided to stay and moved into the little house with her bereaved brother-in-law.

Carol Hilley.

Marie Hilley had been a fugitive for three years when her daughter, Carol, was interviewed for a newspaper update just before Christmas 1982. Carol had recovered from the physical symptoms of the poisoning, but she still had not come to grips with the reality of what had happened. "She wanted me dead for some reason," Carol said of her mother. "I tried to figure it out. I tried to. But it's so hopeless." A little more than three weeks later, her mother was arrested in Vermont.

A formal portrait of Robbi Homan.

Robbi and John Homan had been living in Marlow about five months when they had this portrait made at a studio in Keene in 1981. She was forty-eight, fourteen years older than John, but her employment application gave her birth date as March 25, 1945, and she had told friends at work that she was in her late thirties. There were a few skeptics, but her looks, charisma, and energy made it believable to most who knew her.

John and Robbi Homan at their home in Marlow.

The photograph was taken not long before Robbi's "death."

Robbi L. Homan

Robbi L. Homan, 37, of Marlow died Wednesday in Dallas, Texas, after a long illness.

She was born in Buffalo, N.Y., March 25, 1945, daughter of Hugh and Cindi Grayson, and had lived in Marlow for two years.

Mrs. Homan was formerly employed by Central Screw Co. in Keene and was a member of Sacred Heart Church in Tyler, Texas.

Survivors include her husband, John Homan of Marlow, and two sisters, Teri Martin of Dallas and Jean Ann Trevor of White Plains, N.Y.

Mrs. Homan had requested that her body be donated to the Medical Research Institute in Texas and that no funeral be held. Contributions may be made in her memory to a favorite charity.

Obituary of Robbi Lindsay Homan.

The obituary of Robbi Homan, placed in the Keene Sentinel of November 13, 1982, by Teri Martin and John Homan. Suspicions about the obituary helped lead to the arrest of Teri Martin two months later.

Teri Martin at John Homan's house.

When Robbi alienated John Homan's brother Peter, he and his wife, Shelley, took back the furniture they had loaned John, who had to make do with lawn furniture. After Robbi's death, her twin sister, Teri, soon made herself comfortable at John's, reading and watching television in a lawn chair by the woodstove.

John Homan's portrait of Teri Martin.

Comfortable with his late wife's twin sister, John Homan made a record of their domestic life, photographing Teri in a series of activities around the house.

John Homan, at his house in Marlow, New Hampshire.

The photograph was taken by the woman who called herself Teri Martin. Teri had arrived in New Hampshire several weeks before, saying that John's wife, Robbi, had asked her to come and console him. She ended up moving in with John and finding work at Book Press in Brattleboro. Soon after the picture was taken, Teri was challenged by Trooper Barry Hunter and FBI agent David Steele as she came out of work one day. Her three years and two months as a fugitive were over.

Robert March, owner of Cheshire Employment Services, Keene, New Hampshire.

Many people in Keene, including some of Robbi Homan's best friends, were impressed by the blond good looks and pleasant personality of her twin sister, Teri Martin. Bob March, who had helped place Robbi in her job at Central Screw Company, found a job for Teri two years later. Teri didn't do as well on the typing test as Robbi had, but she displayed the same articulate style and self-confident manner as her sister.

Trooper Barry Hunter of the New Hampshire State Police.

Hunter had wanted to be a trooper since boyhood, when he followed the exploits of Connecticut's legendary State Police detective Major Sam Rome. Hunter was thirty-one, one of the youngest men appointed detective in the New Hampshire State Police, when he was called in on the case of the mysterious Teri Martin. Afterward he received a letter of commendation from the State Police commander. Hunter was left to wonder whether the rest of his young career would ever produce another case as challenging and strange.

Calhoun County Sheriff Roy Snead escorts Marie Hilley from plane at Atlanta airport.

The question of who would go to Vermont to pick up Marie Hilley and who would bring her back to Anniston from the airport, thus reaping a publicity bonanza, became the subject of minor skirmishing among Anniston officials. The sheriff, left out of the Vermont trip, pulled an end run at the Atlanta airport and raced off down a corridor with Mrs. Hilley, getting his picture in newspapers all over the country.

Eddie Motes/*Anniston Star*

Eddie Motes/*Anniston Star*

Marie Hilley, on the way home after three years as a fugitive in New Hampshire, hides her face from photographers at the Atlanta airport.

Assistant District Attorney Joseph Hubbard led the prosecution in the trial of Marie Hilley.

Joe Hubbard was still in his twenties when District Attorney Robert Field assigned him as prosecutor in the biggest case to reach the Calhoun County Circuit Court in years, the trial for murder and attempted murder of Audrey Marie Hilley. The more Hubbard learned about the accused in his pretrial investigation, the more he became convinced that he had come face to face with evil. In his closing statement to the jury, Hubbard gave Marie Hilley the name by which the media made her known to people all over the country: "They tell me that the black widow spider mates," Hubbard said, "and then kills its mate. . . . That's what she reminds me of."

Steve Gross/*Anniston Star*

Officer escorts Marie Hilley into Calhoun County Courthouse for the first day of her trial in May 1983.

Marie's return to Anniston had created a sensation in the city, and the courtroom was crowded with curious onlookers. Although her marriage to John Homan had changed her legal name, Annistonians, including court personnel from the judge on down, knew her as Marie Hilley and continued to refer to her by that name.

Steve Gross/*Anniston Star*

District Attorney Robert Field escorts Carol Hilley from the courthouse after the sentencing of her mother.

Following the trial, District Attorney Field talked about Carol's role in the prosecution of her mother: "There were people who told us we'd never get that little girl to testify. But that little girl has more courage than folks who have been around fifty or sixty years." After the sentencing, Carol met with her mother for a few minutes before she was taken away to prison. "She did what she had to do," Field said, "but she still loves her mother."

Jaguar XKE, and finally the ultimate piece of automotive machinery: a Ferrari that had been raced in the Bahamas, capable of 180 miles per hour without straining. He enjoyed a series of sailboats, including a thirty-two-foot ketch that he chose for its old-fashioned wooden hull and brightwork.

But John did not confine his spending to himself. He arranged for a family excursion to Mexico in a new van bought specially for the trip; rather than join the camaraderie, John stayed behind and worked on the house. Big John returned to the surprise gift from his son of a major renovation.

John gave more conventional presents, too. He bought Linda an expensive electric organ and replaced her rundown 1952 MG-TD with a newly restored 1947 MG-TC, dark maroon with a tan top and gleaming wire wheels. He was generous with friends and even acquaintances. The wife of an attorney who was doing some legal work for John wanted to open a dress shop; John put up the money to help her get started. A friend had some large medical bills and got behind on his other expenses; John loaned him enough to get even and continue repairs he was making on a boat. When Tim Doherty was ready to buy a new sailboat and couldn't sell his old one in time, John loaned him ten thousand dollars without collateral. Tim expected to pay interest on the loan, but John didn't even want to discuss it. It was almost as if John were embarrassed by the money and by the way it set him apart from those who knew about it.

As Judy had made herself available to Big John after his wife died, so Bob Sammartino now ingratiated himself with Judy Homan. Sammartino was a housebuilder who had been involved in minor business dealings with Big John. He told the Homans that he and their father had made a pact: if one of them died, the survivor would see that the friend's children were taken care of.

Soon after the funeral, Sammartino sat with Judy in the Homans' living room. "If you ever need any help, just let me know," he said to her. Greer overheard her stepmother's response: The antiques and Big John's art collection would provide for her security; there was one painting alone that family lore valued at a hundred thousand dollars. What about the children? he wondered. The older children were secure with money they had inherited from trust funds, Judy told him, and the younger children had trusts that would pay their expenses until they turned twenty-one.

Sammartino was persistent. The children should protect their capital by investing it. The Gold Coast area, with Fort Lauderdale at its center, was growing rapidly. Everybody was making money. Real estate, especially, was a gold mine. If they worked together, there was no limit to what they could do.

Judy called a family meeting and invited Sammartino to explain his proposal to John, Minnie, and Greer. He was a licensed contractor, Sammartino told them. There was land available out in Golden Springs, an exclusive section of Fort Lauderdale, and the demand for higher-priced houses was practically unlimited. They could buy a piece of land, put up a house for thirty thousand dollars, and sell it for three times that much. With the profits they could build two or three more houses and go on from there.

Minnie and Greer thought Sammartino's proposal made sense, but they were reluctant to make such a big decision by themselves. Greer found herself wishing their father were alive to tell them what to do. But he was gone, and now they looked to John for leadership. Judy and her friend saw that the older brother was the key to the deal; they concentrated their persuasion on John until he agreed to go along. Minnie and Greer quickly fell in line.

They would all join to form a corporation, Sammartino told them, christening it with a combination of their names. His contractor's license and expertise would make up Sammartino's contribution to the joint capital. The three Homans were to convert selected stocks and bonds into cash and take out a construction loan at the bank, using the remainder of their inheritances for collateral. "Then I'll take care of the rest," Sammartino assured them.

Events moved very fast. Within months of Big John Homan's death, Homart Enterprises had built a model house in Golden Springs. Before the end of 1972, the house was sold for ninety-five thousand dollars. Sammartino reinvested the money in two more houses. One, a model called "The Woodstock," was sold for eighty-seven thousand dollars; an airline pilot flying out of the Fort Lauderdale Airport bought the other for seventy-nine thousand dollars.

The investors were excited about their success. Sammartino talked of constructing warehouses out on State Road 84, using cheaper land closer to the airport and building furnished apartments above them for rental to pilots and stewardesses. He also wanted the corporation to buy a $104,000 house in a luxurious neighborhood out near the Homans'. He and his family would use it as a home; at the same time it would be a good investment for Homart. Greer and Minnie thought it sounded like a good idea, but Judy and John refused to go along, so Sammartino bought a house for himself in Plantation, another expensive section of Fort Lauderdale.

And then—suddenly, it seemed—things started going wrong. Homart was falling a little behind on its bills, John told Minnie and Greer. If they all put up a little more, it would only be temporary. They needed to finish a couple of more houses to get things back on track. John seemed confident that things would turn around by the end of the year.

Sammartino brought checks for the girls to sign; he didn't know yet exactly what the amounts would be; he'd fill those in later. They had been working hard for a year; it wouldn't make sense to give up just because of a little setback. Everything would straighten out soon.

But the demands for money continued and there was little progress on construction. The Homans disagreed about how to proceed. John argued that in business, sacrifices were necessary for success. Judy agreed with him. But Minnie and Greer were worried about the amounts of money they had been laying out. Sammartino had been cashing their checks, but there was little progress on construction to show for it. Meanwhile, the contractor was buying an expensive new house for himself and his family. Notices from impatient creditors were leaking through to the Homans. Everybody was getting edgy, but they agreed to hold on a little longer.

Weeks became months and nothing seemed to change, except that creditors seemed more numerous and strident. At last the Homans went to a lawyer. They had invested more than two hundred thousand dollars in Homart Enterprises. They might as well have mixed the money into the concrete for The Woodstock's foundation. There was nothing left. Homart was an empty shell. They eventually got a lien on Sammartino's new house and began preparing for a lawsuit.

Relations between John and Greer were already strained. He had joined with his stepmother in condemning Greer's relationship with a young man named Rick Parker. Sensing her stepmother's opposition, Greer had tried to move in secretly with Rick. A twenty-one-year-old ought to be able to live with a man she loved, Greer thought; Minnie had already done it. But Judy was incensed by

Greer's deception and offended by an arrangement she saw as morally unsuitable.

"Living in a man's home as his mistress is not a proper relationship," she told Greer. Judy saw herself as guarding the legacy of Big John Homan.

"Your father left us so much," Judy wrote to Greer, trying to make peace, "but from each he extracts a price. That price is responsibility, not just to a family name but to the members of that family. . . . Have you forgotten our discussions about the responsibility the Homans have to each other and the world? Have you forgotten that we (each of us Homans) feel so lucky, that we *owe the world* for our intelligence and wealth? . . . Immortality, according to your father and the Greeks, was achieved only so long as a man's name survived in time *with honor*.

"Do not dishonor our family's name," she pleaded. It had no effect on Greer. She moved in with Rick. When they were married in September, a month after John and Linda, none of the Homans attended.

Reinforcing the existing tensions, the Homart disaster became the fatal centrifugal explosion in the midst of Judy Homan's idealistic vision of noblesse oblige and altruistic family solidarity. Minnie and Greer blamed Judy for introducing Sammartino into the family group and held John responsible for driving them on in the face of Homart's imminent collapse. John blamed Minnie and Greer for their fainthearted reluctance to see the project through to the end; his anger, and Judy's as well, may have been fueled by guilt at having encouraged the younger girls to invest their money in what turned out to be a flop.

Since his mother's death just weeks after his sixteenth birthday, John had always experienced the family as a weight on his shoulders, one he had never felt quite adequate to carry. He had tried to support and to lead, but he had never been appreciated, and nothing had turned out right. Now there was only one path left to him; it was time to turn away. He cut off relations with his stepmother, refused to talk to Greer and Minnie, stopped coming around to see Peter and Todd and Terry. He would make his life in his marriage and with his friends.

John's few close friends were people who shared his interest in cars and machinery. Eventually he became closest with Manfred Krukow, who made a living restoring antique automobiles from the ground up. Of John Homan's family, and a lifetime of friends and acquaintances in Florida, Krukow and his wife, Kathy, were the only ones who eventually came to know Marie Hilley. Later, Krukow became an intriguing but mysterious character in the story, a possible key to one piece of the puzzle, but he refused to speak about what he knew.

John's wife, Linda, had been doing secretarial work at the insurance company when they met, but over the years she had been given more responsibility. Finally she was approaching executive status, and a gap was opening between her life and John's. Business had fallen off at Crown Marine in the middle 1970s. John blamed it on the nationwide economic recession. He shut down operations and got a job with a company that manufactured lighted makeup mirrors, doing simple machine work and assembling the frames, glass, and electrical wiring. Within a year he had quit in a dispute with the owner and started up Crown Marine again. While John's business limped along, Linda's career at the insurance company prospered.

No one ever saw John and Linda argue. John wasn't the type to make a show of his anger. Confrontation made him intensely uncomfortable. Anger, especially his own, caused him to grow quiet, withdraw ever deeper into himself, walk away. It seemed as if he and Linda had just drifted apart, like two children in a swift-flowing river, and then had arrived at their separation through a set of signals, without ever saying much, unable to break the growing habit of silence between them.

One evening late in 1979, Greer, now long and happily married to Rick Parker, made another of her periodic attempts to cross the chasm that had opened between her and John after the Homart fiasco. Greer was bighearted and generous, the most sentimental of the Homans, and the one most upset by the breakup. She called John at his shop and invited him to come over when he finished working; he was reluctant, standoffish, and balky as always, but she could hear as they talked that he was discovering a need to talk about what was bothering him. He and Linda had separated. He was on the phone with Greer more than two hours, and when they hung up, John still hadn't committed himself to coming to Greer's house. When he did turn up a few hours later, she was surprised and deeply pleased. She had no way of knowing it would be more than five years before the next time she even talked to him on the phone, longer than that before she ever saw him again.

He didn't want to talk about the family or their business problems, John warned Greer. But they could get it out in the open and put the tensions behind them, she thought. John was adamant; it was too painful, and it was too late. That was his way: Avoid reenacting the conflict.

It was his marriage that John was ready to talk about. He had tried everything to please Linda; she could not seem to decide what she wanted from him. She had ordered a fence that she wanted put up around her house. While she was away in Ohio visiting her family, John assembled the fence and put it up. When she returned, she walked through the new gate and into the house, never saying a word about the fence. John had asked her how she liked the new fence, he told Greer, and she said she hadn't noticed it.

They had agreed to go out for dinner the next night and talk about John's misgivings. When Linda came home from work at the insurance company, John recalled, he had been thinking about things all day. He was waiting with an announcement.

"I can't live like this anymore," he told Linda. "I'm moving out. I don't know how to make you happy anymore."

Linda looked at him for the first time since the beginning of the conversation, John told Greer, and spoke with what sounded like casual curiosity: "Does that mean you're not taking me out to dinner tonight?"

Part Four

Robbi Hannon Homan

12

A New Life

Even after she was unmasked in Vermont following three years on the run, the woman who began as Audrey Marie Hilley trailed unsolved mysteries in her wake.

From the start in Alabama, she had been pursued by FBI agents and the Anniston Police Department's Lieutenant Gary Carroll. At the end, she was captured by New Hampshire state trooper Barry Hunter and three other officers in front of Book Press in Brattleboro. But in between lay a trail of three years' living, jobs and friends and acquaintances, three years of pretense and deception.

Officially, no one was much interested in those three years. The New Englanders dispatched their captive back to Alabama and returned to more ordinary matters. In Alabama, the FBI did the same, and Lieutenant Carroll joined the Calhoun County district attorney's office in building a case for the prosecution. They had no need for more than the barest outline of Audrey Marie Hilley's activities during her years as a fugitive.

But among those who had known her, the arrest of Marie Hilley provoked intense curiosity: How had she escaped the pursuit of the FBI? Where had she gone from Anniston? How had she met and tempted John Homan?

When the detectives questioned her at the Brattleboro police station, Marie Hilley said she and John had met in Fort Lauderdale early in 1980. In a letter written to a Florida friend soon after the arrest, John placed their meeting in the latter part of February, a little more than three months after Audrey Marie Hilley fled Alabama.

These stories seemed consistent. At the time, the investigators accepted them at face value. But among those who had followed the case most intimately, the police and FBI agents and prosecutors who studied the facts as they emerged, bits of evidence gradually assembled themselves into a different version. The FBI had traced the fugitive Audrey Marie Hilley as far as southeastern Georgia, where they placed her a week or so after she disappeared from Anniston. She had been almost penniless, without transportation, inexperienced at flight. How had she managed to disappear so completely, erasing the trail of her scent like a deer swimming across a stream? In Savannah she had met up with a man. Apparently she had gone off with him. And it was there that the trail ended. There was no further identification of the man, no way of tracking him down.

But what they learned from Carol and Mike Hilley allowed the investigators to approach the mystery of Marie's escape from another direction. Eighteen months earlier, during the summer of 1978, Marie and her daughter had visited Mike and his wife, Teri, in Pompano Beach, Florida. Marie had given up her job and sold her house in Anniston; she had left with the idea of settling permanently in Florida.

As it turned out, she had stayed in Florida only three months. Mike and Teri had been distressed by her behavior. Around the house she had been sullen and withdrawn. She was absent for long periods. She found a job at the business office of the Little General Quick-Mart convenience stores. Many afternoons she came home from work, took a quick dinner, and went out again, not to return until late at night. Some nights she didn't come home after work at all. But she never talked about where she was going or whom she was seeing. Mike was concerned about her but was reluctant to pry. She seemed to be enjoying an active social life, and if she wanted to keep it to herself, that was her right.

Marie had returned to Anniston late in the summer of 1978, unhappy with what she saw as Carol's laziness, disappointed with Florida. Looking for a way to satisfy her constant hunger for money, still seeking escape from a life that was growing to seem more and more a trap, she turned up the heat on her lover, Harold Dillard, the wealthy Anniston businessman. When it looked as if he would not leave his wife, she wrote him a letter. If she could not have the "wild, passionate love" she had shared with Harold, she would settle for the steadiness of her new lover, the man she was about to go away with. "I love his kindness, gentleness, and I respond to his love for me," she told Dillard. She dangled the prospect of Dillard's loss, the new man's victory. His name was John.

But Dillard would not succumb. Now she turned the full force of her sexual manipulation on Calvin Robertson. But he would not leave his wife, either, and Marie was forced once again to invoke a rival in a last-ditch effort to tease, to provoke, to panic her lover into making a commitment. If she could not have the passion and excitement of a life with him, Marie told Calvin, she would settle for a peaceful, stable existence with the "kind and gentle" man who wanted to marry her. His name was John Romans.

The ploy did not work, Marie's desperation grew, and greed and madness led to her attack on Carol. Less than a year later, the traces of her flight led east and south from Anniston, through Georgia, heading in the general direction of the Florida border before dwindling away in Savannah. It was a long way from Fort Lauderdale, more than four hundred miles, and certainly there was no solid evidence. But the investigators were left wondering whether John Homan and Marie Hilley might have made contact eighteen months or more before they later claimed they had, during that summer of 1978 when Marie was living just six miles north of John's Fort Lauderdale home. What else could explain John Homan's extraordinary, unreasoning loyalty? Could it rest on some pact, some shared intrigue going back before the acknowledged beginning of their relationship in late February 1980 in Fort Lauderdale? In that case, what appeared to be a three-year masquerade by Marie, capped by a final deception of extraordinary boldness, aided by an amazing gullibility on John's part, was in fact something quite different, some form of collaboration.

Or was John's devotion simply the love of a depressed, unattractive man who desperately needed some human connection, who found an appealing, sympathetic listener to match his loneliness and isolation, who later felt that only one person had given him affection and a degree of warmth in a hostile world? If so, his must have been a need of exceptional force to give birth to a devotion, or a desperation, that could survive what had turned out to be three years of uninterrupted duplicity. This is the version of the facts, astonishing as John's gullibility came to seem, that Marie and John have steadfastly promoted. And this is the version that, except for a few skeptics, has achieved general acceptance.

Certainly Robbi Hannon's need had seemed to John no less powerful than his own. They had met in a bar, John confided to Roger Williams, his friend in the machine shop at Findings, Inc., in Keene, New Hampshire.

"I wouldn't tell anybody this," John had said, "but my wife was a hooker when I met her."

As soon as Robbi had found that he was a sympathetic listener, John went on, she had confessed that her heart wasn't in it, but she needed to earn some money. In fact, tonight was her first attempt, and he was her first customer. She had left everything behind in Texas; she had not been able to find a job in Florida. And now it had come to this. When he told the story to his friend in New Hampshire, John seemed especially to relish the idea that he had saved her from a life of sin.

This story, or at least the idea that she had hovered on the fringes of prostitution, was reinforced by things Robbi told Claudia Brooks later in New Hampshire. Robbi talked lightly of a prostitute she had known in Florida, though she claimed they had met by the pool at Robbi's apartment complex. The woman had told her it was an easy way to make some money, Robbi told Claudia. Robbi tried to portray herself as an innocent, even slightly shocked, observer of the whore's life, but she was too comfortable with the idea to be quite so distant as that. She knew the terminology of "johns" and "tricks," and when a New Hampshire friend moving to Fort Lauderdale asked for advice, Robbi was able to warn her in detail about the streets and hangouts of whores and pimps. She and Claudia could set up an "escort service," Robbi said, have some fun, and earn extra spending money. She was probably joking, Claudia thought at the time, but later, when she knew more about her friend's life before they had met, she wondered.

Marie's account of her life leading up to their meeting in the Fort Lauderdale bar, as John recounted it to investigators, lent powerful reinforcement to the view of her as a woman in desperate straits. Marie's story made it possible for John, though he was miserable and defeated by life, though his habitual lack of confidence had been deepened by his recent series of failures, to believe she might need him as much as he needed her.

She had been married in Texas at the age of sixteen to a man named Joseph Hannon, she told John. Hannon had been a lawyer, a wealthy man. They had lived well and happily with their two children, Joey and Carol, until their lives were shattered in an instant. Robbi had been driving the children on an errand when a drunk driver ran into the family car. Joey and Carol had been killed. Robbi had been racked by guilt over the children's deaths. During the next few years she had suffered repeated nervous breakdowns and bouts of depression. She had tried more than once to commit suicide. Two years after the auto accident, weakened by his own grief and his wife's collapse, Joseph Hannon had suffered a heart attack and died.

She had fled from the guilt, Robbi told John. She had cut her ties to Texas, left her husband's wealth behind with the memories. She was trying to begin again, to make a new life that would give her the strength to face the past. Eventually she would go back to reclaim her inheritance and face the memories, but for now she needed time to heal. She needed time to forget.

It is easy to imagine Robbi telling John of the horrible power of money and what it had done to her, pleading as they became closer that he help her heal the wounds by treating the past as a lost time, wrapping it in silence until she was strong enough to go back and face it anew. Marie Hilley would have felt enough truth in this need to make the pleading seem genuine.

There would have been a bright, romantic side to Robbi's plea as well. A New Hampshire friend of Robbi's said later that she had an extraordinary knack for saying what her listener most wanted to hear; in Anniston, they said the same thing about Marie Hilley. It was an important element in her ingratiating charm, her almost telepathic ability to sense another person's deepest need, longing, illusion, and instantly take the shape that would let her slip smoothly into the empty space of their life, like a key into a lock. As Robbi became intimate with John, she would have spoken to him of the fresh start they could make, of the warmth and mutual support they could offer each other, of the safe, self-contained place they could create for themselves, just the two of them, in the midst of a world that was often harsh, at best indifferent.

And John would have responded not just with enthusiasm but also with relief. This woman was offering him the opportunity to erase his own sad past, to put the losses and the failures behind him, to wipe them from the record and begin anew. He would be reborn. She would not demand more of him than he could give.

Throughout his life, others had always wished John Homan to be something he was not: His father had wanted a son who could become a professional man, his mother had needed someone to make her whole and stop her self-destruction, his brothers and sisters had needed a substitute parent, Linda had demanded an ambitious man to match her own drive. None of them had known him as he truly was, none had been satisfied to accept from him what he was capable of giving. But Robbi Hannon was coming to know John Homan as the man he was now, and the things she needed from him—acceptance, support, affection—were things he could give her. For the first time in his life, he was being accepted for himself.

The sadness of Robbi's tale did not end with the bitter circumstances of her life in Texas. John's brother Peter seems to have been the first outsider to learn of the threat that hung over Robbi's life.

Peter's hopes of attending M.I.T. had collapsed; he had been accepted conditionally, but lost his chance for admission, as he understood it, when the deposit check sent in to hold his place in the freshman class bounced. He had ended up at Nathaniel Hawthorne, a small college in New Hampshire, but dropped out after a couple of years. When he turned twenty-one in 1975, Peter used part of his inheritance to buy a farm in a nearby New Hampshire town. After fixing up the rambling, run-down farmhouse and selling the property at a profit, Peter bought 110 acres of rocky ground on a hilltop in the town of Marlow. With his new wife, Shelley, he set about clearing pasture and building a house and barn.

Peter had been the most energetic of the six Homans in trying to maintain good relations with his brothers and sisters. Old enough to retain vivid memories of the family's happy times, too young to have been embroiled in the bitter fallout of the Homart fiasco, he regularly phoned Greer and Minnie, encouraged Terry, invited Todd to come live in New Hampshire, and made occasional attempts to break through John's morose silence. Seven years younger than John, Peter had now grown to feel himself more settled, the more mature of the two.

In the spring of 1980, Peter decided to take a brief vacation in Florida; when his housing arrangements fell through at the last minute, Peter persuaded John to put him up at his home in Fort Lauderdale. It was there that Peter met his brother's new girlfriend.

Her name was Lindsay Robbi Hannon, but she preferred to be called by her middle name.

John and Robbi told Peter that they had met at a cocktail party in Palm Beach only a few months before, but Peter saw that their relationship had developed rapidly. They seemed comfortable sharing John's attractive cottage apartment in the elegant Isle of Venice neighborhood. Robbi was working for an accounting firm in West Palm Beach and John had revived Crown Marine, but it appeared that the remnant of John's inheritance was subsidizing the expensive apartment.

Peter thought Robbi strange from the start. She seemed jumpy and eccentric, darting into the bathroom to take a Polaroid picture of Peter bathing in the tub, insisting that he open all his 35mm film canisters to prove that he was not carrying "hard drugs." Within the first few hours of meeting Peter, she had recited for him the tragic, intimate story of her life in Texas.

The next day Robbi revealed to Peter that she was suffering from a brain tumor. It was temporarily under control, but she expected it would eventually kill her. She was determined not to be intimidated by the menace, she said bravely. Now that she had met John, she would make the best of whatever time was left to her. John listened in on these recitations with benign detachment; nothing seemed to cut through the pride and pleasure he felt in this new relationship.

The romance seemed incongruous to Peter. Robbi was an attractive, stylish woman, he thought. It was hard to see why she should be interested in his brother. But John appeared more contented than he had in years, and Robbi, whatever her reasons, seemed happy, too. Peter set aside his misgivings.

Both brothers were appalled by what had happened to Fort Lauderdale; the slow-paced country town and the open spaces of their youth had vanished behind the gleaming façade of new construction driven by outside money. John and Robbi were thinking of moving, making "a fresh start" in a new place, breaking free of the past. Peter encouraged them to consider New Hampshire. The brothers made plans for a summer reunion in Marlow.

Except for Manfred Krukow, whose auto restoration shop was near Crown Marine, none of John's friends or family met his new lover. He kept his plans a secret from the rest of the family. Greer only learned that her brother had left town when she ran into Tim

Doherty in the fall. John had called Tim late in the summer to say he had met a new woman and was moving with her to New Hampshire. He was closing Crown Marine, planning to start over. John and Tim had met for drinks; it had been a long time since they had gotten together. They got a little high reminiscing about high-school days. Later in the evening John talked earnestly about Robbi's brain tumor, the constant medical testing, the danger. He was obviously infatuated with her, determined to help her overcome the illness.

13

A Home in New Hampshire

August 1980 to June 1981

Leaving behind the last tendrils of the sprawl around Keene, New Hampshire, Route 10 heads north toward the little town of Marlow. It is a two-lane country road that seems comfortable with the hilly landscape, one of those unobtrusive thoroughfares so common in New Hampshire, laid over old Indian paths and their Colonial successors. North of Gilsum the Ashuelot River plays a good-natured game of tag with the road, and most of the route seems untouched by the past several decades. There are more gravel pits than roadside restaurants here, in spite of the tourism that flows through from New York and Boston, headed north for Canada. The gas stations are clapboard buildings devoid of oil company neon and banners. There is an occasional house, then a cluster in Gilsum, almost all clapboard. The colored paints that newcomers have discovered and called "Colonial," flat-looking greens and yellows and blues, have made no impression here. The houses are all white.

Robbi and John arrived in New Hampshire late in the summer, riding in John's little red Ford pickup with the white camper cap over the bed, the back crowded with John's tools and metalworking machines. Peter and Shelley were living in a tent on their land, completing the barn for their animals, and just starting on the house, so John and Robbi got a room at the Christmas Trees Inn.

There is little sign of Marlow before the inn, framed by its two tall pine trees. A few hundred yards beyond, the road widens out on one side into a concrete apron with two gas pumps that mark the living core of the town. At one end of a shinglefront building is the tiny post office; at the other is the Marlow Grocery. Besides the services they offer, the post office and the store provide almost the only occasion for regular contact among the five hundred or so inhabitants scattered along the narrow country highways and dirt roads radiating out from Route 10. Even that contact is usually indirect. The post office has a small bulletin board, and in the grocery, Carol Hammann and her clerks form a living message board, chatting amiably with customers, assembling the news from bits of conversation and passing it along.

Robbi and John spent a relaxed few weeks. She helped out at the inn, making beds and setting tables when she was needed, asking for no compensation. John occasionally drove the two miles up a winding, bumpy, dirt road to Peter and Shelley's hilltop farm, where he pitched in on the construction of their house, feeding the chickens, hauling hay for the horse and cow, herding the sheep.

John and Robbi took several trips around New England, exploring the Maine coast with the idea that John might start a new boat business there, but by October they had confirmed their decision to stay in New Hampshire. They could see that Marlow was the kind of New England town where people mind their own business. It was a quiet little spot, just right for getting away from the pressure of change, the crowding and the cold glossiness, of a place like Fort Lauderdale. It would be a good place to start over.

North of the inn along Route 10, past the grocery and post office, houses begin to appear with corrugated metal fronts, or asphalt siding that mimics alternating bricks of gray and pink. A yellowing refrigerator stands outside one house, and, farther along, a pile of gravel is covered by black plastic with tires spread over it like parasites on a carcass.

After a few miles, a homemade sign announces the Stone Pond Cottages, which are actually across the road from the pond. Behind a small parking lot, the owners, Ed and Lillian Bryce, lived in a low house, and fanned out behind them like ducklings with their mother are five one-room cottages. The arrangement is reminiscent of the "tourist cabins" that gave way to the motel thirty years ago in most places, but several of these uninsulated one-room houses are occupied as homes during the warmer months. The temporary tenants are usually newcomers looking for long-term housing, or transient families hoping to find work enough to stay in the area through the rest of the year. By late fall, when Robbi and John went looking for a lace to live, the cottages were empty, the toy dump truck and the ricycles were gone from the yard, and a chill wind clanged the rope gainst the flagpole in front of the Bryces' house.

Robbi and John arranged to rent a little house tucked under the pine trees at one end of the row of cabins. Although it was the same color and only slightly larger than the other buildings behind the Bryces', this house was insulated and intended for year-round occupancy. A small, square structure divided into a combined kitchen and dining area, living room, and bedroom, it looked cozy, if slightly cramped, for a couple living together.

Once they were settled in Marlow, Robbi and John set out to find work in Keene, twenty minutes south. New Hampshire is predominantly a state of small towns like Marlow, the little places with simple white churches and plain Colonial houses that have passed into American mythology as symbols for a peaceful life of rectitude and order. Keene has a lot in common with New Hampshire's few larger places, a dozen or so small cities with populations between ten thousand and twenty-five thousand, many of them former mill towns, that have never come to symbolize anything. These places are big enough to be cities but too small to be urban. They seem undistinguished to outsiders, but they exert a strong hold on those who grow up in them, and they offer refuge to those who would escape the little towns nearby. These people form a web of lifelong acquaintance that gives such a place its identity and much of its attractiveness. Their connections cross all kinds of boundaries—the factory worker knows the president of the company, the priest knows the minister, the detective knows the thieves. They grow accustomed to each other's weaknesses and ambitions, often beginning in grammar school, so that bits of local news may please or amuse or satisfy them but will rarely shock or surprise them. This lends such communities a feeling of stability and confers significance on individual lives.

Like many of these places, Keene looks as if it has been treated roughly by the past few decades. Many local economies in New Hampshire were devastated by the exodus of textile mills to the South in search of cheap labor during the 1950s. In areas closer to Boston, the 1970s saw a revival as electronics and computer-related businesses moved to New Hampshire for the low taxes and country living, but Keene felt only the edge of the flow. Off in the southwestern corner of the state, behind a few small mountains and too far from Boston for commuting, the city was forced to depend on a mixture of modest factories, small and medium-sized service businesses, and a state college. A newer sprawl of fast-food restaurants and auto dealers has kept to an impromptu jumble of highway segments and former farm roads around the edges, leaving the core of the city to make do with what is left of the past.

The center of town is a mixture of late-nineteenth-century brick buildings and plain postwar panel-fronts, with an occasional bland imitation of modern architecture that looks like a concrete wall with window holes in it.

At one end of the downtown area there is a white Congregational church of the kind associated with New England towns, but facing it instead of a green is a long, narrow loop formed by two parallel streets that are joined by cross streets a half mile apart. This arrangement gives the business district the appearance of a small rural speedway modeled on the ellipse at Indianapolis. A crumbling movie marquee, peeling paint on some of the fronts, and an occasional empty store looking like a missing tooth in a tired old woman's smile testify to the brave but precarious nature of the attempt to keep the downtown vital. Robbi must have noticed how much Keene resembled Anniston, Alabama, with its decaying, century-old brick foundries and the heartless commercial strip choking off the struggling downtown businesses.

Though she and John were not married, Robbi used Homan as her surname when she registered with Cheshire Employment Services in Keene. It would be the first of three visits she would make to the agency, almost exactly a year apart. Robert March, who would later take over the business, noticed the attractive, brown-haired woman as she sat down in the small office for an interview with his boss. Her well-modulated voice made her southern accent sound especially mellifluous in contrast with the flat a's and dropped r's of New Hampshire speech. She was unusual for the Keene area, a well-spoken woman, confident and self-possessed, with extremely good shorthand and typing. In an area with a lot of large corporate offices, she would have made a well-paid executive secretary, but there wasn't much call for that in a New Hampshire city of under twenty-two thousand people.

The agency referred her to Central Screw Corporation, a company in Keene that manufactured screws and other fasteners, where a temporary secretarial position was open. It was there that Audrey

Marie Hilley wrote the next chapter in the autobiography of Robbi Hannon. She borrowed a typewriter and created a résumé.

"I was born March 25, 1945, in Buffalo, New York," she wrote, taking twelve years off her age. "My family moved to Texas when I was less than one year old." She had graduated from Sacred Heart Catholic School in Tyler, Texas, in May 1963, and gone to work the next month for Builders Supply Company, a firm that manufactured "prehung wood windows and doors." She had been the company's only secretary, serving the president, vice president, sales manager, and shop foremen. She had worked there until August 1978.

"During the 1975 business recession," she explained, "the owner of the company died, and after trying to keep the business going, the family closed it in 1978. After the business closed, I typed various papers for college students, using different styles, such as Turabian, etc."

No one associated with Audrey Marie Hilley can say what might have made her adopt Buffalo, New York, as the place of her alter ego's birth, unless she imagined it as especially remote and obscure, and thus difficult to trace, but the source of some of these details is not hard to guess at. The birth date, March 25, was that of Lucille Meads Frazier, Marie's mother, in 1912. Marie had a wide experience in business, including typing of all kinds. The Keene area, heavily settled by French-speaking emigrants from Canada in the late-nineteenth and early-twentieth centuries, had a large Roman Catholic population; she could expect many of her co-workers to be Catholic, and one of the three Catholic congregations in Anniston is named Sacred Heart Church. And if she had to write another application, it would be easy to remember the year of widespread business failure and the death of "the owner": That was the year when the big foundry in Anniston had closed, putting Frank Hilley temporarily on leave the week he took sick and died. It had been May 1975.

The Texas associations, which had already appeared in Robbi's stories about her life with Joseph Hannon, are more difficult to trace, but there are clues. Louie Frazier, the twin brother of Marie's father, Huey, had gone West soon after Marie's parents were married in 1931. Marie's children had lost track of most of their grandparents' generation, but Louie was said to have lived in Tyler, Texas, at one time, and there was occasional thirdhand news of relatives in the area.

On her mother's side, Marie had remained in contact until around

1970 with Robbie McCullars, her cousin and the first girl playmate of her youth in Blue Mountain, the mill village outside Anniston. Robbie, who was four years older than Marie, had married a soldier named Daigle and left home when Marie was thirteen. Between other assignments, the Daigles had made their home in Texas. During the ten days while she was free before she jumped bail, Marie had called Robbie's father, who still lived in Anniston, trying to find out her cousin's current address and phone number. Mr. McCullars, aware of Marie's arrest and the charges against her, had refused to provide the information.

Later events suggest that Marie was considering Texas as a hiding place and thinking of Robbie as someone she might persuade that she was innocent and beg for help. At the time Marie was trying to locate her, Robbie Daigle was again living in Texas, and Marie returned to the search later, but she never found her cousin. That did not keep her from exploiting the memory of her childhood playmate. Robbie Daigle learned later that her cousin had taken not only her name (dropping the "e") but also a number of details from her life, weaving them into the protective fabric of her false autobiography. The military background of Robbie Daigle's husband, the fact of an incurable illness that she feared would end her life—Robbie Daigle suffered from diabetes and kidney disease—even time she had spent in Germany, these all turned up eventually in Robbi Hannon Homan's life story. Though Robbie Daigle continued to profess love for her cousin and never stopped feeling a loyalty to the girl she had picked huckleberries with as a child near the Blue Mountain Cemetery, she felt that she had been violated. It was as if a burglar had broken into her life and stolen bits of her identity to sell on the street.

Robbi's work at Central Screw quickly won her permanent status as a customer service clerk, taking orders from major customers and expediting the processing and shipping of large batches of fasteners. Production control supervisors from giant manufacturers—among Central Screw's regular customers were General Motors, Ford, and Chrysler—called to discuss their requirements and place orders. Robbi had to understand their needs and work out commitments to deliver the product—it was amazing how many kinds of sheet-metal screws and other fasteners there were, more than a hundred—and time was important. This required balancing the customers' needs and Central Screw's capacity, so Robbi had to consult with the stock people, who knew what raw material was on hand, and negotiate with the foremen in the shop, who could predict how long it would take to produce an order. Sometimes she had to relay an ultimatum from a buyer—if the order couldn't be delivered by such and such a date, the customer would have to go somewhere else for the product—and the people in the shop felt she was putting pressure on them. Central Screw was saddled with monthly quotas by its parent company, Microdot, and the pressure to produce was constant.

In her complicated intermediary's role between the people in the plant and the customers, Robbi's southern accent helped, and so did the style that went with it. She was cheerful and warm, and she seemed to have friends all over the country among the production control representatives she dealt with regularly. Often she had a joke for them, and it was surprising how vulgar she could be; to a New Englander it didn't seem to conform with the stereotype of well-bred gentility that attaches to the kind of accent that flavored Robbi's speech.

Within a few weeks, John Homan had also registered with Cheshire Employment; he was quickly placed as a machinist at Findings, Inc., a company that made small parts—settings, clasps, catches, and the like—out of precious metals, for use in jewelry.

He had come to Findings without credentials, underselling himself—"I'm not a tool-and-die maker," he said, "but I've fooled around with machines some"—but the next day he brought in a model locomotive with tiny parts he had machined from raw stock, and he was hired. By the end of John's first day at work the supervisor, Joe Massicotte, knew he was good, and he turned out to be one of the best machinists who ever worked at Findings. Joe could show him a design for a tiny clasp to hold the ends of a necklace together, and John would come back in a while with a simple, efficient plan for producing a jig that would clamp and bend a piece of gold stock to form the clasp. John was steady, reliable, always at his bench on time, working without much fuss. He was comfortable there, at ease in a place where the complexity of sophisticated machines could be mastered through solitary ingenuity.

John and Robbi settled into a comfortable domestic routine. They rode together down to Keene each morning. The Ford pickup was their only vehicle, and Robbi did not have a driver's license. The difference in their working days often left one of them killing time at Friendly's Restaurant or Bob White's magazine shop near the bus station. Robbi was an avid reader of romantic novels, and John often bought her a paperback or some novelty item.

At work, Robbi made friends quickly, blending easily into several small groups that ate lunch or took coffee breaks together. She never became a fixture in any one group, but it wasn't long before everybody in the company, from the front office to the shop in back, had taken notice of the newcomer. She was special. Part of it was her appearance. Most of the women were casual about their clothes; there wasn't much contact with the public, and many had homes and families to divert their salaries and their energy from appearances, but Robbi always seemed to take particular care with her looks. Her clothes—blouses and skirts with a sweater or a jacket, often high heels—were carefully chosen and often looked expensive. Her hair and makeup seemed precisely arranged and maintained. You wouldn't say she was beautiful, but she had a fresh, open face and a well-shaped body. It was clear from an occasional comment or a look exchanged between two men as she left the room that many of the men at Central Screw felt she was exceptionally attractive.

But even that didn't do justice to Robbi. There was a vitality to her, an energy, that people responded to. She talked easily with the women, often confiding dramatic stories of her life, but there was something exceptional in her way with men. She was always joking and bantering with them, and she seemed innocent of the reserve that most of the women, both married and single, retained in their relations with male coworkers. Once she had settled in, she especially enjoyed teasing Wayne Mitten, the general manager; he was a devout Christian and most people considered him prudish, but Robbi delighted in telling him a vulgar joke or swearing cheerfully in the middle of a conversation, watching carefully to see the combination of embarrassment and amusement that flushed his face. Some of the men thought there was an element of sexual invitation in her manner, but for the most part it seemed more like the unawed familiarity of a tomboyish younger sister.

At times she had an intensity that seemed almost electric. Her eyes were her most striking feature. Their color and appearance seemed to change with her moods. When she was angry she was implacable, and there was a spark of fury in her eyes that could be almost frightening. When she was cheerful, joking, or radiating the warm regard that captivated both men and women, her eyes glistened as if they were overflowing with her vitality.

Her new friends were intrigued by the story of her life. Many of them had been born and raised within a few miles of where they now lived, graduated from high school in Keene, and gone immediately to work in a mill or factory. Robbi's story seemed to have taken place in another world—it sounded like a romantic novel or a TV soap opera, somebody once remarked to Sandra Peace after a lunch break with Robbi.

Robbi had lived only the first few years of her life with her parents, she told them. When a younger sister was born, her parents sent Robbi to live with her grandparents in Tyler, Texas; they had not felt they could love and support both children. In contrast the grandparents were wealthy, with a large house and a full-time black servant. Her grandfather was one of the most prominent citizens of Tyler and a major benefactor of the private school Robbi attended. When the principal punished Robbi too severely for some infraction, her grandfather demanded an apology. Failing to receive satisfaction, he withdrew Robbi from the school and transferred her, along with his financial support, to the Sacred Heart School, where she later graduated from high school. He had given so generously that a wing of the school was named after him.

Her grandparents had been loving but strict. She recalled being locked in her room for most of a day as punishment for skipping school, and at other times she was made to sit for an hour or more in a darkened room. She recounted one instance of being forced to stand with her hands on a mantel piece and receive several blows with a hickory switch.

Marriage had liberated Robbi from her grandparents immediately after high school. She had been supremely happy with her husband, Joseph Hannon, comfortable in luxurious surroundings, able to provide the best of everything for their two children. Following the auto accident that had killed her husband and children—here the story differed from what she had told John, and the details varied slightly from one listener to another, though rarely in separate tellings to the same listener—she had been placed in a mental institution. She had been unable to cope with the sudden loss of her entire family; even now, she still could not bear to drive a car.

After her release from the mental hospital, Robbi had tried to return to normal life, but the burdens on her had been overwhelming. Before the accident, she had nursed her mother for several years while she struggled against cancer. She had died, and now Robbi's mother-in-law had also developed cancer. In spite of her continued depression and mental confusion, Robbi had felt obliged to care for her late husband's mother. She had broken under the strain. Her sister's husband, now Robbi's next-of-kin, had committed her once again to the mental hospital. She had finally fled the institution for Florida, where she had met John Homan.

Robbi never said much about John's role in restoring her to stability, but she seemed happy with him. She talked often of his small presents and attentions—he would draw her bath and rub her back, she told the women at Central Screw, obviously proud of his devotion but trying to sound as if she took it for granted. Every day he brought her a little stuffed animal or a knickknack for the house.

Although the contrast seemed extreme, Robbi never compared her present existence to her life in Texas. She had been forced to leave behind her husband's wealth, including the house with its circular driveway, a Mercedes-Benz, the proceeds of his insurance, and large holdings in real estate. Even her personal possessions—antiques and furniture, closets full of new clothes—were tied up because of her status as a mental patient. She spoke vaguely of legal proceedings that would eventually release the inheritance.

Robbi and John lived modestly. Besides the battered pickup, their only major possessions were two used snowmobiles they had bought their first winter in Marlow, and a small boat on a trailer. The rented house at Stone Pond was tiny, with the single bedroom, small living room, combined kitchen and dining area, and an outdoor porch that was crowded with the tools and machinery John had hauled up from Florida. Much of the time they were without a telephone, and they owned no furniture. Peter and Shelley had taken Robbi to the friend's barn where their household goods were in storage and invited her to choose a few items to furnish the house.

During their first winter in New Hampshire, Robbi talked about finding a larger place to live. She and John were house-hunting, she reported to friends at work. John told Roger Williams at Findings that they were going to look at a house in Harrisville, a small, pretty community nearby with a handsome restored mill complex surrounding a pond and a green in the center of town. Roger had grown up in Harrisville, and as John described the house he recognized it as the home of childhood friends. It was a beautiful Victorian house on a rolling eighteen-acre farm. With real-estate prices going up the way they were, Roger supposed, it must be pretty expensive. Yes, John confided, it was selling for $110,000; Robbie was due to inherit a lot of money from her husband's estate.

They had looked through the house, Robbi told her coworkers, proudly displaying Polaroid pictures they had taken of the rooms. They would remodel the interior, create a library with comfortable chairs for reading, use the barn for raising horses and dogs. Robbi said the price was ninety thousand dollars. They would have the money when her husband's estate was cleared up.

Robbi had given her name at work as Lindsay R. Homan, and John had listed her as his wife and claimed her as a dependent, but they were not husband and wife. In May 1981 they flew to Fort Lauderdale to be married. Robbi claimed she had a friend there whom she wanted to be her maid of honor, though it was John who had the connections in Fort Lauderdale. Manfred Krukow, who had operated his auto restoration business near John's shop, acted as best man. Krukow and his wife, Kathy, were the only guests present. None of John's family or friends were aware of the wedding or even knew he was in town.

The Krukows flanked John and Robbi for a wedding picture. John was wearing a tie for the first time in years; Robbi appeared untypically fat and frumpy in a shapeless flower-print dress. She looked thirty pounds heavier than she had when she met John just over a year earlier.

John was having trouble with a knee he had injured several years before. He had seen several doctors in Keene without improvement. They decided that Robbi would return to work in New Hampshire while John stayed behind to seek help from a Fort Lauderdale orthopedist who had successfully treated the knee in the past.

Back home in Marlow, unable to drive, Robbi became heavily dependent on Peter and Shelley. Except for some rides she was able to arrange with a Marlow woman who worked in Keene, Robbi asked Peter and Shelley to drive her to work and help her with errands. Shelley took her grocery shopping, and a number of times Peter drove her the fifteen miles to work in Keene and went back to pick her up at night. Exhausted from their farm chores and the construction work on their house, Peter and Shelley felt they had little time to spare; but Peter had worked hard to restore relations with his brother, and he wanted to do what he could for his sister-in-law.

The rides offered uninterrupted periods for conversation, and Peter saw them as a chance to learn more about his sister-in-law, but Robbi was less willing to talk about herself than she had been. She had other things on her mind. Soon she was taking every opportunity to criticize John.

He had married her for the money, Robbi said. Now that the inheritance had been delayed, it was becoming obvious that he had never loved her for herself. Peter was shocked. He had thought they were happy together, and even if she were upset with John, Peter was the last person she should confide in.

At dinner with Peter and Shelley just before John returned, Robbi repeated her complaints. They were disturbed by her bitterness and puzzled about what had caused the change in her sentiments. She seemed unable or unwilling to explain herself, but she talked of divorcing John when he returned. Aware of Robbi's painful past, Peter and Shelley made allowances for her. They held back as she recited her grievances, repressing the temptation to challenge her or stand up forcefully for John. Perhaps when John got back he and Robbi would work things out, Peter thought.

The day after his return from Florida, John appeared suddenly at the top of the hill. He had trusted Peter and Shelley to help Robbi, John cried angrily, and he had returned to learn that she had been forced to find her own rides to work. She had been stranded and they had refused to help out, complaining about all the work they had to do, how little time they had.

Peter was almost speechless. What had happened? What could she have told him? After John had stalked out and driven off down the hill, Peter slowly recovered his composure. With it came a wave of anger. The hell with family relations. He was going down to confront her.

At John's house, Peter tried to remain calm, but it was impossible. John was distant and unreachable. His accusation against Peter had been exactly what Robbi had told him, and Peter was unable to overcome her adamant insistence that they had neglected her. Peter never even brought up her complaints about John.

"You're a liar!" Peter shouted at Robbi finally. He stalked out, never realizing the truth that lay behind his accusation.

Peter Homan was the first person in this phase of Marie Hilley's life to cut through her deception, and though he had barely touched the edge of the truth, he had discovered something essential in her. He had seen that she was capable of the most fundamental lie, one that utterly reversed reality. Peter Homan had not discovered this because he was especially perceptive but because Marie had gone too far. She had lied about something whose truth was too close at hand, and she had not reckoned on John's stubborn sense of grievance. Self-pitying as ever, he had felt forced to confront Peter directly with this latest injury. Peter in his turn, stricken by the injury this outsider was doing to the brotherly unity he had worked so hard to restore, had been driven to confront her. And John had made his choice, breaking the tie of blood in favor of this woman who had let him feel wanted for the first time in his life. His decision foreshadowed a still more costly choice he would be forced to make in the future.

Peter Homan was merely the latest on the list of Marie Hilley's victims. She had begun in childhood, creating a series of fantasies to improve upon her life, to make it more comfortable, glamorous, luxurious. Her fantasies had led her to murder, and they had brought her to a little town in New Hampshire. The price of her illusions was unceasing danger. If she was not constantly vigilant, refreshing her lies, keeping them vivid and consistent, outsiders might see some corner of the truth, might break through and expose her. Peter's curiosity, the time they had spent together, the generosity he was showing to his brother's wife, his need to strengthen the family bond had brought him too close to the reality. He had aroused the destroyer's urge in Marie Hilley. Peter was fortunate that she could not attack him as she had Frank and Carol Hilley.

The method she used had its intended effect. Deeply wounded, Peter and Shelley demanded the return of the borrowed furniture and cut off relations completely.

The break made little difference in the lives of John and Robbi. They had been seeing Peter and Shelley infrequently, and the little social life they had established during their early months in New Hampshire had mostly dwindled away. Their occasional snowmobile outings with Roger Williams and his wife, Terrie, had ceased; Terrie, a tough-minded, outspoken woman who worked as a security supervisor at a bank in Keene, had grown to dislike Robbi intensely. At first she had been entertained by Robbi's self-dramatizing stories—the huge inheritance, the deaths—but she had slowly

come to find them implausible, and she had been offended by
Robbi's insistence on being the center of attention. Terrie had
refused to join them anymore, Roger had felt awkward as part of a
threesome, and the snowmobiles sat rusting in John and Robbi's
yard. They showed little interest in carrying on by themselves, or
taking up other activities.

They were satisfied putting in their time at work, spending their
free hours quietly around the house. They had few friends in
Marlow—they had gotten to know the people who ran the inn and
their landlords at Stone Pond Cottages but never saw either couple
socially. Marlow offered a minimum number of opportunities for
acquaintance: buying stamps from the postmaster, picking up a few
things from the Hammanns at the Marlow Grocery, taking the truck
to a mechanic a few miles up Route 10. Since John did the driving, he
was the one who ran the errands and came to know these people; if
Robbi was with him she usually waited outside in the truck.

Robbi made friends through work but rarely saw them outside.
The only people from Central Screw who ever saw her house in
Marlow were two friends who drove her home when she was
stricken with a migraine headache at work. Even within the office,
her close relationships seemed to decompose over time. Some ended
in neglect, some in bitterness. All came to a breaking point, and it
was never possible to tell, even afterward, who had been responsible.
Had it been Marie, instinctively sensing a danger in closeness and
unconsciously pulling away? Or had it been Robbi, seeing a friend
move too close to some truth she knew would expose her, consciously fomenting conflict?

Robbi's announcement that she was going to Texas came as a relief
to several of the co-workers she had antagonized. She had talked
often about her late husband's estate. Now the preliminary work had
been done, she told friends, and the time had come for her to go
home and settle things. The terms of the inheritance required that she
take up residence in Texas for several months. Her husband's brother
was executor of the will, and he was nervous about her mental state.
Apparently they were going to make her prove that she was
competent to receive the inheritance.

It was August, nine months since she had come to work, and
unlike some of her co-workers, the managers at Central Screw were
sorry to see her leave. She had become a trusted, valuable employee.

"If you ever come back to town and want a job, sing out," Ron

Oja, the executive in charge of personnel, said on her last day. She thanked him, but she wasn't sure how long it would take, or even if she would be back at all.

Apparently that was the one real element in the scenario of her departure. It was only a few months since Robbi and John had been married, but they were already estranged. When she left, John said later, he wasn't sure whether she would come back. And Robbi would claim that several months later, when she decided to return, John discouraged her.

14

Time in Texas

Summer 1981

Judy Cox had gone to Texas to save her life. In her midthirties she had become like a woman of eighty, exhausted, almost crippled by heart disease. In the summer of 1981, as soon as the two boys had finished the year in junior high school, her husband, Gary, quit his job as a security guard and they left their home in Kentucky for Houston. If you were going to risk your life in complicated heart surgery, you might as well get the best. She would be treated by the world-famous surgeon, Dr. Denton Cooley.

The operation went well. Afterward the Coxes took an apartment in Clear Lake City, twenty miles from downtown Houston, while Judy continued postoperative therapy. As she was taking her exercise walk through the grounds of the apartment complex one day, a woman she recognized from previous casual encounters started a conversation. She seemed interested in Judy's medical problems and her recovery. The woman was from New Hampshire, and she was no stranger to life-threatening medical difficulties. She was suffering from a rare blood disease and would be leaving shortly to go to Dallas for treatment by a specialist. In the meantime, she was in Houston working on some legal business. Her name was Robbi Homan.

Judy invited Robbi over and soon they were spending much of their free time together. Robbi was an easy person to have around, sitting comfortably at the kitchen table drinking coffee and talking with Gary and the children, Michael and Kevin. Judy got the feeling that her new friend craved affection and could soak up any attention the Coxes would give her.

When the weather was hot or rainy, Judy got her exercise walking in a mall, and Robbi often joined her. Robbi was always buying something, and she was generous with the Coxes. Picking out a pantsuit for herself, she insisted on buying another for Judy; she brought home a shirt for Gary and a digital Snoopy watch for Michael's birthday. She responded to Judy's protestations by saying that she would be a wealthy woman when the estate was settled. Several times she insisted on buying takeout food for the whole family. She cooked dinner when Judy was tired, and volunteered to baby-sit for the children so that Judy and Gary could get out for the evening.

Robbi had grown up in Tyler, Texas, she told the Coxes, but she had moved to New Hampshire with her husband. They had been the happiest family in the world until Joe and their two children, Carol and Joey, were killed in an auto accident; her eyes grew moist as she talked about them. It had been several years, with long periods in a mental hospital, before she had recovered from the loss.

A few years ago, she had been remarried to a man named John Homan, a boatbuilder, and with him she had slowly reconstructed a semblance of her former happiness. A year or two before, her sister and brother-in-law had died. They had been wealthy, and she was the primary heir. Robbi had returned to Texas to settle their estate. She was working with her lawyer's assistant, a woman named Erin Patterson, to make an inventory of the estate and prepare for the disbursement. Each day she took the bus in front of the apartment complex, headed for the lawyer's office.

Several weeks after they had met, Robbi told the Coxes that she was planning to move. She had been suffering from migraine headaches brought on by her blood condition, and the boys in the apartment above her played the drums, which made her condition worse. She didn't know how long she would be staying in the area, and it was a nuisance looking for a new place. The Coxes talked about it with the children. Robbi had become like a member of the family. She had become especially close to Michael, who thought of her as a new aunt. They invited her to move in with them, taking the spare bedroom.

In long chats around the dinner table after the plates had been cleared away, Robbi talked about the future, what she would do with her life once the estate had been settled. She and John had been thinking of leaving New Hampshire, and Gary Cox had no firm plans for the future. The Homans could move to Kentucky, and Robbi could finance a boat-building business for John and Gary. Robbi herself would like to have a dress shop; maybe when she was recovered, Judy could help her. Robbi made long calls to John from the phone in the bedroom and came back to report that he was enthusiastic about the idea.

Robbi was about to return home, and she was disappointed at the prospect of missing Michael's fourteenth birthday in October. She ordered a special cake with basketball players in colored icing and held an advance birthday party. It was arranged that she would come back with John for Thanksgiving in Houston with the Coxes; afterward they would join the Coxes on their return to Kentucky and scout the prospects for the boat-building business. Robbi talked of taking Michael to New Hampshire with her for the two months. Michael was enthusiastic and his mother was tempted to let him enjoy the adventure, but in the end she decided it was too long for him to be separated from his parents.

A few days before Robbi was due to leave, Judy had just turned off the television and was heading for bed when she heard Robbi whimpering in her sleep. It was unsettling, she thought, hearing those childlike sounds from an adult. After Robbi left for the lawyer's office the next morning, something drew Judy toward Robbi's room; she told herself she was going in to straighten up. The room was neat, as always, the cosmetics lined up on the dresser, paperbacks standing in a row on the table, clothes spaced out evenly in the closet to avoid creasing. As she turned to leave, a piece of paper on the floor of the closet caught Judy's eye. It was a stub from a payroll check, dated the week before. Imprinted on the stub were the name and address of a Houston firm called Gulf Coast Investors. The check had been made out in the name of Robbi Homan.

This new piece of information clashed so directly with what she knew about Robbi that Judy Cox was unable to accept its full implication until she had discussed it with Gary that night: Robbi was working. She had not told them the truth. They tried to imagine some explanation that would make the check consistent with what Robbi had said. Could it be an advance from the estate? It looked like a payroll check. Maybe her pride had kept her from admitting that she was working.

The Coxes talked for hours before reaching a conclusion: Robbi had been a wonderful, generous friend, and she would be gone in a few days; there was no point in challenging her. Perhaps there was some explanation, and she would only feel that they did not trust her. They had nothing to lose by maintaining the friendship.

The entire family took Robbi to the airport. When she turned away to walk through the boarding gate, Judy Cox saw tears shining in her eyes.

A few weeks later, the phone bill came. There was $150 worth of calls to New Hampshire. They had assumed Robbi was reversing the charges.

Judy Cox had saved the check stub she found on the floor of Robbi's closet. She called the number on the stub and asked about Robbi Homan. "Who is this calling?" the woman asked. Judy told her what she knew about Robbi, including her work on the estate with Erin Patterson at the law office. The woman was amazed. Her own name was Erin Patterson, but this was no law office. It was an investment firm and she was the supervisor of the typing pool. Robbi had been working for them since September; she was an exceptional secretary, a perfectionist.

The Coxes were shaken by the news. They had accepted Robbi like a member of the family. If she had lied about her work and the estate, did that mean that everything was a lie, the favors and the presents, the baby-sitting for Kevin and Michael, the birthday cake with the basketball players on it? And what of their plans for the boat-building business? They would have to confront Robbi at Thanksgiving, get it all straightened out before going ahead with any further plans. If she showed up at Thanksgiving.

The Coxes waited to hear from Robbi. A few days before Thanksgiving, Judy got the New Hampshire number off the phone bill and dialed it. The voice that answered was unmistakable: It was Robbi.

"Robbi, this is Judy Cox," she said. There was no reply. "Calling from Houston," Judy added. There was a banging sound, as if the phone had been dropped, then rustling, and a pause.

"Hello, hello," someone said. "Who is this?"

"Robbi? Robbi? Is that you?"

"This is her sister, Teri," the voice said. "Who is this?"

Judy described her connection with Robbi in Houston. She was calling to see about Thanksgiving.

"Oh, yes," Teri said, "she's talked about you a lot. She said you were very nice to her when she was down there; she missed you." The voice was remarkably similar to Robbi's, Judy thought.

"I don't think she is going to make it for Thanksgiving," the woman said ruefully. "Excuse me just a second," she interrupted herself. The muffled sound of conversation came through the phone. Teri seemed to be talking to Robbi. She came back on the line. Robbi wanted to go out of the house, she said.

She resumed the conversation: "Robbi's been back in the hospital," she said. "It was another one of her breakdowns. You probably know about her mental problems?" Judy acknowledged that Robbi had told them about her collapse after the death of her husband and children.

"She just got out. She's come to stay with us for a while, try to get back on her feet." She interrupted herself again for a side conversation.

Judy mentioned their plans to go to Kentucky with Robbi.

"Yes," Teri responded, "she told me about that. She wanted to open up a business with you in Kentucky. It doesn't look like she's going to be able to do any of those things, now. Uh, look," she said suddenly, "I've got to go. She's going outside and it's pouring rain out there. I'll have her call you when she's feeling better. Okay?"

Judy mumbled something and the phone went dead. She realized she hadn't even mentioned the phone bill. Probably wouldn't have made any difference, she thought. She was fairly sure it had been Robbi she was talking to all along, though she couldn't even begin to think why Robbi could be doing such a thing. When she and Gary talked about it, they agreed that it would certainly be the last they would ever hear of Robbi Homan.

They were wrong. They would read about her in the newspaper a little more than a year later.

15

A Twin Sister

Somehow, Robbi persuaded John to accept her back in New Hampshire. How she talked him into it, even her reasons for returning, are unknown. It was not long, however, before the restlessness and unpredictability that had attacked her the previous year in Keene, that had pursued her to Houston and intruded in her friendship with the Coxes, appeared once again. And this time, her fantasies of another, better self, her desire, dating back to childhood, to remake her life and rewrite her own story, took a new and bizarre form.

Her efforts to get reestablished started out in ordinary enough fashion. She went once again to Cheshire Employment Services. It was almost a year to the day since she had first applied there. This time Bob March, who was now owner of the agency, interviewed her himself. She scored seventy-three words per minute on a typing test, with two errors, fast enough for the most demanding employer. He placed her the same day at Cheshire National Bank, as secretary to the president.

By the second week, Robbi was restless. She called Ron Oja at Central Screw and reminded him of what he had said about taking her back.

"I heard you were in town," Oja told her. "We didn't think we'd see you again so soon." The work on the estate hadn't taken as long as she had expected, Robbi said; the lawyer had assigned his secretary to help her. Now the employment agency had placed her at the bank, but there wasn't enough to do.

"Compared to the action you have out there, the banking business is dead," she said. "It's putting me to sleep."

She returned to Central Screw with increased responsibility and higher pay. Oja needed somebody to work closely with automotive customers, handle their special requests and complaints, and keep them off his back. Robbi was perfect for the role, with her smooth southern style and her sense of when to switch from ingratiating charm to a sharp, "Tough shit."

Oja soon became even more dependent on her than before. The pressure of the quotas seemed to build every month, forcing Oja and the other executives to work longer and longer hours. The turnover among key employees was increasing; even the general manager of the factory had crumbled under the pressure and left a few months before. Oja, a big man with a round, friendly face and a relaxed style, seemed increasingly tense. Robbi's ability to handle the needs of the customers kept them from bringing their problems to him, which left him more time for his other responsibilities, overseeing production and customer relations.

Robbi moved smoothly back into the work at Central Screw, as if she had never been away, but her friendships were another matter. It was almost as if she were starting over. Marcy Stabler, one of her first friends there, had left to stay home with her children, and Michele Wilcox had taken another job. Robbi made no effort to stay in contact. Others had grown disenchanted with Robbi and had been relieved to see her go; when she returned they knew better than to succumb to her initial charm. Shirley Leonard, an unmarried middle-aged woman who had lived all her life in Keene, had been put off by Robbi's taste for gossip. She was constantly bringing Shirley stories about which employees were sleeping together, who was cheating on his wife, who got drunk and ended up vomiting outside the Valley Green. It was as if she chose just those items that would most offend the straitlaced older woman.

Jerry Scadova had been close friends with Robbi during her first year, enjoying her stories and gossip, teasing back and forth with her. He called her "Tex" or "Tumbleweed," for her accent, and she called him "Polack." Marcy Stabler had been picking up Robbi's mail for her; Robbi complained to Jerry that Marcy had been opening her letters, and later that Marcy had made a play for John. Scadova thought it was so unlike Marcy that he began to wonder about the truth of other stories Robbi was telling him. Finally, after she had ignored his warning and gone searching through his office files, trying to find figures she needed for customers, Scadova had told her off.

Later he had given her some onion bulbs as a peace offering; she had phoned him from Texas and brought him souvenir gifts, including a piece of cow dung encased in clear plastic and labeled as "True Texas Bullshit." But on her return she was distant again, and Scadova found her impossible to get along with. She often seemed angry at someone in the office, and she was fond of saying, "I don't get mad, I get even."

The pattern of alienation from old friends raises the question again: Was Marie consciously repelling those who were closest to her? This might help to explain the trip to Texas, which removed her from the scrutiny of people like Jerry Scadova and Shirley Leonard. They had heard the story of Robbi's life more than once; each additional telling increased the chances of somebody catching her in an inconsistency.

But if that was her reason for leaving, why did she return to Central Screw? Was it simply the work, boring and confining at the bank, challenging and lively back at Central Screw? Did she think she could control her friendships and contacts to protect herself from exposure?

Or was it merely Marie Hilley's personality forcing its way to the surface? The pattern had been similar in Anniston: warm initial attractions, the emergence of several fond friendships, followed by growing alienation from the closest friends and occasional outright conflict with her coworkers. Marie had changed jobs, houses, and banks, staying one jump ahead of the truth. Perhaps this inconstancy had always been instinctual with her.

Her outgoing personality made it easy for Robbi to find new friends. One was the wife of Wayne Mitten, the general manager at Central Screw. The Mittens were evangelical Christians, and Wayne did his best to watch his language and control his temper at the office, but Robbi saw his impish side and played to it. Fran Mitten had chatted with Robbi when she dropped by Central Screw to pick up Wayne, so she was not surprised when Robbi called to ask about the baby shower for Wayne's former secretary. Fran had been planning the shower, but it had fallen through. Some of the women had bought a gift, and Robbi had been chosen to deliver it. Fran volunteered to drive Robbi out to visit the new mother. The house was far out in the country. On the way they got lost.

Robbi filled the long ride with anecdotes about her life. She came from a wealthy background in Texas. After a nun at Robbi's school had harmed a child with punishment her grandfather thought too severe, he had founded a new school where Robbi and her friends could receive a more enlightened education. But she had been touched by tragedy, the loss of her entire family in an auto accident, and Fran Mitten sensed a great emptiness in Robbi that she was sure religion could fill. She felt her intuition had been confirmed when Robbi brought her recitation to a stunning climax:

"I'm going to die, you know," Robbi said. She gauged the impact of her words on Fran, who sat silent, staring at the road in front of her. Robbi went on to explain that she was suffering from a blood disease. There was no cure. Tears filled Fran Mitten's eyes, but Robbi was calm.

"But I'm not afraid to die," Robbi concluded. "I know I'll be all right." She was brave, Fran thought, but she seemed so isolated and vulnerable. She had no faith, nothing true and enduring to believe in. Fran felt a powerful sympathy for her.

"Robbi," Fran responded, "I'm a Christian and we believe in prayer. I'd like to pray for you."

Robbi's reaction was muted, but she seemed grateful for Fran's compassion. She looked surprised a moment later when Fran spoke again.

"I'd like to do it now, Robbi. Would you mind if we stopped here for a minute?" Robbi looked puzzled, but she didn't protest as Fran pulled the car onto the grass at the side of the narrow country road, into the shadow of some old pine trees, and turned off the ignition.

Robbi bowed her head as Fran closed her eyes and clasped her hands tightly before her face, her arms resting lightly on the steering wheel. She invoked the name of Jesus Christ, praying that Robbi would find the faith and strength to face her trials. After a few moments she straightened up and opened her eyes. They glistened with tears. When she had composed herself for a moment, Fran reached for the ignition key. They drove off to continue their search for the new mother.

Another of Robbi's new friends was Claudia Brooks. Robbi had trained Claudia to take over her job before leaving for Texas. When she heard Robbi was coming back, Claudia's first thought was that she would be fired to make room for her return. But Robbi's new job made that unnecessary, and they became friends. Claudia was aware that other people who had been at Central Screw longer than she had thought Robbi strange or difficult, but to Claudia she had been a patient teacher and a good-natured friend. Many of the other women had been friends for years, always taking their coffee breaks or going shopping at lunchtime in the same pairs or threesomes. It was difficult for a new person to break into these cliques. Now Claudia and Robbi formed a stable unit of their own.

Claudia had never known anybody with Robbi's kind of elegance. Robbi told of picking out the house in Tyler, Texas, with its long driveway encircling the fountain at the front, and redecorating it herself, with antiques and fine fabrics. The inheritance—there had been further delays in Houston, so the money would not be released for a few months more—included a ski lodge in Aspen and a beachfront home in Carmel, California, which Robbi had visited on the way back from Houston. Robbi's twin sister enjoyed the skiing, so they were going to keep the Colorado house, but she had instructed the lawyer to sell the one in Carmel when the estate was settled. It was a beautiful modern house and the scenery was dramatic, but it was too far away, and she didn't like the idea that an earthquake could occur at any time.

There was a glamour to Robbi that Claudia had never seen up close before. She was like a character on *Dallas* or some soap opera. She even had a mischievous, sexy side, with her talk about hookers, her idea of starting an escort service, and the knowing way she flirted and swore with the men at work. She worked only because she wanted to, not because she needed to. "I'm not a person to sit at home," Robbi said once. It reminded Claudia of a woman she had seen on television who won the Massachusetts lottery and said she was going right back to work on Monday.

But Claudia had not known at first of the terrible threat that hung over Robbi. She knew that her friend suffered from migraine headaches. The previous year, before Claudia came to Central Screw, Robbi had gone home early on several occasions. More than once she had disappeared from her desk for long periods and somebody had found her in the lounge off the ladies' room, holding her head and weeping from the pain. Periodically she had missed a day of work or left early to see a doctor; Claudia had heard her arranging appointments.

At first, Claudia thought this was another migraine attack. Robbi was sitting at her desk, just in front of Claudia's. She seemed distracted. She began fumbling through the desk drawers, looking for something. There was a frantic quality to her movements.

"Robbi," her friend asked, "what are you doing?"

"I'm looking for my lunch," she replied.

"What do you mean?" Claudia asked. It was the middle of the afternoon.

"I want to eat lunch," Robbi said.

"We already ate lunch," Claudia told her. She was disturbed by the confused look on her friend's face. "We sat out back and ate lunch at the table."

She stared at Claudia. "We ate lunch? I don't remember . . ." Her voice trailed away.

When Robbi had recovered her composure, she told Claudia about the blood disease. She had been to doctors all over, several in Keene, then to Dartmouth Medical School in Hanover, even to a specialist in Boston, but there was no known cure. The disease was progressive; they didn't know how long it would take, but usually it was fatal. That was what caused her headaches, and occasionally she lost her memory or blacked out.

A month or two later, she told Claudia that she had awakened that morning to find a frightening gap in her memory.

"I can't remember leaving work yesterday," she said, "and I can't remember anything that happened after that." She looked worried. She fixed Claudia with an intense, pleading look.

"If anything ever happens," Robbi asked, "if I start acting strange, just call John at Findings and ask him to come and get me."

Claudia was disturbed at her friend's vulnerability, but the spells were infrequent, and Claudia comforted herself with the uncertainty of the disease's progress. That was how Robbi seemed to deal with it. It could be months, Robbi had said, but it could be many years, too.

Claudia had known of Robbi's twin sister almost since they had met, but it was news to other friends and co-workers. Soon after her return from Texas, Robbi had dropped by to see Marcy Stabler at her home in Keene. Robbi had not made any effort to stay in contact, so Marcy was surprised to hear from her. She seemed to have something she wanted to talk about. After chatting lightly about her trip to Texas and the inheritance, Robbi suddenly turned serious.

"I haven't been feeling well. It's gotten worse," she said. "I've been having blackouts. Sometimes I can't remember anything." Marcy expressed sympathy, and Robbi took it as encouragement to go on.

"I just lose whole areas out of my memory. I blanked out a whole piece of my past, my family. I blanked out my twin sister." She began to weep. "How do you forget your own sister?" she asked, sobbing.

Marcy murmured reassurance, but she was concerned for Robbi. She had talked in the past about a sister who had been favored over Robbi by their parents. Robbi had always resented it. But this new story about the twin was strange and improbable. Could it be the same sister? Robbi talked about Teri with conviction. Was it possible to forget a piece of your life like that, for a sister to drop out of memory like a puzzle piece falling off a table? Robbi seemed confused. Marcy wondered if Robbi herself knew what was true and what wasn't. Robbi promised to call her soon for lunch, but Marcy never heard from her again.

In the spring—at least it is dated May 7, 1982—Marie Hilley wrote the first of two known letters from Robbi to Teri. It was found in pieces a year later in Robbi's papers at Stone Pond. There had been four pages of blue-lined white paper, covered with Robbi's neat handwriting, looking like the composition of a high-school girl. The letter had been torn up, as if to be thrown away, but the pages had been aligned so perfectly and the tears made with such neatness and regularity that the twenty-four strips were easily reassembled into their original form. It was as if the person who tore the letter up had intended that it be easily put back together.

Would Robbi have left the letter for John to find and then have dramatically shredded it later for the purpose of some further deception? Or would she have left the torn pieces lying where John would be sure to find them? Could she have counted on his reassembling the strips and reading the letter? Or was it intended for some other eyes—and some other purpose entirely?

If the letter was intended for John, as seems most likely, it appears to have had a purpose beyond introducing or reinforcing the existence of Robbi's twin sister, Teri. Members of Marie Hilley's family remember finding a letter she had written to an invented lover, in order to communicate some grievance to her husband, Frank, and to make him jealous. If the marriage of Robbi and John Homan was founded on a conspiracy of amnesia about their lives before they met, it also depended on John Homan's long-cultivated determination to suppress, ignore, or run away from personal conflict. If there is anything genuine in Marie's feelings for John, Robbi's letter to her sister reads like an indirect attempt to tell him of her hurt and bewilderment. They have arranged for her to visit Teri in late summer; Robbi is not planning to go back to New Hampshire afterward.

Dear Teri—

Thanks for the call today. You always make me feel better about everything, even if I don't agree. You are very wrong about one thing—John isn't in love with me any more, and I don't know how I really feel about him. We have both changed too much. To answer your question—no, I won't ever go back to him. I will offer him his freedom. It doesn't matter either way to me, as I won't ever marry again. Twice is enough. However, I feel that some day he will want to remarry, and I don't want the hassle of a divorce later on, so now is preferable to me.

Teri, John hurt me very deeply when I was in Houston. The estate was such a mess, and I needed him then more than I've ever needed anyone, but his love is New Hampshire, and he didn't want to come out with me. Then, when I was coming back, he asked me not to. He doesn't want marriage. I haven't figured out why he married me. I guess he had his reasons. Whatever they were, it didn't work. You will be wondering why I came back when he didn't want me. At the time, I was very confused, very lonely, and I still loved him, or thought I did. If I hadn't come back, I wouldn't have lost the feeling I had for him, so, you see, it was necessary. I've left too many things unfinished, and I know from experience that it can go on hurting forever. I didn't want that again.

I hope that he and I will remain friends, but also from experience, I know that we will lose track of each other. I guess this sounds strange to you, since you know that once I cared very much for him, but John isn't the same person I fell in love with, just as I'm not the same, and everything changes—I had really hoped this would work, but I've looked back too long at things that might have been. That has been part of my problem.

He is very aloof now, and I've felt these past weeks that he couldn't wait for me to be gone. I tried to tell him once that he need not feel responsible for me, to live his life, but that only annoyed him, as most everything I do annoys him. We have very little physical contact, and this has made me feel that, in some way, I'm very unattractive. That, too, I don't need any more. I had too many years of that. So much for my love life, or rather, my lack of a love life. Let's get on with other things.

I'm really looking forward to our summer together. If everything goes well, and we don't drive each other insane, then perhaps we can arrange something permanent, until one of us goes on to something else.

Teri, there are two things I don't want to talk about—one is John. I've told you all that I can tell you about that. I don't know what went wrong. I just know that it's over for good, and I'd rather put it out of my mind. The other is Texas. I will go back when I'm ready. The money isn't important to me. All it has done is cause me hurt and a lot of trouble trying to straighten it out. I know it's there if I want it. I also know I can live without it. So if you will stay away from these two subjects, you and I will have little or no trouble.

One last thing about my marriage. I hope I haven't made it sound like it is all John's fault. It isn't—it is just as much mine, so don't have any bad feelings toward him. It was just something that happened. It doesn't hurt any more.

Teri, I called Julie this morning. She was coming out to the house to look at the furniture. I really don't care what you do with it—my days of wanting nice things are over—permanently, I'm afraid. If you want to have it re-done, go ahead, but personally, I think it's silly. I don't want to live there, and you said you didn't, and it will cost quite a lot to move it, especially since I don't want it. If you really want it, I'll try to live with it, and I'll do it gracefully! Does Emma have anything left there? She was very upset when she had to move. Before you leave, will you go through the closet in our bedroom. Bring all the clothes that are nice, and call Mandy to pick up the rest. I don't know what is there, but I'm sure there are things we want to keep. You decide.

I'm so pleased that you are doing so well. I hope the cast comes off soon. It must be awful—so long on your leg.

Take care—see you soon.

Love you,
Rob

Beyond its main purposes—giving life to the character of Teri and showing Robbi's pain to her husband—the letter seems calculated to achieve other ends as well. The warning about discussing Texas seems aimed at John: Robbi must have feared that too much scrutiny of her plans would turn up inconsistencies or require impossible flights of invention on her part. Her indifference to wealth puts off further explanation of her failure to produce the inheritance she has been talking about for more than a year.

In addition, there are things in the letter that ring hollow—the explanation that she came back in spite of John's resistance in order to exhaust her remaining affection and prevent later pain, for example. And the details about the house and furniture, including all the women mentioned incidentally—the letter purports to be written from the twins' childhood home in Dallas to Teri in Houston—are like scenery and minor characters added by the playwright as background for the main action.

But she was building her deception on a foundation that mixed invention with reality, and there are tantalizing nuggets of true feelings here. It was very much in character for John Homan to use aloofness for a shield against anger, as the letter shows him doing; this had consistently been his way with Peter and the rest of his family. And how like the real John it was to express annoyance when his wife told him not to feel responsible for her; of course I'm responsible, he would have said, feeling as he spoke like the sixteen-year-old John Homan whose mother has just died, obligated to care for the younger children yet incapable of meeting the responsibility, needing his mother as much as his brother and sisters.

And Marie Hilley saying, "My days of wanting nice things are over"—this woman who has destroyed her life and those closest to her in pursuit of "nice things" is only describing the life that flight, and perhaps fatigue, have forced her to live. Or has she genuinely changed?

And finally, the long discussion of furniture and clothes, of Julie and Emma and Mandy—a childhood friend of Marie Hilley thinks Mandy may have been the name of a black housemaid in Blue Mountain—and the cast on Teri's leg, all this sounds obsessive, beyond what would have been helpful in establishing credibility. It raises the question that often hovers over Marie Hilley: Were there times when she believed her own inventions, when she became so wrapped up in the story, like a theatergoer suspending disbelief, that she thought the action was real? Was there a form of madness blurring the line between reality and invention for Marie Hilley?

As she rewrote the story of her life, did Marie Hilley recall her childhood, taking threads from her grandmother Susie's deathbed story of twins who died as babies, some overheard whisper about her own stillborn sister, a scrap of family legend about her paternal grandfather Huey's yearning for his twin brother out West? Was she continuing the process, begun in childhood, of becoming immersed in a better version of herself, a Rachel Knight or a Rose White? She had reinvented herself; now she was getting ready to invent a second, better self.

In all this boiling brew of storytelling and invention, there was a mixture of calculation and madness, but even after Audrey Marie Hilley was exposed, it was never possible to tell where one left off and the other began. After her arrest, Marie told Barry Hunter, the detective from the New Hampshire State Police who had pursued her, that she had created the character of Teri Martin, her twin sister, early in 1982. She had done it in anticipation that she might use this other identity at sometime in the future. She was thinking of leaving John Homan, she said, and thought the character of Teri Martin might come in handy.

Marie gave no details about the charade, but John Homan talked with Hunter about his wife's mental state during the two years they had lived in New Hampshire. Soon after they arrived, he said, Robbi had suffered a series of strange attacks. There were periods when she acted "like a one-year-old child," John told the detective. John believed her problems were a result of her upbringing. She had told him about a series of traumatic experiences inflicted on her as a child by her parents. Doctors in Keene and at the Dartmouth Medical School had been no help, John said, and he described their trip to the public mental hospital in Boston, where Robbi had pleaded with him not to make her stay and they had driven back home.

John amplified this account in conversations with Roger Williams, a friend of his at Findings. He confided to Roger that Robbi had spells from time to time in which she talked in the voice of a little girl and acted like a child. She had an obsession with a story about a room with a large fireplace, John said; she had eventually told him that her grandfather had tied her to the mantelpiece over a fireplace and molested her. It was a much darker version of the tale she had told friends about being disciplined with a switch while holding on to the mantelpiece. At other times, John told Roger, the grandfather had tied her in a chair and abused her.

Robbi's attacks might last a few hours or most of the night, periods of trancelike sluggishness alternating with spells of manic babbling and crying. John stood by, he said, comforting his wife and preventing her from harming herself. On certain days John would come to work looking exhausted. "Robbi had another one of her spells last night," he would explain to Roger.

The question of calculation and madness has several layers. The spells of craziness were not essential to the creation of Robbi's twin sister, Teri, unless they were an excuse for numerous visits to the doctor, which later helped to establish the disease that led to Robbi's departure and death. And surely there would have been simpler ways to justify a series of visits to doctors. Robbi could have died without being crazy.

If the spells are not the plausible result of calculation, then perhaps Marie-as-Robbi actually did break under the strain from time to time. When at last she was halted by the police outside Book Press, she gave no hint of resistance. "I'm relieved to stop running," she told Detective Hunter later at the Brattleboro police station. "I'm so tired of it all. It's been so confusing."

Certainly the effort of trying to keep her story consistent while developing the new themes of fatal disease and the twin sister must have caused immense strain. Perhaps there were times when the tension of coping with a phone call from Judy Cox, or an occasional intuition of skepticism from Shirley Leonard or Jerry Scadova or Marcy Stabler, shook Marie's resolve. Perhaps there was madness within calculation, periods when Marie took refuge from her fantasy life as Robbi by loosening her own desperate grip on reality.

There remains the possibility that John was not a dupe but an accomplice in all this. In that case, a question still remains: Was he helping Robbi or Marie? That is, did he know anything of Robbi's life before their acknowledged February 1980 meeting in Fort Lauderdale, as the suspicions about Marie's affair with "John Romans" and her disappearance from Savannah might suggest? Or was he helping Robbi, for some reason she had invented to manipulate him into cooperating, prepare for her disappearance and possible return as Teri? If that were the case, what reason could she have had? Might she have hoped to put another layer of identity between herself and the suspicion that would follow the eventual collapse of her fiction? In spite of the John Romans evidence, which does seem too extraordinary to have been a coincidence, the argument for John as a dupe rather than a conspirator is too strong to be ignored.

For Robbi's spells seem purposeless as a fake. As John and Marie described them to the police, they were too different from the migraines to reinforce the credibility of the "blood disease" that led to the appearance of Teri Martin; they were clearly psychotic episodes. John confirmed the spells independently, describing them to Roger Williams, but neither he nor Robbi seems ever to have mentioned them to anyone else before her arrest; if they were meant to deceive anyone besides John, Robbi would have spread the story.

If John had been her accomplice, he would have gone further than confiding in Roger Williams.

Brushed with madness or not, Robbi pleased her supervisors with the way she handled the increased responsibilities of her job. She was often the first one in the office, Wayne Mitten noticed, sitting at her desk in the big room when he came in at seven-thirty. Often they chatted for a while over coffee before getting to work. She enjoyed talking about her inheritance and how she would use it, about her twin sister and the trips they would take together.

Claudia Brooks noticed that Robbi was spending a lot of time on the phone with Teri. Employees were allowed to use the WATS lines for personal calls during lunch hour, as long as they kept track of the charges and reimbursed the company. Robbi often got permission to use one of the executive offices that lined one side of the large, open office space, shutting herself in for most of the lunch break. She would report that she had talked with the lawyer in Houston about the estate, and increasingly she entertained Claudia with news of Teri. Teri's husband was a military man and she had lived all over the United States, but now they were having marital problems and Teri wasn't sure what she was going to do next.

If the madness was real, it was now leading up to the climax of Robbi's final, and most dramatic, invention. As the months passed, she seemed increasingly worried about her blood condition. She described it to several people as something like the opposite of leukemia—her body was producing too many red blood cells. The headaches became a regular occurrence. She missed a day of work to go to Massachusetts General Hospital in Boston, one of the world's leading medical centers.

"Even the specialists down there don't know what to do," she reported to Claudia Brooks.

But there was hope, she told Claudia. They had told her of a doctor in Germany who was doing the most advanced research in the world on her disease. If necessary, that would be her last resort, she said.

John was playing his part. He applied for passports and called a travel agency in Keene to inquire about flights to Germany.

"Vacation?" someone asked, overhearing a conversation with the travel agent.

"If things don't improve with Robbi, we're going to see a specialist in Germany," John said tersely.

Robbi was working closely with Ron Oja now, and he noticed the deterioration in her condition. She often looked fatigued and wan, with dark smudges under her eyes. The intensity of her attacks gradually increased. Oja knew about her blood disease, but during her first year at Central Screw it hadn't seemed to affect her much. Now the headaches were sometimes so intense that she had to leave work. Somebody from accounting found her one day in the ladies' room, nauseated and crying from the pain. Finally, the headache was so bad that she couldn't see. Oja insisted that she go home. Rather than make her wait for John to finish work at Findings, Oja gave two of Robbi's friends time off to take her home to Marlow.

Slowly the attacks seemed to break down her overall health. She was missing work to go for treatment, too. First John took her to Mary Hitchcock Hospital in Hanover, which was associated with the medical school at Dartmouth. Mary Hitchcock had an excellent reputation, but nothing the doctors there could offer her seemed to help, and they switched to Massachusetts General in Boston. One day she came into Oja's office.

"I'm not doing a good enough job for you," she said. "I'm feeling so weak and tired from all the medication that I can't function anymore." Oja was reluctant to see her leave and concerned about her health.

"I'm going back to Texas to see the doctors there," she said. They had excellent medical care in Houston; she had been treated there the year before. "And if that doesn't work, I'll go to Germany." She told him about the research scientist who had made some progress in treating her condition. The money from the estate would allow her to get the best treatment available. Oja renewed his offer to take her back once again.

It was too bad that she would be so far away from her husband, Oja remarked.

"We decided it made more sense for him to stay here and keep working," Robbi said. "There wouldn't be anything for him to do there. Teri will take care of me."

Once again, she was cutting off her stay at Central Screw after nine months. It may be coincidence, but there was a regularity to Marie Hilley's movements. One co-worker familiar with clerical procedures theorized that Robbi's departures were related to the fact that Social Security registration requires three fiscal quarters for processing; after that, some form of cross-checking would take place that might turn up discrepancies in the records of a person like Robbi Hannon Homan.

Whatever the case, the regularity of her movements presents a curious sidelight to the case of Audrey Marie Hilley, beginning with her exposure in Alabama. Carol Hilley's poisoning reaches its climax in late August 1979; Marie Hilley is arrested in early September. A year later, Robbi Hannon and John Homan leave Florida for New Hampshire in late August; Robbi leaves Central Screw for the first time in August 1981. Now she is leaving Central Screw again in early September 1982.

Another cycle follows the first by three months. Marie Hilley jumps bail in November 1979. She begins full-time work at Central Screw in November of the next year and returns to Central Screw in November of the year after that.

One possible explanation for this regularity involves some form of stress building toward the anniversary of powerful events in the life of Marie Hilley, like the depression that afflicts certain people around the anniversary of a loved one's death. Perhaps she is unconsciously commemorating her arrest, the crushing end of her Anniston fantasy life, with a series of annual leave-takings.

A second theory might see psychological pressure building cyclically within the fugitive, making her increasingly restless and agitated, until it drives her to some form of movement, releasing the pressure and starting the sequence again.

Whatever the explanation, if the cycles were to continue, Robbi Homan was now due for another major move in November 1982.

16

Becoming Teri

According to Marie Hilley's account, she did go to Texas when she left New Hampshire, as she had said she was planning to do, but after only three days in Dallas, she flew to Florida.

Eight minutes before 7:00 A.M. on September 23, 1982, Robbi L. Homan, giving her address as P.O. Box 257, Marlow, New Hampshire, registered at the Howard Johnson's Motor Lodge in Pompano Beach, Florida. The motel was less than three miles from the house where her son, Mike, had lived when Marie Hilley stayed with him four years before.

A few hours later, she left the motel and walked a hundred yards south to Atlantic Boulevard, where she turned and strolled away from the beachfront a short distance until she found the Sandy Head Uni-Sex Beauty Salon. A little more than an hour after that, her hair gleamed under the fluorescent lights, a bright, bleached blonde. She paid the forty-dollar charge with a VISA card in the name of Robbi L. Homan and stepped out onto the street.

Her next stop was the AAA Employment Agency, where she filled out an application. Impressed by her skills and well-spoken, dignified manner, the manager, Mrs. Bertolini, pulled out a job listing that had just come in. They needed someone in a hurry, she said. Within minutes she was on the phone with Mr. McKenzie, the owner of Solar Testing Service.

After talking with him for a minute, she put her hand over the phone.

"Would you like to go out there for an interview right now, this afternoon?" she asked. Seeing that the response was positive, she turned back to the phone.

"She'll be right out, Mr. McKenzie," Mrs. Bertolini said. "Her name is Theresa Martin."

Jack McKenzie was getting desperate. He had been doing everything himself, all the record-keeping and most of the typing, for several weeks, and it was wearing him out. It was an unusual line of work, laying out six-inch squares of painted metal on racks in the sun to test the durability of the paint for auto companies, but he had found a comfortable niche in the market, and his business was growing fast. He had trouble keeping a secretary, however, and as the volume had grown, the clerical work had begun driving him to distraction. He had phoned half a dozen employment agencies and he was ready to accept almost anybody they sent him.

Still, he was impressed by the striking woman who showed up for the interview. He was waiting when she pulled up in a taxicab. Her eye-catching blond hair glowed in the late-afternoon sun, and she showed her legs under a neat, businesslike skirt as she slid out of the taxi. It must have cost her twenty-five dollars to get out here from the beach, McKenzie thought; she must not have realized that Pompano Beach included all the flat, vivid green farmland and country roads extending inland ten miles or more from the tourist hotels on the ocean.

"I don't have transportation," she told him when he remarked about it, "but I'm going to get a car down here soon. My sister lives in New Hampshire, and she has my car. I'll fly up there some weekend and drive it down."

McKenzie quickly satisfied himself that she was well qualified and offered her the job. He didn't bother with a typing test. She accepted when he volunteered to drive her out each day. He lived in Fort Lauderdale, the next city south of Pompano Beach, and it would be easy for him to swing by and get her. She agreed to start the next day. When he drove her back to the beach that night, she had him drop her off along the strip rather than take her home. "I'm going to do some shopping," she said.

The following day, she found a room for eighty-five dollars a week at the Balkan House Motel, a place with fourteen units and a deli out front, down the seafront boulevard from Howard Johnson's. She gave her name as Teri L. Martin. Her address was still P.O. Box 257, but now it was in Laconia, New Hampshire, a small city on Lake Winnipesaukee, about fifty miles from Marlow.

Before eight the next morning, a Saturday, Robbi Homan paid her bill and checked out of Howard Johnson's. Teri Martin turned from the cashier's desk and walked a few blocks down Ocean Boulevard to her room at the Balkan House, a little more than the distance from the grocery to the Christmas Trees Inn in Marlow, New Hampshire.

Jack McKenzie didn't mind providing the transportation for his new secretary; in fact, he quickly grew to look forward to it. The twenty-five-minute drive gave them time to talk. McKenzie had been divorced seven years, and he lived alone in a small apartment. He was spending long hours at work, sometimes six and seven days a week, trying to keep things going, and his social life had reached a low point. He was a big man with a friendly face, but overwork and the constant worry about keeping the business healthy were having an effect. He had gained twenty-five or thirty pounds and developed a slight tremor in his head and neck.

As he got to know Teri Martin, Jack McKenzie found her more and more attractive. She was small but full-breasted, and she dressed in clothes that flattered the curves of her body. She always wore high heels, even after McKenzie had worried out loud about the danger of her getting caught in the mesh pads on the slippery shop floor and hurting herself. She wanted the extra height, he concluded.

McKenzie found Teri easy to talk with. She had been raised in Alabama and the accent still mellowed her speech, though she had moved to New Hampshire several years before to be near her twin sister, Robbi. She and Robbi, whom she called "Rob," shared the extraordinary closeness that many twins experience. One Saturday, Robbi's husband had been taking their children somewhere early in the morning when a drunk driver plowed into the car, killing them all. Robbi had suffered a severe nervous breakdown after the accident and never fully recovered. She was still living in New Hampshire, in a beautiful house surrounded by pine trees, alone except for her English sheep dog and an older woman who came in each day to prepare her meals and clean up. Teri was utterly devoted to her twin, borrowing McKenzie's office almost every day for long lunchtime phone calls—she was scrupulous about reversing the charges, so McKenzie wouldn't get the bills. She would emerge to report in detail on Robbi's latest problem with her helper, or how the autumn was closing in on New Hampshire, bringing out the brilliant colors in the leaves and putting a chill in the breeze.

Teri often talked about the supernatural bond she shared with her twin. When Robbi had gone into labor, halfway across the country

Teri had felt the pains. One morning she turned from her desk and said to McKenzie, "I just got the worst feeling. I know something has happened. I've got to talk to Robbi." She went immediately to the phone. Robbi had passed a night of terrifying dreams and was suffering from an excruciating headache. For the rest of the day, Teri seemed to suffer along with her sister.

"Teri's obsessed with her twin sister," McKenzie remarked to someone in the office. "She just lives for her sister."

McKenzie wondered why such an attractive woman as Teri wasn't married. "Oh," she said, "I was married," and a sad, thoughtful look came over her face. Her husband, apparently an older man, had been a business executive and an avid pilot. The couple had never had children, but they enjoyed being together, taking flying trips all over the country. Her husband had died a few years earlier, and she had decided to leave the memories behind in New Hampshire.

A few weeks after she had started at Solar Testing, Teri came in one morning to report that Robbi had suffered a stroke. She had been taken by ambulance to the Harvard Medical Center in Boston. Teri was planning to fly up to see her over the weekend. After that, she repeated the weekend trip, calling from the office for an airline reservation. She supervised the arrangements for her sister's treatment and return to her home in New Hampshire. McKenzie was impressed by Teri's ability to make the long trip and return to work punctually on Monday morning. She talked again of driving the Mercedes back to Florida after one of these trips, but McKenzie asked her to postpone it until they had cleared up the enormous backlog of work that had accumulated.

Teri was an exceptionally fast typist. She reminded McKenzie of a high-school friend, an athlete taking typing because it was required, who had entered the state typing contest on a lark and won the prize, setting a record. It was like thunder in the office when Teri was going at full speed. Even so, they never seemed to catch up. By the time they finished one job, another had mounted to emergency proportions and he was forced to ask her to begin on it right away. She always agreed graciously, and kept postponing the extra three days' absence that would be needed to drive the car down.

It was obvious that she was above average in competence and intelligence, McKenzie thought. That made her lapses seem incongruous. She seemed distracted at times. He had showed her what to do with the three copies of the weekly inventory, but after a few weeks when they went to get the bottom copies for billing, they were gone. She had been throwing them away. McKenzie recovered some of them from the dumpster, but five thousand dollars' worth of billings was lost. Maybe it's my fault, he thought, everything so rushed. Must be something on her mind.

She couldn't keep the company checkbook straight, either—"Jack," she would cry, "I can't even keep my own checkbook balanced"—so McKenzie assigned it to someone else. Still, he was grateful to have her there. She was fast, willing to do whatever he asked, and always even-tempered. It was amazing how she tolerated the pressure and the chaos, particularly since she didn't need the job.

"I don't have to work," she told him. "I'm doing this because I like doing it, and I have to be busy. I can't bear just sitting around, doing nothing." There was money in her family. She and her husband had lived well and owned a vacation house in Carmel, California; he had left her with an income. She and Robbi had also inherited money from a wealthy relative who died.

About a month after she started work, Teri announced that she had met a couple who were going away and had invited her to use their condominium. She moved out of Balkan House and McKenzie began picking her up at a twenty-six-story apartment building about half a mile away. It was an expensive-looking place, with a large swimming pool at the back, on the ocean side. McKenzie estimated that the cheapest apartment in the building probably cost $150,000. Teri was always prompt, standing in front of the lobby door, often chatting with the doorman, when McKenzie arrived at seven-thirty each morning.

The rides back and forth were becoming the highlight of McKenzie's day. He began entertaining thoughts of a more personal relationship with Teri Martin. There didn't seem to be a steady man in her life. She mentioned a man named John who lived in Palm Beach. They had dated in the past and he had wanted to marry her after her husband died, but she didn't seem interested. One evening McKenzie asked Teri if she had plans for dinner, but she said she had made a date to eat with a friend. McKenzie tried once more, but then abandoned the idea. Dull as his private life was at the moment, he needed a good secretary at the office more than he needed a lover.

And there was something else, a feeling that McKenzie couldn't quite put into words: Teri Martin was a little too glamorous, with her hundred-dollar blouses and her Mercedes, living at the beach during the tourist season on a salary of three hundred dollars a week. Her life was a little too full, too fast, too lavish for his taste, McKenzie thought, and it gave her an aura of mystery, so much of her existence taking place somewhere else, in New Hampshire or Palm Beach or wherever she went after work. They had talked of her staying in Pompano Beach, taking on more responsibility at Solar Testing, but McKenzie knew she wouldn't stay long. She was impossible to pin down, he mused, driving her home one day. There were times when he felt intimidated by Teri Martin, even frightened, McKenzie admitted to himself, as he watched her walk away from the car onto the bustling streets of Pompano Beach.

She began to talk of wanting to live with Robbi, to take care of her. Robbi had developed cancer and she needed more care. She had always been slight, Teri said, and now she was down around ninety-five pounds. One day when Teri got into the car, she could hardly wait to tell McKenzie her news: She was thinking of buying a house. It belonged to the Christoffs, the owners of Balkan House Motel, where she had stayed before moving into the condo. She could bring Robbi and her dog and the woman who cared for her down from New Hampshire. The sisters would live there together.

McKenzie encouraged her. "That sounds terrific," he told her. She would be able to continue working with him and still give Robbi as much time as she needed. On the way home from work they drove out to Lighthouse Point so he could see the house. It had two bedrooms and two baths; the paint was peeling and the roof needed cleaning, the lawn was burned up and would have to be replanted. Even in that condition, McKenzie knew, a house out at the Point would cost a lot of money. Teri didn't seem intimidated by the possibility.

The owner, Peter Christoff, was a short, muscular man in his fifties. The name of his motel and a thick middle-European accent gave away his origins. Christoff told investigators that the house had not been listed for sale, but Teri Martin had found out somehow that he was thinking of selling it. She let him know that she was a widow with the means to live wherever she wanted. She was thinking of moving to the area permanently.

They had hardly begun their tour of the house when she made up her mind to buy it. As they walked through the rooms, she talked to Christoff of the changes she would make, gesturing expansively to indicate the placement of furniture, exclaiming over the vision she was creating of her new home. They would knock out this wall, she told Christoff, and add a wing for her sister, who was ill, and her live-in maid. They would be coming down from New Hampshire.

And what about the price? she asked. They were asking two hundred thousand dollars, he told her. That sounded reasonable, she replied. And how would she be financing it? he wondered. "Oh, that's no problem," she answered, "I'll be paying cash."

"How soon can you be out?" she wanted to know. Christoff was taken aback: they hadn't expected things to happen so fast. He would talk with his wife and let her know right away. She promised to phone in a day or two to make the final arrangements.

Christoff never heard from her again.

She finished her sixth week at Solar Testing and prepared to go to New Hampshire for the weekend. She looked as if she had lost a lot of weight; McKenzie wondered if the pace—working full time, flying to New Hampshire every few weeks, house-hunting in her spare time, and planning for Robbi's move—was starting to wear her down.

Sometime early the next week, she telephoned Jack McKenzie at home. It was eleven o'clock at night.

"Robbi's dead, Jack," she told him. "I'm going to stay here in New Hampshire and take care of things. This is where I belong."

McKenzie had been expecting something of the sort for quite a while now. She had been out of place at Solar Testing, out of place with Jack McKenzie. It was just an interlude in her life. He wished her the best of luck.

Now she sat down to write a letter, the second from Robbi to Teri that has come to light. It covered six pages of small notepaper:

Teri—
I'm afraid I won't make it home, and certainly not to Germany. I want so much to see John again, and I know you have been torn between my wishes and what you feel is right, but I don't want him to see me like this.

I'm trying to hold on until December, but though my mind tells me not to give in, my body is too tired to listen. Writing this is taking every ounce of my energy, but there are things I want you to do.

If things don't work out, please don't call John. Use the ticket and go on to New Hampshire. I don't know what effect you will have on him. After all, we have confused people who lived with us every day, so if he doesn't want you there, please don't feel offended. You could be a painful reminder.

About Mother's house—it may be the only thing I have to give you, but you understand, anything you get from it, rent or sale, half goes to John. I just felt it would be easier to put it in your name since you are here—and there is no doubt in my mind that you will do the right thing.

Teri, I'm sorry I've given you such a hard time. You have been wonderful to me. It's just that I miss John so much. I'm miserable without him and I took it out on you.

When we went to live with Grandfather, I was afraid to go to sleep—I was afraid I would wake up and you would be gone. I've lived with the same fear since I've known John. Now I will wake up some place and both of you will be gone. I want very much for the two of you to be friends. I love you both very much—more than anything else. If you don't upset John too much, please stay with him as long as he needs you. He is so kind, and you need a friend like him, and I think he will need you. He is very sensitive and if I don't make it, he will feel it very deeply. I know you will want to go back to Denver, but you love cold weather, and New Hampshire is a lovely place, so stay for a while, until John gets over the worst.

I don't want either of you to waste time grieving for me. Life is too valuable, and it doesn't last that long.

I don't want to die. I want to get well and learn to live as you and John know how to do.

There is a phone number in my wallet. If things don't work out, that is the number to call. I don't want you to know where they take me. You might live in that part of the country again, and I know it would bother you to know that's where I am. No funeral or memorials. I've lived my life and those things are too painful for the people who love you.

I hope you don't have to read this. I hope I will wake up one morning and everything will be better, but this is just in case things go wrong.

One more thing—buy John a lot of Christmas presents, the one thing, especially, that I told you about. He loves Christmas, and if I'm not there, perhaps I'll come back as a Christmas tree ornament. So, please, no sadness at Christmas. I will know and be very unhappy.

My body is so tired and if it didn't mean leaving John and you, I'm ready to trade it in.

I want you and John to go someplace and have a lavish dinner, even a party. Time is a slow healer, but I know that, eventually, it does heal. Just keep that in mind. Everything passes. Just please take care of John. He is strong about everything—except me.

I love you both—more than anything else.

Rob

Teri—One last thing. I'm not afraid to die. I know the question you would ask. I've tried to live my life without hurting anyone. Maybe I haven't always succeeded, but I have tried, so I don't feel that God will judge me too harshly. I know I haven't lived according to man's rules, but I still believe there is a just and merciful God, and He will judge me accordingly.

I've hesitated about telling you this, but in fairness to the doctors, I feel I must. When I left Houston last year, I knew what was wrong with me. I would have told John, but at the time, he wanted us to live apart, and I knew I didn't have that much time. I was afraid he would take me back out of pity, and loving him the way I do, I didn't want that. But you must never think he wasn't kind. I went back, knowing how he felt, and since that time, I've never been real sure of his feelings. I just know that I love him, and he's the first real happiness I've ever known. He's been wonderful to me. I only regret that the past made me so distrustful, because he never gave me any reason not to trust him. After living those years with Joe, it was hard to realize there are men like John. Any trouble we had was my fault. Don't ever live in the past, Teri—it will destroy you.

At lunchtime Wednesday, she telephoned John Homan at Findings, Inc., in Keene, New Hampshire.

"It's over, John," she told him. His wife, Robbi Hannon Homan, was dead.

The following day, Thursday, November 11, carrying Robbi's letter, Teri Martin boarded a flight for Logan International Airport in Boston, where John Homan was waiting for her.

Part Five

Teri Martin

17

Consoling John

Months later they looked back to the day of the phone call, searching for clues, but there was nothing except the look of dumb shock on John Homan's face as he returned to the toolroom at Findings, Inc.

"That was Teri," he told Joe Massicotte, the supervisor. "Robbi's gone." The brief, almost curt, euphemism—Robbi had "gone," not died, not even passed away—was typical of John. He kept things to himself, and he had seemed always to hold the idea of death at arm's length.

Now, with the phone call from Teri, the last three years seemed in retrospect to lead inevitably to this moment. Teri had spoken of a letter her sister had left, and of Robbi's wish that Teri and John, her only living relatives, console each other. Robbi had spoken of the special closeness of twins, the peculiar emotional bond, almost beyond ordinary sensory communication, and it was easy to imagine that Teri's sense of loss now could be equal to John's, even greater in a way. Robbi's death severed an intimate bond formed even before their birth, forged in the common biological origin of identical twins.

It was typical of Robbi to plan ahead, and she seemed to have thought of everything. She had made all the arrangements herself, Teri reported, leaving phone numbers for Teri to call after her death to put them into effect. She was determined to protect the mourners from the lingering sadness of ceremony, ruling out a funeral or memorial service. Her body was to be donated to the Texas Medical Research Institute. It was the kind of practical generosity familiar to anyone who knew her. And she had told Teri to go to John in New Hampshire, to grieve with him, to help him recover from the loss.

She had missed John—"I'm miserable without him," she had told Teri—and it pleased her to think in her last days of the two people she loved beyond anyone or anything else, together after her passing.

Robbi anticipated that it might be difficult for John, adjusting to the extraordinary likeness of the two women. They had often confused even those who knew them best, including family members and friends, but Robbi hoped the consolation to John of having someone to share the loss would outweigh the eeriness of confronting his late wife's double. Teri, divorced after a long and difficult marriage to a military officer, had little to hold her to Dallas. She had traveled all over the country as her husband followed his career, always ready for the next move, never establishing deep ties anywhere. She loved cold weather—the idea of settling down to read by the fire on a snowy day had always been a romantic vision of tranquillity to her—and New Hampshire seemed as good a place as any.

And so it was settled: Teri would come North on Robbi's return ticket to Boston.

The woman who got off the plane at Logan Airport in Boston was striking, no doubt about it, even if you had never met her twin sister. It was probably the hair that struck John first as Teri came through the door, the kind of bleached color that some associate with gaudiness but that almost everybody notices at a distance, particularly men. Combined with the way she carried herself, it gave her the type of presence that turned heads in a public place. It was a different kind of attractiveness from Robbi's quiet charisma, which worked so powerfully at closer range. Teri was much slimmer than her sister, and smaller all over.

During the ninety-minute ride westward through Massachusetts and north into New Hampshire, they discussed plans for the next few days, beginning the process of getting comfortable being together. They had anticipated this moment, wondering how it would feel to be together in Marlow; now it was clear that it would take time to get used to the reality.

The following day they drove into Keene. Teri wouldn't wait another day to close the book on the life of Robbi Homan.

A couple of blocks down a side street leading away from the center of town stands a modest brick building with a bronze plaque in front identifying it as the home of the *Keene Sentinel*. When a couple arrived that Friday morning with information for an obituary, the receptionist directed them to Diane Nix in the first-floor newsroom. Nix was an editorial assistant, still making the rounds from one job to the next on the paper, hoping eventually to be a full-time reporter. Lately she had been in charge of obituaries.

Most obituaries were phoned in by funeral homes, which collected the necessary information from relatives of the deceased, but once in a while there was no funeral home involved for some reason and word came from another source. The couple stopped in front of Nix's desk and the blond woman held out a page of information, written in a neat, flowing hand. The deceased was named Robbi L. Homan. As Nix scanned the page, the woman began explaining. The reporter was struck by the woman's hair; it was the kind of color that could only be artificial. The man seemed somewhat unkempt, and he seemed to have difficulty concentrating on the conversation.

It was the woman's sister, a twin, who had died. The blond woman introduced her companion as the husband of her late sister. Like many survivors, she seemed to need to talk about the circumstances of the death and her own reaction to it. She had difficulty keeping to the information Nix needed for the obituary. The sister had been with Mrs. Homan when she died in Dallas and had come to Keene to help John Homan through a difficult time. Under Nix's patient questioning they filled in missing details; there was some question about a third sister, a Jean Ann Trevor in White Plains, New York, and the two visitors disagreed momentarily about whether she should be mentioned. The man amended his sister-in-law's account of the illness and they agreed finally on a statement that the body had been donated to the Medical Research Institute in Texas. Through all this they seemed comfortable together, cooperating on the details of the obituary and talking at times as if there were no one else present. Finally Nix had the facts she needed. It was too late for that day's paper; the obituary would have to run on Saturday.

Claudia Brooks had thought often of Robbi Homan, wondering how she was doing and whether she would come back to Keene. Robbi had phoned a few times from Texas, taking advantage of Central Screw's 800 number to save on her phone bill. The treatments, which involved radiation, sounded difficult, but they left plenty of time free for other activities. Robbi's chatty reports made her life in Texas sound more attractive than it had been in Keene. Teri, after her many years of marriage and the strain of her divorce, had established a busy social life in Dallas. The sisters were very much alike, but Claudia had gathered that Teri was more outgoing at parties, enjoying the drinking and conversation at a higher pitch than her twin. One of Robbi's calls came the day after the sisters had been to a party, and Teri was still fragile from the effects of a hangover. Robbi and Claudia had joked about it on the phone, but Robbi rarely took more than a social drink or two, and she had sounded a little bit critical of Teri's excesses. Except for occasional minor differences of that kind, the twins got along well, and Robbi had seemed in good spirits. But that call had been several weeks before, and as Claudia settled down to her work that Friday morning, thoughts of her friend's medical progress, never far from her mind when she was at the office where they had worked together, had given way to the more immediate requirements of work.

Priscilla Gendron was at the switchboard when the call came. She had taken several of Robbi's calls from Texas over the past several weeks and had come to recognize her telephone voice. It was that unmistakable southern accent, so distinctive among the variations of flat New Hampshire voices that dominated conversation at Central Screw. The caller was asking to talk to Claudia Brooks.

"Hi, Robbi," Priscilla responded. "How are you doing down there?"

There was a pause before the voice replied, "This isn't Robbi, it's Teri." Priscilla was puzzled, then embarrassed at her mistake as the caller asked again for Claudia Brooks. It was peculiar that Robbi spoke so formally, and who was this "Terry"? Claudia's desk was near the front of the big office, only a few feet behind Priscilla's switchboard, so rather than use the buzzer, she turned around and signaled for Claudia's attention.

"It's for you. It sounds like Robbi but she says it's 'Terry' or something." There was no sign of confusion on Claudia's face, and she seemed pleased as she picked up the receiver. Priscilla watched Claudia for a moment, looking for some clue to the mystery.

"Is this Claudia Brooks?" the voice asked. It sounded like Robbi, but the smile stiffened on Claudia's face as the caller went on.

"My name is Teri Martin," she said. "I'm Robbi Homan's twin sister."

"Yes? She told me about you," Claudia said, feeling as if time were suspended, still confused about the caller's identity in spite of the explanation.

"I have some bad news," Teri said. She paused. "I'm calling to tell you that Robbi died."

Even as Claudia said "What?," instinctively trying to delay taking in the news for another moment, she was absorbing the reality of what Teri had told her. As Teri went on, reciting the meaningless details that fill gaps in conversations about death, the tears started in Claudia's eyes.

Priscilla stared at Claudia as she put down the phone and stood up. "She died," Claudia said. "Robbi died." And she began to sob.

Claudia Brooks appeared at the door of Ron Oja's office, her face wet with tears.

"Oh, Ron," Claudia cried, "she's dead. Robbi's dead."

As she told him about the phone call from Teri and he tried to comfort her, Oja reflected on Robbi's death. Because of her obvious decline over the previous months, he was not particularly surprised at the news.

"It's a rotten thing," he said, "but it's probably best for her." Claudia looked at him as if eager for some consolation.

"Because of the pain and suffering," Oja went on. "If you were going to live like that for the rest of your life, why bother to be around? I wouldn't want to live like that."

Oja didn't want to add to Claudia's pain, but he couldn't help observing how sad it was that John had not been able to join his wife at the end. They talked for a few minutes more, and when her grief failed to ease, Oja suggested that Claudia take the rest of the day off. She preferred to stay at work, around people who had known Robbi, and she went off to share the news with others.

The switchboard was quiet when the outer door to the lobby opened and John Homan entered with a woman companion. As they approached the window, Sandy Peace recognized the woman's face, though it didn't seem to fit with the pale blond hair.

"Hi, Robbi," Sandy Peace said. The woman blinked and looked back at Sandy without any sign of recognition.

The woman's companion stepped forward and asked if Wayne Mitten, the general manager, was available. That must be John Homan, Sandy thought; she knew of Robbi's husband, though she had never met him. She was put off by his slovenly appearance. She told him Wayne had left, so John asked for Ron Oja. Sandy had noticed that Oja was not in his office, so instead of using the intercom she walked to the back of the shop to find him.

John Homan turned to face Oja as he stepped through the doorway into the lobby. Oja was struck immediately by the grief on John's face.

"I'm sure you've heard that Robbi passed away," John said. Oja made a sound of acknowledgment. Tears started in John's eyes.

"This is Robbi's twin sister, Teri," John said. "She's come from Texas."

The woman was clearly different from Robbi: She was much thinner and smaller, and her face was shaped differently. Still, Oja was stunned at the likeness. As he reached to shake her hand, he couldn't help himself. In spite of the solemnity of the occasion and the obvious sadness of both the bereaved visitors, he said to the blond woman, "Boy, I'll bet you've been mistaken for Robbi many, many times."

Teri acknowledged that he was right. Even their grandparents, who had raised them, sometimes confused the two sisters. She spoke of Robbi's illness and how they had been together at the end. Robbi had spoken fondly of her friends at Central Screw, Teri said, in particular Wayne Mitten and Claudia Brooks. Part of Teri's purpose in coming to New Hampshire was to remember Robbi to her close friends.

"Could I please meet Claudia?" she asked. Oja stopped somebody coming in from lunch and asked them to send Claudia out.

As Claudia stepped through the doorway from the office the little group standing in the lobby turned toward her. Claudia's attention was drawn first to John Homan, who stood next to Ron Oja, tears shining on his face. The sight was enough to set off a fresh flow of tears from her own eyes, and she stepped forward to put her arm around him.

"Oh, John," she began, "I'm so sorry."

John turned slightly, directing Claudia's attention to the figure on the other side of Ron Oja. Claudia became conscious that from the moment she had first glimpsed the three people standing in the lobby she had been avoiding looking at that third person.

"Claudia, I would like you to meet Robbi's twin sister, Teri," she heard John saying, and she was conscious of her gaze turning, against her will, to the small blond woman. The words burst out of her before she could think.

"Oh, my God, I can't," Claudia exclaimed, and looked quickly past the woman. Teri seemed to freeze in place. It was uncanny how much the twin looked like Robbi, and she was even wearing her sister's ski jacket. The sensation was frightening, like looking at a ghost, and Claudia could not bring herself to turn again to face Teri. She was overcome by a fresh wave of sobbing.

Oja looked at her with concern. "Claudia, go into my office and calm down," he said gently. She turned away as if she were under remote control.

Teri seemed momentarily stunned by the force of Claudia's reaction, but she quickly recovered her composure.

"She had a lot of friends here," Teri said. "She liked her job a lot. Do you suppose I could see her desk, where she sat?"

Oja led them into the office and pointed out the desk where Robbi had worked. Claudia Brooks's desk, just behind it, was empty. Robbi had kept a photo of John on the desk, but there was no longer any sign of her presence. Lou Smith passed through, on his way in from lunch. "Hi, Robbi," he said. Teri looked up, a blank stare on her face. Smith appeared embarrassed when Oja introduced Teri as Robbi's twin and told him about her death. The situation was uncomfortable and Oja was eager to get back to work; after a few more minutes of polite conversation, he saw John and Teri back to the lobby door and headed for his office.

Sandy Peace had observed the scene from a distance, still puzzled about what the visitors were doing. As they said good-bye to Ron Oja and walked out the door to the lobby, Sandy joined a small group of women who had gathered at one side of the office, watching the brief inspection of Robbi's former work station.

"What is going on?" Sandy asked, exasperated by the sense that things didn't add up and her inability to figure out what was happening.

"It's Robbi's twin sister, Teri Martin," someone said. "She just wanted to see where Robbi—"

Sandy broke in on the explanation. "What?" she asked. It was as much an expression of her amazement as a question, and she said it loud enough to attract the attention of several people who had just begun to go back to work after watching the visitors.

The other woman was puzzled. She began again: "It's Robbi's twin sister—"

This time Sandy didn't hesitate, and her tone was even more emphatic.

"Bullshit!" she exclaimed, almost shouting. "That's Robbi."

Roger Williams hadn't heard from John since Wednesday. John had come back to the toolroom after the phone call and told Roger the news of Robbi's death. John had sat at his bench after the phone call, listless and distracted, waiting for Teri to call back; she was making travel arrangements. The call came within an hour; after hanging up, John had gone over to Joe Massicotte's bench. "I need some time, Joe," he said, and he was gone. That had been two days before.

Roger was concentrating on his work, trying to leave things in good shape before starting the weekend in a couple of hours, when he looked up to see John in the doorway of the toolroom. A woman was standing beside him. John had his arm around her shoulder, as if to encourage and support her. Her arm was around his waist. As they approached, Roger realized she was the twin, Teri; her hair was blond and she was much thinner, but anyone who knew Robbi would recognize the sister.

As John was introducing her, Roger had trouble concentrating, his mind busy comparing the two sisters and going back over what had happened. It occurred to him that she had made the arrangements and come to New Hampshire in an extremely short time. She and John seemed fastened together. John was trying to get through the awkwardness of the introductions by explaining things to his friend.

"We're both all alone now," he was saying, and he looked down at Teri for confirmation. She returned his gaze with a little smile, and Roger was struck by how close they seemed.

"We're just going to take some time," John went on, "and try to piece our lives back together."

The words were hopeful, but they didn't erase the powerful aura of grief surrounding John; there were dark circles under his eyes, and he seemed constantly on the verge of tears. In spite of his sympathy for John, though, Roger was slightly amused, and even a little impressed, by his friend's good luck.

Man, Roger thought, this guy's planning on spending some time with this girl.

Sandy Peace's exclamation had triggered an uproar at Central Screw. Several employees, returning from lunch, had stopped, curious to see what Robbi's sister looked like. Someone who had come in from the back shop to use the Xerox machine wondered what was happening. "She just left," someone said, and the latecomer ran to the door, trying to get a look at Teri, but it was too late.

Jolene Hoover had come out of the computer room while Ron Oja was showing Teri and John around. She had been friends with Robbi and half expected that Robbi would have told Teri to look her up, but Claudia Brooks was the only person Teri seemed interested in meeting. It was odd, Jolene thought, that Robbi hadn't mentioned her to Teri. Looking on as Teri moved around the room, Jolene began to have a strange feeling: It almost seemed that Teri had avoided looking at her.

As she watched the scattered groups converging around Sandy Peace at the switchboard, an idea took form in Jolene's mind: That wasn't Teri, it was Robbi herself. Peggy Wilson came out of the computer room and stood at Jolene's side.

"Was that Robbi?" Peggy asked. Jolene found herself nodding in reply.

The speculation ebbed and flowed as more employees returned from lunch. The talk turned to the details of the visitor's appearance. Someone mentioned that her teeth seemed different. Jerry Scadova had an answer for everything, relentlessly striking down any argument for Robbi's reliability. He recalled that she had told him and his wife, Marcy, one night over beers at the Village Green that she was going to have her teeth fixed. Gold caps didn't seem attractive to her anymore; she was going to have them capped with porcelain.

Paul Benoit, who was in charge of the computer room, had seen her. "Tell me that isn't Robbi," he challenged. Only Jerry Scadova answered. "Of course it's Robbi," he said.

Scadova had heard enough. He was disgusted with Robbi. He didn't want anything more to do with her. He headed back to his office.

Jolene Hoover and Peggy Wilson had returned to work in the

computer room when Paul Benoit came in. They had sent him out a few minutes before to see the visitor for himself.

"Yes, it does look like her," Paul said with a skeptical laugh.

"Why, don'tcha know," Jolene responded, exaggerating for effect, "it's her twin sister." They all laughed together. The computer room was unanimous. What had seemed an odd thought to Jolene a few minutes before was hardening into a certainty. She pictured the scene: The visitor was even wearing Robbi's ski jacket and carrying Robbi's purse. But what was going on? she wondered. What was the point?

In Ron Oja's office, Claudia Brooks had become calmer, but Ron felt sorry for her. He had always been considerate about employees with medical or personal emergencies during the working day.

"Why don't you go home, Claudia," he suggested. She shook her head. She didn't want to be alone.

"It's kind of dumb for me to go home," she said. "I can work." She got up to return to her desk. She stopped to talk to Shirley Leonard on the way.

Shirley had gone out for an early lunch and had been finishing up some errands. It was a cold day, typical of those early-November warnings that winter sends New Hampshire, and she had been hunched down inside her coat. She had looked up in front of the R and R discount store on Main Street to see John Homan getting out of his white pickup truck. John didn't know Shirley, but she recognized him from the occasions when he had come to get Robbi at Central Screw. He had just parked at the curb, and a blond woman was getting out the other side of the truck—Robbi had gotten her hair dyed, Shirley thought immediately. Robbi looked at Shirley, smiled, and turned her head without speaking. She walked off with John. That was strange, Shirley thought, but then, Robbi was strange anyway.

If anybody at work might be expected to clash with Robbi, Shirley Leonard would be the one. It was hard to imagine two people whose styles were more different. Even the names seemed to come from different worlds: old-fashioned "Shirley," and up-to-date "Robbi," with an "i."

Middle-aged now, Shirley lived with her sister out on Spring Street in the same house where they had lived when Shirley was born. She had come to Central Screw soon after high school and stayed there ever since. She spoke carefully, her voice under tight control, in well-formed and grammatical sentences. The first impression was of a kind, motherly woman, mannerly in an old-fashioned way, but that was deceptive. She could be firm, sometimes stubborn; it was easy to imagine Robbi appearing in a rush with her demands, and Shirley sitting at her desk, moving at her accustomed, deliberate pace, doing things in the way that had been perfectly satisfactory for twenty-eight years and gradually saying less and less in a softer and softer voice until Robbi would stalk away in a frustrated rage. At one time Shirley had been fascinated by Robbi, by her colorful stories of wealth and loss, travel and romance, dramatic collapse and brave survival, but they had come to seem threadbare and illogical, and the charm had worn thin.

Glee was not part of Shirley Leonard's emotional vocabulary, but she felt something close to it in her eagerness to carry the news of her sighting back to the office. She hadn't liked or trusted Robbi for a long time. As she thought about it now, something about the call to Claudia Brooks announcing Robbi's death a few hours before hadn't seemed right. Nothing about Robbi semed straightforward or reliable to Shirley anymore.

"Guess who I just saw uptown," Shirley said as Claudia stopped by her desk. Claudia looked sad and bewildered.

"Robbi?" she asked. There was something in her manner reminiscent of a child flinching from an expected slap.

"Yes," Shirley answered, and described the brief confrontation on Main Street.

"Is it her or Teri?" Claudia asked plaintively.

"It's her!" Shirley said, and in spite of Claudia's gloom, there was a hint of triumph in Shirley's voice.

Jerry Scadova came out of the back room. He had returned to the Engineering Department, where there was a window overlooking the parking lot. He had noticed John and the woman heading for John's white pickup truck. Scadova swore they were both laughing. "Just a minute before, she's all solemn and he's got tears in his eyes," Jerry said, "and then John's holding the door of the truck for her, and she's got a big smile on her face."

Ron Oja wondered how long it would take before the excitement died down. It all seemed ghoulish, he thought, the unhealthy intensity of their suspicion, their avid passion for the story, like the chattering of hyenas over a carcass.

For Christ's sake, he thought to himself, will they leave her alone?

The guy's just lost his wife. There's always some people who will pick anything apart. And nobody was getting any work done. At least it was Friday afternoon; maybe things would settle down over the weekend.

The grocery was a small oasis to the people of Marlow, a way station between home and the outside world—Keene, Claremont, and the other surrounding towns where most residents went to work. Morning and night they stopped for gas and cigarettes, a cup of coffee, some forgotten item for dinner, a candy bar or a newspaper, and with their purchase they got a friendly greeting and a little news. In all of this it was the model of a small New England country store.

Instead of the grizzled proprietor, the lifelong resident and town sage that New England mythology portrays in such a store, however, the Marlow Grocery was owned and run by two emigrants from New York, Carol and Fred Hammann. They had fled the complexity and overcrowding of Long Island five years before, which was enough time for them to become fixtures in Marlow, but not long enough to rub more than the edges off Carol's accent or dull her outspoken urban style.

Carol Hammann was at the counter for her usual midday shift when John Homan came in. The news he had brought of Robbi's condition over the past few weeks had not been good. Carol had not known Robbi well—she usually waited in the truck while John came into the store—but Carol liked John and followed his wife's progress with growing sympathy.

As John held the door and the woman stepped into the store, Carol was shocked at what she saw. The words burst from her mouth:

"Robbi, my God, you've lost so much weight!" Carol exclaimed.

The woman smiled slightly as she stepped toward the counter.

"I'm not who you think I am," she said. "I'm Robbi's sister, Teri Martin."

Carol was confused, then shocked as Teri told of Robbi's death and her own decision to come to New Hampshire. John's eyes filled with tears, and the thought of her quick warm greeting to this stranger brought a delayed flush of embarrassment to Carol's face. Her cheerful frankness of manner, reflecting the detachment of an outsider, ordinarily left little room for embarrassment, but the combination of mistaken identity and tragedy broke through her defenses. She felt sympathy for John and Teri, but she had not known Robbi well enough to feel the loss with great force herself. After a few more minutes of awkward conversation, John and Teri paid for their purchases and left.

Carol couldn't wait to pick up the phone and call Fred with the news. After they hung up, she experienced another rush of sympathy; John had seemed so forlorn and alone in the past few weeks, and Teri was going to help him settle her sister's affairs. It would be a difficult and melancholy time for them; they would probably appreciate some distraction. Carol and Fred had planned to rent a plane and fly over to New York State for the day. There would be two extra seats in the rear. She called Fred back.

"Can we ask them to go to New York with us?" she asked. Fred agreed, and the next time John and Teri came into the store, the arrangements were made.

The story of Robbi's death and Teri's arrival slipped naturally into the flow of local intelligence through the grocery, and Carol Hammann had occasion to mention it to several people who had known John and Robbi, or who just liked to be informed about what was going on in town. It was awkward, and sad, too, that she turned out to be the one who first told the news to John's brother Peter.

In spite of his estrangement from John and his wife, Peter was touched by the news of Robbi's death. Could her passing be an occasion for ending the estrangement? In any case, Peter was moved to offer condolences to his brother. When he got home from work in town that evening he rushed through the farm chores, washed up and dressed carefully to show his respect, and drove down the rough dirt road to Stone Pond.

The Homans had never acquired the ritual or custom to help them approach death comfortably. Their parents had given them little on the subject but disconnected secular aphorisms—children are immortality; care about others while you live because life is short—and then both had died suddenly. Uncomfortable at the prospect of condolence and nervous at the idea of confronting his estranged brother, Peter knocked on the door of the little house. After a moment, the door swung open.

Peter felt as if his heart had stopped. John's wife, the woman who had driven a wedge between Peter and his brother, the woman who had died, stood before him in the doorway.

Peter couldn't keep the words in: "I thought you were dead," he blurted. Could he have misunderstood Carol Hammann's report?

She stood in the doorway for a moment, silent and unmoving, outlined in the light from the living room behind her.

"I'm not Robbi," she said. "I'm Teri." She stepped aside to let Peter in.

There was a television set murmuring in the background; they hadn't owned a TV before. They had been reading, sitting in the lawn chairs they had used since Peter and Shelley took their furniture back after the falling-out. John greeted his brother stiffly, his manner suffused with sadness.

As they recounted the events since Robbi's death, Peter listened with growing sympathy. The three sat at the table in the cramped kitchen alcove, drinking coffee. John was weeping. Peter had never seen his brother cry before. It had become an issue between them when Peter, seventeen years old at the time, had cried on hearing of their father's death. He was pleased for John. He also felt a degree of vindication, and perhaps, too, a little edge of belated triumph—to see that John had also learned, sometime in the past ten years, to let his emotions flow. He looked, in fact, as if he must have been weeping without interruption since hearing about Robbi's death.

Beyond a few reminiscences of her sister and their childhood, Teri said little, allowing the brothers to work out their reconciliation. Peter was pleased at the welcome from John but uncomfortable with the mentions of Robbi; Peter had, after all, begun the estrangement from John by calling her a liar. It was difficult now for him to think kindly of her, even in death, and the memory of her role in the estrangement threatened the good feeling between him and John. After about fifteen minutes, Peter got up to go. He turned to John, prepared to offer a consoling hug, and was further gratified to see that his brother did not pull back. Maybe John was more conscious than before of how few people there were in the world who would offer that kind of consolation. They parted with promises to get together again in the next few days.

At home, Peter started to tell Shelley what had happened.

"She had a twin sister," he said, amazement in his voice. Robbi had not told them much about her family, but she had mentioned a sister in White Plains, New York. She was a model, wealthy and glamorous but unhappily married for many years, then finally divorced. But Robbi had never told them anything about the twin.

Shelley was sorry she hadn't been there to see Teri. She was eager to follow through on the parting agreement between Peter and John to get the two couples together.

Teri wanted to meet the people Robbi had known and see the places where she had lived her life, so different from Teri's. As John guided her around Keene, each visit brought forth vivid images of Robbi and their life together. Everywhere they went, old friends greeted her as Robbi. John stood by quietly as Teri was forced each time to correct them and introduce herself, explaining about the failure of Robbi's treatments in Texas and describing her death. Everybody wanted to reminisce about Robbi.

They stopped in at the Autowize auto supply store owned by Wayne Mitten, the former general manager at Central Screw, and Wayne suggested they go up Eagle Court to the pizza place for coffee. He recalled how Robbi had delighted in teasing him, taking advantage of his prudery, shocking him with vulgar comments about customers' excessive demands. He had clearly enjoyed their special relationship.

At Hilson's Home Center, John introduced her to Roger Champagne, who had owned the Christmas Trees Inn in Marlow when John and Robbi had first come to New Hampshire. Roger and Marie Champagne had been their landlords for those first weeks, and they had become close friends. The Champagnes had sold the inn, and Roger was manager of the Hardware Department at Hilson's. "My God," he said, "if I didn't know any better, I'd think you were Robbi."

During their tour of Keene, John and Teri stopped in at Friendly's Restaurant. Friendly's looked like what it was, a chain restaurant with mass-produced Colonial-style decor, but the reality was closer to what its name suggested. It functioned like a small-town diner, with a regular clientele made up of people who arrived at the same time each day and expected to see others who did the same. Though there was some turnover, many of the waitresses had been there half a dozen years or more, and they formed part of the scene. They would notice if someone didn't come in at his regular time for more than a few days in a row. They didn't know everybody by name, but if they ever had reason to mention a regular customer when he wasn't there—he had dropped a twenty-dollar bill on the seat, or she had left a glove behind—they could refer to the customer by his table number and expect the hostess to know whom they meant.

John and Robbi had eaten most weekday breakfasts and a lot of dinners at Friendly's. If one of them had to go to work early or leave late, Friendly's was where the other one waited.

Shirley Bullard, one of the veteran waitresses, had known them first as booth 18, then as corn muffin and coffee, the simple breakfast each of them customarily ordered. They were both quiet people, and it was some time before she learned their names, but they had eventually gotten in the habit of chatting and joking with her. Shirley and the other waitresses on the day shift who knew the couple had followed John's reports, based on the calls he had received from Robbi's twin sister, through the months of his wife's decline. And one morning the story had culminated with John's despondent account of her death. Now, several days later, he brought Teri in to meet his friends and get something to eat. Teri was much more outgoing than Robbi and seemed more nervous: She left a full ashtray when they got up to leave. Shirley Bullard had never noticed Robbi smoking. She observed that they sat at table 29, across the room from John and Robbi's accustomed place.

John wanted Teri to get to know Roger Williams, his co-worker in the toolroom at Findings and his closest friend in Keene. They met Roger at work and went up the street to the Stage Restaurant. John spoke of the reactions Teri's arrival had produced among friends and acquaintances of Robbi. These people had been amazed at the similarity of the two sisters, he told Roger. It was as if they had never seen twins before. Some had told John in private that she looked like the same person. John's eagerness for Teri to be accepted by his old friends was obvious and touching, but Roger was tense. He was having his own doubts about the situation.

Sitting across the table from Teri, Roger experienced again the uneasiness he had felt during the long, painful period of Robbi's illness in Texas. His friend's suffering had been visible, and Roger had identified with him. Yet he had also felt slightly unsettled. There had been something missing in John's reaction; he had been gripped by a terrible passivity. He acted as if events were taking place on the other side of a transparent wall. At the same time that Roger had felt sympathy for John, he had been impatient with him. Something in his friend's response to the crisis just didn't seem right.

Now there was something about Teri Martin that disturbed him, too. She was so different from Robbi—the hair, the incessant smoking, even her shape—and yet there was something jarring about her, something that just didn't fit. It came to him: her voice, so unnaturally, disturbingly reminiscent of Robbi.

Roger was embarrassed by his doubts: It didn't seem decent in the face of the tragedy John and Teri had experienced. Yet he found his gaze ranging over the restaurant, anywhere but the place it should most naturally fall. He could not look Teri Martin in the eye.

18

The Shadow of a Doubt

Somehow the decision was made: Teri would get a job and settle down with John, at least for a while. John suggested they try Cheshire Employment Services in Keene; he and Robbi had found jobs through the agency.

Teri gave an account of her work history for Bob March, who had twice placed Robbi in jobs. Teri had last worked a year before at Manfred's Auto Specialty in Fort Lauderdale, Florida, John's hometown. For fifteen years before that she had been married to an Army officer and moved repeatedly around the country, holding short-term jobs with a series of companies, an attorney, and a CPA. She had taken the commercial course at Sacred Heart School in Tyler, Texas, where she and Robbi had grown up, and like her sister, she had excellent secretarial skills. Her shorthand was the same—she claimed a hundred words per minute—but she didn't do as well on the typing test. Robbi had scored seventy-five words per minute, with only two errors; Teri could do no better than seventy-three, with thirteen errors. Still, she would not be hard to place. There was always a need for someone with the combination of skills and presentability that Teri offered. She struck March as a very appealing woman, even beautiful. Like her sister, she spoke well, in a businesslike yet genteel voice that would raise her above the average secretarial or clerical employee; no executive, even the most demanding, would be embarrassed to have her representing him to callers. She seemed particular about the kind of job she would accept; it had to be a pleasant environment and something that would use her skills effectively. She wouldn't work just to be doing something, or just for the money.

March quickly found an opening that seemed right for her, at Book Press, across the border in Brattleboro, Vermont. Getting there meant a twenty-minute ride from Keene, but it was an interesting firm—they printed books, some of them best sellers, for major publishing companies—and they needed someone like Teri as an executive secretary. The interview was set for Friday afternoon.

Teri was impressive in the interview, and the personnel manager asked her to come to work the following Monday on a temporary basis as executive secretary to the vice-president in charge of sales. After two weeks her employment was made permanent, and she and John settled into a routine much like the one he had followed with Robbi. They drove down from Marlow for breakfast at Friendly's, and afterward Teri would go over to the bus station. Often they stopped off to get something to read at Bob White's newsstand behind the little terminal, just as John and Robbi had done. Sometimes John let Teri off at the newsstand, where she would kill time while waiting for the bus by picking out paperback historical romances for herself or an aviation magazine for John. In the evening, John picked her up for the ride home, sometimes with a stop at Friendly's first for dinner. Teri Martin had slipped into her late twin's place in John's life like an understudy taking over for a departed actress.

It was the best flight Carol Hammann had ever taken. Usually her time in an airplane offered long stretches of low-level anxiety punctuated by moments of fear. She and Fred went flying from time to time when they had the chance, and Carol kept at it because she enjoyed the outings and the time with her husband, free of distraction. The nervousness was an unpleasant but unavoidable side effect. But the flight to Poughkeepsie with John and Teri was pure pleasure. Carol wasn't quite sure why, but it probably had something to do with Teri's strong, attractive presence and Carol's curiosity about the newcomer.

Carol had gotten over her initial confusion at seeing Teri walk into the store, and she found herself growing to like the newcomer. Teri was an enthusiastic talker, much more outgoing than Robbi, recounting some of her own history and describing events in Robbi's life that Carol had not known about—the deaths of her two children in Texas, her inheritance.

The details of Teri's relationship with Robbi fascinated Carol. She told Teri about an article she had read recently in a women' magazine about a convention of identical twins held in the Midwest There appeared to be a special closeness between twins, something almost supernatural. Teri described times when she and Robbi had been separated and one of them sensed that the other was going through an emotional or physical crisis; these premonitions always turned out to be accurate. Carol asked how the death of one so close had affected Teri. "It's very strange," Teri said, "like having a par of yourself die." Any remaining uneasiness Carol had felt at the strange perfection of the likeness between the two sisters was banished by the stimulating conversation and the pleasure of sight-seeing from the air on a glistening fall day. The lunch in New York State and the return flight passed in lighthearted camaraderie.

But that evening, as Carol thought back over the day, the doubts returned. There had been moments during the day when little inconsistencies had stuck briefly in her mind, like twigs snagging for a moment at the banks of a stream. Now she reassembled them, trying to find a pattern. Teri had never been North before, yet as they crossed into New York she identified the Catskill Mountains, which Carol thought too obscure for an outsider to know about. At lunch Teri mentioned things about Marlow that a newcomer would be unlikely to pick up so quickly. And there was the uncanny resemblance to Robbi, which even extended to gold caps on Teri's teeth; Carol hadn't known Robbi well enough to remember exactly, but she thought she remembered some kind of caps on Robbi's teeth, too. Of course she was the same woman, Carol thought.

"She can tell anybody anything she wants, but that's Robbi Homan," Carol finally said to Fred, but even as she spoke, she doubted herself. Fred wasn't convinced either way. They let the matter drop.

In spite of the pendulum swings of her belief in Teri's identity, it was undeniable that Carol felt close to the newcomer. There weren't many people in Marlow with Teri's sense of a larger world, her fast-moving intelligence, and her sharp, earthy wit. Carol didn't have a friend like her in New Hampshire. In spite of her five years in Marlow and her central position in the community, Carol was still an outsider in some ways. Teri was more like the people she had known on Long Island. There was a definite affinity. The Hammanns made plans to invite Teri and John to join them for Thanksgiving.

Over Thanksgiving dinner, conversation flowed easily. For the first time, Teri spoke at length about her past. She had been married to a military man, she said, an officer. They had been living in Colorado when Robbi got sick. It wasn't a happy marriage; her husband had struck Teri more than once. When he had refused to let her go to care for her twin in Texas, she had simply left him. She had no intention of going back. The sisters had inherited a large amount of money and she was quite ready to take advantage of the independence it allowed her. She talked about all this in a witty, detached style that made her interesting to listen to. When she discussed her marriage, or her difficult childhood, there was no self-pity in it. She spoke from the perspective of a survivor, one who had triumphed over the harsh circumstances of her past.

It was the trauma of her childhood that fueled Teri's argument with Irene Paquette a month later, early on Christmas Eve. The three couples were sitting in Carol's living room, talking in shifting combinations, when a rising tension in the voices of Irene and Teri forced itself into the other conversations. They all fell silent as Irene spoke about a young boy she had been taking care of. Irene was older, a forceful woman, not used to being contradicted. She was a believer in health foods and natural remedies, and when she advised Carol to put honey on her cut finger or grind up seaweed for her children to eat, Carol would nod and say, "Hmm, yes, I'll try that," and smile to herself.

The child she had been caring for had misbehaved repeatedly, Irene said, and when he continued after several warnings, she sent him to stand silently in a room by himself. Irene's manner did not invite disagreement, but Teri was tense with anger. She insisted that what Irene had done was "cruel." As a child, Teri said, her voice shaking with resentment, she had been abused herself. The implication was clear: Irene had been guilty of child abuse. Irene attempted to stem the attack, but Teri was not to be put off. She had lived with her grandparents, she went on, and her grandfather had tied her in a chair and made her sit in the living room all night in the dark. They had been wealthy, she said, but there was no love in the house, and she had been miserable.

Irene protested that she had merely been firm, not cruel, but she wilted before Teri's force. She seemed stunned. The others sat in uneasy silence as Teri talked, and when she had finished, it was difficult to restart the conversation. The Paquettes waited the minimum time politeness would allow, and then stood up to leave.

"Jeez, do you know who you just argued with?" Carol asked Teri when the door was safely shut behind the Paquettes. "Nobody argues with Irene."

Teri could see that Carol's indignation was ironic. There was more amusement, even admiration, than displeasure in it. As her own anger continued to subside, Teri began to appreciate the humor in her choosing the formidable Irene Paquette to argue with.

"I nearly died," Carol went on, exaggerating for effect. "I was so embarrassed."

Teri laughed, but her voice was serious as she spoke: "I feel very strongly about that, about being cruel to children."

"Well, next time keep your 'strongly' to yourself," Carol said in her rough New York way. She had the feeling that Teri understood the mixture of appreciation and mild shock that she felt. "Now I have to face Irene, and you don't. You can go dancin' off."

Carol couldn't remember a time when her family had felt like having any outsiders around late on Christmas Eve while the children opened their presents, but Carol had wanted to make an exception for Teri Martin. There was something in the way Teri had stood up to Irene that appealed to Carol in an unexpected way.

Teri and John fit comfortably into the Christmas Eve celebration. Teri got along well with the children. Carol noticed that Dawn, who was sixteen and choosy about whom she liked, seemed particularly relaxed with Teri. They talked easily about Dawn's boyfriend, and Dawn listened attentively when Teri told her he sounded unreliable and she should forget about him.

The Hammanns had given Dawn an electric typewriter for Christmas, and Teri sat next to her as she tried it out, offering pointers. Carol wanted to take a picture of the occasion for a keepsake, but Teri leaned back, leaving Dawn alone in the picture.

Terrie Williams had made her mind up even before Teri appeared. She had seen enough on their snowmobile outings: Robbi was a phony, and nothing that involved her could be taken at face value. Roger disagreed, and they even got in little arguments about it.

"You don't trust anyone," he said to her, and they both knew there was an element of truth in it. Terrie Williams was naturally unsentimental and impatient with indirection. As a young child, when she had failed to get along with her father, she packed her own little suitcase, walked out, and went across the road to live with her grandparents. And stayed. This element of her personality was reinforced by her work. In a bank, it paid to be consistently skeptical about human nature.

But slowly Roger's own doubts about Robbi grew, and they discussed each day's developments with the enthusiasm of faithful soap opera viewers. They shared a good laugh when he came home and told her about the twin sister. Terrie Williams was from Texas, and her maiden name was Theresa Martinez. Robbi's "twin" was from Texas and her name was Teri Martin. She seemed to have stolen bits of her identity from Roger's wife.

But Roger found himself seduced from time to time by the reality of John's grief and by Teri's self-confidence. John had been truly love-struck with Robbi, and when Roger had pressed him about going to Texas to see how she was and find out once and for all what was true and what wasn't, the reasons for John's resistance had seemed credible. First it was money, then it was Robbi's pride, then it was their shared aversion to the ceremonies of grief. And finally, underlying it all, giving plausibility to this extraordinary reticence they shared, was the tacit understanding John and Robbi had constructed at the very beginning of their time together: Each had a past filled with pain, and neither wanted to relive what had gone before. They would live in the present.

John had displayed his own doubts about Robbi's inheritance and other details of the story. "I've had some questions from time to time," he said once when Roger pressed him about trying to validate something Robbi had told him, "but it doesn't make any difference. I don't want to know." He was content with her, and he didn't care if the inheritance came through; they didn't need the money to be happy. Roger thought John might be afraid of what he'd learn, but he kept the thought to himself. Even after Roger's belief in Teri Martin began to erode, he would find himself listening to John talk about her and thinking, I can believe this, I can see it from his point of view.

In the end, it was his wife's account of the VISA card incident that settled things once and for all in Roger's mind.

Terrie Williams was working as supervisor of the tellers at the Monadnock Bank's branch in the Hillside Shopping Plaza. She was seated at her desk behind the line of teller windows when she looked up to see Teri Martin step through the gateway into the business area. As the blond visitor headed for the desk of the VISA account supervisor, her eyes swept past Terrie Williams without pausing. At least she's good at that part, Terrie thought. When Teri had finished her business and left the bank, Terrie Williams strolled over to her colleague at the VISA desk, Nancy Giovanni.

Nancy had opened a VISA account more than a year earlier for Robbi Homan, she said, and Robbi had died in Texas. Her twin sister, Teri Martin, had just come in to see about closing the account and getting a card of her own. Nancy had told her that if she would bring them a death certificate for Robbi, the bank would pass her outstanding debts into an estate account and the balance would be taken care of by the bank's insurance. Terrie Williams began to laugh. She explained that there was no such person as Teri Martin, that the woman was Robbi Homan. Nancy Giovanni was incredulous.

"I opened that account for her," Nancy said, "and she died. Her obituary was in the paper. That's her twin sister."

Terrie Williams repeated her assertion that Robbi Homan and Teri Martin were the same person. Nancy seemed offended. She was equally sure that her observation of the twin sisters could not be mistaken. Professional pride was involved. Bank officials are expected to be more acute than the average person in observing and judging behavior. Nancy explained patiently about the estate account. Terrie Williams, irritated at Robbi's long history of deception, was in no mood to be diplomatic.

"Forget it," she said, "there isn't going to be any estate account, because that woman is not dead."

She was stunned by the force of Nancy's response. Anywhere but in the middle of the bank, with a midday flow of customers and bank officers all around, it would have been a full-fledged shout.

"The poor woman is dead," Nancy hissed. "Let her rest in peace."

"Okay, okay," Terrie responded, taken aback but determined to stand her ground, "you believe what you want to believe, and I'll believe what I want to believe." She paused.

"All I want is an apology when you find out the truth," Terrie said. She made it as forceful as she could, standing in the middle of the bank. "And you will!" she concluded.

Terrie was willing to wait. It was only a matter of time. She was sure of that.

As Ron Oja had hoped, the weekend had quieted some of the uproar at Central Screw provoked by Teri's visit. The obituary verifying the report of Robbi's death, which appeared on Saturday morning, further dampened the enthusiasm of some of the skeptics. But Sandy Peace was not ready to let the matter drop.

As she listed the arguments for doubting Robbi's death, Peace drew additional observations and bits of speculation from others. Shirley Leonard was convinced that the woman she had seen on Main Street was Robbi, no matter what color her hair was. And how logical was it, asked Edna Brown, an outspoken woman who had clashed with Robbi over minor office matters, that a woman would fly two thousand miles to console a man she had never met? But what about the difference in her teeth? someone asked. That would be an easy thing to have a dentist do, came the reply. And anyway, no two people could agree on which sister had what caps and what fillings on which teeth. Teri had a scar that looked just like one that Robbi had. But who notices scars? And somebody saw them laughing in the parking lot. Sure, but maybe she told him a joke to cheer him up.

Someone had brought a copy of the obituary, and they pored over it: "Robbi L. Homan, 37, of Marlow died Wednesday in Dallas, Texas, after a long illness."

"It's all just too pat," Sandy Peace murmured.

And what about the name? Priscilla Gendron asked. What *about* the name? someone wanted to know. In addition to serving as receptionist and covering the switchboard, Priscilla had worked in personnel, and she remembered seeing Robbi's name on her records. Robbi was only her middle name. Her legal name at Central Screw was Lindsay R. Homan. Why should it be different in the obituary? But newspapers make mistakes, someone offered. But how do you get an obituary if someone hasn't died? That was the real question, somebody responded. The buzz of speculation coursed from desk to desk throughout the large office, overflowing into the back shop, widening to touch almost all of the 125 employees.

At first, Ron Oja viewed the disruption with detachment. But as days went by and the dispute failed to moderate, he became increasingly concerned. There seemed to be intense feelings developing between several employees who felt strongly that Robbi was trying to carry out some kind of deception, and a few who were prepared to accept Teri and put the matter to rest. The tension was threatening to make a martyr out of Claudia Brooks.

There was no malice in it; quite the contrary, in fact. Claudia was a cheerful, outgoing woman who had made a lot of friends in the fifteen months since Robbi had trained her to take her place at Central Screw. It was just that Claudia had accepted the idea of Robbi's death from the first minute she received Teri's phone call, and the doubts of her coworkers and friends at Central Screw seemed bizarre to her.

"Don't you see the difference?" she would say, ticking off the details of looks and habits—hair, weight, teeth, eyes, smoking, everything she had seen or heard about—that distinguished the two sisters. She had talked to Teri on the phone, she had followed Robbi's illness. The whole thing seemed so strange: Why would anyone fake all that? Who ever heard of anything like that happening?

At first they tried to discuss it with her, but the only effect was to press each faction more firmly into its own corner, narrowing views on both sides and heightening the tension in the office. The loudest voices belonged to those who saw deception in Teri's arrival. Those who initially took her appearance at face value either gradually became persuaded by the doubters or withdrew in the face of their certainty. It became difficult to adopt any position other than suspicion. All but the doubters were learning to keep their views to themselves. All except Claudia Brooks. Seeing the loneliness of her position, others in the office began to feel sorry for her. They stopped bringing up the subject of Robbi Homan and Teri Martin.

Claudia began to feel that people were avoiding her. One day she went in to see Ron Oja.

"You know, something funny's going on," she said. "Nobody's talking to me. I don't think they're mad at me, but . . ." Her voice trailed off. Oja wanted to help, but there wasn't much he could say.

Next, a few of the skeptics took up their doubts with Oja. Maybe they should alert the police.

"Don't be ridiculous," Oja replied. "Robbi's dead. Let her rest in peace." He didn't want to disturb things any further by arguing with them, but it was obvious that he felt they were acting like busy-bodies, creating tension that wasn't doing anybody any good.

Oja's response had little effect. Throughout Central Screw, skepticism cascaded into doubt and then into suspicion, which focused on the obituary. Why not put the office to work checking out the obituary? The idea filtered in to management. When the answer came back, it was clear and direct: "Leave it alone. Robbi's dead. We don't think it ought to be pursued, so this company is not going to pursue it." It was time to let the matter drop and get back to business.

Sandy Peace wasn't surprised, but she wasn't satisfied, either.

Management had closed their minds on the subject. If management wasn't interested, the women could pursue it themselves. It would be easy to check out the facts in the obituary. The little group looked it over again:

Robbi L. Homan

Robbi L. Homan, 37, of Marlow died Wednesday in Dallas, Texas, after a long illness.

She was born in Buffalo, N.Y., March 25, 1945, daughter of Hugh and Cindi Grayson, and had lived in Marlow for two years.

Mrs. Homan was formerly employed by Central Screw Co. in Keene and was a member of Sacred Heart Church in Tyler, Texas.

Survivors include her husband, John Homan of Marlow, and two sisters, Teri Martin of Dallas and Jean Ann Trevor of White Plains, N.Y.

Mrs. Homan had requested that her body be donated to the Medical Research Institute in Texas and that no funeral be held. Contributions may be made in her memory to a favorite charity.

They could begin by trying to verify Robbi's death. Jolene Hoover, who worked in the computer room, had grown increasingly skeptical since Teri had failed to show an interest in looking her up. She had a friend in Texas; she could call and ask him to see if there was a Medical Research Institute in Dallas. Sandy Peace would call directory assistance in Dallas and see if she could find the institute, and she could also try Tyler, Texas, to see if anybody there knew about Robbi.

Nobody wanted to antagonize Ron Oja and the rest of management. But it might take a lot of telephone calls all over the country to find the answers. Central Screw had WATS lines, but if management had no sympathy or patience for the enterprise, the calling would have to be done secretly. Feeling like naughty children, both guilty and excited, the women began investigating.

No one who had seen Robbi and Teri could resist comparing them. After his visit to pay condolences to John, Peter Homan had talked with Shelley about Teri, and when the two couples finally got together several days later he found himself cataloging the differences between the twins. During long evenings sitting across from Robbi as the two couples played cards and Monopoly during John and Robbi's first months in New Hampshire, Peter had been fascinated by a tiny black slash mark on the iris of Robbi's left eye. Teri didn't have any such mark. Shelley was more impressed by the differences in personality; Teri was more physically vigorous, eager to experience a New England winter, and enthusiastic about trying cross-country skiing. Robbi had shown irritation when John bought her skis for their first Christmas—she made it clear that she would have preferred a mink coat—and if she had ever gotten over her antipathy to cold weather, it had been after Peter and Shelley knew her. Teri shared Robbi's pleasure in reading; when they stopped by, Peter and Shelley were likely to find her sitting in the lawn chair, smoking, with a book in her lap. Teri watched television more often, she smoked more heavily, and she seemed less interested in housekeeping—the living room had a permanently cluttered look these days—but John didn't seem to mind the difference.

Peter was relieved at the reconciliation with John and pleased for his brother's sake that John was growing comfortable with Teri. They seemed to get along well, and while they were not demonstrative, they seemed increasingly affectionate toward each other. John let it be known at first that he was sleeping on the floor in the living room, leaving the bedroom to Teri, but within a few weeks he confided to a friend that a certain intimacy had developed between them and that those arrangements were no longer necessary.

One weekend John was seized by an urge to make a record of his new companion and their tranquil domestic scene. Getting out the camera, he caught Teri in a leopard-spotted housedress, moving round the house, working at the stove, sitting in her chair by the wood-burning stove. Finally he moved in for a portrait, the close attention of the camera forcing her to look off to the side, the knuckles of one hand placed with studied casualness against her chin. She seemed comfortable, relaxed, and a bit tired. She had been through a lot of changes in the past few weeks.

It seemed a good time for an evening out. Robbi had instructed Teri to go somewhere with John after her death and have a lavish dinner, even a party, to help begin the healing process. It wouldn't be lavish, but it would be nice to have dinner with a few of Robbi's friends at the Valley Green Restaurant. The lounge in the Valley Green Motel was a place she and John had gone for drinks with Jerry and Marcy Scadova, Claudia Brooks, Ron Oja, and other people from Central Screw. Teri phoned a few days before Thanksgiving to ask Claudia and her boyfriend, Lloyd Peters, to join her after work the next day. John would come as soon as he got finished at Findings.

Lloyd had been watching the effect of Teri's arrival on Claudia, and he was emphatic when she asked him to go to the Valley Green with her. Claudia had been in emotional confusion since the first phone call from Teri, and it didn't make her easy to be around. He had no idea what was going on, but the whole thing seemed ominous, like a poker opponent's hole card, and he didn't want any part of it.

"I ain't going," he said.

"I'm not going unless you go with me," she said, appealing to his sympathy. She wanted moral support.

"I'm not going with you, and that's it," he repeated. "The whole thing is weird. I remember Robbi the way she was, and that's fine, that's how I'm going to leave it."

"But I'm not sure if it's Robbi," she answered, realizing as she said it how greatly doubt had grown in her. She knew she would go without him, if she had to.

Claudia recalled the stories Robbi had told, during the calls from Dallas, about Teri's drinking.

"Whenever I went out with Robbi, she had one drink, and that was it," she told Lloyd. "Maybe Teri will have more drinks. This is going to be the night I find out." Lloyd didn't seem excited about the prospect, but Claudia grew increasingly nervous as she thought about meeting Teri.

At work, still looking for psychological support, Claudia asked Ron Oja to join the party for a drink and bring his wife, Sue. Oja was fascinated by the opportunity to see Teri again, to look her over. He accepted the invitation and phoned Sue.

"Sue, you've gotta see this," he said, and described the situation.

"I can't have a drink," she said. "I've got to make dinner."

"The hell with dinner," he said, "we are going to have a drink."

After work, Oja dropped Claudia off at the Valley Green and went home to pick up Sue. At the door of the lounge, as Claudia's eyes became accustomed to the dark, she spotted Teri at a table to the side. She stood up, as if to make herself visible to Claudia, but then gave no sign of recognition. Claudia walked to the table.

"Are you Claudia?" the blond woman said. She acknowledged the greeting and sat down. The anticipation had made Claudia extremely self-conscious. She wanted to inspect Teri closely but wondered if she would be caught at it.

As the conversation got under way, Claudia found herself beginning to relax. Teri reached into her purse and took out a pack of cigarettes; Claudia's eye was immediately riveted to the package. They were Merits, the same brand that Robbi smoked. She wondered if Teri noticed her interest. Would Teri feel she was being spied on? Would she challenge Claudia, even attack her? Teri lit her cigarette and went on talking animatedly. There was no sign that she felt anything was amiss.

After a while, John joined them. Teri continued to reminisce about Robbi. John's eyes glistened at the memories of his wife, and Claudia once again felt sorry for him. He seemed endlessly sad. When the Ojas came in, Ron introduced Sue to Teri and they shook hands. After a few minutes of polite conversation, the Ojas began to feel that they were not expected to sit at the table, so they excused themselves. Since it was dinnertime and they had nothing at home, they went into the dining room.

"Her hand was freezing," Sue said when they were sitting down. "And that's Robbi." She was convinced, without doubt.

"No, it's not," Ron said, equally sure. They settled down to dinner. After a while, Teri and John came into the dining room with Claudia. The situation was a little awkward, but the three made no move to join the Ojas, choosing a table in the Ojas' line of sight. "She sure doesn't act like Robbi," Ron said, noticing her subdued manner. She looked a lot smaller, too.

Even after the three had ordered dinner and started eating, Claudia was still uncomfortable, but she was determined to find out what she could. She had been talking mostly with John, and she found it easier not to look directly at Teri; it was hard to find things to say to this woman. She forced herself to observe details of Teri's dress and behavior. She was wearing Robbi's jacket, a gray ski parka with stripes on the sleeves. Claudia's scrutiny was interrupted when Teri got up to go to the ladies' room. John turned his sad gaze on Claudia. He had heard that some people doubted Teri's identity.

"Don't you notice the difference?" he asked her. It was a plaintive question, an echo of her own plea to her co-workers at Central Screw in the days after Teri's appearance. Now it sounded hollow to Claudia.

"Aren't her eyes different," John said, trying to prompt her. He wanted her to see it, but Claudia was not convinced. The uncertainty was making her resentful, even angry. All the pressure of her doubts, the pain of her growing isolation during the past few weeks, overwhelmed her desire to offer John some reassurance.

"No, she looks like Robbi to me," she said to him, defiance in her tone. She seemed to be telling herself as much as she was answering John. "She's still not drinking, and she's still smoking those same damn cigarettes."

She needed some resolution of her doubts, needed it with an almost physical craving. When Teri returned, she would try a test.

Claudia and Lloyd Peters had been separated for more than a year when Robbi left. Claudia had regularly confided in Robbi about the breakup with Lloyd and about another man she was seeing. Robbi had counseled her to straighten things out with Lloyd: "You're crazy," she had said, "get back with him." Now that she and Lloyd were together again, the man she had been seeing was calling her, asking her to go out with him. As she told John about the latest developments, Claudia watched Teri, trying to provoke a reaction, to catch her in a slipup. Even some facial expression or gesture might be revealing. But Teri listened without any visible reaction. Nothing. She might as well have been made of stone.

After dinner, John and Teri drove Claudia home in the little white pickup. It struck her that Teri had nursed the same drink from the time Claudia joined her through the whole evening.

"I'm going shopping the day after Thanksgiving," Claudia said. "If John has to work, do you want to go with me, over to

317

Manchester or someplace?" Claudia felt something pushing her beyond the lurking sense that there was a sinister quality here, something to be avoided. Teri said she would enjoy it and promised to call the next day. The call never came. Claudia went shopping with her mother and a friend.

She had offered friendship and Teri hadn't even had the decency to call her, Claudia thought. Maybe the people at work were right, maybe there was something fishy about all this. She found herself curious for the first time to know what was going on with Sandy Peace and the others, all the phone calls and whispering about the obituary.

At work the next week, Claudia's co-workers were eager to fill her in on the latest developments but still wary about her feelings.

"You know, Claudia," Sandy Peace began, "I don't want to break your heart about this . . ." She hesitated. Something had changed in Claudia. She was ready to hear what they had learned.

They had taken turns making the calls, using the WATS line. One would cover the reception window and the switchboard, serving as a lookout, while another was calling from one of the executive offices. Each time a new piece of intelligence came in, they held whispered conversations in the ladies' room, analyzing its significance and deciding who would take the next step.

Some of their efforts had been inconclusive. They had examined Central Screw's telephone records, looking for some trace of Robbi's frequent, long lunchtime calls. They found nothing to confirm her calls, but they abandoned the effort when it became clear that she probably used the WATS line; WATS calls were not itemized.

Sandy had called Dallas information to see if there was a listing for Teri Martin. There were two. At one, there was no answer for days on end. At the other number, a woman finally answered.

"Do you have a sister named Robbi?" Sandy asked.

"No," came the emphatic reply, "Who the hell is this?" Sandy was nonplussed.

"I'm sorry, I must have the wrong number," she blurted, and hung up abruptly.

But other efforts added weight to their skepticism about Teri Martin. Jolene's friend in Dallas had checked the hospitals, looking for a Medical Research Institute. It had taken him several days of calling to find out that there was no such place. Sandy had called information in several Texas cities, with the same result. Next she had reached a reporter at the newspaper in Tyler, Texas.

"I'm calling from New Hampshire," she said, "and we think there's something really weird going on up here." She explained the situation, telling him about Robbi's death and the auto accident that caused the deaths of her husband and children in Tyler. Nobody knew their last name, but the husband's name was Joseph and it had happened between five and eight years before. Could he help them? The reporter was intrigued and promised to check into it. He could start off by telling them that there was no Sacred Heart Church in Tyler. He called back several days later to say there was no record of a Robbi Homan dying November 10, or anytime around then. He had searched the newspaper's files, also, and found no record of any accident like the one they described.

Jolene had asked her friend to check obituaries and coroners' records that might show deaths anywhere in the Dallas area. That, too, had failed to turn up anything that might have to do with Robbi.

Each new bit of evidence cut a little deeper into Claudia Brooks's conviction that Teri was Robbi's twin sister. But if she wasn't Teri, then she was Robbi. And if she was Robbi, what was she trying to pull? And what should they do about it?

Claudia's friends were relieved that she seemed to be listening to reason. Now it was time to take the next step. Sandy Peace was ready for another approach to Ron Oja. Claudia knew someone on the police force. Maybe she could take it up with him.

Sandy Peace didn't want to challenge him; there was no point in making an issue of it. She had been around the other managers enough to realize how much store they put in business judgments. They had hired Robbi and worked with her for two years; management had given her a lot of responsibility, relied on her, put a lot of confidence in her. She had been an exceptionally valuable employee. It would be hard for them to change their minds. But the group was confident that the evidence they had assembled would back up their early suspicions. And as they laid it out for him, Ron Oja's skepticism slowly gave way to curiosity and then to fascination. He seemed impressed.

As he considered the evidence, Oja agreed to make some calls of his own. Chaparral Industries acted as a sales representative for Central Screw in Texas. Oja was on the phone with them regularly. Maybe they could find something.

Oja talked to a woman named Patty, one of his contacts at Chaparral. "Hey, Patty," he said, feeling a little silly, "I'd like you to do me a favor." He asked her to double-check on the Medical Research Institute and see what she could find out about the Sacred Heart Church in Tyler, or maybe somewhere nearby.

It was several days before Patty called back. She had been busy, but she had made some calls on Ron's request, and she couldn't find a Sacred Heart Church in the Tyler area, or a Medical Research Institute anywhere. And the delay had given Oja more time to get used to the idea that his confidence in Robbi might have been mistaken.

Almost without thinking about it, Claudia Brooks had begun edging up to the idea of doing something herself. She and Lloyd were invited for dinner by an old friend, Tommy Dale, a patrolman in the Keene Police Department. Claudia told the Dales about Robbi, about her illness, and how her twin sister had shown up with news of her death. They were fascinated by the story. No one else believed she wasn't Robbi, Claudia said. What could someone do to check up in a case like this?

Tommy made some suggestions: You could write to the coroner in Texas and ask for a copy of the death report, or you could check with the bureau of vital statistics in Dallas, he said.

They talked about it some more and then moved on to other things. At home later, the idea came back to her, but she didn't have the strength to struggle with it anymore.

"I'm sick of the whole mess," she told Lloyd. "I haven't seen her again, she didn't call me when she was supposed to. The hell with it." Maybe they were doing something illegal, but it didn't really matter. She didn't want to get into it anymore. And she pushed it out of her mind. But that was not to be the end of the matter for Claudia Brooks.

Lloyd was working late at the state liquor store one evening, helping to manage the pre-Christmas rush, when Claudia drove into the parking lot to pick him up. As she pulled up in front of the store, a car just ahead slowed down almost to a crawl. Impatient to pick up Lloyd and get home, she pulled out and moved in front of it, but as she did the car moved away from the curb and came around next to her, as if playing leapfrog. Wondering what was going on, Claudia looked out to see Bob White, the owner of the newsstand near the bus station downtown. White had once worked with Lloyd at the liquor store and they had known each other a long time, but Claudia was unprepared for his first words, spoken without greeting or preamble. She had barely gotten her window rolled down when he spoke.

"What the Christ is going on?" White said gruffly.

"What do you mean?" she asked.

"What is this shit with Robbi Homan?" he went on. Claudia was still not sure why Bob White should be asking about Robbi.

"She comes into my store every day. She's waiting for a bus to go to Brattleboro. I know it's Robbi."

Claudia recalled the many occasions when she and Robbi had walked upstreet at lunchtime, stopping at White's, where Robbi would buy cigarettes or Necco wafers. She knew Robbi and John went in often for magazines and paperbacks. After Claudia had introduced them, Robbi got in the habit of passing the time of day with Bob White whenever she was in the store.

White had seen Teri on the street outside the store, a day or two after she arrived, and simply figured Robbi had dyed her hair. When he saw Robbi's obituary White said to his wife, "That's a lot of baloney. I just saw her in town." Somebody at Central Screw had mentioned it to White in the store; all the people who worked with Robbi seemed just as confused as he was. Claudia was a good friend of Robbi's. What the hell was happening?

"I don't know," she said, exasperated. She was annoyed at having the question brought so forcefully into her life again. Even more, she was thrust once more into the frustrating uncertainty of a few weeks before.

"I'm so confused I don't know whether I'm coming or going," she told White.

"Well, is it the same person?" he wanted to know.

"I don't know if it's the same person, I don't know who it is." They chatted a few minutes about possible motives.

If it is the same person, what is she proving? Claudia wondered. What are they going after? Insurance money or what?

Bob White had no more idea than Claudia did, but if Robbi's best friend didn't believe in Teri's identity, there had to be something funny going on. Somebody ought to do something about it. But what? Nothing obvious occurred to him, and with Christmas coming on, the question had to compete with the pressure of work and the pleasures of the season. The mystery of Teri Martin slipped from Bob White's mind.

19

The Hunt

When he stopped in at Bob White's newsstand to pick up his copy of the *Boston Globe* the day before New Year's Eve, Bob Hardy didn't have anything much more pressing on his mind than the weather. Even thieves seemed to slow down during the holiday season; things had been quiet at the Keene Police Department for the past few days. As a senior detective in the department, Hardy was due for a four-day break surrounding New Year's Day. He was an avid skier, but this winter had been a disappointment so far. Most years he would already have had a few weeks of skiing by now, but this winter the snow was late. It was the second year in a row, and people were talking about a snow drought.

Bob White had something besides the weather he wanted to talk about. He was a man who wouldn't sit still long for any foolishness, and something obviously was bothering him. He told Hardy a little bit about a woman at Central Screw and her twin sister, some question about her identity.

"It seems funny to me," White said, "and I'm not the only one." He was making change for a steady stream of customers while they talked. "Can I come down and talk to you later?" They arranged for White to drop by the police station when his relief person came on in the afternoon.

Hardy was a veteran, a man who had gone a long way on a quiet, friendly manner and a steady consistency. His low-key style absorbed little incongruities—the trendy, metal aviator frames of his glasses, the pipe he smoked at his desk—leaving the impression of a homey, placid man. The wash of gray in his black hair had the same effect on the little Clark Kent curl at his forehead. When Hardy admitted that he kept the paperback copy of *Name Your Baby* on his desk for help in filling out reports because he was a "terrible speller," there was no sign of false modesty in it.

As White began to outline the story for him, Hardy quickly concluded that it didn't fit any of the ordinary categories—robberies, assaults, thefts, and the like. This one presented itself more like a scatter of stones dumped in a New Hampshire meadow, with no obvious way to fit them together into a wall.

John Homan himself had reported his wife's death to White during a visit to the newsstand, and her obituary had been in the paper a day or so later. After seeing Teri Martin on the street, White had been first amazed, then quickly suspicious, about the extraordinary likeness to Robbi. White knew several people at Central Screw—they were regular customers at the newsstand—and over the following weeks they had added weight to his own skepticism. Jerry Scadova agreed with White that it was the same person, and Scadova had known Robbi a lot better than White had. Some of the people at Central Screw had been checking on the obituary, and they couldn't confirm any of the facts. Just the other day, White said, he had run into Claudia Brooks, who was Robbi's best friend, and even she had doubts about the blond woman's identity.

"I don't know what's going on, but I'd bet there's some kind of hanky-panky there," White concluded.

Hardy was intrigued, and eager to get started looking into it. He had known Claudia Brooks for a number of years, and she seemed like a logical person to start with. He called her at Central Screw.

Claudia laughed ruefully when she heard who was on the phone. Ever since her conversation with Tommy Dale, the police officer, she had been half expecting to hear from someone at the Keene Police Department.

"How'd you hear about it?" she asked Hardy. He told her about the visit from Bob White, and Claudia recalled her conversation with White in front of the state liquor store. So it wasn't Tommy. The word was getting around.

"Can I come over and see you?" Hardy asked. It was still a sensitive issue at Central Screw, and Claudia didn't want to stir things up again. She offered to go home for lunch and meet him there. It was too late for that day, and Hardy was going to be off duty through the holiday weekend. They agreed to meet at Claudia's house Monday at noon.

There wasn't time to do much more before the end of his shift, and Hardy postponed thinking about it seriously until he had a chance to get more background from Claudia.

Over a sandwich Monday at her first-floor apartment in a small, brown, frame building a half mile from the center of Keene, Claudia ran through the story for Hardy.

"You know," she said, almost as an afterthought, "I understand that she comes down from Marlow and goes into Friendly's every morning for breakfast. I saw her there myself one morning."

"I looked right at her," Claudia said, "and she looked right at me. She didn't smile, or say 'Hello,' or anything. I didn't know what to say. So I walked right by."

"Do you want to go to breakfast with me?" Hardy asked. The lighthearted manner of his invitation masked a growing curiosity; he was eager to see what the woman looked like. Claudia was reluctant. It sounded like a situation with the potential for pushing her into another uncomfortable confrontation with Teri Martin. Hardy needed her to point Teri out to him, though, and she agreed to think about it.

There was no obvious pattern to the case, Hardy thought, no handle to grab it by. In situations like this, he had learned to fall back on investigator's routine. He called the Bureau of Records and Statistics in Austin, the capital of Texas, requesting a search for any record of Robbi Homan's death. A series of calls repeated the attempt at Central Screw to find a Medical Research Institute in Texas, with the same result. He called Robert DiLuzio, a longtime acquaintance, at Foley's Funeral Home in Keene, and asked him to check into Texas procedures for verifying and reporting deaths. Maybe the reports of the Homan death had gotten lost in some bureaucratic dead end. Finally, Hardy walked over to the *Sentinel* to get a copy of the obituary. Maybe something solid, like facts on a piece of paper, would bring some pattern to the situation.

By early afternoon the day after his visit to the *Sentinel,* Hardy's telephone ear was starting to feel battered, but calls to the police department and the newspaper in Tyler, to hospitals and churches, had produced no further trace of Robbi Homan. It was starting to look as if the woman had gone to a lot of trouble to change her identity, and that suggested someone on the run.

It was time to get other law-enforcement people involved. He called Ed Blair at the New Hampshire office of the Internal Revenue Service; maybe it was some kind of tax fraud. Blair agreed to look into it, and Hardy promised to send him a copy of the obituary. At the Cheshire County Sheriff's Department no investigator was available; they were still closed for vacations and the New Year break.

Finally, Hardy called the New Hampshire State Police barracks in Keene. Hardy's jurisdiction didn't extend to Marlow. Maybe they could get a trooper up there and find out something from the Homans' neighbors. Hardy had often worked with a state police investigator named Larry Migneault, but he was off duty. The dispatcher referred him to Trooper Barry Hunter.

As he filled Hunter in on what he knew, Hardy felt the need to keep an open mind, but one possibility pushed itself insistently forward. When he had finished his account of what was known about Teri Martin, Hardy mentioned the Manning-Levasseur gang. There was hardly a cop in northern New England who hadn't kept this radical group near the top of his list of unfinished business; Hunter knew immediately what Hardy was thinking about.

Thomas Manning and Raymond Luc Levasseur were the leaders of one of the last political terrorist groups surviving from the early 1970s. They had called themselves the United Freedom Front and the Jonathan Jackson–Sam Melville Group, the latter after two radical convicts killed in prison. The group had roots in New England—Levasseur had been born in Maine, and members had served time in the New Hampshire State Prison. Manning and Levasseur were wanted for the armed robbery of a bank in Portland, Maine, in 1975, and along with others they were suspected in a series of bombings of corporate offices and military installations. But the thing that made them infamous among law-enforcement officials was the murder of a New Jersey state trooper just a year earlier. The FBI and investigators from each of the six New England states had set up a sixteen-member task force based in Boston with the sole assignment of pursuing the half-dozen or so remaining members of the gang, and the state of New Jersey had offered a reward of one hundred thousand dollars.

One of the fugitives was Thomas Manning's wife, Carol. A native of Sanford, Maine, she was wanted with her husband in the Portland bank robbery. Hunter caught the quickening of interest in Hardy's description. They agreed to get together and go over the information Hardy had accumulated. After Hunter notified his supervisor about the case, he made the five-minute drive to the Keene Police Department.

The two detectives looked over the FBI flyers to refresh their memories about Carol Manning. The photographs showed a tall, thin woman with brown hair; according to the flyer, she would have passed her twenty-sixth birthday the day before. Teri Martin was said to be about five feet, six inches and 125 pounds, her hair possibly dyed. She was supposed to be in her late thirties, but estimates of age had to be treated with care; a lot of people weren't very good at estimating ages, especially of a woman. The rough description they had of John Homan—thin, with a mustache and long, dark hair—was a match for Raymond Levasseur. The obvious next step was to get a look at Teri Martin and John Homan. They agreed that Hardy would follow through on his breakfast with Claudia Brooks; Hunter would try to get a look at John Homan. The investigation would have to be carried out under extraordinary security; Levasseur and the Mannings were all considered extremely dangerous; they were likely to be heavily armed and very sensitive to any sign of pursuit.

They agreed to divide up a series of calls to check the rest of the facts in the Robbi Homan obituary. Hunter had good connections in Marlow from the days when he was just starting in the state police; he had rented a room on Stone Pond Road from a woman who took in rookie troopers on temporary training assignment at the Keene barracks. He would go up there when he left Hardy and see what he could find out. Hardy would see if they could get into Book Press. They would talk again the next day.

Claudia Brooks was still reluctant when Hardy called her that evening about the breakfast at Friendly's, but in the end she agreed to help him out. She wasn't going to come alone, though. She would ask Jeanne House to go with her. It was like the time at the Valley Green. She would need the security of someone familiar if she was going to face Teri again. The woman was taking on an ever more ominous cast in Claudia's mind.

The next morning, Hardy picked Claudia up at home and drove to Friendly's, where they met Jeanne in the parking lot. It was six forty-five. Jeanne was a moody person; today she seemed even more nervous than Claudia. The two women went inside and sat down. A few minutes later Hardy followed, feigned a chance meeting, and joined them. They ordered coffee and chatted, trying to appear relaxed. After a few minutes, Claudia suddenly stiffened.

"Here she comes," Claudia whispered. She nodded to the back of the restaurant, thirty feet away, where a blond woman was coming out of the ladies' room. Without taking his eyes from Teri Martin, Hardy asked Claudia a series of questions about Robbi's purse, whether she carried it in her hand or under her arm, and which arm she normally carried it under. Why does he care about her purse? Claudia wondered.

Even as he was checking out the possibility that the blond woman might be carrying a weapon in her purse, Hardy was eliminating the possibility that she was Carol Manning. She was a minimum of ten, maybe fifteen years too old, at least a couple of inches too short, and too full in the face; there was no similarity at all to Manning's high cheekbones and thin, almost horsey face.

There goes the only idea we had for this whole business, Hardy thought, continuing to watch her, chatting with Claudia and Jeanne. He finished his coffee while Teri Martin stood at the back of the restaurant for a few minutes, talking with two of the waitresses. When Teri started toward the door, Hardy thanked his companions, waited a brief interval, and followed her out.

Hardy kept his distance as she walked along West Street toward the bus terminal. He watched from outside while she waited for the bus. After she had gone, he went inside. All the bus station employees seemed to know her story: She was the identical twin of a Marlow woman who had recently died in Texas. She took the eight-o'clock bus every morning to Brattleboro, where she was an executive secretary at Book Press, but she wouldn't have to ride the bus much longer; she was having her own car, a Mercedes, shipped to her from Texas. Hardy headed for his office and more phone calls.

Carol Hammann had something she wanted to say to Teri Martin. She had seen Teri several times since Christmas, but no good opportunity had presented itself. The incident with Irene Paquette hadn't dominated the quiet pleasure of John and Teri's company Christmas Eve, and the Hammanns had invited them to come back the next day.

John and Teri had opened their presents at home Christmas morning, sitting on the floor by the wood-burning stove. John took picture of Teri sitting amid a clutter of wrapping paper and opened presents. She was smiling, and the cheerful scene was in keeping with Robbi's wishes.

Later they joined the Hammanns again. Teri contributed a bowl of fruit and a delicious potato salad she had made herself. They had brought presents for the children, leg warmers for Dawn and a small train for Peter, who was twelve.

Since then, Teri had come into the store with John several times. Robbi had always stayed in the truck while John came in, but Teri was more sociable. They had chatted comfortably, but Carol didn't want to speak her piece in front of anyone else.

One cold evening after New Year's the store was empty when Teri came in with John. Carol saw her chance to set things right. They chatted a bit before she felt ready to say what was on her mind.

"You know, Teri," she began, "when you first came here, I never believed you were different." Teri listened with interest. Carol was a little uncomfortable, but she was determined to go on. As she spoke, it felt like a confession.

"I thought you were Robbi, and just changed your name." Teri continued to stand silent.

"But every day I see you," Carol went on, "I can see more and more difference between you two."

Teri didn't say much, and the conversation moved on to more casual talk, but Carol was glad she had gotten it off her chest.

Barry Hunter was at his desk early the day after his evening in Marlow. He hadn't learned anything very helpful from the visit. He had talked to several people, and they all knew the story of Robbi Homan's death and the arrival of her twin sister. They seemed to take Teri Martin at face value: Except for the blond hair, she was a dead ringer for Robbi. Afterward, Hunter had driven along Route 10, past Stone Pond Cottages; at least he could get a look at the house where the Martin woman and John Homan lived. But the house was mostly hidden by pine trees, and he hadn't been able to see much from the road, except that it looked small.

Hunter spent the first part of the morning on the phone. The owner of Findings, Inc., agreed to let him in to take a look at John Homan; they arranged it for later in the morning. Directory assistance had no listing for Jean Ann Trevor, Robbi Homan's sister in White Plains, New York, so Hunter called the New York State Motor Vehicles Bureau and asked them to check automobile registrations and drivers' licenses. The New York Bureau of Records in Albany began a search for a listing of twins born to the Graysons in 1945. At last it was time to get out of the office.

In the parking lot at Findings, Hunter took off his sports jacket, removed his tie, and opened his collar. He would pose as a working visitor, an inspector of some kind. Inside, he learned that John Homan was at his workbench in the toolroom. Hunter asked permission to wander a little bit before moving in close to Homan; like a new child on the playground, he wanted to stay at the fringes for a while to let people get used to his presence. The owner led him from the office into the workroom, where Hunter strolled for several minutes among the assembly workers seated at the long tables.

When he finally completed his circuit and moved into the toolroom, Hunter spotted John Homan immediately from the description: a thin man, bald at the front and top of his head, with black hair hanging down in the back. He was at his bench, working on an electric motor. Hunter moved around the room, feigning interest in the electrical outlets and ventilation of the shop, surreptitiously examining Homan in detail as he went. Hunter paid particular attention to Homan's hands and feet; they often told a lot about a person's identity. Homan wore a workingman's heavy shoes, and his hands moved naturally over the bench. There were no obvious scars or marks, but there was a line of grease under his fingernails. He looked like a man comfortable at what he was doing, without self-consciousness about his role or his surroundings. In spite of the mustache, there was only a vague resemblance to Raymond Levasseur, and none at all to any of the other members of the gang. Hunter was left without any doubt: John Homan had nothing to do with the Manning-Levasseur group.

Just after noon, Hunter met Hardy for the drive to Brattleboro. Criminal activity often crossed the Connecticut River, which forms the boundary between New Hampshire and Vermont, so Hardy had no trouble finding someone at the Brattleboro Police Department to help arrange a visit to Book Press. He had called Hardy back to say that the people at Book Press had been reluctant. For some reason they seemed extremely sensitive to any outside attention, but they had finally agreed to the visit.

As they pulled into the parking lot after the twenty-minute drive rom Keene, Hunter made sure his tie was in place once again; a isitor here would be a little more formal. Book Press occupied a ow industrial building faced with a pinkish-gray exterior. A glass howcase in the lobby held copies of best sellers in glossy covers, ooks printed by the company. The executive who had arranged the isit met the two investigators at the front office; they chatted for a ew minutes, going over the facts about Teri Martin's employment t Book Press. She had been working there a little less than two nonths, and they were very pleased with her performance.

When the detectives had finished recording the information, the xecutive led them into the manufacturing area. It was a space the ize of a warehouse, filled with the hum of working machinery. Teri Martin worked in a section at the rear walled off for office space. Hunter knew their look at her would be brief; they would attract too nuch attention if they tried to go into the office area. As he walked ast the large window in the office wall, Hunter glanced noncha- antly inside. He saw a well-dressed, attractive blond woman vorking over papers at her desk. There was something about her hat didn't quite fit there; she was almost overdressed for this mall-town New England atmosphere. But she didn't have much in :ommon with the pictures of Carol Manning. He put Teri Martin lown as five feet, four inches tall, 120 pounds, thirty-five to forty ears old.

On the drive back to Keene they mixed speculation about Teri Martin with relaxed conversation about police work, the frustrations of seeing their cases through the courts, their shared enthusiasm for ishing, and Hardy's children, who were only a few years younger han Hunter. Maybe the Teri Martin thing involved some form of raud, a big credit purchase or land mortgage in the name of Robbi Homan that would be paid off by insurance if she died. Over the next few days they could look into Robbi's debts and any large urchases. Hardy had a three-day break coming up and they parted with an agreement to get in touch after he came back to work.

The skiing was still poor, almost nonexistent, at Stratton, Brom- ey, and Okemo, the mountains in Vermont that Bob Hardy could reach in a short drive from his home near Keene. He puttered around the house or walked in the woods, trying to distract himself from the puzzle of Teri Martin. Nothing worked. Even the woods were eerie, the trees stripped and rigid in winter's grip but standing amid an unnaturally snowless blanket of long-dead leaves. Pacing along the dirt trails near his house, standing on the footbridge over the Ashuelot River, watching the sky for some sign of darkening clouds, Hardy was visited again and again by images of Teri Martin. All those phone calls and inquiries about birth dates and churches, real-estate deals, insurance manipulations, credit-card fraud, and the only thing they had turned up was a bank card with a forty-four-dollar balance outstanding. It was like holding the tail of some animal you couldn't see. All his cop's instincts told Hardy there was a tiger on the other end, but so far there was no damn way to prove it.

It wasn't the sort of thing Sally Tomlinson would do, striking up a conversation with a stranger on a bus. She preferred to keep to herself, read a book or just look out the window and think, but the blond woman liked to talk, and it was hard to put her off. After a while the woman introduced herself—her name was Teri Martin, and she lived in Marlow—and talked a little about how she had come to New Hampshire; it all sounded peculiar to Sally, but she didn't mind listening. The woman had lived an interesting life. When Sally mentioned that she didn't take the bus every day, that she drove to Brattleboro two or three days a week when her husband didn't need the car, Teri wondered if she would like to have a rider. Sally hadn't done anything about looking for a passenger, but she had thought about it and liked the idea of sharing the cost of gasoline. She was a special-education teacher at the Beacon Street School in Brattleboro, and her husband worked for the state of New Hampshire; they didn't make a lot of money.

Teri was a reliable passenger, always ready, standing in front of Friendly's when Sally's little white Honda Civic station wagon arrived in the morning. It was an easy twenty-minute ride, most of it on a widened, modernized road, up a rising series of hills and then down into the valley of the Connecticut River, before crossing to Brattleboro on the Vermont side. Teri liked to talk about herself and her past. She had come from the South after her sister's death and stayed on with her brother-in-law. She spoke of the warm relationship John Homan had enjoyed with her twin sister, Robbi. They had never had an argument, she said: "Can you imagine that, never having a fight? I can't imagine it."

Sally thought she seemed out of place in New Hampshire. Her

makeup was skillfully applied, but heavy—Sally wore none at all—and the bleached hair seemed gaudy against the somber palette of a New England winter. Her clothes were flimsy, polyesters and dressy shoes, often high heels, that would seem fitting in Keene only at a garden party on the half-dozen hottest days of summer. The gloves and lightweight boots she sometimes wore seemed like afterthoughts.

Sally made it clear there was not to be any smoking during the ride; it was her car, her space, and she just didn't like the smell. Sally knew Teri smoked, but Teri took the prohibition in stride and never mentioned it again. Maybe her talking was a substitute for the smoking. She went on about Robbi, her strange illness and the treatments, and about the grandfather who had raised them in Texas. He was a wealthy and powerful man who virtually "owned the town" where they lived, and he was used to having his way. He was always punishing them, and Teri had taken the brunt of it. Robbi was the "good sister," the well-behaved one, at least in his eyes, and Teri was the one who was constantly causing trouble.

At first, Sally found the stories interesting, but little by little they began to make her uncomfortable. It was strange about this kind of relationship, one based solely on the mutual convenience of sharing transportation. You could learn so much about a person, things you would ordinarily hear only from someone you had grown close to over a long time. With Teri, the more personal the stories became, the more intimate the revelations of tragedy and trivia, private thoughts and deep emotion, the wider the gap that Sally felt opening between them.

Teri spoke of watching movies on television and reading paperback Gothic romances and horror stories. Sally read realistic novels about contemporary life, and classic writers like Proust, and she disliked television, particularly the violent programs that Teri sometimes talked about. They didn't really have much in common, Sally thought. Once or twice it seemed that a minor detail in one of Teri's stories had changed in a second telling, and at other times the stories seemed to merge with the books and movies she talked about. Gradually the image Sally had developed of Teri seemed to loose its sharpness, like a picture slipping out of focus.

Routinely wary anyway, Sally became uneasy, then distrustful of her passenger. It wasn't something she would do anything about; the feeling was too vague. But one day when Teri offered her a coconut macaroon cookie from a box she was taking to work, Sally refused. She made an excuse, said she wasn't hungry, but it rang hollow, even in her own ears. The fact was, she just felt a kind of animal aversion, like a cat inexplicably walking away from a fresh bowl of food. She was relieved when Teri said she expected her car to be delivered soon from Texas so she would be able to share the driving. It would be a good opportunity to cut back on their relationship, maybe even end it altogether. It was getting too uncomfortable.

Barry Hunter always liked going in to work, but this Monday morning there was a special anticipation in it. It was almost a week since he had come into the Teri Martin investigation, and he didn't know much more than when he had started. Maybe if they went back and began again with the basic facts, something would turn up. He phoned the Vermont State Police and talked to Mike LeClair. LeClair was a detective Hunter had worked with before, and he was glad to help out. Hunter filled him in on the little they had learned about Teri Martin, pointing out all the gaps in the story. He asked LeClair to check Vermont tax records to find her birth date and Social Security number. They could compare them with Robbi Homan's and see where that might lead. While he was at it, LeClair said, he would run a routine fugitive check.

It was frustrating, Hunter thought, but it was fascinating, too. This was the kind of mystery, appearing suddenly amid everyday events and ordinary people, that had drawn him to police work in the first place. From the time he was in junior high school, Hunter had never wanted to do anything but be a detective. Growing up in Connecticut, he had been fascinated by crime stories in the newspaper. He had come to idolize Major Sam Rome, the legendary chief detective of the Connecticut State Police. Hunter had followed Rome's career, his repeated successes in breaking cases that had stumped police throughout the state, his growing reputation for infallibility. Later he had realized that Rome was a cop of the old school, honest and shrewd but willing to use brute force or deception to ferret out information or get a confession. Hunter had graduated summa cum laude from the University of New Haven with a degree in criminal justice. The kind of professional procedures Hunter was trained to use had seemed softhearted to Sam Rome; he had been unable to adjust to Supreme Court decisions and changing values that expanded the rights of criminals. Toward the end of his career, Rome had been like the last survivor of an extinct tribe. Hunter had learned to reject Rome's methods while honoring his memory.

At thirty-one, Hunter was well started on the kind of career in police work he had always hoped for. Most troopers served long apprenticeships in uniform before becoming detectives; Hunter had been selected after only three and a half years, and now he had been appointed as an instructor at the New Hampshire Police Academy. He was tall and fit, with the rectangular good looks of a figure on a military recruiting poster. A light dusting of gray was just visible in his black sideburns, and the serious young boy he had once been was still visible in his face and manner; he was not humorless, but he rarely smiled. It was easy to imagine him someday—younger than anyone before him, perhaps—becoming what he had aimed for since that first fascination with the exploits of Sam Rome: chief of detectives. For now, though, he was absorbed in the present, quick to say he had the best job in the state police—investigating major crimes—and never more captivated by the hunt than he was in the case of Teri Martin.

Today, however, that meant another day with the telephone and little to show for it. Hunter arranged to meet LeClair Tuesday morning over in Springfield, Vermont, to go through everything again and decide what to do next. But when they sat down in the little room at the Springfield Police Department, LeClair had only negatives to report. Nothing yet from central records. There was no trace in Vermont tax registrations of a Teri Martin employed at Book Press. Maybe her records hadn't gotten into the main file yet; they would check the new registrations. It was all they could do, keep following what they had. Hunter handed over copies of the obituary and an employment application for Teri Martin. The meeting ended without any resolution. A lot of these meetings had as much psychological value as practical effect. The cops talked about suspects and descriptions and evidence, but there was another message that came through: You're not alone, keep going, there's bound to be a break sometime.

The break came on Wednesday. Vermont State Police headquarters reported that they had a match for LeClair's description of Teri Martin, a woman wanted for trial on federal drug charges. Her name was Terry Lynn Clifton, and she had a long list of aliases. One of them was Melissa Martin. Now, finally, they could move. Hunter agreed to meet LeClair a little after noon at the Vermont State Police barracks in Chester, thirty-five miles north of Brattleboro. LeClair was having the records rushed down from Montpelier.

They were professionals, just investigators doing their jobs, they would say, but a tide of excitement swelled beneath the surface of routine procedure as they went over the descriptions with Sergeant Bob Hains, LeClair's supervisor. The fugitive was a white female, date of birth February 25, 1947. Almost thirty-six, within Hunter's estimated range of Teri Martin's age, and Homan and Martin, the twins, used a birth date of March 25, 1945. Clifton was five feet, three inches tall and weighed 115 pounds. An inch and five pounds smaller than Teri Martin. Close enough, and Hunter had only seen Martin sitting down, anyway. Clifton had brown hair, like Robbi Homan, and blue eyes. Nobody had gotten close enough to see Martin's eyes. The names put a little extra wrapping on the package. Fugitives often spun out permutations of their aliases; running down a list of a.k.a.'s on a wanted bulletin was often like one of those word games where you change one letter at a time and end up with a new word. They'd keep their own first name for a while, with a series of changing last names, then keep one of the last names and change the first name and middle initial a few times, then change the spelling of the last name. Clifton was using the name Terry, and one of her old aliases was Melissa Martin. She had been identified recently in a small town in central Vermont when she tried to get false identification papers. By the time the state police were notified, she was gone, and the trail soon went cold. Now maybe they would close two cases at once and make a good federal bust in the bargain. And solve the mystery of Teri Martin.

They were in LeClair's jurisdiction and he needed to get a look at the suspect. Hunter couldn't match the picture of Terry Lynn Clifton to his memory of Teri Martin, but now that he had something specific to look for he wanted to see her again. With the clear federal connection, they had to get the FBI into it. LeClair called Dave Steele at his office in Rutland, forty miles north.

"I think we've got something here that'll interest you," LeClair said, and briefly described the mystery of Robbi Homan and the tentative match of Teri Martin to the fugitive Clifton. They were about to go look at her; if they made a bust on the federal charges, Steele would probably want to come along.

It sounded interesting, Steele thought, but he wanted to make sure it was worth the trip. The temperature was close to fifty degrees outside, the day was gloomy, and there was sure to be fog in the mountains later as the warm air settled on the cold earth.

"You think we have to do it this afternoon?" Steele asked.

"I think so, Dave," LeClair answered. "We really ought to have a look at it now." There was no telling when a fugitive might get spooked and take off. LeClair had the feeling, for no particular reason he could explain, that this one wouldn't keep.

That was enough for Steele. He had worked with LeClair before and had confidence in his judgment. He'd notify his supervisors in the FBI division office over at Albany, New York, and leave right away.

While they waited, LeClair phoned a detective friend at the Brattleboro Police Department and asked him to arrange a visit to Book Press; maybe with the local connection they would get a little calmer response at Book Press than Hunter had a week earlier. Hunter and LeClair wanted to do someting, to start moving. They would head for the Brattleboro Police Department in separate cars, then drive to Book Press together from there once the arrangements were made. Hains would bring Steele down as soon as he arrived at the state police barracks. The FBI agent didn't know his way around Brattleboro.

It was close to three quarters of an hour, down along the Connecticut River, a quiet ride, few cars on the interstate. This was peaceful country, even on a gloomy day, with its little farms on the Vermont side, an occasional herd of cows or a few horses, every few miles a picturesque barn or a small settlement across the river in New Hampshire, everything looking self-contained, somnolent under lowering skies. Where did drugs and wanted posters and fugitives fit into this picture?

Hunter and LeClair arrived at Book Press around three o'clock. The contact person met them at the door and ushered them into the big press room, with its high ceilings and deep, rolling clatter. Apparently they were used to visitors there, representatives of publishers, suppliers of papers and ink; nobody paid much attention to Hunter and LeClair, just two guys in coats and ties. They walkd past the giant rolls of paper stacked near the presses, toward the offices in back. Teri Martin was seated at her desk again, Hunter noted. The woman was a no-nonsense worker, he thought; she never looked up. He looked hard for something more than a rough

correspondence to the picture of Terry Lynn Clifton; he still couldn'
see her eyes.

"What do you think?" he asked when they were outside again
There were a lot of similarities, LeClair responded, but she didn'
look like the photograph. Hunter had to agree.

"Good-looking woman," LeClair said, "but she's got to be
older than thirty-seven. Hard to tell, though, with all that
makeup."

They sat in the car at the back of the Book Press parking lot
mulling over the possibilities. The Brattleboro Police Departmen
checked LeClair's headquarters for them and called back on the car
radio: Steele was on his way down from the barracks with Hains
They had nothing on the woman except a couple of confused
people who had talked to Bob Hardy, and a lot of unverifiable
information in an obituary. Nobody Hunter had talked to was
even suspicious of the woman until he started asking them
questions. There was no evidence of anything illegal, no justifica-
tion for arresting her. Sam Rome would have gotten her alone in
a quiet, secluded place and stared her down, insinuating that he
knew the deepest secrets of her soul and had enough on her to
hang her three times over, letting her imagine him capable of
fiendish, unrelenting tortures until she broke down and cried and
admitted committing every unsolved crime in three states. But
things just didn't work that way anymore. They could stop her
and ask to talk to her, pretty much the way anyone on the street
could stop another person, but if she didn't want to talk to them,
she didn't have to. She could just walk away.

Steele and Hains drove into the parking lot around four o'clock
and pulled into a parking place next to Hunter and LeClair. They
rolled down a window of each car and talked about what they were
going to do. LeClair and Hunter told Steele about the weakness of
their identification. He agreed that there was no probable cause for
arrest. Should they stop her? If she was a fugitive and refused to talk
with them, she would be alerted. She could take off anytime. They'd
have no way of stopping her unless they followed her every minute.
But there were so many gaps in her identity, and they weren't
getting anywhere with the investigation. Maybe if they challenged
her it would create some kind of break in the case. It was decided:
They'd wait for Teri Martin and confront her when she came out of
work.

*   *   *

The contours of Sally Tomlinson's face were flat, like a three-dimensional model of some almost featureless terrain, and they were matched by her soft, toneless voice. Her nervous manner seemed to reflect the strain of keeping things under control. The tension showed itself in a defensive, suspicious nature.

The four big men in the parked car at Book Press had instantly seemed ominous to Sally. As she sat at the end of the walk waiting for Teri, it was all she could do to keep from jamming the accelerator to the floor and fleeing. After the men had intercepted Teri—"I've got a ride, I'll see you later," Teri had said before driving off with them, as if it were the most natural thing in the world to go away in a car with four strange men on a moment's notice—Sally sat in her car at the curb for a long time before she felt composed enough to drive home.

The next day, still uncertain about what she had seen, Sally called the Brattleboro Police Department before going to work.

"The strangest thing happened," she told the officer, and recounted the events in the parking lot.

"That woman was a fugitive," the policeman told her. "You won't ever be picking her up again."

Part Six

Unmasking

20

A Decision

"That's so ridiculous. Why would I do that to my own daughter?"

The words hung in the overheated air of the small interview room. Her own daughter, Hunter thought. This small, blond woman with the pleasant manners was wanted for the attempted murder of her own daughter.

And murder. The computer said she was also wanted for murder. Hunter looked up from the ragged piece of teletype paper, trying to match Audrey Marie Hilley with the words on the report from the national crime computer. His gaze was drawn to the window behind her. Not even five o'clock, and the winter dark had already settled hard. The room seemed colder suddenly.

LeClair perched on a desk near the door while Hunter absorbed the information on the teletype report. He turned from his own silent examination of the woman as Hunter looked up. Steele, the FBI agent, came in after a minute. He stood behind them, holding the door open. The two state police detectives followed him back out into the hall.

Steele had called Alabama to confirm the charges. In addition to the attempted murder of her daughter and two bad-check cases, she had been charged with murdering her husband. She might not even know about the murder case; she had been charged after she jumped bail on the other cases. They quickly divided the work. Steele would deal with the Alabama authorities and then arrange for the fugitive to be held overnight. Vermont was LeClair's jurisdiction, so he would take care of the arrest formalities. Hunter was the most familiar with the details, from his investigation across the border in New Hampshire; he would lead the questioning. They would stay away from the Alabama cases, concentrating on what they needed for her arraignment as a fugitive.

She was sitting quietly, seemingly unaffected by the sudden collapse of her masquerade. LeClair told her she was now under arrest as a fugitive and recited her rights. She didn't need a lawyer, she said; she was willing to talk without one; she had promised them in the car that she would tell them all about it.

Hunter primed her with basic questions. She responded easily, in a matter-of-fact voice: Yes, she was wanted in Anniston, Alabama, she had been a fugitive for three years. Teri Martin was an alias, Robbi Homan was an alias, too. As she talked about meeting John Homan in Florida and coming to New Hampshire, Hunter tried to imagine her as a murderer. It didn't fit, he thought; she was wrong for the role, too small, too genteel, too cooperative. Where was the force, the anger?

She spoke so smoothly, Hunter thought, in that soft voice, her story sounded almost as if she had rehearsed it. Maybe she's been getting ready to confess for a long time, he speculated.

She had started laying the groundwork for Teri Martin's appearance about eight months ago—May 1982—thinking she might use the identity eventually. She had been considering leaving John.

"Did he do anything to make you want to leave him?" Hunter asked.

"No, in fact it's just the opposite," she replied. "He was a good husband, loyal. I just felt I had to get away from him. I didn't want to involve him in all this. I thought if I just faded away it would be easier for him."

She had left him in early September and staged Robbi's illness, leading up to her death in Texas November 11, two months ago. Actually she had been in Florida, changing her identity to Teri Martin, the twin sister.

"How did you do it?" Hunter asked. He was intrigued by the differences between Robbi and Teri that so many of her friends had argued about, a fleck in her eye, caps or gold teeth, a different brand of cigarettes, her drinking habits. And some of the reports, especially about her teeth, had conflicted. She gave a small laugh.

"I bleached my hair and I went on a diet," she said.

"That's all?"

"That's it." She smiled vaguely, like an actress recalling a satisfying performance.

"It's a relief," she said after a moment. "I'm tired. It's been so confusing."

Hunter asked about her return as Teri Martin. He was calling her Audrey. It was ironic: For the first time in three years somebody had discovered her true identity, and they were calling her by a name she hadn't used for more than forty years. She didn't correct him.

She had told John that Robbi wanted her twin sister to come to New Hampshire and console him, she said. She came back, put the obituary in the *Keene Sentinel,* and took up a new life with John as Teri Martin. He had never realized it was all a hoax.

"Why did you do it?" Hunter asked the question that had been bothering him from the first, the one that nobody had been able to answer, even the people who had questioned the reality of Teri Martin from the first. "Why did you come back after leaving him?"

For the first time in her narration, she hesitated, looking away for a moment before she spoke.

"I don't know," she said simply. She seemed to sense that the question needed more of an answer.

"I kept trying to decide whether to keep running or give myself up," she said. Hunter waited for her to explain further, but she was silent. Maybe she meant she had left for Florida intending that she wouldn't come back, then changed her mind.

It would remain one of the great mysteries in the story of Marie Lilley: Why did she leave John Homan when she was apparently settled in her marriage, secure in her job, living comfortably, if not lavishly, in a tiny, remote town in a place where no one was likely ever to find her?

And why invent the twin sister, a ruse that took so much energy and calculation to carry off?

And why, most puzzling of all, once she was well away, free in a new life as Teri Martin, did she return to New Hampshire, where her masquerade was certain to undergo close scrutiny? She could have remained free in Marlow forever as Robbi Homan—even the FBI agents believed no one would ever have caught her—and once away, she could have settled in Florida with little fear of discovery.

The investigators had no official interest in why Audrey Marie Lilley came and went as she did; their responsibility was simply to send her back for trial on the charges in Alabama. But the questions about her life in New Hampshire would not go away. Months later, when Mike LeClair speculated about the mysteries within the mystery of Teri Martin, his mind went back to the few minute while they were going through her possessions, making an inven tory. She had responded to their earlier questioning with calm animation; now she seemed deflated and listless.

LeClair held up a piece of paper with half a dozen names followed by strings of numbers.

"What's this?" he asked.

"Social Security numbers," she responded with a wan smile "New identities." She was matter-of-fact, as if everybody spent few hours each day deciding who they would be next week. "On wears out, you use another one."

"Did you use them?"

"They're for the future." She paused. "Or rather, they were Won't have to do it, now." She considered for a moment. "It's hard To keep setting up new identities. There's so much. Social Security bank accounts, taxes . . ." Her voice trailed off.

LeClair unfolded a letter. It was from the office of the Interna Revenue Service in Manchester, New Hampshire.

"You were trying to get an extension?"

"Yeh, just put it off for a while. They always get you eventually. just got tired." She looked away.

If it were some combination of fatigue and fear of pursuit tha drove her from New Hampshire and her life with John Homan, the the identity of Teri Martin could serve a dual purpose. Teri would be the one who explained to John what had happened to his wife Robbi, cutting off any curiosity that might cause him to follow he trail. With his taciturn nature and his denial of death, John would be particularly vulnerable to this deception. And Teri Martin, with her ready-made life story and her Social Security number, would become the costume for the next role of Marie Hilley.

But then why, free and settled in Pompano Beach, the ground work solidly laid for the death of Robbi Homan and a clean break from Keene and Marlow and John Homan, did Marie Hilley return to New Hampshire as Teri Martin?

Her employer Jack McKenzie, the person who knew her best in Florida, never saw any inconsistency in her stories, but there were signs of strain: her five-thousand-dollar mistake at work, the bizarre house-buying charade, the complicated shifting back and forth of her plans for Robbi, her ailing twin.

Was there something that frightened Teri Martin away from her

lorida life, some menace in the part of her existence that Jack
McKenzie never saw, her life after hours? Did some current in the
shady street life she had described so knowingly to her New
Hampshire friends threaten to trap her, carry her off? Or was it just
the ceaseless effort of deception finally exhausting her immense
energy and ingenuity for duplicity, making the quiet, obscure life in
Marlow that she had abandoned seem once again like a comforting,
safe haven?

"We're going to want to get John over here and talk to him,
Audrey," Hunter told her.

"John doesn't have anything to do with this," she said. "He
doesn't know anything about my past." They remained silent.
"Does he have to be involved in this?" she asked plaintively. She
looked from Hunter to LeClair and back. "He doesn't know
anything," she repeated.

Hunter put it as gently as he could: "We need to talk to John, just
to be sure we have all the relevant facts. You'll get to talk to him."

"I don't want to talk to him," she said. She saw the surprise on
their faces. "I've already hurt him enough. I don't want to hurt him
any more."

LeClair directed her to call her husband and ask him to come to the
station. After what his wife had said, John Homan wasn't under
suspicion, but just in case, LeClair told her what to say on the phone.
She wouldn't have to talk to him when he arrived, the detective
assured her.

John was waiting for her at Friendly's, where her ride from Book
Press was to drop her off.

"John, I'm at the Brattleboro police station," she began.

"What's going on?" he asked.

"I need a ride home. Can you come and get me?"

"Are you all right?"

"Yes, I'm fine. I'll tell you all about it when you get here."

He promised to leave right away. She must have been in an auto
accident, he thought. It had begun snowing lightly. At least she
wasn't hurt.

While they waited, she filled in the details of her meeting with
John, the story she had told him about her life as Robbi Hannon
before they met, and her two trips to Texas. She had never been to
Tyler, Texas, the hometown she had chosen for Robbi Homan, she
said, but it was near Dallas, and she thought there was a Sacred Heart

Church—"Robbi" was a member—somewhere between the two
places. There was no reason for John to doubt any of it; he had never
been to Texas.

"I'd rather not talk to him," she said again. "I don't want to put
him through this. He's been good to me. You can just take me
away."

Her reason had changed; now she wanted to spare John the pain of
a confrontation. Hunter thought that John deserved to see her, if he
wanted to, to hear it directly from her. They discussed it for a few
minutes, but she seemed unconvinced.

"I don't think I can do it to him," she said. "He probably won't
want to see me, anyway."

"We'll see when he gets here," Hunter said finally. "I'm quite sure
he's going to want to see you."

Hunter went out to see if John had arrived.

In the hallway, he ran into David Steele. "All hell broke loose,"
the FBI agent told him. Within a few minutes of his call to the FBI in
Alabama, the phone had started ringing. It seemed like every
newspaper and television station in the South wanted to know about
Audrey Marie Hilley. Steele had been on the phone almost without a
break.

As John Homan walked through the door of the old brick
police station, a man in a coat and tie stepped into his path and
introduced himself. Another man joined him from the other side,
and they steered John past the dispatcher, through a small office,
and into a large officers' room. Posters of missing children smiled
down from the walls. They pulled four desk chairs into a small
group in a corner. An old steam radiator clanked and chuffed
behind a desk.

"Mr. Homan, we need to ask you some questions."

"What's going on?" he asked. "Where's my wife?"

"She's fine," one of the detectives said. "You'll get to see her in a
minute. We want to ask you a few questions first." They were joined
by a third man. One of the men leaned forward to speak.

"Mr. Homan, do you know an Audrey Marie Hilley?"

"Huh?" He seemed genuinely puzzled.

"Audrey Marie Hilley. Is that name familiar to you?"

"No, I never heard of it."

Hunter took over the questioning. He asked John to tell how he
had met Teri Martin. John gave a brief account of meeting Robbi in

Florida, the move to New Hampshire, her death, and the arrival of her twin sister.

"Okay now," he said when he had finished, "what's this all about?"

Hunter glanced at Steele and LeClair. They were ready for him to carry on.

"John," Hunter said, "I have to tell you: Teri Martin and Robbi Homan are the same person."

"They're twins," John responded.

"They're the same person," somebody repeated. Hunter watched carefully, looking for any hesitation or sign of evasion. There was none. John Homan was a man in possession of an absolute certainty. And he wasn't about to let it go.

"Look, I don't know where you get your information," John said, leaning forward for emphasis, obviously making an effort to be polite, "but it's just wrong. I lived with the woman, and now I live with her sister."

"John, we're not making this up." Hunter waited a moment. John did not respond. There was no gentle way to tell him.

"She told us this herself, John," Hunter said. "It isn't just our suspicion. She told us all about it."

"The whole story," one of the other detectives added.

Their words seemed to press John back in his chair. He looked from one face to another, as if searching for a sign of dissent. He shook his head.

"I lived with her," he said. "It can't be."

"You can ask her yourself," someone said. "She'll tell you."

"I still wouldn't believe it," he said. A faint hollow note had crept into his denial.

"There's more, John," Hunter said. "Robbi Homan is not her real name."

John just blinked at him.

"Her real name is Audrey Marie Hilley."

He seemed to recognize the name they had asked him about at the beginning of the interview.

"She's wanted by the police in Alabama," Hunter continued, watching closely for some sign of guilty knowledge. John sat still, stunned but unyielding, like a wounded bull staring at the matador.

"She's wanted for murder and attempted murder."

There was a long silence. John Homan's disbelief seemed genuine
Hunter thought. He wondered if anything in Robbi Homan's life
with John could provide a link to Audrey Marie Hilley. After a few
moments, he asked John if there had been anything unusual in their
life together.

John said nothing more about the Alabama charges, but he seemed
to be searching for things that might have a bearing on his wife's
behavior. She had experienced a lot of mental problems during their
marriage, he said. She had spells when she behaved "like a one-year-
old." He thought it was related to mistreatment she had received as a
child. They had gone to numerous doctors, and he had almost put
her into the Massachusetts Medical Institute. As he talked, John had
the dull look of a man in shock.

The three detectives questioned him a little longer. Finally they
seemed satisfied.

"Okay," someone said, "thanks for your help. You're free to go
now."

"Wait a minute," John later remembered saying. "It's not quite
that simple. Where's my wife?"

One of the detectives looked surprised. "You've gotta be kid-
ding," he said. "You still want to see that bitch? After all you know
about her?"

John glared at him. "I want to see my wife." He seemed to have
made up his mind about something.

Steele escorted him down the hall to the small office where they
had interviewed Audrey Marie Hilley. She was sitting quietly. The
FBI agent sat near the door, as far away as he could get in the small
room. John took a chair facing his wife, their knees inches apart. In
John's account, she spoke first.

"Did they tell you, John?"

"Yes."

"Well, I don't expect to ever see you again, but could you do me a
favor? Would you get me some clothes from the house?"

"Wait a minute," he said, "it's not quite so simple as that."

She looked at him intently.

"Did you do it?"

"Of course not," she replied.

"Then I'm not going anywhere."

As Steele watched, they leaned close together, talking in a
murmur. They had been warned against any physical embrace or

emotional outburst. Marie Hilley described this moment to her daughter, Carol, a few months later.

"I love you, dummy," she recalled John saying. "I have to get the best defense I can for you."

"Most people," Marie added to her daughter, "would have walked away."

Marie's statement neatly summarizes the enigma of John Homan's behavior and the main reason so many of those who knew John and his wife continue to wonder about his complicity in some part of Marie Hilley's long career of deceit. Could a man who knew nothing at all about his wife's deceptions have learned what John Homan learned at the Brattleboro Police Station and then made the decision that John Homan made?

For what John Homan learned in those few minutes changed his past, and the decision he made would change his future. He learned that Teri Martin was not his wife's twin, but a hoax carried out by his wife. He learned that his wife was not dead, that her death had been another hoax. He learned that his wife was not the person she had claimed, but a woman from Alabama. He learned that the woman from Alabama was a fugitive, wanted by the police and the FBI. He learned that the crimes she was accused of were murder and attempted murder. And he learned that the attempted-murder charge involved her daughter and that the murder charge involved her husband.

And in that moment, John Homan decided: "I'm not going anywhere," he told her. And he kept his word, long past the point where ordinary measures of loyalty would have been exhausted.

Could a man make such a decision without some prior knowledge, some deeper involvement? Even Marie Hilley said it: "Most people would have walked away."

John was typically reticent on this point, probably recognizing the implausibility of his explanations, but he made an occasional attempt to rationalize it for a friend or, in a rare moment when he relaxed his guard, an interviewer. The explanation carries more than a hint of Marie Hilley's genius for making herself into the person her listener needs to love.

As his wife, John explained, Marie had wanted only two things: a committed relationship filled with love, and his own happiness. It was her concern for him that had led to her capture. "If she had left things alone and not tried to get out of my life to spare me this problem," he said, "we would still be living happily in New Hampshire."

"We had three basically wonderful years," John said. His wife's spells of madness, the marital tension after they returned from Florida, his reluctance to take her back after her first trip to Texas—all this had shriveled in John's memory to the modest qualification of "basically." "She is the best thing that ever happened to me," he exclaimed.

They were so close, he said, so devoted, that the constant deception had become an unbearable strain on her. She wanted to confide in him, he said, but she could not, "for fear that I might hate her."

If she had not been arrested as Teri Martin, she would have been gone in a few weeks. She had planned to work only long enough to save the money for "a ticket out and enough to live on."

She had been accused in Alabama of things "I honestly believe she didn't do," John went on. Falsely accused, deserted by her family and friends, she had fled. Now she would no longer be alone. He would stand by her.

The one thing that makes this explanation believable is the one thing that John Homan does not mention: He had virtually no alternative. His parents were gone, he had cut himself off from his hometown, his stepmother, and his brothers and sisters in Florida. He and Robbi had retreated gradually even from the occasional social contacts of their first months in New Hampshire. He was once again estranged from his brother Peter. He had maintained only the most superficial relations with friends from work, neighbors, and acquaintances in Marlow.

The only person in the world who needed John Homan, whose need was so uncomplicated and so desperate that there was no danger of failure in trying to help, was Audrey Marie Hilley. For John Homan, the choice was simple.

21

News of Murder

With the details from the National Crime Information Center computer report, Dave Steele had reached Wayne Manis at the FBI office in Anniston. Steele introduced himself as the agent covering Vermont. A folksy midwesterner, he had absorbed a little of the laconic Vermont style.

"Do you have a case open down there by the name of Audrey Marie Hilley?" he asked Manis.

"We sure do," Manis replied eagerly.

Steele drew out the anticipation: "Are you still looking for her?"

"We sure are," Manis answered, beginning to sense that this was not a routine call for information.

"Well, would you like to talk to her?" Steele asked.

"You got her?" Steele could hear the excitement in the other agent's voice. He described the steps that had led to the unmasking of Teri Martin. Manis told him about the hunt for Marie Hilley. She had been gone three years, and it was still one of those cases that people talked about in the courthouse or over a beer after work. A few weeks before, the local paper had published a long article titled "Mystery Still Surrounds Marie Hilley's Disappearance."

When they had finished, Manis called Gary Carroll at the Anniston Police Department. Carroll had told the newspaper reporter that Marie Hilley had an unusual ability to "melt into society." Unless she broke the law, which she was unlikely to do, finding her would be "just a matter of chance."

The two investigators agreed: This was a matter of chance that deserved a special celebration.

* * *

Joanne Klinger was dying to call Claudia Brooks, but she made herself wait. She had been up since five o'clock, making lunches and getting ready for the early shift, and she knew Claudia would be up around six-thirty. The minute hand was still a little short of the six when she gave in.

"Claudia, it's me. Have you heard the news?"

"What news?" Claudia's groggy response reassured Joanne. She would be the first to pass the word.

"I think your friend Robbi just got picked up for murder."

"What?" It was a shriek. Claudia had recovered her normally boisterous wakefulness with one word.

"I've been up for hours and I couldn't wait to call you. They just arrested someone named Audrey Hilley from Marlow."

"What for?"

"She murdered her husband in 1975. I'm sure it's Robbi. She was working at Book Press in Brattleboro. She had a false identity."

Claudia was shaken. She had worried and puzzled over Robbi Homan and Teri Martin for two months, considering every possibility she could think of, but she had never come even close to something like this: Teri Martin—Robbi, she corrected herself—was a fugitive, wanted for murder. So, they were right, Sandy Peace and the other doubters, the whole Teri Martin thing was a fake.

Everybody's always said I was too gullible, she thought. I guess they were right.

Claudia ran to turn the radio on. When she was ready for work, she took it with her. She wanted to be the one to bring the news; she could be a good loser. But a small knot of people was already talking about it when she arrived. Shirley Leonard, the quiet spinster who had become Robbi's bitter antagonist and scoffed at Teri Martin, came in a bit after Claudia. She had not heard.

As Claudia told her, Shirley's eyebrows rose. Even Shirley was amazed at the charges against Audrey Marie Hilley.

"Murder?" she exclaimed. "I'd believe it if it had to do with money, she always talked about money. But murder?"

Finally Claudia joined a group as someone told Sandra Peace, the strongest of the doubters, the one who had led them in the private investigation of Teri Martin and the obituary of Robbi Homan. She took the news with grace, as if she really had known all along. She was one person who had a right to act that way, Claudia mused.

The excited exchanges of the latest bits of information continued through the morning, punctuated by shouts and laughter as new arrivals were brought into the circle. As it was beginning to quiet down later in the morning, another element was added: Reporters from the New Hampshire, Vermont, and Boston newspapers, Associated Press, and United Press International had begun hop-scotching around the big office by telephone. By afternoon, television reporters and camera technicians were taking employees aside for interviews. It would be a few more days before reporters from the supermarket tabloids started showing up, the *National Enquirer,* the *Globe,* the *National Examiner.* Still later, Robbi Homan's coworkers would read about her, and about themselves, in the pulp crime and detective magazines.

Robbi's supervisor, Ron Oja, described John Homan's arrival in the lobby of Central Screw with Teri Martin after the death of her twin sister, his wife: "He's standing there crying as he's telling me this. I'm kind of a dumb son-of-a-pup and I'm gobbling this all up. It goes to show you what you know about people, or what you think you know."

Don Parpan, the general manager of the plant, told a reporter that Robbi Homan had been an exceptional worker. "Frankly, everyone around here is shocked," he said. "It's wild. It certainly is."

Peter Homan was surprised to hear from his brother. It was Carol Hammann who had told Peter about his brother's wife, when he stopped at the grocery around noon the day after the arrest. He had gone home immediately to tell Shelley and then called his sister Greer in Fort Lauderdale. It hardly seemed real.

"Greer," Peter said, "before you see this in the papers, you ought to know: John's in big trouble."

He considered calling John to offer help, but there had not been any recent contact. If he wants me, Peter decided, let him call me this time.

When John telephoned, more than a week had gone by since the arrest. Peter had already stopped expecting to hear from him.

They made awkward small talk for a minute or two before John declared himself: "I'm standing by her," he told Peter. They had taken her back to Anniston and he would be leaving for Alabama in a day or two. He had spent four hundred dollars on phone calls, talking with people, including "Marie's family"—he already seemed comfortable with the new name for his wife, Peter reflected. He had reached her daughter, Carol, and her son, Mike, John said. All but one person said he should stay with her. Peter was curious, but John didn't name the lone dissenter.

Peter wished his brother well, but secretly he was amazed at John's unquestioning trust. It wasn't only that she had deceived John so completely; there also was the question of the poison. Peter and Shelley had speculated about John's safety. Arsenic could be given in food and drinks. She had poisoned her first husband, Peter remarked to Shelley: "Why not go for two?" But John seemed completely unconcerned.

He wouldn't have time to clean out the house, John said; there would be food left in the refrigerator. They were welcome to it if they would come by and turn off the electricity. Peter thanked his brother and wished him well. It was a strangely low-key parting, Peter thought. John had made his choice; Peter was sure it would take his brother far from the reach of the family bond Peter had worked so hard to restore. The occasion seemed to call for more of a leave-taking. But John was in a hurry. Peter realized he didn't know what to say anyway.

A few days later, Peter and Shelley let themselves into Robbi and John's house at Stone Pond. After tidying up a little, Peter went to the refrigerator and began removing bottles and containers. After a moment he stopped, puzzled. He stared into the refrigerator.

"Shelley, come here a minute," he called. She came around the counter from the living room, where she had been putting magazines in a box.

"Look at this," Peter said. Shelley stared into the refrigerator for a moment.

"So?"

"What do you see?" he asked her. He gestured at the door shelf.

"I see a bottle of olives, a jar of mayonnaise . . ." She was humoring him. She looked at him quizzically. She could see by his expression that he wasn't satisfied.

"What am I supposed to see?"

"Look inside. Now what do you see?"

She turned to the interior of the refrigerator and began naming the items on the top shelf.

"I see a bottle of catsup, a jar of mayonnaise, a bottle of olives . . ."

She stopped. She looked back at the door. A bottle of catsup stood in the middle of the top shelf.

"Oh, my God . . ." she breathed. She pulled a package of Velveeta from the bottom shelf of the door. Peter knelt down and thrust his arm into the refrigerator. He withdrew it. There was a package of Velveeta in his hand.

They sorted excitedly through the remaining contents. Pickles, salad dressing, several more items, all were duplicated, one in the door, one in the refrigerator's interior.

They stood up and looked at each other.

"Do you think . . . ?" she said.

"I don't know." Peter realized that he had lowered his voice almost to a whisper.

"John's got enough problems already."

"What shall we do?"

"We could take them to be analyzed."

After several more minutes of discussion and speculation, they gathered all the contents of the refrigerator in two cardboard boxes and drove off to the Marlow town dump.

Part Seven

The Trial

22

The Missing Piece

There wasn't much time to think about it when you were working ten-hour days, seven days a week, but every once in a while it struck Joe Hubbard: This was shaping up as the case of a lifetime, and he wasn't even out of his twenties yet.

In fact, when the case began, Hubbard reflected, he hadn't even started law school. That was in 1975, the year Frank Hilley died, and Hubbard had just graduated from Auburn. When Marie Hilley was arrested the first time, he had been a year out of Cumberland Law School in Birmingham, already working in the prosecutor's office in Anniston, so he had known about her. But the idea that four years later he would be the assistant district attorney assigned to prosecute her for murder and attempted murder, with all of Calhoun County and a lot of the United States watching, took a little getting used to.

He had started on the case the day of her arrest in Vermont. It was late in the afternoon, and he was getting ready to go home. Through the open doorway he heard a secretary answer the phone in the outer office.

"They found her?" she exclaimed. "Where?" She was almost screaming with excitement. "Vermont!"

Something clicked in Hubbard's mind. The only fugitive missing long enough to create that kind of excitement, he thought, the one person all of Calhoun County was still wondering about . . . He leaned forward to look out the office doorway, already knowing what she was going to say. The woman put her hand over the phone and called to Hubbard: "It's Marie Hilley! They've found her in Vermont."

Hubbard had gone to the files to refresh his memory; it seemed he

had hardly taken a break from the Hilley case in the four month
since. His tall, lanky frame and boyish face gave the impression of
country lad wearing his first suit, but that was deceptive. A vetera
defense attorney in Anniston called Hubbard "one of the best tria
lawyers I know of." Six years in the prosecutor's office had brough
him face-to-face with all the great variety of moral corruption tha
human beings can achieve. Since the liquor laws had changed ther
weren't as many illegal drinking clubs, with their murderou
Saturday night brawls, but there was still plenty of work for si:
prosecutors, four more than when Hubbard had started. There wer
people around the courthouse who said nothing had changed mucl
since the days when Anniston was called the small-town murde
capital of the world. Hubbard viewed all this with detachment an
wry humor. It amused him to recall that when he changed caree
goals from pharmacy to law, his father, a retired civil servant an
farmer, had said, "Well, I don't know, son. I had hoped that all o
my boys would grow up to be somebody that could help people.'

The assignment to the Hilley case had been a great vote o
confidence from the district attorney, Bob Field, considering all th
attention it was going to get. Hubbard had grown up aroun
Anniston, but he had never seen Marie Hilley until he went up tc
New Hampshire in January with Field and Gary Carroll and th
matron. Marie hadn't looked like much, he had thought at the time
a tired, plain woman, now almost fifty, but that wasn't the rea
Marie Hilley. The months of investigation had slowly revealed a
woman of enormous energy, ingenuity, and personal magnetism
She had carried out each new deception with extraordinary daring
and self-confidence. They would have to be at their best to expose
the reality behind her façade of illusion.

Gary Carroll had already pierced Marie Hilley's carefully unde
structed myth, and he was happy to join the team working under
Hubbard on the prosecution. Four years earlier, Marie Hilley had
been a presence in his life, with her frequent complaints abou
prowlers, nuisance phone calls, and other minor incidents. He had
come to like her and enjoy her company. As her stories had
crumbled before the facts, the detective had steadily revised his view
of Marie Hilley. Once she had been exposed and charged in the
poisoning of her daughter, he had begun to dig deeper into her life,
anticipating prosecution. That had been cut off by her flight, but he
had taken part in the search, and he had begun again after her capture

Vermont. Now the detective knew her better than anyone else outside her family; he knew her charm, and he knew her capacity for deceit.

On the way back from New England they had stopped at Kennedy Airport in New York for a layover. Marie had promised to cooperate, so they had let her go without handcuffs, but Carroll was uneasy. As she wandered through the airport with the Anniston police matron sent to escort her, stopping to thumb through a magazine or examine the souvenirs, Carroll had followed her everywhere. She had recovered much of her vigor and self-confidence in the days since her arrest. She turned repeatedly to glare at him, annoyed at his persistence, but Carroll had refused to be diverted. He had followed her to the door of the ladies' room, waited outside, and continued following her when she came out. People were deceived by her reasonable, articulate manner and delicate looks; he had been fooled himself. But he had learned: There was iron determination in her, and a tireless genius for deception. Carroll never relaxed until she was back in the Anniston city jail. Three years, and she was finally back where she belonged.

While she was a fugitive, there had been little to do on the case, but Carroll rarely went very long without thinking about her, wondering where she was, hoping some slip or lucky break would expose her. At last it had happened, and now she was there at the center of his life again.

The investigators had gathered financial records and insurance policies, conducted interviews in New Hampshire and Florida, gathered analysis reports on the suspected arsenic containers, talked to doctors and nurses, and lined up testimony from Carol and Mike Hilley, Freeda Adcock, Eve Cole, and others about how the poison could have been administered to Carol Hilley and her father. But one loose end to the case was still bothering the detective. He discussed it with Joe Hubbard.

In her long discussion with Carroll a few days after her arrest in 1979, Marie had denied giving her daughter an injection at Carraway Hospital. The detective persisted, asking again and again. Each time, she repeated her denial. Carroll asked once more and finally Marie gave in: It was Phenergan, a nausea suppressant. She had acquired it through a woman she had met in the lobby. The woman's name was Mrs. Hill. She had gotten the Phenergan from her daughter-in-law, who was a nurse on the third floor of the hospital. Her name was

"Toots." Earlier, Carroll had tried to find "Toots" or identify Mrs Hill, without success.

It was the middle of May, with only two weeks to go until the trial; what if Marie brought in Mrs. Hill and the mysterious Toots to testify that she really had paid them six dollars for medication to make her daughter feel better, at a time when the doctors and nurses who had treated Carol for six months hadn't been able to do anything for her? It would reinforce Marie's pose as the devoted loving mother desperately seeking some comfort for her beloved child, going to any lengths to find help. It could be a serious blow to the prosecution. Hubbard agreed with Carroll: It was worth trying again.

At the hospital, Carroll waited in an office while someone disappeared to make the search. Finally a clerk returned with the four-year-old patient records. No one knew a nurse called Toots, but Marie had claimed that Mrs. Hill was visiting a family member at the hospital when they met in the lobby. Carroll began poring over the piles of admission records for the weeks Carol had been a patient, searching for someone named Hill. He had to hope it was her husband, or somebody else with the same name.

The records were starting to blur and run together when the name caught his eye: "William D. Hill." He hadn't really expected to find it, Carroll reflected, as he wrote down the information.

Hazel Hill didn't recognize the name Marie Hilley. She had been at the hospital visiting with her husband. The night they had told her he was going to die, she had finally left him asleep and gone downstairs to the waiting room. She remembered a brown-haired woman who sympathized with her. The stranger began to talk about her own problems: Her daughter was in the hospital, and the doctors couldn't find out what was wrong with her. Now they were forbidding her to visit the girl, her own daughter, she told Mrs. Hill indignantly, and they wouldn't allow her to be checked out, either. The woman was going to get a lawyer and make them release her daughter.

Did you ever help her get some medicine? the detective asked Mrs. Hill. No, never, she replied. Do you know anybody named "Toots"? Sure, she answered, that's my husband's cousin's wife; she works at the hospital.

Toots's real name was Lillie Boyd, and she had been working as a clerk on the third floor at Carraway Methodist Hospital when

Hazel's husband died. In addition to being distant cousins by marriage, they had been neighbors; after getting off work each day, Toots had gone upstairs to visit with Hazel and her husband in the last weeks of his life. Once or twice they had met in the lounge downstairs where other visitors waited. She had never heard of Marie Hilley, a six-dollar payment, or any medication.

One more escape route cut off, Carroll thought with satisfaction, heading back to report to Joe Hubbard what he had found.

The prosecutor was pleased, but even so, it was not going to be an easy case to prove. For one thing, it was a lot older than the typical case: The murder had happened eight years before, and even the attempted murder had been almost four years ago. That made it much harder to find witnesses and revive memories; even routine things like locating bank statements and doctors' office records were more difficult.

Beyond those problems, there was the method of the crimes. Among all the types of killing, poisoning stood by itself. It was so indirect, the violence in it was so deeply buried. There was no single, dramatic, easily visible act that could be isolated. Especially with Frank Hilley: All they had was Freeda Adcock's memory of her brother talking about Marie learning to give him shots. In the case of Carol they had more to work with: They would have Carol's testimony, and her friend, Eve Cole, had seen Marie give Carol an injection. Even more important was Marie's admission in the interview with Gary Carroll; her own words would be a crucial element of proof. Still, poisoning would be much harder to illustrate for a jury than something more direct, like a shooting or a stabbing.

At first the motive for the poisonings had been obscure, somehow related to money but difficult to document. With six weeks to go before the trial, Hubbard and the DA's chief investigator, Charles Winfrey, had started uncovering the patterns in Marie's bank accounts and insurance policies. Slowly, like a chill fog taking shape over a field, the outline of her design emerged from the stacks of canceled checks and policy applications. First her husband, then her daughter, her own flesh. In spite of his experience as a prosecutor, Hubbard was horrified at what they were finding.

Behind the pattern of manipulation was a woman capable of the most coldhearted calculation and cruel greed. The consequences were most poignantly obvious in Carol Hilley. Hubbard had spent a lot of time talking with Carol, trying to understand what had happened. He had developed great admiration for her courage. Physical therapy and the passage of time had restored normal movement in her arms and legs, though the bottoms of her feet would always be ultrasensitive, and there were days when she had trouble buttoning her shirt or fastening a belt buckle. She was twenty-three years old, but her thin face and tiny frame combined with her preference for blue jeans and T-shirts to make her seem much younger, reinforcing the impression of sadness and vulnerability that clung to her.

For there was no therapy that could help with the mental anguish, and the passage of time just seemed to make it more intense. Carol was confronted in every waking moment with two facts that just could not be made to fit together: Marie Hilley was her mother, who had given birth to her and raised her, who had cared for her when she was sick, taking her from one hospital to another, one doctor to the next; and Marie Hilley had poisoned her, nearly to death. Which was true? They could not both be true, could they?

Carol seemed racked with the contradiction, and her mother's actions might have been designed to deepen the agony. Carol went to visit her at the county jail in Anniston; afterward Marie sent Carol a long letter, full of deep maternal love:

> I'm afraid I wasn't fair to you when you were growing up. I loved Mike, but you were so very special, and I'm afraid I was too protective of you. . . . I thought there couldn't ever have been a baby as beautiful and perfect as you.

Everything was "peaceful and predictable," Marie wrote her daughter. "And then my world fell apart." Her husband died, then her mother, and then Mike moved away.

> . . . and I realized that somewhere along the way, you had sort of moved into your own world, and I felt more alone than I've ever felt. I didn't know how to reach you, and I realize now that I held on too tightly.

Of course, Marie added, this was "natural for most mothers where a daughter is concerned."

And indeed it was, in Marie's carefully edited version, just the normal response of a mother and daughter to death in the family and the turbulence of adolescence. There is no reference in the letter to the idea that the father's death might have been anything but a tragic oss, or that the mother could have attempted mortal harm against her daughter.

There are two oblique references in the letter to Marie's flight and he charges against her:

> I know I've cried a million tears these past three years. I wanted to see you and talk to you so bad, but . . . . I was afraid to try to contact you. . . . I considered suicide very seriously, several times, and I knew if I didn't do that, some day I might see you again, and you would love me, but if I was dead, and you ever needed me, I wouldn't be there.

And later Marie talks about the money she and John have been told hey will receive from publishers for telling their story. "I don't know and I don't care," she writes, "other than what I can do for you with it."

Marie's years as a fugitive and the charges that put her behind bars become nothing more than opportunities to illustrate her deep devotion to her daughter.

Carol answers in kind, her block letters in sharp contrast to the controlled, flowing hand of her mother: "Mom, The letter you wrote me means a lot. I will keep it forever." She promises to drop off a book of crossword puzzles and a tablet of writing paper. She has something difficult to tell her mother: "I can't come to visit with you until the trial is over." But they can keep writing and talking on the phone.

Carol is desperate to keep her mother's affection: "I hope because of this you won't change your mind about talking to me at all. I still want you to call me whenever you want. I do like hearing from you cause I worry about you when I don't hear from you, plus because I love you."

Yet, at the same time, Carol had found the resolve to cooperate with the prosecution, accepting the need to stop visiting her mother, undergoing long interviews with Joe Hubbard and the other investigators, recalling her months of anguish in painful detail, supplying bits of fact and insight for the wall of evidence that was slowly rising around her mother.

As the picture of Marie Hilley's cunning heartlessness emerged in his own mind, Hubbard had warned Carol of what was coming: "In that trial, I'm going to have to say some terrible things about your mother," he told her, knowing of her continuing devotion to her mother, not wanting to hurt her further. Carol had accepted it as one more unpleasant necessity.

Yet Hubbard knew it would be difficult to show a jury what Carroll and others had told him, what he had only come to see for himself in the painstaking accumulation of evidence over several months.

"You know," one of the doctors who had treated Carol said to Hubbard, "the main problem you're going to have with proving this case is getting a jury to believe that a mother would actually do something like that to her own daughter."

With only a little more than a week left until the trial, Hubbard knew the doctor was right. The stacks of documents, the bank statements and insurance policies, the lists of dates when checks were written and hospital stays ended, the dry recitation of the defendant's coming and goings—where in all this was the picture of Marie Hilley's cruelty, her greed, her vicious indifference to everyone and everything except her own desires?

That was when Hubbard got the break that helped bring the picture of Marie Hilley into focus. As Hubbard told the story later, it was a combination of whim and persistence that led him to a woman named Priscilla Lang. However it happened, Hubbard learned more from Lang than he had ever expected. She had been Marie Hilley's cellmate in Anniston. There was a story that Lang had talked about escaping, before being transferred to the Cullman County jail a few weeks earlier. Hubbard and Charles Winfrey, the investigator, were nearby on other business.

"We ought to give it a shot and go see that girl," Hubbard recalled saying.

"We're as close as we'll ever be," Winfrey replied.

At twenty-five, Priscilla Lang was already a veteran of the Alabama penal system. She had served time for assault and battery, several types of involvement with stolen property, and manslaughter. The manslaughter, reduced from a charge of murder, involved a man who claimed in Lang's hearing to have raped her friend. The two women lured him to the woods with a promise of sex and Lang took revenge with a .22-caliber pistol, for which she was sentenced to a year and a day in jail. She had been in the Calhoun County jail serving a ten-year sentence on theft charges that involved stealing and cashing large numbers of checks in a multistate ring; they had taken stores in Anniston alone for close to a hundred

ousand dollars. Related charges of theft and forgery awaited her in
x other Alabama counties. Cullman County, where she was now
waiting trial, was one of them. A guard took Hubbard and Winfrey
ack to Lang's cell.

"You probably don't know me, ma'am," Hubbard recalled
eginning the conversation, "but I'm assistant district attorney in
alhoun County." He introduced himself and Winfrey.

"I know you were a cellmate of Audrey Marie Hilley in Annis-
n," he continued, "and we came by to see what you might be able
o tell us about an escape attempt." The woman lowered her head.
He seemed to have inside information.

"Do you know anything that might help us?" The question was
ore direct.

"Yes, sir, I do " It was Marie Hilley who had proposed the plan,
ang said. Later, Lang quoted Marie: "A lot of people are going to
et hurt in this trial and I just don't want to stay around and watch
." Marie had claimed that she could get her cousin Doug, in North
Carolina, to send her a "jewel string," which Lang described as a
exible saw that could cut through steel. They planned to saw
hrough the "row bars" of their cell and flee. Marie knew a house
earby where they could break in to get money. But the plot had
een aborted by Lang's transfer in mid-April from Anniston to
Cullman County.

It was very interesting, Hubbard thought, but not much help with
he prosecution. As long as we're here, he later recalled thinking, we
ight as well ask about it.

"Did she ever say anything about what she had done to her
usband and daughter?"

"She told me she didn't do it."

"Anything else?"

"She didn't know why y'all were charging her with it."

"Did you talk about it any more?"

Lang considered the question. After a moment, she seemed to
each a decision. Lang had a child of her own, and Hubbard liked to
hink that even this hardened criminal was capable of horror at what
er former cellmate had done, and sympathy for the victim, her
hild.

Marie had undergone strange alterations of personality, Lang told
he two men. Ordinarily she was talkative and outgoing, but
ccasionally she would become withdrawn, complaining of a terrible

headache. Afterward she would seem a different person, cold and distant, with a powerful, commanding manner.

They had been together a few weeks before Marie told Lang what she was charged with, and a week or two more before they discussed her case in any detail. At first she had continued to maintain her innocence. Actually, Marie claimed, she had been framed. She was being made the scapegoat for the real killer. It was her sister-in-law who had done it.

But in the next few days, Marie's tone had changed, and what she proceeded to tell Priscilla Lang added the missing dimension to Hubbard's portrait of Audrey Marie Hilley. Priscilla Lang would be the final witness in the prosecution's case, Hubbard decided, like the last touch of paint from an artist's brush.

23

A Victim Speaks

f the prosecution was faced with making sense out of too much
material, Wilford Lane had the opposite problem. Marie Hilley's
defense lawyer didn't have very much to work with.

Anniston had been anxious with speculation that Marie would get
off by pleading insanity. Everybody knew she was the kind of
woman who could talk anybody into anything, and the stories of her
amazing plots and personality changes would make it easy to believe
she was out of her mind. How could anybody do that to her family,
especially her daughter, not to mention impersonating a bogus twin,
if she weren't crazy?

But the prosecution had preempted the insanity defense. Taking
note of the speculation, District Attorney Field had requested a
psychiatric examination for Marie Hilley. As far as anyone could
determine, the request was unprecedented. It was always the defense
that initiated psychological exams. But the court allowed the tests,
limiting them to a simple finding on whether the defendant was
competent to stand trial. After a few hours of interviewing, a
psychiatrist and a psychologist found that Marie Hilley was capable
of understanding the charges against her and aiding in her own
defense. No one would ever have doubted it, and the exam said
nothing about whether she was clinically insane, or ever had been,
but the finding cut the heart out of any chance to portray her as being
in the grip of mental illness.

Most people who knew Marie Hilley thought she never would
have allowed that, anyway.

"She'd rather spend her life in jail than ever admit there was

anything wrong with her mentally," one acquaintance said. "She h
too much pride for that."

That left Will Lane with two basic approaches. Once the prosecu
tion proved that Frank and Carol Hilley had indeed been poisoned,
they got that far, the defense could try to show that someone besid
the defendant had done it. Marie had implied in her conversatio
with Priscilla Lang that her sister-in-law, Freeda Adcock, w
involved in a plot and was trying to pin the blame on Marie. Th
defense could develop that idea, or some similar alternative theor
about how the poisoning happened. Along with that, they could tr
to undercut the prosecution's case, discrediting its witnesses an
evidence, leaving enough room in the minds of the jurors fo
"reasonable doubt" about Marie Hilley's guilt.

Lane had filed several motions for "discovery" of items that woul
make up the prosecution's case. The judge had turned down one o
these requests, for a synopsis of any statements made by th
defendant, without explanation; that decision would result in
shocking surprise for the defense attorney, and one of the turnin
points of the trial. The motions for fingerprints, handwritin
samples, articles taken from Marie Hilley's purse, and tests fo
poison were granted.

It didn't seem like much to work with, the prosecution's evidenc
and the jury's "reasonable doubt," but Will Lane was used to bein
the underdog. He had been born to the role. His family wer
struggling farm folks from south Georgia who had moved t
Anniston when he was a boy. Like Joe Hubbard, the prosecutor
Lane had gone to high school in Oxford, just south of Anniston, an
to law school in Birmingham.

But Lane had gravitated toward the opposite side of the bench
from Hubbard. Lane was a few years older than his rival and a fev
inches shorter, with the square shoulders and blond hair of a former
high-school fullback, now grown red-faced and overweight. H
liked to cultivate a raffish air, drinking Old Forester bourbon out of
paper cup in his office after hours, swigging Mylantin to make up fo
his erratic eating habits, lighting a cigarette while the one before i
still smoldered in the ashtray, putting his feet up on the desk, an
telling stories of the assorted misfits and habitual offenders who
made up the bulk of his clientele, like the drunk who shot and killed
a man over a bowl of butter beans.

There was another side to Lane that came as a surprise, however,

ompassion for the sinner that emerged in his gentle counseling of a
aurch elder who had embezzled funds from the congregation's
easury and couldn't find a way to confess, or his sympathy for a
omeless man charged with assault after a bar fight. Lane was more
omfortable fighting for a lost cause than representing the establish-
aent and upholding the rules of society.

Another lawyer had referred Marie Hilley to Lane for help with
er check-fraud cases. Lane had been working with her to raise
aoney to make restitution, when she was arrested on the charge of
etempted murder. What had looked like a routine case for the
nall-type listings in the local paper had turned into a magnet for the
ational media.

Will Lane had been under siege by reporters, but he had kept his
aoughts to himself. Marie Hilley had already gotten enough
ablicity, which couldn't possibly help her defense. She was main-
nining silence, too, and she had turned down a television station's
equest to tape parts of the trial.

"I don't want to see this thing tried in the newspapers," Lane
ad told a reporter soon after his client was returned from New
Iampshire, and he had lived by his word.

The silence only deepened the aura of mystery that surrounded
Marie Hilley. As the trial opened, the old courthouse in Anniston
ummed with speculation: was she going to take the stand? Lane
vasn't saying, which heightened the sense of expectancy.

Nobody around the red-brick courthouse could remember any-
ning like it. Lines of spectators had begun forming an hour before
ne trial was due to begin, filling the second-floor rotunda outside the
eavy wooden doors of Courtroom One, snaking back down the
wo curving staircases to the lobby. Many in the crowd were older
nen, but the largest number were middle-aged women, dressed for
n outing, their hair freshly done. Somebody who worked in the
ourthouse dubbed them "the blue-hairs," and the name stuck for
he duration of the trial. They came from all over Calhoun County,
nd almost everybody seemed to know the defendant or a member
f her family. Even the few without some connection had been
ollowing her case so long that they felt they knew her; everybody
eferred to the defendant by her first name. Almost none would
dmit it, but there was no question what had brought most of them
o the courthouse.

"They want to see Marie tell her story and name names," one

woman in the crowd said, cheerfully assigning her own motive t
the others. If her dramatic flight and fugitive years were not enough
it was common knowledge that Marie Hilley had enjoyed affair
with some of Anniston's most prominent men.

"She slept her way through the front page of the newspaper," one
of the more candid observers said, exaggerating the facts but not the
expectations of her fellow spectators. The story had all the juice and
incident of a TV soap opera.

Judge Samuel Monk III, the handsome, dark-haired Circuit Court
justice presiding, had put unprecedented security measures into
effect. He had announced that the special procedures were for crowd
control, not security, but no one was convinced. Why were bailiffs
with metal detectors checking every spectator at the door?

Three benches at the front had been reserved for the media,
leaving close to three hundred seats downstairs and another 120 in
the balcony. By the time Joe Hubbard stood to begin his opening
argument, most of them were filled.

The jury of twelve men and two women, enough to provide for
two alternates, watched Hubbard with rapt attention. They had just
spent their first night at the Anniston Holiday Inn, where they would
remain, sequestered, for the rest of the trial. The anticipation of what
they would see and hear had overcome their distress at learning late
the day before, when the jury selection had ended, that they would
not go home to their families until they had rendered a verdict.

It had been a mild surprise to the legal community that Will Lang
had not moved for a change of venue because of the publicity; the
judge had cut him off when he tried to explain his thinking in pretrial
arguments, but the expense and inconvenience of moving his base
out of Anniston weighed heavily. John Homan had dedicated the
remainder of his inheritance to his wife's defense, but the original
amount, close to $150,000, had dwindled sharply. It would not allow
for any expensive legal maneuvering.

Hubbard wasted little time in preliminaries. "This diabolical
plot," he opened, "by this cold-blooded killer, began, ladies and
gentlemen, in May of 1975." He described Frank Hilley's illness and
rapid decline, followed by the defendant's frequent changes of
residence. Carol Hilley had graduated from Anniston High School,
he told them. "In April of 1979, her nightmare began."

Hubbard laid out the long progression of Carol's mysterious
illness, the months of wandering among doctors and hospitals, the

advance of her pain and paralysis, culminating with her three weeks in the psychiatric wing at Carraway Hospital, with the endless batteries of tests and interviews. Earlier, she had received an injection from her mother; four to six days before her discharge, she received two more, Hubbard said, "supposedly to help her legs so she could go home."

Instead, her condition worsened. Her mother removed her from the hospital against the physicians' advice and took her to the Holiday Inn. The next day, her mother took Carol to the emergency room at the University of Alabama Hospital in Birmingham. "Unable to walk, having to hold on to her mother, in a state of total deterioration," she was admitted to the hospital. There, finally, after being tipped off, a doctor found the signs of arsenic poisoning.

Hubbard recounted Marie's arrest, the searches of her various belongings and the discovery of arsenic, the exhumation of Frank Hilley, the finding that his tissues held a hundred times the normal amount of arsenic. The prosecutor briefly outlined the defendant's flight and recapture three years later.

In closing, the prosecutor alluded to the uncritical element in the public curiosity about Marie Hilley: "You're not going to be looking at a folk hero," he warned, "you're going to be looking at a cold, calculating, diabolical killer."

If you look objectively at the evidence, he assured the jurors, "When you're finished with this trial, you'll have no problem, I submit to you, no problem in deciding that Audrey Marie Hilley should be convicted of the murder of her husband and the attempted poisoning of her daughter.

"And at the close of this trial, you'll know why she did it. And it will scare you to death."

Hubbard folded his long frame into a chair at the prosecution table, next to his boss, Bob Field, the broad-faced, kindly looking district attorney. Field would speak barely a word in the courtroom throughout the trial, but he became the only major figure who provided regular commentary and speculation to the press. District attorney is an elective office in Alabama.

Wilford Lane had also enlisted a partner, a square-jawed young Anniston attorney named Tom Harmon. In addition to practicing law out of an office down the hall from Lane's in the Radio Building, Harmon served as a judge of the Police Court, where he displayed a stern waspishness that contrasted with his otherwise friendly, relaxed style. Harmon had lived in Anniston several years with his wife, a native of Calhoun County, his Nebraska twang fading comfortably into an Alabama drawl. As he rose to speak for the defense, his lean, concentrated look provided a nice counterpoint to the air of disheveled informality that clung to his florid partner at the defense table.

Harmon immediately revealed the direction the defense would take by drawing the jury's attention to the "presumption of innocence" due the defendant in a criminal case. It was the obligation of the prosecution to prove its case "beyond a reasonable doubt," he pointed out; anything less should result in the freedom of the defendant.

The defense's version of the facts turned Hubbard's presentation on its head. Even the defendant's name was different. Tom Harmon was referring to her, correctly, as "Mrs. Homan"; in his opening statement, the prosecutor had called her Marie Hilley. Along with the rest of Anniston and all the news media, the prosecution continued to use her former name throughout the trial. Except for the bailiff, once, the two defense attorneys were the only ones ever heard to use her correct name, and even they would slip occasionally as the trial went on.

Harmon passed briefly over the initial finding that Frank Hilley had died of viral hepatitis, and the later discovery that arsenic had killed him. He picked up Hubbard's account of Carol's illness. Her mother had searched endlessly for help, refusing to give up. Even at the end, rather than take her daughter home, Mrs. Homan had sought out another hospital. Hardly the action of a woman trying to kill her daughter, his tone clearly implied.

Now Harmon moved to the crucial core of the defense's argument. In the selection process the previous day, he reminded the jurors, the prosecutor had asked jury candidates whether they would be "prejudiced" if they learned that Carol Hilley had smoked marijuana, or that some witnesses "may have engaged in some acts of homosexuality."

"We would expect the evidence in this case to show that Carol Hilley had serious psychological problems," Harmon went on, "that Carol Hilley has used drugs extensively, especially marijuana, and has admitted on at least one occasion that she's been using harder drugs . . ." Harmon paused to let this new view of the defendant begin to take shape for the jurors.

". . . that Carol Hilley is in fact either, as Mr. Hubbard indicated, a homosexual, or has engaged in homosexual activities." Another pause.

"In addition to which, we expect the evidence to show that Carol Hilley has, on at least three occasions, attempted suicide."

The defense's line was clear. They would undermine the prosecution's proof in the murder case; time and a lack of evidence were on their side. In the attempted murder of Carol, they would attempt to show the defendant as a solicitous, loving mother. They would try to change the flow of argument, to make Carol a defendant in the jury's minds. Audrey Marie Hilley's freedom would depend on portraying her daughter as drug-ridden, sexually unstable, and suicidal, the kind of person who was capable of doing serious damage to herself, nearly to the point of death.

"Marie Hilley doesn't have to prove her innocence," Harmon reminded the jury. "The burden is on the state to prove their case beyond a reasonable doubt." Harmon's repetition made the defense sound more dependent on the hope of the prosecution's failure than on anything they could do themselves. That impression, as it turned out, was correct.

The defense would have an early chance to try out its strategy. The prosecution called as its first witness Carol Marie Hilley.

Her mother turned to watch Carol enter the courtroom. There was a warm smile on Marie's face, the look of a hostess welcoming a young matron to a Garden Club tea. The dramatic images of the peroxide blonde convoyed back to Alabama in handcuffs were now no more than bits of the legend; the familiar dark brown hair framed her face in neat waves. A ruffled white blouse contributed to the illusion, but Carol hardly seemed to notice her mother's cheerful gaze. Her walk was normal but stiff, betraying her nervousness. She had dressed for a different occasion from her mother, in a blue, button-down Oxford-cloth shirt and white slacks.

Hubbard eased Carol into her testimony, asking the details of her age and work, before turning to Frank Hilley's death. As the questioning came closer to the day of her father's death, Carol paused frequently for breath, as if she were hyperventilating. She had been sleeping on the couch in the living room, Carol said, when her brother, Mike, awakened her at four in the morning and told her that their father had died.

The questioning proceeded smoothly into the moves from house to house that Carol and her mother had made after Frank's death, and on to the beginning of her illness. It had been the night of the junior-senior prom.

"Well, it was real, real slight the night of the junior-senior. I was sitting there and I never even really had to tell anybody about it because I wasn't—it was just very slight nausea, is all it was, until the next day." In answer to Hubbard's questioning, she admitted smoking marijuana at the party after the prom.

The next day she had been sick off and on during the day. "And then it got worse that night, so I went back to the hospital myself."

Hubbard led her on, through the months of illness, the repeated hospital stays, the cycles of rising hope followed by despair, the low points a bit lower each time as the doctors and medications failed to provide relief.

"Now, Carol," Hubbard asked, an edge of tension showing in his tone, "did, at any time, your mother have the occasion to give you an injection?"

"Yes." Eve Cole had been present, she said. Did Carol remember how it came about?

"Yes, sir, I remember. I was real bad throwing-up sick. I was feeling real bad, you know, just—I was wanting somebody to do something for me, because I just could not lay still. I could not lay there. And—so my mom said that she could get something that would make the nausea go away. And so she went—left and came back with that syringe and then gave it to me." The injection was supposed to ease her nausea; it didn't work.

Carol had not looked directly at her mother since entering the courtroom, but when she spoke her name she inclined her head slightly toward the defense table, where Marie sat between Will Lane and Tom Harmon. Carol had phoned her mother in the months since the prosecution's ban on visits, but they had not been together in the same room until today.

The questioning moved on to her stay in the psychiatric ward at Carraway Hospital, under treatment by Dr. Elmore. Hubbard asked about the first injection she had received at the hospital, how her mother had led up to it.

"I wanted to go home," Carol replied. "The doctors were telling me it was in my head and I could not go home until I could walk out of the hospital or gain, you know, fifteen or twenty pounds, and it didn't look good either way. So my mom said one time there was this little girl, that her mom had the same problem—or, the mom said her little girl had the same problem, and she gave her this, and it helped the little girl. And you know, she said she had gotten it from a clinic somewhere and she gave me another one, saying it would help my legs."

A few days later, Carol recalled, her mother had given her the second injection. She had the syringe ready, loaded, in her purse. At first, she only injected part of the contents, a cloudy white liquid. After a while, they had discussed it, and her mother had retrieved the syringe from her purse and injected the rest.

Carol's thin, soft voice was difficult to hear at times. The normal rustling of the spectators had ceased. In the tense silence it was easy to imagine Marie Hilley moving around the hospital room, straightening the magazines, fussing over the flowers, stealing sidelong glances at her daughter, gauging the effect of the first injection, trying to decide whether another was needed or whether the impact would be too dramatic, deciding finally that she could accelerate the process without risking exposure.

Her condition had worsened, Carol said, and finally her mother had removed her from the hospital, promising to take her home after the night at the motel. The next morning she had reneged on the promise.

"We're not going home until we find out why you can't walk," her mother had insisted. Carol admitted that she had been "rather cantankerous," in Hubbard's words, about her disappointment that she was not going to spend the night, at last, in her own bed. Her mother had slapped her, she said, "because I wouldn't shut up about it."

Carol told of checking into the University of Alabama Hospital, the discovery that she was being poisoned, and her eventual release.

Hubbard then went back to another incident of suspected poisoning. Carol recalled the trip to Gadsden to pick up the Camaro Marie had promised to buy her with the fifty thousand dollars from Frank Hilley's stock. On the way she had gotten sick and her mother had stopped to get some Maalox. Marie had served it to her from an empty Tylenol bottle in her purse. The medicine had frothed up as it was poured into the little bottle.

"It made me sicker, you know," Carol said. "And it burned real bad going down and everything." Hubbard had no further evidence about the incident, but it was meant to contribute to the weight of suspicion.

Now Hubbard moved to take the sting out of the defense's attempt to discredit Carol:

"Now, Carol, at some time did you have the occasion to take some Tylenol? A large amount of Tylenol?"

"I took five." She was matter-of-fact.

"Was that after you became ill?"

"I—it was in between. I wasn't feeling good that day. That's why I was in my bed."

"Okay, did you try to kill yourself on that day?"

Carol laughed. "Yeah," she admitted. Her manner was so casual that it was hard to take the idea seriously. Five Tylenol? It sounded like the normal dosage for a hard day and a bad headache. Hubbard also moved to undercut the defense's image of Carol as a drug-abuser: She had voluntarily told the doctors at Carraway about her use of marijuana, she testified, before Judge Monk called for a break. It was midmorning.

During the break, Lane and Harmon called a bailiff and shifted the heavy wooden defense table ninety degrees. When the jurors returned, they found the defendant and her two lawyers facing them head-on across the space below the judge's bench. As Carol resumed testifying, the expressions on her mother's face provided a commentary on the evidence they were hearing from the stand.

Marie was restrained as Hubbard briefly finished his questioning of Carol and Will Lane stood for the cross-examination.

Lane led Carol through an account of the repeated moves after her father's death, then the trips back and forth to the hospital. The defense attorney seemed to be probing for vulnerable areas: He asked about her use of marijuana, her drinking the night of the prom, her rebellious behavior, and the falls in the corridor at Carraway Hospital, then her account of the injections at home. He elicited details and probed for inconsistencies; the result was a more vivid picture of the young girl at her mother's mercy, grateful for what she thinks is care born of love. Her mother had ordered her not to tell anyone about the injections. Carol recalled the indiscretion that eventually led to her mother's exposure.

"Eve called and asked me how my legs were, and I said, 'Mom has given me a shot for my legs.' "

"You, in fact, walked down to the nurse's station," Lane challenged her. He was referring to her trips to the telephone. "You made it to the nurse's station, did you not?" He was trying to show that the accounts of her pathetic physical condition had been exaggerated to win sympathy.

"Yes, sir," she replied.

"You walked down there, didn't you?"

"I didn't exactly walk, no. I had help getting down there and I would hang on to the wall to get down there."

Lane asked about her weight. She had weighed a mere "eighty-something pounds" before leaving the hospital, she said; her normal weight was 107 or 108. Even now she only weighed ninety-six. The two-digit weights sounded ludicrous for an adult, heightening the impression of Carol's frailty and vulnerability. Lane's questions were turning against him.

The attorney elicited Carol's account of the Maalox incident, Marie's trips for baby food and pizza while Carol was in the hospital, and other examples of the mother's attentions to her daughter. Hubbard took over briefly, mentioning a woman named Dorothy Austin; Carol had lived with her in Jacksonville, a few miles north of Anniston, the summer after her mother's arrest.

When it was the defense's turn again, Lane returned to the attack, seizing on the reference to Dorothy Austin. Carol and her grand-mother, Lucille, had been living on $380 a month from Frank Hilley's Social Security survivor's insurance. Dorothy Austin had been working occasionally at Jacksonville State, bringing in a hundred dollars a month. Carol had paid the rent and other common expenses.

"You were having some problems with her at that time, and you attempted to move out, is that right?" Lane asked.

"I was wanting out of a situation I was in because I jumped into it because I didn't have anywhere else to go. And I jumped into living with somebody I didn't know very well. And—"

"What situation was it?"

"She was into drugs real bad and stayed in trouble a lot, so . . . and she didn't want to work and go out and help me with the bills and things. So I wanted out from living with her." They had lived together eight months or so.

"And she was into drugs real heavy?"

"Maybe not into hard drugs real heavy, but she was into smoking a lot of pot, and she had it in the house all the time."

"And you never did . . . you never did engage in it, did you?"

"Oh, I smoked it, yeah. But I didn't want a lot of it in our house at one time. And so I didn't want, you know, all of that in my house with me living there, no."

Carol's distinction between what sounded like casual smoking of marijuana and the serious crime of large-scale possession had the opposite effect from what the defense had hoped for: It made her sound both candid and innocent. Lane pressed on to his goal.

"There wasn't any hard—so-called hard drugs involved in it?"

"No, sir. She had been involved with hard drugs prior to this, like years before. Like when she was fifteen or sixteen. And it sort of affected her mind a little bit. And I didn't like living with her."

"Did you know her when she was fifteen or sixteen?"

"No."

"When did you first meet her?"

"When I went back to school from the hospital. I met her in one of my classes. Her and another girlfriend of hers . . . the girl that she was in the class with, her boyfriend, I met them all together."

"She is in fact a homosexual, is she not?"

"To my knowledge, yes."

"And you lived with her and supported her for seven or eight months?"

"I did not support her."

"No further questions."

There was a flurry of excited chatter and movement among the audience as Carol stood to leave the witness chair.

Several knots of spectators formed in the rotunda after the morning session, opening bag lunches brought from home and soft drinks from the machine downstairs. So that was it, that was what all the talk about drugs and homosexuality was aimed at. The morning's testimony had pumped new energy into their speculation. The defense had laid down the first broad strokes for its own portrait of Carol Hilley.

The first part of the afternoon was given to testimony from Carol's doctors describing her treatment and explaining their inability to find the cause of her symptoms. Poisoning of any kind is so unusual that physicians rarely consider it as a possibility; the white lines in the fingernails and toenails that indicate the presence of arsenic were not dramatic enough to catch their attention.

The testimony was solid but undramatic. It was a hot day and the air conditioning in the old courtroom, balky at best, was having a hard time coping with the unusually large crowds. An old man in the back of the room could be seen nodding off, jerking back to consciousness, and finally surrendering to sleep.

The testimony of Marie's sister-in-law, Freeda Adcock, added a colorful new element to the trial. She had channeled her anger at the death of her brother into a single-minded pursuit of the killer. It had been Freeda who passed on to the doctors Eve's tip about the injections, and later she had searched Marie's belongings for possible sources of arsenic. Like her sister-in-law, Freeda was a small woman, neat and prim. She was slow to understand the prosecutor's questions, but once under way she was hard to stop. Her resentment of the poisonings spilled out in answers that frequently went beyond what she had been asked.

She was describing her visit to Frank in his bedroom a few days before he died:

"When I walked in, he was rubbing his left arm. And his arm was red. In the middle part of his arm."

"Did he say anything to you at that time, while Mrs. Hilley was there?" Hubbard asked. He was leading to the single most crucial piece of evidence in the case of Frank Hilley's death.

"He made the statement that—"

Will Lane interrupted: "I'm going to object." Freeda's testimony would be hearsay, Lane claimed. Judge Monk anticipated the looming battle. He called for a recess. It was thirty minutes before he emerged from his chambers with the two attorneys. When Hubbard resumed his questioning, he established that a conversation had taken place between Freeda and her brother, but he avoided asking the witness what was said. Freeda was clearly eager to tell him:

"What type of condition was your brother in at that time, this, his physical condition?" Hubbard asked.

"He was in a nervous condition. I'm sure his nerves had been affected by his sickness. And he made one or two statements to me and—" Hubbard had to cut her off.

"You had some conversation with him at that time?"

Hubbard went on to elicit her description of Frank's death and then moved ahead to Carol's illness and Freeda's finding out from the doctor that Carol had been poisoned with arsenic. Two weeks later Freeda had gone with her then-husband, Charles, and her daughter, Lisa, to the back room where Marie's things were stored. Hubbard asked why.

"We were going there looking, to see what we could find, is the reason we went there." Freeda glared defiantly at her sister-in-law. Marie shook her head, as if resentful at the intrusion on her privacy.

In Marie's cosmetics case, Freeda had found a prescription pill bottle labeled "Esidrix." It contained a clear liquid. The next day, after church, she had taken it to the police station.

"Did you handle that bottle or its contents in any way?" Hubbard asked.

"In no way. In fact, I thought it was water. I did—"

Will Lane jumped in: "I'm going to object."

"I'm saying too much," Freeda interjected, inexorable. There was a titter from the spectators. Freeda looked chastened.

Two weeks later she had searched other possessions of Marie's that were stored in the garage and the small building behind the house.

"What places in the house did you remove items from?"

"There was a chifforobe that had a key to it." She paused. When no one said anything, she spoke up. "I'm really afraid to make any comments." Hubbard invited her to continue. She went on to describe the second search.

"On a Sunday evening, my daughter and myself went downstairs, we went through—we had never gone through all of the things that we had down there. We went through—we were searching to see what we could find. And at that particular time we found some baby food and some arsenic in a sack. And so we—"

Lane cut her off again. "I'm going to object to the conclusion on her part, that she found arsenic, and ask that it be excluded and the jury be instructed."

Freeda would not be squelched so easily: "We did find it," she insisted. There was a burst of laughter from the audience. When it was quiet, the judge sustained Lane's objection and ordered the jury to disregard Freeda's conclusion that what she had found was arsenic, but the point had been made.

Responding to Hubbard's questions, Freeda described the bottles. Along with the baby food, there was a white plastic container labeled Cowley's Rat and Mouse Poison. Freeda remembered it as Croley's Rat Poison, but her testimony had introduced two of the three containers holding arsenic that had been found in Marie Hilley's possessions.

The session ended just before five o'clock. Afterward, attention cused on Carol Hilley's testimony and the emotional pressure she as being subjected to by her role.

"It's obvious to me," Joe Hubbard told a reporter, "and I think it to the jury, also, that she was telling the truth about what appened to her. We're very concerned about Carol and the fact that he has testified in a case involving her mother, but she held up very ell."

Hubbard began the next day with brief technical testimony by a olice officer who had received the poison bottle from Freeda dcock. It was like a five-finger exercise before a concerto. Dr. rian Thompson was next, beginning the slow buildup to the climax ter in the day.

Thompson had been a resident in neurology at the University of labama Hospital in Birmingham on September 19, 1979, when he as called down to the emergency room to meet the Hilleys— Audrey and Carol," he called them. It was late morning.

Carol had been extremely thin, unable to control her feet, ffering from nerve palsy and numbness up to her knees. She was nable to feel a pinprick in her hands, and they were numb up to the rists. The deep tendon reflexes—the ones that respond to a doctor's ubber hammer—were gone from both her legs and hands. He had ade a preliminary diagnosis of "peripheral neuropathy"—nerve amage—and begun studies to find out more, when he received a hone call late in the afternoon from Freeda Adcock.

Thompson's testimony about his conversation with Freeda was are, but what she said had moved him to reexamine Carol. Now e was looking for Aldridge-Mee's lines, the white strips that form the fingernails and toenails when arsenic is present.

"So, at that time did you reach a second diagnosis?" Hubbard sked.

"Yes."

"And what was that?"

"It was arsenic poisoning."

The simple words seemed to carry a hush through the courtroom. fter the long ordeal that Carol Hilley and Freeda Adcock and the ther doctors had described the day before, the truth had finally been iscovered. Thompson's tests had later found fifty-two hundred icrograms of arsenic per hundred grams of Carol's hair. The upper mit of normal occurrence, from the traces of arsenic common in

drinking water and other environmental sources, was sixty-fiv
micrograms. Carol's symptoms, the nausea and vomiting along wi
progressive nerve damage, were consistent with extended exposu
to moderate amounts of arsenic taken orally. The only dire
treatment had to be undertaken within twenty-four hours of th
poisoning. It had been too late to treat Carol Hilley.

With the medical sequence of Carol's poisoning complete
Hubbard now turned to other matters. The prosecution called Mik
Hilley to the stand.

Marie's son had the attributes of an ideal witness. Just thirty, N
was a minister of the Christian Church in Georgia, neatly dressed
a suit and tie, comfortable with speaking in public.

Tightening a Noose

Unlike his sister, Mike Hilley had attained some distance from his mother, both physical and psychological. His pastoral duties included counseling members of the church; he had grown comfortable with psychological explanations of why people acted as they did. He had not come to understand his mother's behavior, but he thought of her as sick and needing treatment. His religious conviction and his psychological training were coming together in the conclusion that his mother must admit her guilt and her need for help; then she could be treated. And then, only then, could he forgive her.

Mike was convinced that his mother had poisoned him the day he forced her to look for Harold Dillard and make good her promises about the money from Frank Hilley's stocks. His sudden, violent sickness fit the pattern perfectly. She had also poisoned Terri, he believed, probably repeatedly, during her pregnancy. Marie's rich potato soup, loaded with beets and tomatoes, made up specially for Terri, the bouts of abdominal pain, nausea, and vomiting, again the familiar sequence appeared, though the motive was not as clear. Marie may even have been responsible for Terri's miscarriage. Perhaps she had feared losing Mike to his wife and child, as two years later she had resented Carol's attempts to make her own way.

But there was no way to confirm these suspicions, and his mother had given no sign of confession or repentance. Her arrest and her subsequent failure to resolve the anger and distrust had been seeping through the family, eroding the blood ties among those closest to her. Carol and Aunt Freeda had seen Mike as aloof and unsympathetic. Mike had viewed Carol as confused, sadly incapable of admitting what had happened to her and achieving a clean separatic from her mother. Freeda and Aunt Jewell Phillips had misu derstood Mike's attitude and his phone calls in connection with I mother's bail, concluding that he believed her innocent and soug her freedom. Mike thought his aunts insufferable busybodies bent unreasoning vengeance for the murder of their brother.

It was Frank Hilley's death that provided the initial focus of J Hubbard's questions to Mike. They led up to Mike's departure fro his father's hospital room around nine o'clock Saturday night. home in bed he had been uneasy about leaving his mother to care f her husband alone. Returning with his grandmothers, walking ahe of them, he had entered the room.

"I looked over and I thought, you know, something doesn't lo right. And I walked over to where my father was lying. There was fan blowing the sheet. . . . I went over closer to where he w lying, to the other side of the bed, and it didn't appear that he w breathing."

His mother had appeared to be asleep in the chair when he entere When he turned to speak to her, she was awake, looking at him.

"I don't think Dad's breathing," he said to her, and rushed off find a nurse. When he returned, the room had filled with nurses ar other hospital personnel. His father was dead.

Marie had been listening impassively. Now she raised a handke chief to her eyes and dabbed fitfully as Mike described the scene.

The questioning moved to new subjects. Mike testified brief about Carol's illness, then recounted his insistence that his mother g to the FBI about the supposed extortion plot against her—she ha used it to explain her financial problems, Mike said. He told learning about the injections and overriding Carol's denials that h mother had given them to her. Will Lane used his cross-examinatic to clarify some details, and Mike was excused.

Like his sister, Mike Hilley had hardly acknowledged his mother presence while testifying. Now he left the courtroom withou looking at her. He was required to remain available for anothe appearance. The defense was planning to call him back as its firs witness.

Whatever Freeda and Jewell might think, Mike had identifie clearly with his mother's defense in one way: He was refusing to ad to the buzz of notoriety by talking to the press. His actions ha already been misunderstood within the family; he had no confidenc

t any reporter could fathom the complex mixture of love and fear
held for his mother, and how it had affected his actions. He wasn't
e he understood it himself. It was strange, but his own dilemma
med much more remote than the problems church members
ught him almost daily.

Mike Hilley disappeared from the vicinity of the courthouse, not
be seen until it was time for the defense to begin its case. When he
return it would be with a totally unexpected impact on his
ther's cause.

Dr. John Elmore, the psychiatrist who had searched for a psycho-
ical explanation of Carol's problems, followed Mike Hilley on the
nd. He outlined the physical symptoms and his attempts at
gnosis. Finally, he said, Mrs. Hilley had come to his office to talk
out her daughter.

"And would you say that the tone of that conversation was a
asant one, or was there some disagreement between you and Mrs.
lley?" Joe Hubbard asked.

"I think that—I don't think it was a heated-disagreement thing. I
nk Mrs. Hilley registered dissatisfaction with the way things were
ing at the hospital."

"Do you remember any specific complaints that she had?"

"She thought that her daughter wasn't improving, which obvi-
sly was the case. She felt that the nurses hadn't been sufficiently
eful about her, and that sometimes she had fallen and had hurt
rself, which Mrs. Hilley felt could have been prevented."

"Did she register with you any complaints about her not being
owed to visit Carol?"

"I don't remember having restricted her from visiting Carol. I do
member that I once asked her—suggested that it would be better if
didn't. But I don't think we ever absolutely forbade her to do
t."

Mrs. Hilley had asked him what could be wrong with her
ughter.

"And did you tell her what you felt could be causing Carol's
mptoms?"

"I told her that things such as malnutrition, vitamin deficiencies,
d lead or other metal poisonings might do that."

The conversation had taken place late in the morning. Marie
lley had removed her daughter from the hospital that afternoon.
e defendant need not have known that arsenic was a heavy metal,

in the same chemical group as lead. The word "poisoning" wou have been sufficient to set off alarms.

Hubbard asked the doctor about Carol's depression and her dr use, again displaying the prosecution's confidence that this wou not become the telling point the defense hoped to make of it.

Tom Harmon followed for the defense. His tone was courteous he questioned the doctor about Carol's drug use, but his th eyebrows lowered in a no-nonsense police magistrate's look t displayed his disapproval to the jury. Yes, she had used marijua "excessively," Dr. Elmore conceded, and she had experimen with methaqualone, a widely abused sedative, and she had be depressed enough to be considered suicidal.

Hubbard returned for recross-examination, asking Elmore for details. The doctor searched his notes.

"I don't find any record of suicide attempts. Her mother said t Carol had told her several times that she wanted to die. And mother said that she had found a note written to her deceased fat [saying] that she was wanting to die. I don't believe I have any rec of any history of any suicidal attempts." Except for Carol's ha hearted attempt with the Tylenol, the impression that she w suicidal had been mainly her mother's creation.

The morning ended with a series of witnesses establishing deta of Marie's arrest and the inventory of her purse. Among the items the purse had been a brown medicine bottle. The state lab had fou a residue of arsenic in the bottle. Along with the rat poison and t Esidrix prescription container Freeda had found, the small brow plastic container documented Marie Hilley's possession of arseni

John Homan was spotted talking briefly with his wife during lunch break. He had been conspicuous during the jury selectio sitting in the fourth row, following the questioning closely, occ sionally jotting a note, but since then seemed to have thought bett of his high visibility. He had been seen from time to time walki beside Marie as she was led back downstairs to her cell during a bre or at the end of the day, but during the testimony he had kept distance. His lank, black hair, weedy frame, and pale countenan helped complete the impression of a ghostly, hovering figure.

After the lunch break, Hubbard guided several witnesses throu the details of Frank Hilley's treatment and exhumation, befo calling Gary Carroll to the stand.

Marie looked up from her notepad as the Anniston detecti

ered the courtroom. She had been conferring frequently with her
rneys, occasionally writing a note and pushing it along the table
where they could see it. Some in the courtroom had concluded
t she was masterminding her own defense, but the afternoon's
imony had been routine so far and she had seemed preoccupied
h her notepad, moving her pencil in broad strokes that suggested
was sketching. Now she watched Gary Carroll intently as he
k the witness stand.

he detective described the phone call from the Birmingham
tor telling him about the discovery that Carol was suffering from
nic poisoning. Carroll had then called the state toxicologist and
d him the description of Frank Hilley's symptoms in the days
ore he died. The toxocologist had advised Carroll that the
nptoms were consistent not only with infectious hepatitis but also
h arsenic poisoning.

"All right, sir. And after you had advised him of those develop-
nts, what did you do then?" Hubbard asked.

"I talked with Marie Hilley on September the twenty-sixth, 1979,
he presence of Captain Remer."

Will Lane looked quizzically at Marie Hilley. She shrugged
htly and turned back toward the witness stand.

he detective was responding to a question: "I went to the city jail
I checked her out and brought her down to the office."

"All right. After she was brought—or you brought her to your
ice, did you read Mrs. Hilley her Miranda rights?"

"Yes, sir, I did."

"Did you—"

Wilford Lane was on his feet interrupting: "Your Honor, at this
e may we approach the bench?"

As Lane stepped out from behind the table he glanced again at his
nt. She did not meet his eyes.

After the lawyer and judge had conferred for a few minutes, the
ge called for the bailiff and turned to the jury.

"All right, ladies and gentlemen," he said, "we need to examine an
dentiary question which is based entirely upon rules of law. It
ds to be done outside of your presence. I'm going to ask you to
ase follow Mr. Lakey, he'll take you upstairs to the jury room,
I you will be brought back in just a few minutes."

At the defense table the two lawyers were deep in discussion with
ir client. When the jury had left the room, Wilford Lane rose to

question Lieutenant Carroll on *voir dire*, a hearing to establi
whether his evidence would be admitted. Lane seemed confide
but there was a new wariness about his manner. He guided t
testimony to the point where Carroll, Captain Buzz Remer, the ch
of detectives, and Marie Hilley had seated themselves in Carro
office.

"Did you have a conversation with her at that time?"

"Yes."

"What was your conversation?"

"Well, first of all, I advised her of her Miranda warning."

"Okay, and then what did you do?"

"I asked her if I could interview her and tape-record the intervie
and she agreed to do so."

"And what did she tell you?" The question betrayed Lan
growing curiosity. It didn't sound like a lawyer's question. B
Marie had not mentioned the interview to her lawyers at first. A
now she had just told them that she was in the office with Carroll a
Remer no more than ten minutes or so. She had said nothing abou
tape recorder.

"What did she tell me?" Carroll was taken aback by the questio
The detective was an experienced witness and he knew it was
lawyer's first commandment never to ask a question witho
knowing the answer. The defense attorney could not possibly kno
what he was getting into.

"Yes," Lane replied, showing more confidence than he felt. I
had no choice.

"This is about, approximately, two hours of it. Do you want n
to begin now?"

The spectators erupted in laughter. It had been a quiet afterno
and the humor allowed for a release of energy. Will Lane did n
look amused. The trial had been developing well up to this point, I
thought. What the hell is going on?

Lane seemed to take notice for the first time of a thick sheaf
paper in the detective's hand. He gestured at it.

"Is that her statement there?" he asked.

"Yes, sir."

Lane filled in for a minute with questions about how and whe
Carroll had given Marie the Miranda warning about her right
Finally he came to the point.

"Did she sign any sort of statement?"

"No, sir."

"Did you make a recording of it?"

"Yes, sir," Carroll replied.

"Do you have that recording with you?"

"Yes, sir."

That was it. There was not going to be an easy way around the tape. Lane and Hubbard approached the bench again. Lane asked for another recess.

The defense attorneys felt as if they had been ambushed. Marie Hilley's uncontrollable instinct for concealment had led her to deceive her own lawyers about the interview with Gary Carroll; perhaps she had even deceived herself, editing the memory to make it support the illusion that she was safe, invulnerable.

They had no choice, Lane concluded. They would have to listen to the tape in *voir dire*, see what was in it and just how damaging it might be, then decide what to do next.

Lieutenant Carroll had brought the cassette and a tape recorder. The entire attention of the courtroom seemed to be focused on the small cassette as the attorneys gathered at the judge's bench and started the tape, but the tension soon dissipated. The sound quality was weak and the voices on the tape carried poorly in the muggy air of the courtroom. It was difficult to understand from more than a few feet away.

The playing took close to ninety minutes. The tape ended with Gary Carroll asking Marie about Mrs. Hill and "Toots," the women she had said supplied the medicine for Carol's injection:

"And then when I go to the daughter-in-law she's going to tell me that she's given medicine—her mother-in-law some medicine for your daughter?"

"She'd better tell it," Marie responded, "because that's what she did." She was still speaking in the soft voice she had used throughout the interview.

"Marie, would you be willing to take a polygraph examination?"

"Yes," she answered, and the recording ended.

Lane resumed his questioning of Lieutenant Carroll. The attorney sounded as if he was thinking on his feet. When he had finished with the witness he asked that the court provide a transcript. The judge asked what the grounds were for his request.

"There are parts of that tape that were not audible that I would like to be clarified," Lane replied. "We're going to—we have not yet, but we intend to, if the state offers only part of the testimony, we're going to ask that the whole be made available outside of what certain—few certain parts that we feel are totally irrelevant to the case." The defense attorney had made his decision: Marie's lack of candor had left them open for a sandbagging. There seemed to be no grounds for keeping the interview out of evidence. Rather than let the prosecution pick out only the parts that would be most damaging to Marie Hilley, the defense would seek out segments that could benefit the defendant and try to exclude the rest as irrelevant.

It was too late to go any further that day, though. Judge Monk adjourned the court and retired to his chambers. The spectators stood to leave, subdued by the long session and the monotonous drone of the tape recording.

When the judge entered the courtroom the next morning for the fourth day of the trial, the crowd of spectators was smaller. Some had been discouraged by the slow pace of the previous day, the long breaks while the lawyers wrangled with the judge over dry legal questions, the difficulty of hearing, the close air of the courtroom. They were to miss the most anticipated moment of the trial.

The bailiff called Audrey Marie Homan to the stand.

The jury was still absent. The defense was going to try to get Marie's statement excluded by showing that she had not been properly advised of her rights by Gary Carroll and that she had felt threatened.

Marie Hilley's thirty minutes of testimony became an anticlimax for those who had hoped to see the image of evil and hear torrents of salacious gossip, but her testimony would be just as revealing for anyone who cared to pay attention.

Tom Harmon spent only a few minutes drawing out the defendant's claim that Lieutenant Carroll had failed to tell her that she was entitled to a lawyer, or warn her that the discussion was being recorded. Then it was the prosecution's turn.

Joe Hubbard must have been affected by listening to the defense attorneys address their client:

"Mrs. Homan," he began, "you had been arrested before—excuse me." He started over: "Mrs. Hilley, you had been arrested before September fourth, hadn't you?"

For thirty minutes, Hubbard led her skillfully back and forth like a trainer with a show dog. Had the lieutenant failed to recite the statement of her rights before starting the recording? Then why was he heard on the tape saying, "With these rights in mind, would you be willing to answer questions I might ask?" Had she cooperated only because she saw Lieutenant Carroll as impersonal and antagonistic? Then why was she heard again and again on the tape calling him "Gary"? Was she afraid the detective would hurt her if she didn't talk with him? Then why did she say to him, "I know you're not trying to hurt me."

She had been afraid that Lieutenant Carroll would mistreat her because she had known him a long time and he had mistreated her before, she said. Then how was it that the detective said to her on the tape, "I've never mistreated you or anything" and she replied, "No, Gary"? Lieutenant Carroll had told her previously that attempted suicide was a felony in Alabama and that her daughter could be prosecuted, Marie responded; she had cooperated to protect her daughter from arrest. Then why had she not objected?

"I objected the whole time," she replied.

"Well, if you told Lieutenant Carroll, when he told you his job was not very pleasant and he would rather be doing something else right now . . . you said, 'Well, I'm not objecting to it,' then which time are you telling the truth?"

She had no effective response. Under Hubbard's relentless questioning, Audrey Marie Hilley had been revealed scuttling from answer to answer, searching for some way to reshape the reality of what had happened. But this time, no fiction could replace the truth, no lie could save the day. This time, this one time, her own voice had been preserved, her own words had been set forever upon the page. For a woman who had lived so much of her life spinning a web of verbal fantasy, it was a crucial moment. She had been trapped, at last, by her own creation. After several concluding minutes of dueling between the attorneys, Judge Monk ruled against the defense: The statement would be admitted.

But first it would have to be edited. There were sections that might be prejudicial to the defendant that the two sides agreed were irrelevant: The detective had emphasized to Marie how "pitiful" Carol's condition was, Marie had admitted having occasional "mental lapses" and admitted that she might "need some help," the detective had speculated that there might be "another side" to Marie that could have poisoned her daughter, and they had discussed the prowlers and fires and the extortion plot that had kept her in frequent contact with the police.

In the final passage removed from the transcript, the detective was asking her about the nuisance phone caller she had reported to the police:

"Do you think it's possible that this person might not exist? That it's just an imaginary person that you've made up?"

"No, I don't think that," she responded.

"You don't think that's possible?"

"Well, if all these other things they are saying about me is true, maybe it's possible, but I can't believe my mind is that deranged."

"Why can't you believe that?"

"Well, would you want to believe that about yourself?"

"No, but, ah, you've got to realize, you know, that things might not be, you know, what they seem."

"Well, if they are not," Marie had answered, "then I want somebody to get me back to what's real."

The exchange could not be admitted as evidence, but it said as much about the true character of Marie Hilley as any single bit of evidence brought forth at the trial. She was speaking hypothetically—"if these things are true," "if things are not what they seem"—but it was her closest approach to acknowledging the mixture of the real and the imaginary that made up her world.

It was late afternoon before the edited statement could be retyped and photocopied. The time was filled with technical witnesses testifying about the autopsies of Frank Hilley, the arsenic found in his body, and other matters. Engineers from two local radio stations had patched a tape player into the courtroom speakers. By the time the transcripts were ready for the jurors it was close to five o'clock, the usual end of the court day. The ranks of spectators had thinned out considerably. Once again, the audience hearing the voice of Marie Hilley would fail to match the anticipation of her appearance.

Addressing her as "Mrs. Hilley," Lieutenant Carroll began by asking her about the events leading up to Frank's death, then the death of her mother a year and a half later. She denied giving any injection to Frank, but she had learned from Doris Ford, the neighbor who was a nurse, how to give injections of morphine to her mother, Lucille. At the time of the interview, the police had suspected Marie of causing her mother's death as well, but later the arsenic levels in Lucille's body had turned out to be higher than average but not enough to cause death. Marie's admission that she was familiar with the technique of giving injections stood by itself, however.

The detective was heard next leading her through an account of Carol's illness. Now he was addressing her as "Marie."

"Do you have any idea how she got arsenic poisoning?"

"I certainly do not."

"Have you ever given her any medication?"

"I gave her a shot of Phenergan that Dr.—oh, you mean what pills and—?"

"Well, any kind. You said you gave her a shot of what?" Carroll had started to go on before realizing the significance of what she had said.

"A shot of Phenergan, when Dr. Donald was sick, and he recommended—when I took her to the emergency room, before they admitted her, they gave her a shot of Phenergan. And then Dr. Donald gave me some to give her if she got sick again, so many hours later."

She had administered the shot in July, she said. That would have been the one that Eve Cole had witnessed at home; Marie would need some explanation if Eve ever told the police about it. Phenergan was the nausea suppressant. And Dr. Donald had died in August, a month before the interview with Lieutenant Carroll, so Marie would have been aware that her story would be difficult to check.

The detective asked whether she had given Carol an injection in the hospital. She had given her Thorazine tablets, Marie said, but no injection. He repeated the question.

"But you never administered any shot to your daughter while she was in the hospital?" She repeated her denial, a simple "No."

Carroll asked about insurance policies on Frank and Carol. After a few minutes, he returned to the question about injections at the hospital. He had already asked her five times.

"And you're telling me you never gave Carol a shot while she was in the Carraway Methodist Hospital over there, Marie?"

"No, I didn't."

"Marie, Marie, you gave her a shot over at Carraway Methodist." His insistence must have made her suspect that he had some other information about what had happened at the hospital.

"Okay," she said at last, "it was Phenergan."

The detective would not accept the answer. "No, that's not what you gave her, Marie."

"I didn't give her anything poisonous. I've never given her anything poisonous."

"Well, why did you lie about that?"

"Well, she was in the hospital, she was a little nauseated, and I did not want her to have to stay because she was vomiting. She didn't vomit." It didn't sound like an answer to the detective's question. She had lied, she had been heard on the tape lying, she had admitted the lie, and she had been unable to explain it away. It was a crucial step in the exposure of Marie Hilley.

In response to the detective's questions about where she got the medication, Marie first said the source had been a doctor, then a nurse. In her soft voice, she was heard weaving the tale of her six-dollar purchase from Mrs. Hill and her daughter-in-law, "Toots." It was all very plausible, in spite of Lieutenant Carroll's skepticism.

Carroll asked her again and again whether she had poisoned Carol. She was just as puzzled as he was about what had happened, she said, repeating her insistence that she could not have done such a thing. She was a loving mother, she had struggled all summer to find out what was wrong with Carol. She was heard briefly breaking down, weeping. After close to an hour and a half, the detective had exhausted every approach he could invent to persuade her to confess. The recording ended.

It was past six o'clock, but two more witnesses had been waiting all day, and the judge wanted to get them in before dinner. The trial was already one of the longest ever held in Anniston, and it looked as if there were several days still to go. It was also one of the most expensive, with the jury eating and sleeping at the Holiday Inn, and bailiffs on duty twenty-four hours a day. The county wasn't used to this kind of expense.

The bailiff called Lillie Boyd to the witness stand. Marie had been busy with her notepad, sketching again, but she stared at the witness as she walked to the stand. Will Lane and Tom Harmon turned to Marie; Lane raised his eyebrows in a question. "I don't know her," Marie said.

Lillie Boyd was "Toots." Joe Hubbard led her efficiently through her testimony. She was a clerk, not a nurse, she had visited with her cousin, Hazel Hill, she had never received six dollars or procured medicine for Hazel Hill or anybody else, she had never met Marie

Hilley. She had no access to medication. The defense declined to cross-examine.

The next witness was Hazel Hill, a gray-haired woman wearing glasses. This time Marie had something to offer.

"That's Mrs. Hill," she told her attorneys as the small woman passed the defense table. Her voice was loud enough for the jury to hear.

Mrs. Hill's appearance was almost as brief as her relative's. She had been visiting her husband at the hospital. "They had told me he wouldn't make it," she said. She did not remember meeting a woman named Marie Hilley, but she had talked with a woman in the lobby about her daughter.

"Mrs. Hill, would you recognize this woman that you talked to if you saw her again?" Hubbard asked.

"I think so, yes."

"Point her out, please, ma'am."

She squinted out at the courtroom, searching for a moment, before her eyes settled on the defense table. She pointed.

"Right over there," she said. Marie was sitting between her lawyers. She smiled slightly and nodded.

Mrs. Hill confirmed Toot's testimony: There had been no medicine or syringe, and no discussion of getting any.

It was almost seven o'clock by the time Mrs. Hill finished her brief appearance. The strain showed on the faces of the jurors as they retired to dinner. It had been the longest day of the trial, much of it quiet, even monotonous. But for those who were sensitive to the flow and nuance of the testimony, there had been a decisive change in the atmosphere.

The attorneys on both sides felt the shift acutely. The defense had been rocked the day before by the extent of Marie Hilley's discussion with Lieutenant Carroll, and today the edited tape had been played for the jury. Until today, the picture in evidence of Marie Hilley as a conventional housewife and mother had remained unblemished. The details of her discussion with Carroll, the admission that she had given her daughter injections both at home and in the hospital, were less important than the overall impression they gave of her character. The tape, along with the testimony of Lillie Boyd and Mrs. Hill, had shown Marie lying, not just once or twice, but again and again, systematically, remorselessly lying.

As Marie Hilley rose, she placed her pad of paper briefly on a chair and leaned across the table to talk with someone. The pad fell open to a drawing of the judge at his bench, presiding over the court. She had skillfully applied an apelike cast to his features. Below the drawing, she had lettered in a title: "Judge Monkey."

Afterward, the district attorney, Bob Field, could barely contain his satisfaction at the day's events. It had been like "tightening a noose around the neck, slowly but surely," he told a reporter.

25

Intimate Crimes

The length of the previous day's session and the intensity of the revelations seemed to have sapped the strength of everybody involved. The mood was listless as Thursday's testimony saw a procession of witnesses laying down the details of physical evidence, countering Marie's claims that Frank Hilley's medication had come from the late Dr. Donald, contradicting the illusion Marie had tried to create that she had been kidnapped from the motel in Birmingham while on bail in 1979.

An expert from the Department of Forensic Science testified that Carol had been poisoned over a period from four to eight months long; it had been a few days short of five months from Carol's first noticeable symptoms, the day after the junior-senior prom, to the day Dr. Thompson found the Mees' lines in her fingernails. The hair of a victim's head retained the deposits of arsenic as the hair grew out, the witness went on. The length of the hair containing poison provided a rough measure of the duration of the poisoning, the gaps showed when the dosage had been interrupted, the density of deposits showed how much poison the victim had taken in. Carol Hilley had received lighter doses at first, for a period of two to four months. Later she had received heavier doses, for another two to four months. The amounts of arsenic in Carol's hair ranged up to a hundred times normal.

Joe Hubbard sketched the figures and percentages for each half inch of hair on a blackboard set before the witness stand. Will Lane objected frequently; he seemed now to be fighting a rearguard action, hoping to control the damage, trying to establish possible points for appeal if things should go against them. Marie Hilley was taking fewer notes, rarely talking to her lawyers. She seemed listless, deflated, as though the revelations of the day before had killed some part of her personality by exposing it to the light.

There was one more blow to come. Two officials from Liberty National Life Insurance Company appeared. Recording their testimony on the blackboard with white chalk, Hubbard laid out the dates and amounts of the payments Marie Hilley had made on the various insurance policies held by her family members. She had told Gary Carroll that she had allowed the policy on Carol to lapse, continuing only her own. Sandra Cummings, the company's policy administrator, described the coverage. Marie Hilley had taken out two policies in the summer of 1978, eight months before Carol became sick. One covered herself, twenty-five thousand dollars of life insurance, twenty-five thousand dollars for accidental death, with Carol as beneficiary. The other provided the same coverage on Carol, with her mother as beneficiary.

In the summer of 1979, while Carol was sick, premium payments on both policies came overdue. A two-month premium on her own policy would have been $114.30, on Carol's $132.98.

Hubbard had run out of writing room. He called for another blackboard. Mrs. Cummings continued. In August, more than a month late, she had received a check to cover both policies for July and August. Later in the month, she had received another check from Mrs. Hilley. It was to continue only one of the policies for the following two months, September and October. The amount was $132.98. It was for the policy on Carol Hilley's life.

But the extension had not taken effect. The check had bounced. She had returned it to Mrs. Hilley, the witness testified. On September 6, a week after the coverage was to have terminated, another check arrived. Marie Hilley had delivered it in person to the company's office in Birmingham. In preparing for the trial, Hubbard had noted that on that date Carol Hilley had been a patient on the psychiatric floor at Carraway Hospital in Birmingham, her mother hovering nearby, disappearing from time to time on unspecified errands, but he could not point out the correspondence at this point in the testimony.

The check delivered in Birmingham included two months' extension on Marie's coverage and four months on Carol's, Mrs. Cummings testified. It had never taken effect. Once again, the check had been returned by the bank. This time it was marked, "Account Closed."

But that was not the end. Eleven days later, another check had arrived. This one, like the first, was for $132.98, the amount of the policy premium covering Carol Hilley. Mrs. Cummings had never even bothered to deposit the check, she testified. It had been written in the same account as the previous one. Marie Hilley had exhausted her goodwill at the Liberty National Life Insurance Company. Mrs. Cummings had sent the check directly back to Mrs. Hilley.

The day ended with New Hampshire State Police Officer Barry Hunter and David Steele, the FBI agent from Vermont, testifying about Marie's masquerade as Robbi Homan and Teri Martin. They described picking her up at Book Press in Brattleboro. After they had questioned her at the police station, on the way to the prison in Rutland that night, Steele said, driving through the mountains, they had talked briefly about the charges against her. She had no idea what could have happened to Carol, she had told him. She recalled that her mother had once bought some poison to kill squirrels that were infesting the yard; maybe Carol had somehow gotten hold of the poison.

When court was recessed for the day, the district attorney was even more confident than he had been the day before. "I feel like, if we quit today, we get a conviction," he told a reporter. "But you can't predict what a jury will do," he added quickly, like a man knocking on wood.

It had been another long day, it was the end of the week, the jurors had been in isolation since Monday morning, but there would be no rest yet. Testimony resumed Saturday morning, with bank officials bearing records of Marie Hilley's accounts. Three different Anniston banks were represented, and one from Florida.

Joe Hubbard stood once again at the blackboard, writing down the numbers, erasing and correcting, like an accounting teacher with a complex lesson to get across. The board filled up quickly with the prosecutor's scrawl, a dusty welter of dates and dollar amounts with notations. The bankers' recitations seemed dry and pointless at first, but the prosecutor's intentions slowly emerged.

Marie Hilley had repeatedly overdrawn her accounts, moving from one to the next as her checks bounced, writing a draft on a new account to restore one that was overdrawn, covering one bounced check with a worthless check on another account, closing an account and continuing to write checks on it. Through the summer of 1979, as Carol Hilley had edged ever closer to death, her mother had been on the brink of financial collapse.

The testimony matched up smoothly with Mrs. Cummings' description the previous day of Marie's payments on the insuranc policies. Scurrying from the hospital to the bank to the insuranc company to a new bank and back, like a trapped fugitive under sieg in an empty house, she had tried desperately to cover all the hole where reality might surge through and put a stop to her scheme Over the defense's repeated objections, interrupted again and agai by murmured conferences at the bench, Hubbard had forged anothe link in the chain of motive.

It was near time for the defense to begin its case. Speculation ha mounted again about whether Marie Hilley would testify on he own behalf. Her appearance on *voir dire*, unseen by the jury, limite to testimony on whether the tape recording was admissible, ha merely whetted appetites. And as the prosecution's case had steadil acquired substance, the perception had grown that the defendan would have to do something dramatic to knock it down.

"She's their main, or their only, hope," Bob Field had said in on of his regular briefings with the reporters. "But I don't know wha they'll do." He acknowledged the risks. "Just sitting here an listening to all the evidence, I really wonder: If I represented he what would I do?"

But the prosecution had two more witnesses before retiring, on with some unfinished business, the other with the biggest shock o the trial to date. After lunch, Freeda Adcock returned to the stand

Now, nearing the end of the trial, an important weak spot ha become apparent in the case against Marie for the murder of he husband. There had been nothing to establish that Frank Hilley ha ever received arsenic by injection or other means; as far as th evidence was concerned, the act of murder had not even taken place The defendant could ask the judge for an acquittal even before th case went to the jury; in the absence of evidence that someone ha administered poison to Frank Hilley, the motion would have a excellent chance of success. The prosecutor was going to fight fo Freeda's account of what her brother had said to her in his bedroo before he died.

As he had during her earlier appearance three days befor Hubbard guided Freeda's account to the point where she entered th room to find Frank sitting on his bed.

"He was rubbing his arm in the middle and he had a red circle. She pointed to the crook of her arm.

"And what, if anything, did he say at that time, when you went into the room?"

As he had on Tuesday, Will Lane leaped to his feet, objecting. Any account of what Frank Hilley said would be hearsay evidence, inadmissible. The jury was ushered out and the attorneys braced for the argument. First Hubbard, then Lane, questioned Freeda, rehearsing what she would say, examining whether it should be excluded from the prohibition against hearsay. After twenty minutes, Judge Monk had made up his mind. He addressed Wilford Lane:

"I'm going to overrule your objection and allow it in." He summoned the jury. Hubbard repeated the last part of his introduction before returning to the point where he had left off the questioning:

"What, if anything, did Mr. Hilley say at that time?"

"He said that Dr. Jones has told Marie she'll have to learn how to give me shots at home." There had been a red spot, a large circle, in the crook of his arm, and he was rubbing it as he spoke. Freeda had taken over the rubbing for her brother. The implication was clear: Marie had already begun giving him the shots she said Dr. Jones had prescribed.

"What, if anything, did he say then?"

"He said, 'Freeda, I'm sicker than I've ever been in my life, and if something's not done for me, I won't be here long.'" Freeda would never forget the pain in her brother's eyes. A few days later, he had died. For four years, what he told her had seemed like a morbid prophecy of his own death. Now it had come to seem like an accusation of murder.

The crowd of spectators had grown again, supplemented by Calhoun Country residents unable to attend during the workweek. Among them a reporter discovered the judge's mother. Mrs. Monk did not ordinarily attend trials, but this one was special. One couple had cut short their usual week of vacation in Augusta, Georgia, to attend the trial. Freeda Adcock's testimony had been brief and the spectators were just absorbing its significance when the prosecution called its final witness.

She was a young woman with a square face and dark blond hair cut short. She wore the collar of her blouse over the lapels of her summerweight jacket. Her clothes looked a little too large for her.

The witness's name was Priscilla Lang. She was the woman Joe Hubbard and his investigator had found in the Cullman County jail.

Hubbard opened with her criminal record. She mentioned the ten-year sentence she was presently serving for her role in the check-passing ring and then listed her previous convictions for manslaughter and for handling stolen property.

Lang had been in a cell at the Calhoun County jail when Marie Hilley was brought in, she said. Later she had been moved into the same cell with the defendant. At first Marie had denied the charges against her, blaming it on her sister-in-law. A few weeks later, the subject had come up again.

"And what, in fact, did she tell you at that time about whether or not she had done the events that she was charged with?" Hubbard's anticipation had scrambled his language slightly.

"That she had poisoned her husband and attempted to poison her daughter."

An excited whisper rippled through the courtroom. As Hubbard spoke again, it was cut short.

"When she told you that she had, in fact, poisoned her husband and attempted to poison her daughter, did she tell you why, in fact, she had attempted to poison her daughter?"

"Yes, sir." The stillness in the courtroom was complete.

"And what reason did she give you for attempting to poison her daughter?"

"That her daughter was a lesbian." Lang spoke in a monotone. Her face was expressionless. Hubbard pressed on.

"And did she tell you why, in fact, she had actually poisoned her husband?"

"That her husband was taking up for her daughter, Carol, and she was jealous of her."

At the defense table, Marie Hilley glared at the witness, her eyes wide in an expression of amazement.

"Did she tell you how, in fact, she poisoned her husband and her daughter?"

"Yes, sir. With arsenic."

"Did she tell you how she went about doing that?"

"By putting a little at a time in their food."

Hubbard allowed a momentary pause for the words to make their impression, before finishing his questioning.

"I believe you said that you had left Calhoun County jail on April the thirteenth?"

"Yes, sir."

"The last conversation that you had with Marie Hilley prior to that, did she tell you whether or not she had done those crimes?"

"Yes, sir."

"What did she say?"

"That she had done them."

Hubbard turned toward his seat, satisfied. "That's all," he said.

Wilford Lane looked stunned. There had been no chance to anticipate Priscilla Lang's testimony, to prepare for it. In cross-examination he tried to highlight her criminal background, emphasizing her many convictions. He drew out a repetition of her testimony, probing for inconsistencies.

As Lang repeated Marie's statement about Carol's lesbianism and Frank's defense of his daughter, the defendant shook her head and rolled her eyes ostentatiously in a pantomine of disbelief. She leaned over to Tom Harmon, whispering in a voice loud enough to be heard in the first rows of the courtroom.

"I can't believe this," she said. As Priscilla Lang stepped down from the stand, Marie slammed her pencil to the table.

Lang's testimony had provided the dramatic ending that Joe Hubbard had wanted for the prosecution's case. Now it was the defendant's turn. It was the middle of the afternoon when the defense called its first witness, Carol Hilley.

The questioning was brief. Wilford Lane's questions were designed to show that Marie had tried to provide for her daughter during the summer of 1979, buying Carol furniture and a car, paying her medical bills. The effort was undercut when Carol mentioned that the hospitals were still dunning her, four years later, for unpaid charges from the summer she was poisoned. Her mother had not paid any of those bills.

After a few minutes, Lane released the witness. Perhaps the closing crescendo of the prosecution's case, with Freeda Adcock's memories of her brother and Priscilla Lang's account of Marie's confession, had distracted the defense attorney. Judge Monk was finishing his instructions for the jury's weekend when Lane realized that he had not reserved the right to recall Carol Hilley. The real opening of the defense's case would have to wait until Monday morning. They would work on Carol a little harder at that point.

If Marie Hilley had suffered reversals in court, she was not without her supporters. It was her birthday, and back at the jail a cake was brought in. Marie had spent many hours talking with the guards, especially the women, during the quiet evening hours when they had little to do. Her natural persuasiveness had taken its usual effect. It was so obvious, they thought, in the way she talked about Carol and Frank, just from the kind of ladylike, considerate person she was, a churchgoing woman interested in the guards and their families, easy to talk to, so different from the usual run of prisoners, the Priscilla Langs of the world—this woman could not have done what they were accusing her of. Some of the guards had come to agree with Marie: It looked as if she was being made the victim of a frame-up. She shared out small pieces of the birthday cake and chatted about everything except what was uppermost in everybody's mind: What would the defense do to raise the heavy burden of a week's testimony?

Outside the courtroom, the events of the day had shaken Wilford Lane out of his silence with the press.

"Priscilla Lang is a liar," he told reporters.

The district attorney was put in the awkward position of defending Priscilla Lang's integrity, along with that of the prosecutors. There had been no concessions given in return for her testimony, Bob Field told the press—the dropping of some remaining charges or lenient treatment in court had been mentioned, but there was nothing to it. Lang had testified, Field said, "because she wanted to tell the truth."

"She told us we had nothing that we could offer her," Field explained, leaning hard on the credulity of his listeners.

Surprise and indignation had loosened Wilford Lane's tongue on the subject of Priscilla Lang, but on the question that had been the focus of public attention all week, Lane still refused to speak. His audience was left with the impression that no final decision had been reached about whether Marie Hilley would testify. Could there be disagreement in the defense camp? One rumor had it that Will Lane and Tom Harmon wanted Marie to testify but that she was resisting, fearing the kind of exposure that Joe Hubbard had subjected her to during her *voir dire* appearance. The busy market in rumors was also providing for the opposite conclusion: Marie's pride had been piqued and she was eager to testify, confident that she could restore her reputation, but the attorneys, seeing the weaknesses in her story and chastened by the *voir dire* experience, were reluctant to put her on the stand. All the courthouse gossip agreed on one point: The defense would be dealing from weakness on Monday morning. They would

d something spectacular, like Marie's own account of what had
opened, to recover.

On Monday morning, the trial had overlapped into a week set
de for civil trials. No Calhoun County trial in memory had run so
g. The opening of the defendant's case was delayed until after
ch while Courtroom One was being used for other matters. It
s midafternoon when Mike Hilley took the stand for the defense.
Will Lane's questions established that Mike and his father had been
se, playing golf regularly and spending time together.

"Do you have an opinion as to whether or not your father would
ow your mother to have given him a shot?" Lane asked.

"My opinion?"

"Yes."

"No."

"He would not have?"

"Not in a normal state of mind. No."

t wasn't much, but it was the first indication that there was
ything implausible about Marie giving Frank an injection of
enic. Lane moved on to other matters: the threatening note Mike
d found on the door of his mother's house in circumstances
licating she could not have put it there herself; Mike's search of his
other's possessions, which had failed to turn up any medicine
ttle, a week before Freeda searched those same possessions and
orted finding a medicine bottle containing arsenic; the threat
ainst his mother made by Jewell Phillips in her phone call to Mike.
all sounded like a series of disconnected incidents, but Lane was
parently trying to portray a conspiracy against Marie by Freeda
lcock and Jewell Phillips, seeking revenge for their brother's
ath. Lane had won back a little ground from the prosecution.

"Your witness, Mr. Hubbard," Lane said confidently. It was the
gh point of the day for Marie Hilley's cause. The defense attorneys
re about to receive their final major surprise of the trial; this time
was not their client's doing.

"Mike, on September the twenty-first, 1979, did you inform Mr.
lph Phillips of some of the strange occurrences that you felt were
ppening with your mother?"

Mike was shocked. Ralph Phillips was the coroner. Mike had
itten to him the day after his mother's arrest outside Carol's
spital room. Before the trial, Mike had talked with Joe Hubbard
out the letter; Mike had been concerned that it could be used to

damage his mother. Mike had understood the prosecutor to prom
that the letter would not be introduced.

But Hubbard needed the letter now to counteract Mike's opinic
offered to Wilford Lane, that his father would not have allow
Marie to give him shots. Hubbard handed Mike a copy of the lette
first page.

Wilford Lane interrupted: "If I may, I would like to see the
before he starts." He was even more surprised than Mike Hilley.
their pretrial discussions, Mike had never mentioned the letter
Lane; apparently, Lane was concluding, he had been much mc
helpful to the prosecution. "He craw-fished on us somethi
terrible," Lane would later say of Mike Hilley. The letter had be
typed, single-spaced. Lane had time for only a quick look. The fi
three paragraphs described events leading up to the death of Fra
Hilley.

Hubbard asked Mike to read the last paragraph on the page.

"An autopsy was done by Dr. Ratanaubol," Mike read. "I nev
saw a copy of the autopsy results, only what Mother told me. S
said that Dad had died of kidney failure. There was an approxima
settlement from his employer, Standard/Union Foundry, for for
thousand dollars. Today the money is gone, and I have no idea hc
or where it was spent." The actual figure had been thirty-o
thousand dollars.

Hubbard went on to other matters before returning to the lette

"Now, Mike, you testified earlier that you did not believe th
your father would allow your mother to give him injections if he w
in his normal state of mind. Is that correct?"

"That's correct." Hubbard reminded him of the letter to t
coroner.

"Did you state to Coroner Phillips, at that time, that 'It is n
belief that she probably injected my dad with arsenic as she h
apparently done to my sister'? Did you make that statement?"

"If that's in the letter, yes." Mike was reluctant to acknowled
the stark statement of his suspicions. He had also written in t
letter, "It is my belief (and I pray that I am wrong) that my mother
mentally unbalanced. I know that she loves her family, but h
mental condition is causing her to do many weird things. . . . I lo
her and do not want to see her hurt or in trouble. I believe wheth
she did these things or not, she needs to get psychiatric care. I wou
like to get help for her, as I am sure she needs it. However, I want

d out the truth concerning my father's death and the events that
ve happened since that time."

Mike Hilley's complex and fragile relationship to his mother and
r crimes, the mixture of love and fear and compassion, had been
ttened under the ponderous machinery of justice. It was ironic: In
e prosecution's hands, he had become the ally of his aunts, Freeda
d Jewell, who had falsely suspected him of being their enemy. And
the same time, he had antagonized the defense by refusing to press
r his mother's freedom. Neither side could allow for a middle
ound.

Joe Hubbard was gently insistent: "Review the last part there,
ike, if you would." Mike looked at the letter. He nodded.

"Did you make that statement?"

"Yes." The inference was inescapable: At the time, in the midst of
the visible evidence of events and feelings, Mike Hilley had
ncluded that his mother had murdered his father and that she had
ed to do the same thing to his sister.

26

The Black Widow

It was the following afternoon before the sparse parade of witness[
for the defense concluded, but the impression was left that little
significance had happened after Mike Hilley finished his testimon[
Hope for a dramatic, last-minute appearance by the defendant h[
dwindled with the trickle of minor point and counterpoint worke[
out by the attorneys through the last several defense witnesses. Th[
two sides were playing out the string. It would all rest now with th[
concluding arguments.

The prosecution led off. Joe Hubbard stood and looked out ov[
the courtroom. The number of spectators had dropped off again [
the expectation that Marie Hilley would testify had faded, but it w[
still a sizable crowd for a Tuesday afternoon. The jurors, perha[
invigorated by the prospect of an end to their isolation, watched hi[
attentively. They had given the impression throughout the trial of [
earnest, dutiful group. Perhaps they were just waiting for someboc[
to make sense of what they had heard, to create a pattern from th[
clutter of evidence.

Hubbard began in an apologetic mood. He was going to be usir[
the blackboards a lot, he told the jurors, particularly to get the dat[
straight. Time, chronology, was crucial in the case of Audrey Mar[
Hilley.

"Her motive was based on time," he told them, watching intentl[
as if to measure their responses individually in the first minutes of h[
presentation. "How she went about poisoning her husband and ho[
she went about poisoning her daughter was based on time. We'[
going to take this piecemeal, and we're going to go down throug[
the chronological sequences.

"Be patient with me, because I assure you that when you listen to his argument and the evidence you've heard and you put them together, you're gonna know that you're not dealing with your average, ordinary housewife." Hubbard's voice grew cold.

"You're dealing with a cold, calculating, cunning killer." The alliteration gave his words a hard, sharp sound.

Hubbard's voice grew softer. He had another bit of business before laying out the facts of his argument.

"Now I'm speaking in front of Carol Hilley, who is seated over here," he went on. "I told her before I started this argument that I was going to say some terrible things about her mother, and it hurts me to have to say it. But Carol has been through a lot, she's tough, she can take it.

"So when I refer to her mother as a cold, calculating killer, and somebody who was so devious that she injected arsenic into that girl's system, then I hope possibly she can understand a little bit of what I'm trying to say. She loves her mother, no question about it, you can see by reading those letters she wrote. She loves her mother, and that bond will never be broken and shouldn't be broken. God meant for that bond to be there.

"Maybe in her mind she will always love her mother, just like she did the day she was born." Hubbard inclined his head toward Carol. "She didn't break that bond. Marie Hilley broke that bond when she decided to take it into her own hands, into her own selfish hands, and dispose of the child that she bore, for nothing but money."

There it was, the outline of the prosecution's portrait of Marie Hilley, her offense against the most sacred laws of nature, her unquenchable greed. Now Hubbard lowered the emotional pitch and began setting out the events leading to Frank Hilley's death. Marie Hilley had been sitting with her husband in the hospital when their son, Mike, arrived and found that he had died. The autopsy had been completed and Frank was no sooner in the ground than Marie Hilley had applied for the insurance on her husband.

"And they sent it to her, no questions asked, thirty-one thousand dollars. She's home free, and she knows at that time that arsenic poisoning can get by a doctor. Can get by *three* doctors. *And* can get by the pathologists who do autopsies.

"What does that do to make her bolder?" The prosecutor regarded the jurors for a moment, like a teacher searching out the bright student who could provide an answer.

He listed Marie's series of residences and resumed the narrative with her purchase of the insurance policy on Carol "on July the twenty-seventh, 1978." It was three years after Frank's death, but Hubbard's account made the events flow together as if they were continuous, natural sequence. Carol's mysterious symptoms followed the next spring; in August, after four months of medical treatments and hospital stays, Carol is still hard in the grip of illness.

"August is when she gives Carol her first injection. Carol is hurt, suffering, and in pain, and her mother gives her an injection which she says will make her feel better, which it doesn't." It makes her legs weaker and more painful.

A month later, Hubbard continued, Carol was in Carraway Hospital. Struggling frantically on the outside to keep her insurance in effect, in the hospital Marie gave her daughter two more shots, swearing her to secrecy. Carol broke her promise and told Eve Cole, and the events leading to Marie Hilley's exposure were set in motion.

Hubbard interrupted his account and looked intently at the jurors. "Thank goodness for that," he said, "because if not, we would be trying two murder cases." He let the jurors imagine the narrow margin of Carol Hilley's escape, then resumed the narrative.

Dr. Elmore informed Marie that the logical next steps in diagnosis included tests for heavy-metal poisoning. That same afternoon, Marie removed Carol from the hospital. The next day, instead of taking her daughter home, Marie Hilley checked her into the University Hospital.

"She was in a strange hospital on September nineteenth," Hubbard went on, "and about to undergo all of these tests again, and Marie Hilley just wants one more shot at her: 'If I can keep her in this hospital just a little while longer, I can get the insurance money.'

"But on September twentieth, Sergeant B. A. Woods saved Carol Hilley's life. He may not know it, but he did. He arrests Marie Hilley at the hospital and takes her to Birmingham city jail, where she is picked up and brought here to Anniston."

Hubbard reviewed the exhumation of Frank Hilley and the discovery of the physical evidence, including the three containers holding traces of arsenic. Released on bail, Marie moved into a motel in Birmingham under the name Emily Stephens.

"Frank's autopsy results haven't come back yet, but Marie Hilley knows the outcome before it ever comes back. She knows they've oking for arsenic, and if it's there, they're going to find it, that oison in Frank Hilley's body. And she knows it's there.

"So in contrast to what Mr. Lane will tell you, I submit to you, dies and gentlemen, that that woman realized right then and there, The jig is up, I've got to get out of here.' " Marie staged her own idnapping and disappeared.

The prosecutor briefly traced her flight to New Hampshire, the hanges of identity, first to Robbi Homan, then to Teri Martin, and e arrest. In all of this, he told them, punching out the words for mphasis, she had been "cold, calculating, cunning."

"And she devised a plan, and she thought it would work, but verything she did was to hide herself and her guilt of this particular rime, and to keep you, ladies and gentlemen, from getting her own here in this court so that we could try her and put an end to his story."

And for a long time, he reminded them, she had gotten away with

"It bothers me, and it should bother you, ladies and gentlemen, at Frank's murder was really just discovered four years after his emise. And this woman continued to be in existence, continued her vil ways, I might say, because she was bolstered by the fact that our octors were unable to diagnose what was wrong with Frank Hilley. m not holding them at fault. They were doing their job, but they ad no reason to suspect arsenic poisoning, they didn't know the nancial trouble this woman was in, they didn't know that she had our bank accounts in arrears, they didn't know that she had written two-thousand-two-dollar-and-ninety-eight-cent bad check to Moss urniture on a closed account. And they didn't know that she was oing everything she could to keep the twenty-five-thousand-dollar isurance alive on Carol Hilley, betting on her to die." Hubbard's oice had risen with these last words. He glanced over at Carol gain.

"And the whole time, Carol was a tough nut to crack. Carol vould not die. Carol kept struggling, just like she kept struggling or nine months after they found arsenic in her, through the physical herapy, doing all she could to get back." He outlined Carol's rowing paralysis, the doctors' insistence that her problem was sychological. "And she knows it's not, and she knows she's no razier than you or I, and she knows it's about to get to her."

Hubbard was pressing the jurors to identify with Carol Hilley,

because now he was going to discuss the rest of Marie Hilley
motive, and in the process he would have to risk losing the
sympathy for her victim.

"But the doctors didn't know about the insurance, they didn
know that Marie Hilley had pulled it off once before, when she kille
her husband. If the doctors had known that, or suspected that, the
would have been able to do something much quicker than they did

"And, ladies and gentlemen, they didn't know that Marie Hille
had a notion in her mind that her daughter was a homosexual. It wa
a deep and abiding suspicion, and she didn't like that idea."

The prosecutor was treading carefully. There had been no ev
dence that Carol Hilley was a lesbian or bisexual. It was a priva
matter, in any case, and Carol was understandably sensitive about i
All he needed to demonstrate was that Marie Hilley had believed he
daughter was homosexual. The prosecution had made that poi
with Priscilla Lang's testimony, and Mike Hilley had testified tha
when his mother called him from the prison in Vermont, after thre
years' absence, one of her first questions had been, "Is Carol still
homosexual?"

Hubbard anticipated reservations about the complexity of th
motive he was describing.

"Many of you ladies and gentlemen would say, 'Do these motive
make sense? Mr. Hubbard, you have presented two motives in th
case. Which one are you traveling with?'

"And I submit to you that I am traveling with both of them.

"Here is a woman that is so cold and callous about her ow
daughter, who hates the possible life-style that her daughter migh
have chosen, who thinks so little of her, that she'd be willing to ki
her."

Marie Hilley had stared at Hubbard throughout his presentatio
rarely looking away, her face expressionless, as if she were the on
sitting in judgment.

"She's embarrassed, she's ashamed of what she thinks her daugh
ter is. And she thinks, 'If I've got to kill my daughter, let's make
profitable.' And she did, she tried to."

Hubbard had been talking for close to an hour, and he was read
to stop. He went back briefly to capture a single image of th
defendant to leave with the jurors.

"While she was putting that poison into Carol's body from Apr
1979, to September 1979, she was playing the loving mother, th

416

loting mother, carrying her to the hospital, taking her to the doctor, when she knew good and well that Dr. Jones couldn't diagnose arsenic poisoning in Frank Hilley—didn't have a reason to—and she thought, 'If Dr. Ratanaubol could do an autopsy and not find arsenic poisoning, I'm home free.' And she kept playing the doctors just like a violin."

Hubbard knew he would have another chance to speak after the defense had presented its closing argument. His voice took on a matter-of-fact tone as he moved toward his conclusion.

"Mr. Lane will speak to you, ladies and gentlemen, in a few moments, and I'll sit down. If you use your common sense in this case, you can't look at all this evidence in one glance and comprehend it all. But when you take it all together, which is what you should do, you'll see nothing but a woman who *is* nothing. And whatever you ladies and gentlemen decide to do to her is not enough. She'd kill her own flesh and blood and sell her own daughter for twenty-five thousand dollars.

"The evidence points to that, ladies and gentlemen, beyond a reasonable doubt, to a moral certainty. We ask you to close the chapter on this particular case the way it should be closed, and that is with a guilty verdict in both of these cases, first-degree murder and attempted poisoning. Thank you."

There was a rustling and shifting of weight among the spectators. Hubbard had built an impressive structure of motive and evidence. It would be difficult for the defense to overcome it. A number of spectators left, satisfied that their view of Marie Hilley could not be much changed or improved by anything to follow.

Wilford Lane's presentation did little to contradict that expectation. His low voice and deliberate speech gave the impression of resignation. The shape of his argument added to the feeling that he was struggling desperately, without much hope, to find some weak spot in the prosecution's case.

The defense attorney took up the witnesses one by one, probing for the inconsistent or improbable in their testimony. Where the prosecution had begun with a story to tell, the narrative of Marie Hilley's life and crimes, Lane had none. The defense's alternative explanations of events, that Carol Hilley had poisoned herself with drugs, or that Freeda Adcock had framed Marie in revenge for her brother's death, had never taken hold. Neither explained Frank Hilley's death, and both were implausible. Carol had seemed bewildered but brave, a recreational user of drugs, never seriously suicidal. Freeda had seemed angry about her brother's death but almost comically scatterbrained, more Lucy Ricardo than Lucretia Borgia,

Lane must have sensed the lack of shape and tension in his presentation, or perhaps he hoped a dinner break would help focus the jury's attention on the final section of his statement. A few minutes after six o'clock he interrupted his speech and turned to Judge Monk.

"Can we take a break now?" he asked.

The judge seemed surprised. "Do you want to?"

"Yes," Lane answered.

The interruption made little difference. After dinner, Lane resumed his attack on the key points of proof. He was relying on the requirement that the jury find the defendant guilty "beyond a reasonable doubt," hoping that some little chink of uncertainty could be opened in the wall of belief the prosecution was attempting to construct.

"Throughout this case," he told the jury, "we've heard about everything in the world about Marie Hilley over here. We've heard about everything but the issues in this case. There are two issues being decided: One is, 'Did she attempt to, or did she, kill her husband by arsenic poisoning?' The second is, 'Did Marie Hilley attempt to kill her daughter with arsenic poisoning?' Those are the issues. They've led us halfway around the world with that, and still haven't proven it.

"Now, the burden is on the state, it's not on the defendant to prove. The burden is on the state. There is no burden whatsoever resting on her shoulders."

Lane ended with what sounded like a peculiar digression. Perhaps he was trying to remind the jury of who, besides Marie Hilley, might have been responsible for what had happened. Or perhaps it was an attempt to turn the sympathy of the jury from Carol Hilley to the defense.

"In closing, I'm going to tell you, Mike testified up here yesterday. He said he was threatened, he said he was afraid of Jewell, who had made threats on his mother's life, he was afraid of Freeda, he was afraid of Carol. Let me tell you right now, I'm serving notice on Freeda Adcock, on Jewell Phillips, on Carol, that I'm not afraid. I'm not afraid of them at all. If they try to hurt me, or any of my family

's going to be awful bad for them, because I'm not afraid of them,
nd I know you-all are not either. And I know you-all will render a
ir and just verdict, and you will acquit the defendant in this case."

Lane turned toward his seat. It was a puzzling ending, strangely
relevant to the defense of Marie Hilley.

Once again Joe Hubbard rose, and this time his mood had
hanged. Throughout most of his earlier presentation he had re-
nained laconic and impersonal, with few flourishes and little emo-
on. Now six months of work was nearing an end. The emotional
ontrol he had exercised for so long could be relaxed. His feelings
bout the case, about the killer and her victims, suppressed during
is earlier presentation, could be channeled into his final effort at
ersuasion.

"Mr. Lane has told you that I would come to you and bring you all
inds of theories for you to ride on in this case," Hubbard began,
and he has made it quite clear that he stands amazed at the evidence
nat we have put on and the theories we have espoused in this case.

"And I don't blame him, because when this case began, that
'oman sitting over there"—he gestured at Marie Hilley, who
ontinued to regard him balefully—"thought she had a shoo-in. She
ought she was going to come out of this case a folk hero.

"But instead, she's going to come out of this case what she is,
/hich is a murderess, somebody lower than a snake's belly. Some-
ody who would take their own kin, their own husband, and worse
nan that, I must say worse than that, their own daughter, and kill
nem like a fly for a little bit of money, because she doesn't agree
/ith the life-style of a child."

Now his voice thickened with contempt. "And Mr. Lane had the
all to stand before you and attempt to tell you that Carol was killing
erself."

Hubbard ranged over Lane's argument, challenging the defense's
kepticism about Priscilla Lang, pointing up the absurdity of casting
reeda and Jewell as killers, rehearsing the evidence of arsenic and
njections and bank accounts and insurance. Again and again he
eturned to the heartlessness of Marie Hilley. She had tried once to
ill her daughter, Hubbard told the jury, and now in court she was
ssaulting Carol again.

"It's the worst crime I can imagine," he said, "for a mother to
reak all the rules of a mother-daughter relationship and try to kill
er own offspring for a little money. And now she comes into court

and tries to crucify Carol by saying she's a pervert and she's a psych
and that she has framed her mother."

Of course Freeda and Jewell had been angry at Marie and anyon
they thought was helping her, Hubbard said. It was the most natur
thing in the world.

"You've got to understand, ladies and gentlemen, that this is
family matter. They had found out that one woman has killed a ma
that's very important to them, a forty-five-year-old brother c
down in the prime of life . . . and three and a half years later the
find out who did it, and she's not only done that, she's now, the
believe, poisoning her own daughter, their niece. I can perfect
understand that. I'm sure you can, too."

As he approached the end of his argument, the end of the tri
Hubbard's voice grew harsh. Marie Hilley had tried everything
escape judgment, he said. Her true nature was revealed most clear
in the interview with Gary Carroll.

"She's the type of woman that'll blame it on her daughter, and o
her sister-in-law, and *any*body but herself, and she'll squeez
through any crack she can squeeze through to get you people
believe that." His voice took on a note of sarcasm. Marie Hilley ha
been confident that no one could expose her. "'Check it out,' she sa
to Gary Carroll, 'check it out.' Gary checked it out and found out sh
was *bogus*, and she was telling nothing but lies and hate.

"She's like a black widow spider." Hubbard turned speculativ
like a scientist examining a specimen. "They tell me that the blac
widow spider mates, and then it kills its mate. And there's no reaso
for it. That's what she reminds me of, that's what this case remin
me of.

"I told you in the opening argument that this case, when yo
found out the facts and the motive behind it, would scare you t
death. And I mean, it does scare me to death, and I hope it does scar
you to death. That a woman could be so cold and callous as to ki
her own husband, attempt to kill her own daughter, and to do it fo
the reason that she did it: because she didn't like her daughter
alleged life-style, and she did it for thirty-one thousand dollars th
first time and twenty-five thousand dollars the next time, simpl
because she was hurting for money. Now that scares me to death.

The law required only that Hubbard show that Marie Hilley ha
killed her husband and tried to kill her daughter, and that he explai
to the jury why she had done those things. But now the youn

sistant district attorney felt the need to go beyond the requirements
the legal process, to say something about that part of her crime
at went even beyond the ordinary business of the law. He
counted the warnings he had received that it would be difficult to
ake a jury accept that any mother could do what Marie Hilley had
ne. Wilford Lane interrupted.

"Your Honor, I'm going to object to his testifying to facts that are
t in evidence at this time."

"All right," Judge Monk answered, but the objection was insig-
ficant. The point had been made and the prosecutor was rolling
ward a finish.

"Well," Hubbard resumed, as if there had been no interruption,
et me just tell you what I feel about this, ladies and gentlemen, and
ou can draw your own conclusions from it." He paused to gather
eath; the jury, sensing a climax and an ending, seemed to breathe
ith him.

"Some people, contrary to popular belief, are evil." The word
unded old-fashioned, unfamiliar, out of place in a courtroom, and
t now, when the time had come to put the final touch to the
ortrait of Audrey Marie Hilley, it was the only word that would do.

"They are just, basically, evil, and they are motivated by nothing
cept their own selfish desires. And it doesn't make any difference
hether it's a daughter, a husband, a cousin, or a total stranger,
hatever stands in their way, it goes."

Hubbard returned to his ordinary courtroom manner to tell the
ry what he expected.

"We've proved to you beyond a reasonable doubt that the
fendant is guilty of the crime of first-degree murder, and we know
ou won't turn her loose. We've proved to you beyond a reasonable
oubt that the defendant is guilty of the crime of attempted
oisoning; I know you won't turn her loose. All I ask of you is that
ou do your duty, as you've sworn to do. You'll never have a case
ith any more evidence. I ask you for a guilty verdict in both of
ese crimes. Thank you."

It was past nine-thirty. The judge's final instructions to the jury
ould have to wait until morning. As Judge Monk prepared to
smiss the jurors for the night, Carol Hilley sat on a bench behind
e prosecution table, weeping. The jurors filed from the room.

Marie Hilley stood to leave the courtroom with her guard. She
ught her daughter's eye. She smiled warmly at Carol and mouthed

the words, "I love you." She gestured with her head toward th
hallway leading to the catwalk that connected the courtroom to th
jail, beckoning Carol to meet her.

Carol shook her head. "I can't," she whispered. She covered he
face, her shoulders shaking with sobs, as her mother walked from
the room. Bob Field and her Aunt Freeda moved quickly to Carol
side, placing their arms around her, offering comfort.

There was no sign of emotional strain on Carol's face as Judg
Monk read his charge to the jury the next morning. She seemed t
have achieved some resolve. Perhaps she had somehow conclude
her own trial the day before, reached her own verdict. Perhap
hearing the evidence in the words of others, listening to th
concluding arguments, she had finally found the understanding t
begin separating herself from her mother.

The jury retired at midmorning. The crowd thinned gradually. I
felt as if the remaining spectators had just settled down to wait fo
the verdict when the word rippled through the halls: "They'r
coming back." It had been less than three hours. John Homan
spectral and impassive as ever, took a seat as the jury filed into th
courtroom. The defendant's son, Mike, was nowhere to be seen.

The jury foreman was a forty-seven-year-old fireman at th
Anniston Army Depot named Keith Croffoot. He stood facin
Judge Monk and read the verdict:

"We, the jury, find the defendant, Audrey Marie Hilley, guilty c
murder in the first degree, as charged in the indictment in this case
and we fix her punishment at life in the State Penitentiary."

Marie Hilley drew in her breath, frowned, and lowered her head
The jury was polled and the foreman turned to the second verdict

"We, the jury, find the defendant, Audrey Marie Hilley, guilty c
attempt to poison, as charged in the indictment in this case." The
had voted only once on each charge, one of the jurors told a reporte
later.

As her mother was led from the courtroom, Carol Hilley spok
earnestly to Bob Field. She was dry-eyed and composed, in contra
to her demeanor at the close of the previous day's session. Th
district attorney told reporters later that Carol had asked to see he
mother.

At the sentencing hearing, Judge Monk confirmed the life term o
the murder charge and imposed the maximum sentence, twent
years, on the charge of attempted murder.

Invited to comment before being taken to the Alabama Women's Prison, Audrey Marie Hilley murmured a few words.

"I'm sorry, I can't hear you," Judge Monk replied.

"I still maintain my innocence," she repeated.

Epilogue

By any ordinary standard, conviction and sentencing should have brought the drama of Marie Hilley to a close. But Marie had long since converted her whole existence into drama, with constantly shifting guises and rapid changes of scenery and costume. Now there was no going back, and only death could bring this tragedy to its end.

Audrey Marie Hilley became prisoner 135272 at the Julia S. Tutwiler State Women's Prison in Wetumpka, Alabama, on June 9, 1983, but her presence continued to shadow the days of all those whose lives she had touched.

In the outer circle of those who would never be free of Marie Hilley were former schoolmates, friends, fellow workers, people in Alabama and New Hampshire, in Florida and Texas and Vermont, who had known her as a bright, pretty child, a charming, outgoing woman, an efficient worker, a wife and mother, a friend. Marie's conviction and sentencing left many of them unsettled. There was a good deal of gossipy banter and jokey curiosity about the ingredients of a dessert she had brought to share at work or a cup of coffee she had offered during a visit in her home. For some, this light talk bore an undercurrent of real anxiety—what could small amounts of arsenic do to the body? people wondered—though they rarely spoke of their concern. But there was something else, something harder to identify, for Marie Hilley had shaken the underlying structure of ordinary life, disturbing patterns so basic that they were like air or water, never noticed until they were threatened by some insidious poison.

For daily life—in Anniston, in Keene, in any community any-

ere—depends on a fundamental honesty, a plainness of approach.
er time, each person presents the reality of himself to others as an
umulation of fragments. A smile, a frown, a confidence, a bit of
ignation, a show of reliability, a display of pride or disappoint-
nt, all these add up to the truth of a person. We depend on the
egrity of each separate impression as a building block for our
ture of an individual, for our sense of all the people around us, for
· idea of the world we inhabit.

he exposure of Marie Hilley as a woman who had murdered her
band, who had brought her daughter near death, who had
bably used poison to assault many other relatives and acquaintan-
, was the exposure of our unquestioned assumptions, and of their
nerability. Marie Hilley had lived a hidden life. Her pose as a
ventional homemaker, worker, friend, good citizen of the com-
nity had been an outright lie, from start to finish. Her whole
ble life had been a deception. Which meant that every transaction,
ry act of friendship, every word she had ever uttered was a lie.
d yet, of all people, she had seemed so believable—special,
n—a person whose character was written right there on her face
d in her manner.

io for those who had known Marie Hilley, the question must slip
gewise into some corner of consciousness: If so much of what
eared to be true about Marie Hilley was false, if so much that
med obvious and factual was merely illusion, then who else might
something vastly different from what they seemed, what other
itine assumptions of daily life might conceal some gathering
nace or threat of evil?

or some, the worry that trailed in Marie's path was more
ailed, more immediate. Arsenic had been discovered in the bodies
Marie's mother and mother-in-law. The amounts were not large
ugh to have directly caused death, but the poison was known to
a trigger of cancer, and it was cancer that had killed both women.
addition there were the police officers who had visited Marie's
use to take her complaints of prowlers and crank calls; Marie
ways had a pot of coffee ready when they arrived, and at least two
them had experienced stomach pain, vomiting, and loss of weight
ring that time. Then there were the neighbors whose children,
quent visitors at the Hilleys', had suffered from chronic, unex-
ined health problems that disappeared after they moved to
other neighborhood. And there was the case of Sonya Gibson.

Sonya Gibson was Carol Hilley's friend from church who had d
suddenly nine years before in a helicopter ambulance on the way
the hospital in Birmingham. She had been eleven, three ye
younger than Carol. She had died only three days after becoming
An autopsy determined that death had been caused by a raging vir
accompanied by inflammation of the lining of the heart. But in 19
four years later, her family had learned that Marie Hilley, th
onetime neighbor and the mother of Sonya's friend, had be
arrested on suspicion of committing murder and attempted murd
by poison. And rumors were rife that Marie's poisonings had
stopped with her husband and daughter. Sonya's family recalled th
Sonya had often visited the Hilley home, that Marie Hilley h
seemed particularly eager to have her as a guest for Carol, and tl
during the Christmas holidays of 1973 Sonya had stayed at l
friend's house and taken a number of meals there.

Sonya's mother had never seen her doubts resolved. She had d
while Marie Hilley was still a fugitive, a year before her trial a
conviction in the poisonings. Within days after the trial, Distr
Attorney Field was considering reopening the case of Sonya Gibso
The girl's grandmother was eager to know what had happened, c
way or the other. "I know you're not supposed to disturb the dea
she told a reporter, "but I would like to know. It'll either reli
your mind or give you more to think about."

But Sonya's father, who had recently suffered a heart atta
objected to the possibility that his daughter's body might
disturbed. Marie Hilley had been sentenced to terms of life p
twenty years in jail; there was no further point in prosecuting her
Sonya's death. "What good would it do?" he asked. The exhumati
was delayed while the district attorney investigated the chances
finding traces of poison in a body buried for nine years, but the sto
fed the flow of gossip and speculation that continued to surrou
Marie Hilley.

Freeda Adcock, Frank Hilley's sister, talked about Marie in
restrained way. Freeda had been divorced and had moved to a mob
home in Weaver, just outside Anniston. Seated stiffly in her n
living room, wearing a pale orange sweater set and crisp polyes
slacks, Freeda spoke calmly as she recalled the years when she a
Marie had been close friends, but occasionally her anger ca
through. Her posture of gentility sagged slightly and her li
tightened when she spoke of her brother's death: "Marie took h

y from us, took him before his time." Freeda's daughter, Lisa
nter, had displayed her anger more directly, telling a reporter
r the verdict, "She got off too light. She killed my uncle,
soned my grandmother, poisoned Carol. They were all real special
ne. I think she should have gotten the electric chair or life without
ble."

isa was not alone in her vengeful temper, but other members of
rie's family responded more with fear. One couple, apparently
gining that Marie might somehow escape from prison or send an
nt seeking revenge for their opposition, was said to have aban-
ed the sunny but exposed rooms at the front of their house,
ving their bed and television and a hot plate into a refuge at the
k, protected from the view of outsiders.

heir reaction, and the hushed, careful way many of those who
known Marie Hilley talked about her, bespoke a fear that seemed
n outsider to be exaggerated and inappropriate. Marie had never
mitted direct violence against anyone, had never used a gun or
fe, and now she was locked up in jail. What was there to be afraid
Nobody who knew Marie seemed to think of it that way. To
m, she was more of a specter than a person, a malignant spirit, an
arnation of evil. Calm, systematic analysis didn't tell you any-
g about Marie Hilley, they would say. She was the kind of force
t invaded your mind when a sound outside the house brought you
denly from sleep at 3:00 A.M., a force beyond nature and the
light world. There was her remarkable skill at manipulation, her
lity to set aside feeling, her anger, her immense willpower. She
uld find a way, she would escape, she would somehow get free;
hing was beyond Marie Hilley. And she would threaten those she
ught had harmed her.

Within a month, Tom Harmon and Will Lane had filed a request
t Judge Monk overturn the verdict and grant their client a new
l. When that request was denied, the lawyers presented their case
the appeals court. The grounds were technical. The brief argued
t several procedural errors had been committed at the trial, but the
orneys were pinning their main hopes on an assertion that Marie's
hts had been violated: Gary Carroll's examination of her purse at
police station and the search of her belongings by Freeda Adcock
Moore Avenue that turned up evidence of poison had been illegal,
y claimed.

Lieutenant Carroll, who had come full circle, beginning on

friendly terms with Marie Hilley and ending as the key investiga
who brought her to justice, was nervous. The case had been
obsession, its conclusion the highlight of his career. Next to a map
the world above his desk, Carroll had hung a mounted copy of
Anniston Star story on Marie's capture, with its headline, "The La
Chapter in Marie Hilley Saga." What if now all that effort by
prosecution were thrown out because a court decided that an act
Carroll had thought of as standard investigative procedure I
infringed on the defendant's rights? Carroll would never be co
pletely comfortable until the appeal was resolved.

Not everybody who knew Marie was convinced of her guilt.
part-time guard at the county jail had spent long hours talking w
Marie during the months she was being held for trial. When she w
not needed at the jail, the guard ran a dry-cleaning business with I
husband, and customers told her things about Marie, her family, a
friends; many had positive memories of Marie and bits of evide
that seemed to suggest other explanations for what had happened
Frank and Carol. Gradually the guard had come to share I
prisoner's outlook. Marie Hilley was a good person, she kne
outgoing and honest, as normal as the rest of us; she couldn't ha
done those terrible things. Even the trial could not change
guard's view of the prisoner who had become her friend. Those w
shared her view had become fewer as each day of the trial brou
new evidence to light, but even now there were those who could
believe a woman like Marie Hilley was capable of committing
crimes of which she had been accused. None of these supporters
Marie Hilley, however, approached John Homan in the intensity
their faith.

John had followed his wife to Anniston soon after her arre
abandoning most of his possessions to storage in New Hampshi
He hovered in the background throughout the trial, refusing
discuss the case with reporters, taking the opportunity to confer w
his wife and her lawyers in a hallway or walk with Marie and I
guard to the car that returned her to the jail each evening. One day
was seen lurking at the edge of a group discussing the case with
out-of-town reporter in the hallway during a break; occasiona
John put in a comment, enjoying the fact that no one in
discussion seemed to recognize him.

John had gotten a job as a toolmaker with a small manufacturi
company in Oxford, the next town south of Anniston. Eventually

ok up long-term residence in two rooms at the Heart of Anniston
n, formerly the Jefferson Davis Hotel, a run-down establishment
the decaying heart of the city. On alternate Sundays, when Marie
as eligible to receive visitors, John faithfully made the 180-mile
und trip, getting up early in order to arrive promptly for the eight
clock start of visiting hours.

In spite of his reluctance to speak in detail about his life with Marie
illey, much of what John did say sounded practiced, as if he had hit
a way of seeing things that looked good in the press and had
emorized the words for future use. Speaking of his unaccountable
yalty, John would say, "This is all about just one thing. It's a
ur-letter word that a lot of people don't like to hear." He would
use to let the impression grow that the word might be vulgar, then
ish the thought with an arch smile. "The word is 'love.' " About
s wife, John repeated what he had said to a New Hampshire
porter: "She's the best thing that ever happened to me. She's never
ne anything to harm me."

In the fall of 1983, the case of Sonya Gibson was closed. Her body
ntained only the small amounts of arsenic considered normal.
'ithin a month, Marie Hilley was writing to Judge Monk, asking
s help in getting admitted to the prison work-release program. She
d been ordered to make restitution for the bad checks she had
ssed, Marie reminded the judge. "I am innocent of the [poisoning]
arges against me," she wrote, "and I can only hope that someone
ill tell the truth. But until, and if, that happens, I would like to be
orking so that I can start restitution." Judge Monk denied the
quest, replying that he had no authority in the work-release
ogram, but the news fueled the speculation about Marie Hilley's
turn to the community. She would become eligible to be con-
dered for parole in 1990, after serving about one third of her
ntence. The universal reaction around Anniston when the subject
me up over the following months was indignation. Seven years?
r what she did? They should never let her out, the consensus went.
e Hubbard, who had led the prosecution, seemed to agree, but he
as more restrained and less concerned. Marie Hilley's prosecutors,
w enforcement officials, and the general public of Calhoun County
ould make their opposition heard, he was sure. What was not so
ear was whether parole and prison officials would listen.

The widespread belief, and fear, that Marie Hilley could success-
lly manipulate the prison officials as she had so many others, which

seemed so overblown to an outsider, appeared to Annistonians to
confirmed by the news that circulated periodically in her hometov
The press reported that she was studying accounting to augment l
office skills. During her second year in prison, word reach
Anniston that she had worked her way into the trust of pris
officials. In the coffee shop across from the courthouse they w
saying that Marie had become secretary in the warden's office a
achieved special trustee status. The accounts of her legal appeal
the conviction that sooner or later she would find a way to regain l
freedom.

Both of Marie's children faced that prospect with anxiety. Ca
had abandoned her studies in criminal justice and no longer expec
to continue her education. She was working as a stock clerk i
warehouse at the Anniston Army Depot. Her modest salary v
enough for the ordinary demands of living, and later she was able
make a down payment on a sporty red Nissan Pulsar, but she v
beset by an ironic vestige of her ordeal: Since her mother v
insolvent, the hospitals were dunning Carol for payment on seve
thousands of dollars in hospital bills accumulated during her illne
Eventually she arranged to pay five dollars a week.

Carol's weight had recovered only to ninety-five pounds, still
pounds below what it had been before her five-month illness, bu
was stable. She had occasional problems with fine motor coor
nation—putting on earrings could be a problem—but she walk
without a limp and had almost completely recovered most of l
strength and coordination.

But Carol's physical stability was not matched by her postu
toward her mother. When Marie's long campaign of poisoning h
ended and Carol was freed, at first she had resisted believing t
facts. The idea that her mother could assault her in this way was
monstrous to fully assimilate right away. But gradually she h
come to accept the reality of what had happened. At the same tin
she had continued to feel a daughter's love for her mother. Af
Marie had settled in at Wetumpka, they had exchanged letters a
talked regularly on the phone. Carol had sent small gifts and l
mother had responded warmly. Marie had never said anything ab
the poisoning, and Carol was too timid to bring it up.

Carol swung between loyalty and fear, sometimes within t
space of a sentence. She would talk cheerfully at one minute ab
visiting her mother in prison, and muse in the next about wl

uld happen if Marie, after serving her time, wanted to come and e with Carol: "I'd be crazy to let her come here and stay. I'd be aid to leave my house." She paused to consider what she had just d, as if concerned that she might be considered disloyal for ressing fear. "Not because I might worry about what she might t in the food, not anything like that. But, you know, there's other ys to deal with things." The vague words were a screen between rol and the idea that her mother had tried to kill her, that she ght try again, might find some other method. "You don't have to it the same way," Carol said thoughtfully. As long as Marie was ve, Carol would never be free of the fear that her mother might n against her once more. She was a defiant, even brave, young man, but it would take more than courage to heal the unspeakable ury her mother had done to Carol.

Marie's son harbored similar feelings, but for different reasons. w established as the respected pastor of a Protestant church eral hours from Anniston, the Reverend Michael Hilley still had son to fear his mother: She had told Carol that she would "get" se who had put her in prison, and Mike was sure that his timony at the trial had placed him in that category. And Marie had ated to Mike that she might try to reach him through his children. ke and Terri Hilley could not forget the mysterious stranger wling around their porch in Tennessee. It was possible to imagine arie luring a grandchild from the school yard and fleeing. And re was the knowledge that she had not confined her assault to rol. The memories of the unexplained illnesses Mike and his wife d suffered amidst the atmosphere of anxiety and hostility that rrounded Marie were still strong.

But the complexity of Mike Hilley's feelings toward his mother s not solely a product of fear. There was another dimension for arie's son, a moral dilemma. From an early age he had stood off m his mother. He had never been so dependent on her emotional pport as Carol, who was younger and female, less able to separate rself from her home. As the emotional climate deteriorated and arie became increasingly erratic, Mike was already living away m home. He had distanced himself from his mother, both ysically and psychologically. Eventually he married and started a nily of his own.

In his ministry, Mike had been called upon to counsel members of congregation. He had become interested in psychology. Speaking with relatives on the phone, visiting Anniston, observing the slow expanding patterns of chaos in his mother's life, Mike grew incre ingly concerned with her welfare and made frequent attempts to h her. He had become convinced that she needed psycholog treatment. Yet he had been forced to stand by, helpless, as cascading revelations of her deceit culminated in the exposure of attacks on his father and sister.

After his mother's conviction, Mike came to feel that in order achieve reconciliation with her family, she must admit her guilt she could confess, admit her responsibility, and show contrition she would accept treatment for the terrible impulses that had led to this assault on her family, they would be able to forgive her support her in the effort to recover.

But Marie never admitted guilt, never tried to explain what happened, refused even to talk about the accusations in any det She insisted on her innocence. Her stubborn refusal to yield mained an insurmountable barrier between Marie and her son. M was torn between love and the need to see his mother expiate sins. When at last he visited her in prison, the conversation v friendly, polite, but superficial. Nothing had changed, and barrier of her intransigence remained between them.

In the spring of 1985, the Alabama Court of Criminal Appe upheld the conviction of Audrey Marie Hilley. The decision said case had involved a "tragic and bizarre series of events," but th had been no reversible error in the trial. The five judges w unanimous. Marie and her lawyers determined to take their app on to the Alabama Supreme Court. The state's highest court v considered liberal in matters of evidence, generally sympathetic the kind of argument Tom Harmon and Will Lane had devised Marie's appeal.

The state had provided a transcript and covered other costs Marie's appeals. The initial defense had exhausted whatever lit money she had retained from her financial maneuverings and Jo Homan had volunteered to cover the rest. The state supreme co agreed to hear the case. In the fall of 1985 Harmon and Lane appeal in Montgomery to present their arguments before the court. Th invoked the recent Rhode Island decision in the case of Claus Bülow, who had been acquitted of attempting to murder his wi Sunny. The principles of evidence were similar, they contended, a Marie should be similarly treated. Joe Hubbard argued the prose

's case and afterward pronounced himself "confident" that the
dict would be upheld. The only spectator familiar to Anniston
okers was a thin, balding man with a mustache and a curtain of
, black hair hanging over his collar. John Homan was still
ding by his wife.

ohn had become a spectral figure around Anniston. He was still
ng at the Heart of Anniston Inn and working at the manufactur-
company. He could often be seen at the Waffle House on
intard Boulevard where he took breakfast and dinner most days,
sing a cup of coffee, chatting idly with the waitresses and
ulars. He found a local lounge that offered two beers for a dollar
Tuesday nights; he always seemed to be hovering at the edge of a
up. He appeared to have no close connection to Anniston or any
ts people. His brother Peter had called a few months before to tell
n that his possessions would have to be moved from the friend's
n in New Hampshire where they were stored. On the trip north
n had fallen asleep at the wheel and driven off the side of the
erstate somewhere in Virginia. His pickup truck was a total
ck. He had hitchhiked the rest of the way, arriving at Peter's
ne like a figure returned from the grave, mud and caked blood
ging to his hairline and staining his flannel shirt.

he last of the goodwill Peter Homan had painstakingly recon-
cted with his brother seemed finally dissipated after the trip.
ere had been some misunderstanding about which of the brothers
ned certain of the stored items, but the real barrier was John's
olute loyalty to Marie Hilley. He had made belief in her innocence
ondition of his own friendship. "If you don't support my wife,
don't support me," he said.

year later he had wrecked another pickup. Again he had escaped
ous injury, but the apparent pattern of self-destruction and
wing isolation seemed ominous. He had almost no contact with
rol Hilley or any of his wife's other relatives in the area. Late in
5 he had gone to Fort Lauderdale to visit Manfred Krukow, the
e contact he had maintained with his hometown. Hoping to
cape and relax," John had asked his friend to keep the visit secret
m John's family and former friends, but somehow word had
ked out. A week after returning to Anniston, John had received a
l from his sister, Greer, who was upset that he had come to town
d failed to contact his family. John was furious at the person who
believed had mentioned his visit to Greer; it was sufficient cause

for him to remove the person from his dwindling list of frie
"There are only about three people in the world I can trust," he s
speaking in the weary monotone that had become customary
him.

Over a beer in the lounge of the Downtowner Motor Inn, J
muttered darkly about a conspiracy of Anniston's elite that
believed lay behind his wife's arrest and conviction. "It's the
who live up there on the hill, the East Side," he said. Marie
worked for powerful people, she knew their secrets. They had
out to get her, and so far they had succeeded.

"You know why I'm staying in Anniston?" he said at one po
"To get the whole story." He would not talk further about how
conspiracy had operated or who was responsible, but eventually
promised, the story would come out.

"The pressure is tremendous," John said. There was a long pa
while he gazed down into his beer mug. He sighed. "I'm a se
excuse for a human being," he said, holding out his hand paralle
the table. He seemed to have a slight tremor. "I haven't been abl
hold my hand steady for more than a year now."

Four years ago, John said, on the basis of his inheritance he
been good for a personal line of credit of one hundred and f
thousand dollars. Now, one tenth that amount would barely co
his debts for Marie's legal fees.

When Marie's innocence had been proved and she was releas
John said, he would like to go somewhere new, a place where t
were unknown, and start over. There would be no point in goin
Florida or New Hampshire, any of the places where they had frie
from the past. "There's no one I care about," he said, "no one at a

Marie Hilley had constructed a fantasy world, where true was f
and false was true, where respected citizens were conspirators
Marie, the ultimate deceiver, was a victim of the deceit of oth
And in one crucial moment, confronted with a choice in
interrogation room of a Vermont police station, John Homan
stepped through the looking glass to join his wife, to live in
world, leaving the remains of his previous life behind forever.

Counterfeit though it was, John's portrait of his wife as an inju
innocent was no more improbable than the all-powerful Ma
Hilley envisioned by the average Anniston resident. Yet the popu
view turned out to contain a large measure of truth.

Prison records obtained many months later by John Ronne

orter for the *Anniston Star*, portrayed a startling new chapter in rie Hilley's career of deceit and manipulation. In the fall of 1983, hin just months of her arrival at Tutwiler Prison, guards were ed off that she was plotting an escape. Along with another victed poisoner and two other inmates, the story went, she was nning to drug the coffee of a night-shift guard and flee. "She stantly talks of escape," the guard reported to Warden Kathleen lt. Early in 1984, the warden took the rumors up directly with rie, who persuaded the warden that she had been the victim of a ow inmate's lies.

A few months later, a guard reported that Marie Hilley had roached her with a report of another escape plot. This time Marie s informing on a fellow prisoner, who she said had asked to row a dark blouse for camouflage in a nighttime escape and was king for acid to help cut through window bars.

n the late spring, Marie's security classification came up for iew. Soon after her arrival at Tutwiler, she had been assigned to rk at a computer terminal, processing information for state ncies; the pay was a standard twenty-five cents an hour. Soon she l been classified as a medium security prisoner. When the question revising her classification to minimum security arose less than a ur later, a new warden, Jean Hare, was joined by other administra-s in recommending that there be no change. Taking note of rie's dramatic flight after her first arrest in 1979, the prison icials concluded that increasing the prisoner's freedom of move-nt so soon might provoke "negative community reaction."

Marie complained to Warden Hare that she had been denied the ange in status only because of malicious rumors spread by two rsons at the prison, one of them a guard. The protest had no mediate effect, but a year later the change was made: Audrey rie Hilley was placed on minimum security status. That meant was eligible to leave the prison. Her first outing was a trip of veral hours with eight other inmates, accompanied by an assistant rden. The group enjoyed a meal at the Tiki Village Restaurant in ontgomery, the state capital seventeen miles from Wetumpka. It l taken Marie two years to go from convicted murderer to trusted soner.

Not everybody at the prison was impressed by Marie Hilley's new tus. A year later, in the summer of 1986, a guard captain went on ord as believing that the prisoner represented an escape risk. She was opposed to Marie Hilley's being allowed to participate in community project or outside work that did not include c supervision, the captain wrote.

A month later a prisoner's statement to a guard reinforced opinion. Marie Hilley was planning to take advantage of a outside the prison in September to make her escape, the prisoner reported.

Alerted to the rumors, Marie fought back in characteristic fashi with a letter to Warden Hare. She turned the facts upside do portraying herself as the injured party and taking the offensive: ' to escape rumors, I have no way to defend myself against this sor thing. I have worked hard to keep a good record here. I have ne learned to live with lies. I have no desire to make my life m difficult than it already is, and running for the rest of my life is exactly my idea of living. I feel I have proven my trustworthi over the year-plus I have been going out."

During the next few months, Marie kept up the crusade rehabilitate her reputation. Her appeal to the Alabama Supre Court had been turned down. There had been talk about an appea the United States Supreme Court, but there seemed little hope n of overturning the conviction. Marie appeared resigned to mak the best of existing circumstances. She was campaigning for adm sion to the next level of trust accorded to selected inmates, where could be permitted an eight-hour leave from the prison without escort. In December she wrote to the warden, "All I'm asking does it really matter whether one tries to follow the rules regulations and keep a good, clean record? I feel like I'm play some sort of game where no one has explained the rules."

With characteristic perceptiveness, Marie had fashioned perfect approach to fit the openings in the personality of person she wanted to manipulate. The warden approved eight-hour pass for Audrey Marie Hilley. "I'm counting on y not to let me down," she wrote to Marie. The warden underli the last four words.

A few days later, after completing her eight-hour leave with incident, Marie sent a note to the warden. "I have a lot to gain handling this privilege the right way," Marie wrote, "and eve thing to lose if I don't. So you have no cause to worry about letting you down." In January 1987, with four successful eight-h leaves behind her, Marie wrote to the warden once more: "Ag

nk you for my passes. I will never take advantage nor abuse any
vilege you give me."

By the following month, Marie had qualified for the next step
vard freedom. On Thursday, February 19, she walked out of
twiler Prison to begin a three-day furlough. She never returned.
ohn Homan picked Marie up at the prison and they drove to
niston. It was the first time in almost four years that Marie had
ne farther than the seventeen miles from the prison to Mont-
mery. The drive took less than two hours. Marie called Sheriff
y Snead Thursday night as required by the conditions of her
lough, to inform him of her presence in his jurisdiction. Other-
se, the couple tried to keep their presence in Anniston inconspicu-
s, John Homan said later. Marie made no attempt to contact her
ighter or other relatives. She and John spent most of their time in
in's room at the hotel, going out for walks after dark.

Marie was due back at Tutwiler four o'clock Sunday afternoon.
nday morning she told John, according to his account, that she
nted to go without him to visit the graves of her parents. They
anged to meet at the Waffle House at ten o'clock. The couple left
 hotel together around nine. Soon afterward, John was seen
ting alone at the Waffle House.

Sometime late in the morning, John approached the front desk
th a note addressed to Marie. He appeared upset. The note
ntained phone numbers and asked her to call John or the sheriff.
 a little short lady comes in here," the clerk remembered John
ving, "please give her this."

Before noon Sheriff Snead received a phone call from John
man. John sounded agitated. He asked the sheriff to come to his
om at the hotel. He refused to say why, and the sheriff didn't press
n.

When the sheriff arrived, John handed him a piece of paper
vered with writing in Marie's distinctive, neat hand. John had
ited for Marie at the Waffle House past the time set for their
eting, he told the sheriff, then returned to his room to find the
ter under the pillow. The authorities later released an edited
rsion:

Dear John,
    I hope you will be able to forgive me. I'm getting ready to leave. It

will be best for everybody. We'll be together again. Please give me an hour to get out of town. Destroy this note.

The note went on to say that a friend named Walter was drivi Marie to Atlanta. From there they would fly to Canada, where would employ her in his business. When she had gotten settled a saved some money, she would contact John through a woman New Hampshire and they would be reunited. They would find new place and begin their life together again.

The sheriff dispatched deputies to check bus terminals, ta companies, and the airport. If they moved quickly, maybe th could head her off before she slipped away. But the search turned no sign of Marie Hilley.

Sunday evening the night clerk at the hotel took a phone call f John. The caller was a woman. John was not present to take the ca The clerk reported to the sheriff that the caller had sounded li Marie Hilley. Other than the call and the note, the sheriff said, investigators had nothing to work with.

District Attorney Bob Field was outraged. "Marie had a know record of being a runner," he said, "and various federal and sta governments spent years trying to apprehend her. With all th information, she was given a three-day pass without supervision Field said he was considering opening a grand jury investigation in the prison officials' decision to issue the furlough. "With her tra record, it's unbelievable that they would let her out."

Prison officials refused to talk to the press, but the Alabar Commissioner of Prisons launched an internal investigation.

John Homan was cooperating with the authorities, but he had lit to say to the press. Asked what he thought Marie would do, replied in typically inhibited fashion: "You're asking me to speak f her, and I can't do it."

The authorities had checked with Carol and Mike Hilley, but the was no suspicion that any member of Marie's family had be involved in her escape. None of Marie's relatives wanted to spe publicly about her flight, but the chorus of protest grew steadily ov the next few days as the people of Calhoun County learned th prison authorities had never suspected what each of them h known: Marie Hilley was not to be trusted. Even Judge Sam Mon who had presided at Marie's trial, pronounced himself "appalled Radio talk shows were flooded with calls. One talk show ho

nmarized the feelings of his callers: "The emotions are one
ndred percent anger, hostility, frustration, and a sense of futility
ected toward the state prison officials who let her go." An editorial
he *Anniston Star* exemplified local sentiment: "Anyone hereabouts
ıld have told the prison and parole board that if you give Marie
ley a three-day pass you shouldn't expect to see her again."

Thursday morning prison officials were preparing to seek a
rrant charging Marie with flight across state lines. Someone who
ew Marie had reported seeing a woman resembling her Sunday
ght in a store in Tennessee. It was the authorities' only solid lead,
t the suspicion that Marie had left the state would allow them to
ng the FBI into the search.

Anger and concern for his family had spurred Mike Hilley to break
silence regarding his mother's escape. She had threatened him and
family, Mike said, and yet prison officials had been lax in
orming him of her escape. He had asked the local police to provide
tra patrols around his house, and he was prepared to defend his
nily physically if necessary. He would not hesitate to turn her in if
showed up in his town, Mike said, but he didn't expect it to
ppen.

'I don't think they'll ever hear from her again," he said. "She's a
ry clever person, and she can become just about anything she wants
become, changing her looks and blending into the environment."
ke was not alone in this belief. She was long gone, the local
1sensus had it, and this time they'd never find her. She was just too
ver, and after her last escape, now she was experienced as well. She
ıuldn't make the same mistake again. FBI agent Cecil Moses sounded
pared for a lengthy pursuit. He noted that the average federal
zitive remained at large eighteen months. He was already talking
out the stages of a search: If Mrs. Hilley hadn't been found in six
onths, "wanted" flyers would be distributed nationwide.

Around one-thirty that afternoon, Sue Craft was driving toward
r home on Post Oak Road in the Blue Mountain section of north
nniston when she saw a person on the open back porch behind the
use of her neighbor, Barbara Thomason. The person appeared to
trying to break into the house. There was no sign of anyone at
me. As Mrs. Craft drew closer, the figure appeared to be a woman
her knees, groping for the door handle. Mrs. Craft drove on to
home of another neighbor, Janice Hinds, who was sewing when
arrived.

They called the Anniston Police Department and drove ba
through a chilling drizzle to the Thomasons', where they found t
woman slumped on the open porch near the door. Her clothes we
soaked through. Her hands were a blotchy pink and purple. She h
been wearing moccasinlike boat shoes. One of the shoes had co
off and she was holding it in her hand.

Mrs. Hinds asked the woman her name. "Sellers," the strang
replied. Her car had broken down, she went on, pointing down t
road. How had she gotten to the porch? Mrs. Hinds asked. "I walk
part of the way and crawled part of the way," she answered. H
speech was slurred. She tried to put her shoe back on but failed a
crumpled to the surface of the porch. The two women found a she
of plastic and wrapped it loosely around her. Sue Craft found herse
reluctant to look at the woman. Her bangs were plastered to h
forehead and there were spots of mud on her face. She had thi
delicate hands with long fingernails, and the little finger on her rig
hand was bent into an unnatural position. It wouldn't straighten o
The overall effect was of a woman buried alive who had clawed h
way free.

Officer Billy Lett arrived a few minutes later. At first he thoug
the woman slumped under the plastic must be drunk. Or perhaps s
was in a diabetic coma. They propped her in a sitting position agai
the wall of the house and waited for the ambulance, which arriv
shortly. As they were removing the plastic sheet and preparing
put the woman into the ambulance, Officer Lett noticed her soake
mud-spattered clothes. She was wearing a zip-up jacket and slack
They matched the outfit described in the fugitive poster for Ma
Hilley.

Sue Craft and Janice Hinds both knew Audrey Marie Hilley. M
Craft had been a senior at Anniston High School in 1950 wh
Audrey Marie Frazier was a junior. She had followed Marie's sto
in the newspapers and television since then. Janice Hinds's husba
had grown up across the street from Marie Frazier, and h
sister-in-law had served as matron at the county jail in Annisto
while Marie was being held there before her trial. Neither Sue Cra
nor Janice Hinds recognized the filthy, incoherent figure slumped
the porch.

Gary Carroll had been called to the hospital to see if he cou
identify the woman. It was just short of ten years since Ma
Hilley's phone calls had brought Lieutenant Carroll to her house

estigate the first of her nuisance complaints. He peered intently at
e prone figure as the attendants carried in the stretcher. She lay
otionless, but an oxygen mask covered her face and he was unable
see enough to tell if it was Marie. She had suffered a heart attack as
e ambulance arrived at the hospital.

Carroll followed while the attendants rushed her to an intensive
re area. As they removed the oxygen mask to insert a tube, her
otched, muddy face was exposed for a moment. There was no
estion. "It's Marie," Carroll said. Nobody seemed to be listening.

She was suffering from hypothermia, an extreme drop in body
mperature. The typical late February weather had been frigid for
veral days, with nighttime temperatures hovering just above
ezing. A cold wind had dropped the effective temperature well
low the freezing point. Exposed to frequent, chilling rain, her
dy had been unable to retain heat.

As the word spread, a group of reporters and cameramen gathered
the hospital waiting room. Carroll was joined by other police
ficers and members of the sheriff's department. District Attorney
b Field was there and Assistant District Attorney Joe Hubbard,
e man who had prosecuted Marie Hilley. Hubbard's comparison of
arie to a predatory spider in his closing summation to the jury had
ck. Newspapers had picked it up and now she was known all over
e country as the Black Widow.

It was after five o'clock when Hubbard stepped before the swelling
wd of journalists.

"We have just been informed by hospital personnel," he said,
at the efforts to revive Mrs. Hilley from the very serious
akened condition that she was in when she arrived here at the
spital have been unsuccessful." She had been pronounced dead at
6 P.M. She was fifty-three years old.

The news of Marie's death seemed to soften the anger provoked
her deeds. Janice Hinds's reaction was typical. When her husband
me home after work, Mrs. Hinds told him about the woman who
d collapsed on the Thomasons' porch earlier in the day. A strange
a occurred to her. "Honey," she said to him in an offhand way,
ouldn't it be strange if she was Marie Hilley?" When she heard a
w hours later that the helpless, disheveled woman had in fact been
r former schoolmate, Mrs. Hinds was badly shaken by the news.
ll, her first thoughts were for Marie Hilley's need.

"I know she was a convicted murderer," Mrs. Hinds said, "but all

I could think of was that there was a lady that needed help. I ju
hope she had time to make it right with the Lord."

But Marie Hilley's passing did not dampen the outrage at tł
furlough system that had allowed her to be released. The commiʃ
sioner of prisons announced tighter rules for granting leaves aɪ
rigorous provisions for notification of local authorities. In additioɪ
he said, he had sent a letter of reprimand to the warden at Tutwil
who had approved the final furlough of Audrey Marie Hilley. The
was talk of convening the Calhoun County grand jury in Annistoɪ
to look into the possibility of criminal charges.

In the days after her death the coroner concluded that Marie h₂
been in the woods for twenty-four to thirty-six hours before she w
found. It appeared that she had walked along the abandoned tracks
the Louisville and Nashville Railroad from downtown Anniston
Blue Mountain. There were large bruises and scratches on her kne
and legs, evidence that she had fallen to her knees and crawled f
some distance. A hospital official described the progress of hyp
thermia: attempting to compensate for the drop below norm
temperature of 98.6 degrees, the body speeds breathing and initiaɪ
shivering to generate heat. With a further fall in temperature, bloc
vessels in the arms and legs shut down, causing the extremities
become colder but redirecting blood to the vital organs. Metabolis
speeds up to create additional heat. Serious complications beg
when body temperature drops near 94 degrees. Breathing slows aɪ
becomes shallow. As the brain is starved for blood, mental capaci
dims and the victim becomes confused and irrational. At arouɪ
90 degrees shivering stops, body temperature drops more rapidl
and mental capacity deteriorates further. Soon the heart is affect₄
and may begin rapid, irregular vibrations that can lead to a he₂
attack.

This graphic description of Marie Hilley's painful final hours w
shocking to those who had followed the dramatic story of her liɪ
not only because of the drawn-out agony of her passing but becauʃ
of its sharp contrast with what had gone before.

"It's unbelievable," District Attorney Field said. "This go
against everything she's done in the past. The biggest escape artist
this area in ten years, and what does she do? She ended up crawliɪ
in the woods." The further irony was plain: Known for a scrupulo
concern for her appearance, a master manipulator of languaʒ
always in control of herself and her surroundings, Audrey Ma

lley stumbles through her final hours in filthy disarray, mumbling
d incoherent, to end huddled and helpless beneath a plastic sheet.
But if Marie Hilley's death was in most ways a contradiction of
erything that had preceded it, in one essential way it was utterly
nsistent with her life: How she had intended to escape, where she
d been, why and how she had arrived at the porch of an empty
use in Blue Mountain, all of this was hidden in mystery. In death
in life, Marie Hilley was keeping her secrets. John Homan had
lunteered to take a lie detector test, and while the results were not
nounced, authorities appeared satisfied that he had not been
volved in his wife's attempt to flee. Nothing he told investigators
d any light on the final questions about his wife. Sheriff Snead
mmarized the story of Marie Hilley: "It started out as a mystery,
d it looks like it's going to end as a mystery."

But the sheriff was talking about facts, about evidence, about the
d of information that could be examined and validated, that
uld stand up in a court of law. That had never been the kind of
ormation that described Audrey Marie Hilley. The kind of
ormation Sheriff Snead and other investigators were seeking had
n Marie Hilley's lifelong enemy. She had learned long ago to
sh such facts to the very edges of her life, to expel them from her
rsion of reality, and to replace them with a set of invented truths
re to her perverse liking. The truth about Marie Hilley lay
newhere behind the protective screen she had woven from the
satisfied urges of childhood and the fantasies of her later years.

Marie had jumped bail, faked her own kidnapping, eluded capture
three years, changed her identity several times, impersonated her
n twin sister, and lived for extended periods in three states, and
: at the end she could get no farther than Blue Mountain, a few
les outside of Anniston. How could a woman of Marie Hilley's
t, determination, and experience in flight have failed so completely
make an attempt at escape?

Like everything else important about her, the answer was proba-
hidden from Marie as it was from others, but her history is filled
th evidence of a tendency toward self-destruction. She held a
zen excellent jobs but none lasted; usually they ended in the wake
petty disagreements and tensions Marie fomented with fellow
rkers. She had a gift for friendship, yet she rarely remained close
anyone for long; friendships, too, disintegrated under the pressure
her testiness and antagonisms.

It was as if some part of her could not comfortably accept the hi‌
regard and affection of others. Perhaps she felt subconsciously th‌
she did not deserve these forms of approval, believed that she w‌
somehow flawed and therefore unworthy, and found ways‌
destroy the good opinion of others. Even her fantasies, the cov‌
stories she told about her identity, were replete with sudde‌
life-threatening illness, tragic accident, and untimely death. Ea‌
imagined incident was an assault on her precarious well-bein‌
taking away her loved ones or threatening Marie herself.

And in the masquerade as her twin sister, Teri Martin, Marie h‌
even staged her own death, a symbolic act of self-destruction.‌
the circumstances, Marie's decision to head deeper into Annist‌
rather than turning away, to move toward danger rather th‌
heading for safety, to walk away from the center of Anniston alo‌
the abandoned railroad tracks rather than steal a car or head for t‌
highway, seems not strange but almost inevitable.

Finally, there were clues to the mystery of Marie Hilley in t‌
choices that led to her death, in the particulars of where she w‌
going and where she ended up. Perhaps she walked along t‌
abandoned railroad tracks because they seemed to offer a sa‌
sheltered route, but the porch where she collapsed was in Bl‌
Mountain, the mill village section of Anniston where she had grow‌
up. In her childhood, the Louisville and Nashville Railroad h‌
carried goods from the nearby textile mill where her parents h‌
labored to provide a life for their daughter better than their own. S‌
ended little more than a mile from her childhood home, a fe‌
minutes' walk from the cemetery where she had run among t‌
headstones and played in the grass with a pack of cousins a‌
neighborhood children. It was here that Marie Hilley's lifelo‌
campaign of menace and deception had its origins, where some m‌
of heritage and experience formed her murderous character. And‌
was here that her destruction reached its finish. Audrey Marie Hill‌
had come full circle.

Though she died without admitting her crimes before those close‌
to her, Marie Hilley's death promised the possibility of a resoluti‌
for her son and daughter. Carol would never again be forced‌
grapple with the problem of how close she could let her moth‌
come, how far she could bear to go in helping Marie after pris‌
And for Mike, his mother's death put an end to fear and the tensi‌
of her unacknowledged guilt.

The chill rain that had hastened Marie Hilley's death continued off and on during the days before her funeral. It was falling once again as the small group of mourners gathered at Forestlawn Gardens for the burial ceremony. The time and place had been kept secret to protect the family from the curious and the morbid. Two reporters had learned the details but they were kept at a distance by funeral home personnel. John Homan was there, hovering in the background. Carol Hilley stood erect at the graveside. Presiding over the service was the Reverend Michael Hilley.

Audrey Marie Hilley was buried in the grave that had been set aside for her at Forestlawn Gardens many years before, next to her first husband, Frank Hilley, the man she had murdered with poison.